Eugene Onegin

A novel in verse by

Alexander Pushkin

Translated and with a commentary
by Roger Clarke

ALMA CLASSICS
an imprint of

ALMA BOOKS LTD
3 Castle Yard
Richmond
Surrey TW10 6TF
United Kingdom
www.almaclassics.com

An earlier version of this translation, in prose, first published by Milner and Co. in 1999 and later republished by Wordsworth Editions in 2005
This revised edition first published by Alma Classics in 2011
Reissued with further extended revisions by Alma Classics in 2015
Reprinted 2017

English translation © Roger Clarke, 2011, 2015
Introduction and commentary © Roger Clarke, 2011

Printed and bound by CPI Group (UK) Ltd, Croydon, CR0 4YY

ISBN: 978-1-84749-417-7

Contents

Alexander Pushkin (1799–1837)

Abrám Petróvich Gannibál,
Pushkin's great-grandfather

Sergéy Lvovich Pushkin,
Pushkin's father

Nadézhda Ósipovna Púshkina,
Pushkin's mother

Natálya Nikoláyevna Pushkina,
Pushkin's wife

The Imperial Lyceum in Tsárskoye Seló,
which Pushkin entered in 1811 (VIII, 1–2)

Ilya Repin's illustration of Onégin and Lensky's duel

Self-portrait in the margin of a manuscript
page of *Eugene Onegin*

Introduction

Russians regard Pushkin as their greatest writer, and his novel in verse *Eugene Onegin* as his greatest work. Moreover, as one Russian writer, Avrahm Yarmolinsky, once has put it, *Onegin* "has long been recognized as the parent of the Russian novel, the source to which the full stream of Russian fiction must be traced". For these reasons *Onegin* ought to occupy a pre-eminent place in the literature not only of Russia, but of the wider world too.

Yet outside Russia, certainly among the English-speaking peoples, *Onegin* is little read and little known. Even those with a live interest in wider European literature and civilization will commonly encounter it through Tchaikovsky's operatic adaptation, rather than through Pushkin's original verse novel. Why should such an important – and interesting, and beautiful, and moving, and amusing – work as *Onegin* have remained till now so unfamiliar to the generality of English-speaking readers?

I discuss this question in detail in the Translator's Note on page 396. In brief, nearly all previous translations of *Onegin* into English have attempted to replicate the same verse form – stanzas, metre, rhyme scheme – as Pushkin's original. Adherence to Pushkin's complex rhyme scheme, in particular, has frustrated the clear, natural and accurate rendering of the author's words for the English reader. Vladimir Nabokov recognized this in his edition of 1964, but his controversial translation, though literally accurate, can hardly be characterized as clear or natural.

In my new version I have taken a different approach. Like Nabokov, I have freed myself from the shackles of rhyme; but, while I have retained Pushkin's fourteen-line stanzas and something of his word rhythms, I have given absolute primacy to the accurate reproduction of Pushkin's meaning and intonation in a clear, fluent and modern English that matches the original's clear, fluent and modern Russian. In this way I hope that *Eugene Onegin* can at last be enjoyed in the English-reading world both as a novel and as poetry, and that Pushkin's work will attract more and more the admiration and enthusiasm it deserves.

The translation is followed by an extensive commentary – the fullest, apart from Nabokov's, that has appeared in English. Although I have not attempted to repeat Nabokov's exhaustive analysis of *Onegin*'s antecedents in French and English literature, I have of course drawn extensively on him and other commentators, English and Russian, in compiling my notes. The commentary also contains, however, much new material, notably on structure and on the significance of the epigraphs, which I hope will intrigue both students and general readers who wish to penetrate below the surface of this many-layered work.

Notes and commentary (pp. 293*ff.*) are arranged under chapter and stanza numbers.

– Roger Clarke
March 2011

Note on the Present Edition

My bilingual edition of *Eugene Onegin* was first published in 2011. It is now being reissued by Alma Classics, and I have taken the opportunity of the reprint to touch up the translation here and there, mainly to improve the rhythms, and to add a few details to the commentary.

– Roger Clarke
March 2015

Eugene Onegin

Pétri de vanité il avait encore plus de cette espèce d'orgueil qui fait avouer avec la même indifférence les bonnes comme les mauvaises actions, suite d'un sentiment de supériorité peut-être imaginaire.

– Tiré d'une lettre particulière

ПОСВЯЩЕНИЕ

Не мысля гордый свет забавить,
Вниманье дружбы возлюбя,
Хотел бы я тебе представить
Залог достойнее тебя,
Достойнее души прекрасной,
Святой исполненной мечты,
Поэзии живой и ясной,
Высоких дум и простоты;
Но так и быть — рукой пристрастной
Прими собранье пестрых глав,
Полусмешных, полупечальных,
Простонародных, идеальных,
Небрежный плод моих забав,
Бессонниц, легких вдохновений,
Незрелых и увядших лет,
Ума холодных наблюдений
И сердца горестных замет.

DEDICATION

I had no thought to amuse a disdainful world;
but friendly interest I do prize,
and you, my friend, I'd like to have presented
with a token worthier of you,
yes, worthier of your noble spirit,
so full of sublime imagination,
of lively, limpid poetry,
of lofty ideas and of simplicity.
But there it is. Be kind:
accept this batch of patchy chapters,
half-funny and half-sad,
idealistic, down-to-earth –
the slapdash product of my leisure hours,
my sleepless nights, my momentary inspirations,
of a life blighted ere its prime,
of a mind's chilling observations,
and of a heart's experience of pain.

ГЛАВА ПЕРВАЯ

И жить торопится и чувствовать спешит.
—*Кн. Вяземский*

1   «Мой дядя самых честных правил,
    Когда не в шутку занемог,
    Он уважать себя заставил
    И лучше выдумать не мог.
    Его пример другим наука;
    Но, боже мой, какая скука
    С больным сидеть и день и ночь,
    Не отходя ни шагу прочь!
    Какое низкое коварство
    Полуживого забавлять,
    Ему подушки поправлять,
    Печально подносить лекарство,
    Вздыхать и думать про себя:
    Когда же черт возьмет тебя!»

2   Так думал молодой повеса,
    Летя в пыли на почтовых,
    Всевышней волею Зевеса
    Наследник всех своих родных.
    Друзья Людмилы и Руслана!
    С героем моего романа
    Без предисловий сей же час
    Позвольте познакомить вас:
    Онегин, добрый мой приятель,
    Родился на брегах Невы,
    Где, может быть, родились вы
    Или блистали, мой читатель!
    Там некогда гулял и я:
    Но вреден север для меня.

CHAPTER ONE

In a hurry to live, in haste for experience.
– Prince Vyázemsky

1 "Man of the highest principles, my uncle...
When he fell ill in earnest,
he won respect – he couldn't have
thought up a better way.
His example is a lesson to us all...
But, God! – how boring
to sit up with a sick man day and night
and never move one step away!
What base hypocrisy
to try to amuse a man half-dead,
straighten his pillows,
solemnly offer medicine,
make sympathetic noises – and keep thinking,
'When *will* the Devil take you?'!"

2 These were a young scapegrace's musings,
as he rode post-haste through the dust –
heir, by the sovereign will of Zeus,
to all of his family's wealth.
You fans of my Lyudmíla and Ruslán,
I'd like to have you meet
without preamble or ado,
my novel's hero –
Onégin, a good friend of mine,
born in St Petersburg by the Nevá,
where you, my reader, maybe too were born
or made your name.
I was once out and about there too –
but the north disagrees with me now.

11

3   Служив отлично, благородно,
Долгами жил его отец,
Давал три бала ежегодно
И промотался наконец.
Судьба Евгения хранила:
Сперва *Madame* за ним ходила,
Потом *Monsieur* ее сменил.
Ребенок был резов, но мил.
Monsieur l'Abbé, француз убогий,
Чтоб не измучилось дитя,
Учил его всему шутя,
Не докучал моралью строгой,
Слегка за шалости бранил
И в Летний сад гулять водил.

4   Когда же юности мятежной
Пришла Евгению пора,
Пора надежд и грусти нежной,
Monsieur прогнали со двора.
Вот мой Онегин на свободе;
Острижен по последней моде,
Как *dandy* лондонский одет —
И наконец увидел свет.
Он по-французски совершенно
Мог изъясняться и писал;
Легко мазурку танцевал
И кланялся непринужденно;
Чего ж вам больше? Свет решил,
Что он умен и очень мил.

5   Мы все учились понемногу
Чему-нибудь и как-нибудь,
Так воспитаньем, слава Богу,
У нас немудрено блеснуть.
Онегин был по мненью многих
(Судей решительных и строгих)
Ученый малый, но педант:
Имел он счастливый талант
Без принужденья в разговоре
Коснуться до всего слегка,
С ученым видом знатока
Хранить молчанье в важном споре
И возбуждать улыбку дам
Огнем нежданных эпиграмм.

3   Onégin's father had served the state
     with "honour and distinction" (as they say),
     then lived on credit, gave three balls a year,
     and finally went broke.
     But Fate was looking after young Eugene.
     A governess fussed over him at first;
     then a *monsieur* replaced *madame*.
     The boy was mischievous, but sweet.
     The French *monsieur* (a God-forsaken cleric),
     not wanting to harass the lad,
     cracked jokes through all his lessons,
     spared him the rigours of morality,
     scolded him lightly for his pranks –
     and took him on outings to the Summer Park.

4   But once Eugene attained the age
     of rebellious adolescence –
     that age of hopes and tender moodiness –
     monsieur was shown the door.
     My friend Onégin now was free!
     He had his hair cut to the latest fashion,
     dressed like a London *dandy*,
     and took a look at high society.
     He could speak perfect French
     and write it too,
     dance the mazurka gracefully,
     and bow with elegance –
     what more could you desire? Society judged him
     clever, and awfully nice.

5   We've all tried fitfully to study
     some random subject in a random way;
     so in our circles it's not hard, thank God,
     to dazzle folk with erudition.
     Society's instant pundits
     (and they were many) reckoned Onégin
     a well-read chap – a know-all even.
     He had the happy knack in conversation
     of touching naturally and lightly
     on all and every topic,
     holding his peace in serious debate
     with an expert's knowing look,
     and making the ladies smile
     with the flash of a sudden jibe.

6   Латынь из моды вышла ныне:
       Так, если правду вам сказать,
       Он знал довольно по-латыне,
       Чтоб эпиграфы разбирать,
       Потолковать об Ювенале,
       В конце письма поставить *vale*,
       Да помнил, хоть не без греха,
       Из Энеиды два стиха.
       Он рыться не имел охоты
       В хронологической пыли
       Бытописания земли:
       Но дней минувших анекдоты
       От Ромула до наших дней
       Хранил он в памяти своей.

7   Высокой страсти не имея
       Для звуков жизни не щадить,
       Не мог он ямба от хорея,
       Как мы ни бились, отличить.
       Бранил Гомера, Феокрита;
       Зато читал Адама Смита
       И был глубокой эконом,
       То есть умел судить о том,
       Как государство богатеет,
       И чем живет, и почему
       Не нужно золота ему,
       Когда простой продукт имеет.
       Отец понять его не мог
       И земли отдавал в залог.

8   Всего, что знал еще Евгений,
       Пересказать мне недосуг;
       Но в чем он истинный был гений,
       Что знал он тверже всех наук,
       Что было для него измлада
       И труд, и мука, и отрада,
       Что занимало целый день
       Его тоскующую лень, —
       Была наука страсти нежной,
       Которую воспел Назон,
       За что страдальцем кончил он
       Свой век блестящий и мятежный
       В Молдавии, в глуши степей,
       Вдали Италии своей.

6   Latin's gone out of fashion nowadays.
      Yet, to do Onégin justice,
      he knew enough of it
      to make out an inscription,
      expatiate on Juvenal,
      and end a letter with *vale*;
      and he could quote (not faultlessly, it's true)
      two lines from the *Aeneid*.
      For him there was no urge to delve
      deep in the dusty archives
      of world historiography;
      but anecdotes of earlier days,
      from Romulus to now,
      he memorized with ease.

7   Onégin harboured no sublime ambition
      to wear his life out writing verse;
      indeed, for all our pains, he never learnt
      to tell an iambus from a trochee.
      He'd no use for Theocritus or Homer.
      Instead he took to reading Adam Smith,
      and mastered the inwardness of economics:
      that is, he could lay down the law
      on what it is a nation lives on,
      what makes it prosper,
      and why it has no need of gold
      when output more than covers costs.
      Onégin's father couldn't make him out,
      and went on mortgaging his lands.

8   I haven't time to itemize
      all that Onégin knew.
      He was a genius, though, in one thing:
      of this he'd a surer grasp than of any branch of study;
      from earliest youth
      it had been his work, his torment and his joy;
      day in day out it had occupied
      his aching idleness.
      I mean the Art of Love –
      the art that Ovid celebrated,
      and for which he ended
      his glittering and turbulent career
      a martyr on Moldavia's empty plains,
      remote from Italy, his home.

15

9 ....

10 Как рано мог он лицемерить,
    Таить надежду, ревновать,
    Разуверять, заставить верить,
    Казаться мрачным, изнывать,
    Являться гордым и послушным,
    Внимательным иль равнодушным!
    Как томно был он молчалив,
    Как пламенно красноречив,
    В сердечных письмах как небрежен!
    Одним дыша, одно любя,
    Как он умел забыть себя!
    Как взор его был быстр и нежен,
    Стыдлив и дерзок, а порой
    Блистал послушною слезой!

11 Как он умел казаться новым,
    Шутя невинность изумлять,
    Пугать отчаяньем готовым,
    Приятной лестью забавлять,
    Ловить минуту умиленья,
    Невинных лет предубежденья
    Умом и страстью побеждать,
    Невольной ласки ожидать,
    Молить и требовать признанья,
    Подслушать сердца первый звук,
    Преследовать любовь, и вдруг
    Добиться тайного свиданья...
    И после ей наедине
    Давать уроки в тишине!

12 Как рано мог уж он тревожить
    Сердца кокеток записных!
    Когда ж хотелось уничтожить
    Ему соперников своих,
    Как он язвительно злословил!
    Какие сети им готовил!
    Но вы, блаженные мужья,
    С ним оставались вы друзья:
    Его ласкал супруг лукавый,
    Фобласа давний ученик,
    И недоверчивый старик,
    И рогоносец величавый,
    Всегда довольный сам собой,
    Своим обедом и женой.

9   ....

10   How soon he'd learnt to act a part!
      – to hide his hopes, exhibit jealousy,
      destroy belief and re-establish it,
      affect resentment or despondency,
      haughtiness or humility,
      attention or indifference.
      He was adept at languishing in silence,
      at speaking out with blazing eloquence,
      and at writing a lover's artless billets-doux.
      Obsessive in his feelings and affections,
      he was yet able to forget himself.
      The look his eye gave could be curt or tender,
      bashful or bold – and on occasion
      could gleam with an obedient tear.

11   How well he'd taught himself to play the novice,
      startle the innocent in jest,
      scare them with opportune despair,
      charm them with pretty blandishments,
      catch the right moment for emotion,
      and marshal argument and passion
      to overcome the scruples of the young!
      He'd lie in wait for a stray sign of fondness,
      entreat, demand a declaration,
      capture the heart's first shy response,
      keep up love's pressure, clinch
      there and then a secret rendezvous...
      and later in the stillness give her
      tuition one to one.

12   How soon he'd learnt to stir
      the hearts of practised flirts!
      Were he to wish
      to eliminate a rival,
      what cutting slanders he put round,
      what traps he set them!
      But husbands he put blissfully at ease:
      they stayed his friends;
      indeed, all made a fuss of him –
      the cunning ones (ex-pupils of the same school),
      the old suspicious ones,
      and those conceit had blinded to their state,
      so satisfied they'd always been
      with themselves, their dinners and their wives.

13, 14   ....

15   Бывало, он еще в постеле:
     К нему записочки несут.
     Что? Приглашенья? В самом деле,
     Три дома на вечер зовут:
     Там будет бал, там детский праздник.
     Куда ж поскачет мой проказник?
     С кого начнет он? Всё равно:
     Везде поспеть немудрено.
     Покамест в утреннем уборе,
     Надев широкий боливар,
     Онегин едет на бульвар
     И там гуляет на просторе,
     Пока недремлющий брегет
     Не прозвонит ему обед.

16   Уж тёмно: в санки он садится.
     «Пади, пади!» — раздался крик;
     Морозной пылью серебрится
     Его бобровый воротник.
     К *Talon* помчался: он уверен,
     Что там уж ждет его Каверин.
     Вошел: и пробка в потолок,
     Вина кометы брызнул ток;
     Пред ним *roast-beef* окровавленный,
     И трюфли, роскошь юных лет,
     Французской кухни лучший цвет,
     И Страсбурга пирог нетленный
     Меж сыром лимбургским живым
     И ананасом золотым.

17   Еще бокалов жажда просит
     Залить горячий жир котлет,
     Но звон брегета им доносит,
     Что новый начался балет.
     Театра злой законодатель,
     Непостоянный обожатель
     Очаровательных актрис,
     Почетный гражданин кулис,
     Онегин полетел к театру,
     Где каждый, вольностью дыша,
     Готов охлопать *entrechat*,
     Обшикать Федру, Клеопатру,
     Моину вызвать (для того,
     Чтоб только слышали его).

13, 14 ....

15   Here's how a day would pass. Onégin
would still be in bed when messages were brought him.
"What? Invitations?" Yes indeed,
three houses sought his presence at soirées;
at one there'd be a ball; elsewhere a youngsters' dance.
Which would my playboy friend dash off to?
Where'd he begin? No problem there:
easy to make a quick round of them all.
But first, in morning dress
and wide-brimmed hat Bolívar-style,
Onégin rode off to the Boulevard
and took a stroll there out of doors
until his ever-wakeful watch from Paris
chimed out the hour for dinner.

16   Now it was dark. He climbed aboard a sleigh;
"Make way! Make way!" the shout rang out;
and frosty dust
besilvered his beaver-skin collar.
He rushed to Talon's, quite sure
that Kavérin would now be there waiting.
As he walked in, a cork hit the ceiling,
and vintage champagne gushed out in a flood.
Before him were spread *roast beef* carved rare,
and truffles – that treat the youngsters love,
finest flower of French cuisine –
and ever-fresh Strasbourg pâté,
with ripened Limburg cheese
and golden pineapple slices.

17   The friends were thirsting for still more champagne
to wash down the hot fat of cutlets,
but the chime of Onégin's watch informed them
the new ballet had now begun.
Onégin, theatreland's malign trendsetter,
the wayward worshipper
of witching actresses
and honorary citizen backstage –
Onégin dashed off to the playhouse,
where all, in uninhibited excitement,
were ready to applaud each entrechat,
hiss wicked Phèdre and Cleopatra,
and encore good Moëna – their one aim,
to get their voices heard.

18   Волшебный край! там в стары годы,
      Сатиры смелый властелин,
      Блистал Фонвизин, друг свободы,
      И переимчивый Княжнин;
      Там Озеров невольны дани
      Народных слез, рукоплесканий
      С младой Семёновой делил;
      Там наш Катенин воскресил
      Корнеля гений величавый;
      Там вывел колкий Шаховской
      Своих комедий шумный рой,
      Там и Дидло венчался славой,
      Там, там под сению кулис
      Младые дни мои неслись.

19   Мои богини! что вы? где вы?
      Внемлите мой печальный глас:
      Всё те же ль вы? другие ль девы,
      Сменив, не заменили вас?
      Услышу ль вновь я ваши хоры?
      Узрю ли русской Терпсихоры
      Душой исполненный полет?
      Иль взор унылый не найдет
      Знакомых лиц на сцене скучной,
      И, устремив на чуждый свет
      Разочарованный лорнет,
      Веселья зритель равнодушный,
      Безмолвно буду я зевать
      И о былом воспоминать?

20   Театр уж полон; ложи блещут;
      Партер и кресла — всё кипит;
      В райке нетерпеливо плещут,
      И, взвившись, занавес шумит.
      Блистательна, полувоздушна,
      Смычку волшебному послушна,
      Толпою нимф окружена,
      Стоит Истомина; она,
      Одной ногой касаясь пола,
      Другою медленно кружит,
      И вдруг прыжок, и вдруг летит,
      Летит, как пух от уст Эола;
      То стан совьет, то разовьет
      И быстрой ножкой ножку бьет.

18   Ah, theatre, land of enchantment!
It was there, years back, that Fonvízin sparkled,
that daring master of satire, liberty's friend,
as did that great adapter Knyazhnín.
There Ózerov would share with young Semyónova
the nation's spontaneous tribute
of weeping and applause.
There our Katénin resurrected
Corneille's majestic genius.
There caustic Shakhovskóy
released his buzzing swarm of comedies.
There Didelot, too, won his crown of acclaim.
And there – yes there, as I lurked backstage,
my own young days sped by.

19   You actresses I worshipped! What are you, where are you now?
(How sad it is I have to ask!)
Are you the same still? Or have some other girls
succeeded (without superseding) you?
Shall I hear you sing again in chorus?
Shall I see a Russian Terpsichore
leap up with verve and inspiration?
Or maybe my dejected gaze
will find no familiar face on the dreary stage:
so I'll focus my opera glasses
in disillusion on an alien world;
I'll watch the frivolous spectacle with indifference,
yawn quietly,
and think back on the past.

20   The theatre was full; the boxes glittered;
stalls, pit – the whole place seethed.
Up in the gods folk clapped impatiently.
With a swoosh up went the curtain.
There, radiant, light as air,
encircled by nymphs,
spellbound by the string-player's bow –
there stood Istómina.
With the toe of one foot on the stage,
the other she gently gyrated;
then up she leapt, and off she flew,
flew like fluff on a puff of the wind;
now she'd twist, now she'd untwist, her waist
and deftly tapping one foot with the other.

21 Всё хлопает. Онегин входит,
    Идет меж кресел по ногам,
    Двойной лорнет скосясь наводит
    На ложи незнакомых дам;
    Все ярусы окинул взором,
    Всё видел: лицами, убором
    Ужасно недоволен он;
    С мужчинами со всех сторон
    Раскланялся, потом на сцену
    В большом рассеянье взглянул,
    Отворотился — и зевнул,
    И молвил: «Всех пора на смену;
    Балеты долго я терпел,
    Но и Дидло мне надоел».

22 Еще амуры, черти, змеи
    На сцене скачут и шумят;
    Еще усталые лакеи
    На шубах у подъезда спят;
    Еще не перестали топать,
    Сморкаться, кашлять, шикать, хлопать;
    Еще снаружи и внутри
    Везде блистают фонари;
    Еще, прозябнув, бьются кони,
    Наскуча упряжью своей,
    И кучера, вокруг огней,
    Бранят господ и бьют в ладони —
    А уж Онегин вышел вон;
    Домой одеться едет он.

23 Изображу ль в картине верной
    Уединенный кабинет,
    Где мод воспитанник примерный
    Одет, раздет и вновь одет?
    Всё, чем для прихоти обильной
    Торгует Лондон щепетильный
    И по Балтическим волнам
    За лес и сало возит нам,
    Всё, что в Париже вкус голодный,
    Полезный промысел избрав,
    Изобретает для забав,
    Для роскоши, для неги модной, —
    Всё украшало кабинет
    Философа в осьмнадцать лет.

21   The whole house cheered... Now, enter Onégin,
stepping over legs between rows.
He trained his opera glasses sideways;
scanned boxes of ladies he didn't know;
ran his eye along every tier;
took it all in. But faces and dresses
disappointed him dreadfully.
He greeted the men on all sides with a bow;
next, greatly distracted,
he glanced at the stage,
turned quickly away – and yawned.
"Time to get rid of the lot," he muttered.
"I've put up with ballets a good long time,
but now even Didelot bores me stiff."

22   Cupids, demons and dragons were still
prancing noisily round the stage;
weary footmen were still
dozing on furs in the porch;
spectators were still incessantly stamping,
snuffling, coughing, hissing and clapping;
everywhere lamps
still glistened within and without;
horses still fidgeted, feeling the cold,
and chafed at their gear;
and coachmen still clustered round fires,
running down masters and slapping their palms.
But Onégin had left already;
he was riding home to change.

23   Let me now draw you a true-to-life picture
of the inner sanctum
where this exemplary pupil of fashion
would dress, undress and dress once more.
All that the haberdashers of London sell
to meet the demands of extravagant fancy
and ship to us over the Baltic
in exchange for timber and tallow;
all that chic entrepreneurs in Paris,
with an eye to good business,
devise to amuse, to pamper
and to divert with idle pleasures –
all this adorned the dressing room
of our aesthete aged eighteen.

24 Янтарь на трубках Цареграда,
Фарфор и бронза на столе,
И, чувств изнеженных отрада,
Духи в граненом хрустале;
Гребенки, пилочки стальные,
Прямые ножницы, кривые
И щетки тридцати родов
И для ногтей и для зубов.
Руссо (замечу мимоходом)
Не мог понять, как важный Грим
Смел чистить ногти перед ним,
Красноречивым сумасбродом.
Защитник вольности и прав
В сем случае совсем неправ.

25 Быть можно дельным человеком
И думать о красе ногтей:
К чему бесплодно спорить с веком?
Обычай деспот меж людей.
Второй Чадаев, мой Евгений,
Боясь ревнивых осуждений,
В своей одежде был педант
И то, что мы назвали франт.
Он три часа по крайней мере
Пред зеркалами проводил
И из уборной выходил
Подобный ветреной Венере,
Когда, надев мужской наряд,
Богиня едет в маскарад.

26 В последнем вкусе туалетом
Заняв ваш любопытный взгляд,
Я мог бы пред ученым светом
Здесь описать его наряд;
Конечно б это было смело,
Описывать мое же дело:
Но *панталоны, фрак, жилет,*
Всех этих слов на русском нет;
А вижу я, винюсь пред вами,
Что уж и так мой бедный слог
Пестреть гораздо б меньше мог
Иноплеменными словами,
Хоть и заглядывал я встарь
В Академический словарь.

24   He'd amber-stemmed pipes from Istanbul,
a table of china and bronzes,
and (special delight of the over-refined)
perfumes in cut crystal jars.
There were combs, too, and small steel files,
and scissors both straight and curved,
and brushes of thirty kinds
for nails and teeth.
(Rousseau, by the way, that eloquent crank,
could not comprehend
how a man of standing like Grimm
could clean his nails in his caller's presence.
The defender of freedom and human rights
was in this case not right at all –

25   for you *can* be a capable chap
and still take care that your nails look nice.
Why pick a pointless quarrel with your times?
It's custom dictates how humankind behaves.)
My friend Onégin, like Chaadáyev,
feared jealous criticism
and took excessive trouble with his dress;
in short, he was a fop.
He used to spend three hours at least
in front of mirrors,
emerging from his boudoir
just as though Venus on a whim
were off to a fancy-dress ball
in male attire.

26   Having engaged your inquisitive gaze
with the latest taste in *toilette*,
I *could* now regale the literary world
by describing Onégin's manner of dress.
That would be rash, I'm sure.
It's my job to describe, that's true;
but in Russian we have no words
for *pantalons*, *frac* and *gilet*;
and it's with shame that I observe
my threadbare style's
already far too patched
with foreign words,
despite the time I once spent browsing
in the Russian Academy's Lexicon.

27   У нас теперь не то в предмете:
Мы лучше поспешим на бал,
Куда стремглав в ямской карете
Уж мой Онегин поскакал.
Перед померкшими домами
Вдоль сонной улицы рядами
Двойные фонари карет
Веселый изливают свет
И радуги на снег наводят;
Усеян плошками кругом,
Блестит великолепный дом;
По цельным окнам тени ходят,
Мелькают профили голов
И дам и модных чудаков.

28   Вот наш герой подъехал к сеням;
Швейцара мимо он стрелой
Взлетел по мраморным ступеням,
Расправил волоса рукой,
Вошел. Полна народу зала;
Музыка уж греметь устала;
Толпа мазуркой занята;
Кругом и шум и теснота;
Брянчат кавалергарда шпоры;
Летают ножки милых дам;
По их пленительным следам
Летают пламенные взоры,
И ревом скрыпок заглушен
Ревнивый шепот модных жен.

29   Во дни веселий и желаний
Я был от балов без ума:
Верней нет места для признаний
И для вручения письма.
О вы, почтенные супруги!
Вам предложу свои услуги;
Прошу мою заметить речь:
Я вас хочу предостеречь.
Вы также, маменьки, построже
За дочерьми смотрите вслед:
Держите прямо свой лорнет!
Не то… не то, избави боже!
Я это потому пишу,
Что уж давно я не грешу.

27   But this is by the by.
　　　We'd better hurry to the ball,
　　　where Onégin has already dashed
　　　at breakneck speed in a hired carriage.
　　　Coaches were parked in rows
　　　in a slumbering street by darkened houses.
　　　Their double lamps
　　　diffused a cheerful light
　　　and scattered rainbows on the snow.
　　　A splendid mansion sparkled
　　　with encircling lanterns.
　　　Across the plate-glass windows shadows passed,
　　　and transient silhouetted heads
　　　of ladies and male fashion freaks.

28   Onégin drove up to the porch.
　　　He darted past the doorman,
　　　flew up the marble stairs,
　　　smoothed his hair with a hand,
　　　and entered the crowded ballroom.
　　　The blare of music was flagging already;
　　　a mazurka held the company's attention;
　　　on every side was noise and crush;
　　　a cavalry officer's spurs were jangling;
　　　the dainty feet of pretty ladies
　　　flashed by, and tracking their alluring footsteps
　　　there flashed the menfolk's ardent glances too;
　　　and screeching strings drowned jealous whispers
　　　from fashion-conscious wives.

29   In my days of fun and flirting
　　　I used to be madly fond of balls.
　　　There's nowhere safer to declare your love
　　　or slip a letter into someone's hand.
　　　Respected husbands,
　　　I offer you my services:
　　　I beg you, mark well what I say;
　　　I want to warn you in advance.
　　　And you too, fond mamas,
　　　keep stricter watch over your daughters;
　　　hold your lorgnettes up straight!
　　　Or else... or else, God help you!
　　　(Why do I write this? Well it's long now
　　　since I have misbehaved.)

30 Увы, на разные забавы
    Я много жизни погубил!
    Но если б не страдали нравы,
    Я балы б до сих пор любил.
    Люблю я бешеную младость,
    И тесноту, и блеск, и радость,
    И дам обдуманный наряд;
    Люблю их ножки; только вряд
    Найдете вы в России целой
    Три пары стройных женских ног.
    Ах! долго я забыть не мог
    Две ножки… Грустный, охладелый,
    Я всё их помню, и во сне
    Оне тревожат сердце мне.

31 Когда ж, и где, в какой пустыне,
    Безумец, их забудешь ты?
    Ах, ножки, ножки! где вы ныне?
    Где мнете вешние цветы?
    Взлелеяны в восточной неге,
    На северном, печальном снеге
    Вы не оставили следов:
    Любили мягких вы ковров
    Роскошное прикосновенье.
    Давно ль для вас я забывал
    И жажду славы и похвал,
    И край отцов, и заточенье?
    Исчезло счастье юных лет,
    Как на лугах ваш легкий след.

32 Дианы грудь, ланиты Флоры
    Прелестны, милые друзья!
    Однако ножка Терпсихоры
    Прелестней чем-то для меня.
    Она, пророчествуя взгляду
    Неоцененную награду,
    Влечет условною красой
    Желаний своевольный рой.
    Люблю ее, мой друг Эльвина,
    Под длинной скатертью столов,
    Весной на мураве лугов,
    Зимой на чугуне камина,
    На зеркальном паркете зал,
    У моря на граните скал.

30   Sadly, I've wasted too much of my life
on various frivolities.
But balls I would still love today,
if they weren't so bad for morals.
I love the youngsters' recklessness,
the crush, the glitter and the gaiety –
and I love the careful way the ladies dress.
I love their dainty feet as well –
though in all of Russia you'll hardly find
three pairs of shapely female feet.
Ah! one such pair I've long tried to forget –
but even now, though sad and chill at heart,
I still remember them,
and still in dreams they stir me deep within.

31   Fool that I am, will I forget them
at any time, in any place, in any wilderness?
Those dainty feet – where are they now?
Where are they treading springtime flowers?
Groomed in the sumptuous idleness of the East,
they've never left their print
in dreary northern snows:
the luxurious feel of yielding carpets
– that's what they loved.
Was it so long ago that for their sake
I was forgetting my thirst for fame and honour,
my homeland, and my loss of liberty?
My youthful happiness has vanished now, though,
like her light footprint on the meadow grass.

32   A Diana's naked breast, a Flora's blooming cheeks,
dear friends, are indeed delightful;
but the dainty foot of a dancing Terpsichore
for me is somehow more delightful still.
A girl's foot promises the gaze
a reward beyond all price,
and with its hints of beauty draws behind it
a swarm of uncontrollable desires.
I love it, dear Elvína,
whether beneath long tablecloths,
or on the meadow turf in spring,
or on the fender of a hearth in winter,
or on a ballroom's polished parquet floor,
or by the sea on granite rocks.

33 Я помню море пред грозою:
Как я завидовал волнам,
Бегущим бурной чередою
С любовью лечь к ее ногам!
Как я желал тогда с волнами
Коснуться милых ног устами!
Нет, никогда средь пылких дней
Кипящей младости моей
Я не желал с таким мученьем
Лобзать уста младых Армид,
Иль розы пламенных ланит,
Иль перси, полные томленьем;
Нет, никогда порыв страстей
Так не терзал души моей!

34 Мне памятно другое время:
В заветных иногда мечтах
Держу я счастливое стремя…
И ножку чувствую в руках;
Опять кипит воображенье,
Опять ее прикосновенье
Зажгло в увядшем сердце кровь,
Опять тоска, опять любовь!..
Но полно прославлять надменных
Болтливой лирою своей;
Оне не стоят ни страстей,
Ни песен, ими вдохновенных:
Слова и взор волшебниц сих
Обманчивы… как ножки их.

35 Что ж мой Онегин? Полусонный
В постелю с бала едет он:
А Петербург неугомонный
Уж барабаном пробужден.
Встает купец, идет разносчик,
На биржу тянется извозчик,
С кувшином охтенка спешит,
Под ней снег утренний хрустит.
Проснулся утра шум приятный,
Открыты ставни, трубный дым
Столбом восходит голубым,
И хлебник, немец аккуратный,
В бумажном колпаке, не раз
Уж отворял свой *васисдас*.

33   I recall the sea before a storm:
how I envied the waves
running in boisterous succession
to cast themselves lovingly at her feet!
How I longed at that moment to join the waves
and touch those dear feet with my lips!
No, never in my fervent youth's
most ardent years
had I longed with such anguish
to kiss a young Armida's lips,
or the roses of her burning cheeks,
or her languorous breasts.
No, never had such an outburst
of passion rent my heart.

34   Another time too comes to mind.
Sometimes in my most cherished dreams
I thrill to hold a stirrup for her...
and feel her foot between my hands.
Again my imagination boils;
again the very touch
sets blood aflame within my weary heart;
again, the torment; again, the love! –
I'm chattering on, though: that's enough
of celebrating girls who know their power.
The passion and the poems they inspire –
those women just aren't worth it.
Witches they are: their words and looks deceive –
as do their dainty feet.

35   Well, and Onégin? Half-asleep,
he was riding from ball to bed.
By now the restless city'd been aroused
by the dawn drum roll.
Shopkeepers getting up;
street sellers on the move;
cab-drivers sauntering to the rank;
an Okhta dairy girl hurrying with milk churn
and crunching fresh snow underfoot –
the cheerful bustle of morning had sprung to life;
shutters were opened; blue columns of smoke
rose up from chimneys; and already
the ever-punctual German baker, cotton-capped,
had served folk through his *Halbtür* more than once.

36   Но, шумом бала утомленный
      И утро в полночь обратя,
      Спокойно спит в тени блаженной
      Забав и роскоши дитя.
      Проснется за полдень, и снова
      До утра жизнь его готова,
      Однообразна и пестра.
      И завтра то же, что вчера.
      Но был ли счастлив мой Евгений,
      Свободный, в цвете лучших лет,
      Среди блистательных побед,
      Среди всседневных наслаждений?
      Вотще ли был он средь пиров
      Неосторожен и здоров?

37   Нет: рано чувства в нем остыли;
      Ему наскучил света шум;
      Красавицы не долго были
      Предмет его привычных дум;
      Измены утомить успели;
      Друзья и дружба надоели,
      Затем, что не всегда же мог
      Beef-steaks и страсбургский пирог
      Шампанской обливать бутылкой
      И сыпать острые слова,
      Когда болела голова;
      И хоть он был повеса пылкий,
      Но разлюбил он наконец
      И брань, и саблю, и свинец.

38   Недуг, которого причину
      Давно бы отыскать пора,
      Подобный английскому *сплину*,
      Короче: русская *хандра*
      Им овладела понемногу;
      Он застрелиться, слава Богу,
      Попробовать не захотел,
      Но к жизни вовсе охладел.
      Как *Child-Harold*, угрюмый, томный
      В гостиных появлялся он;
      Ни сплетни света, ни бостон,
      Ни милый взгляд, ни вздох нескромный,
      Ничто не трогало его,
      Не замечал он ничего.

36   Tired out, though, by the noisy ball, Onégin
turned morning into midnight
and slept on peacefully in blissful darkness
like a cosseted, carefree child.
Past midday he'd wake up; once more
till morning his routine was settled,
monotonous in its variety,
tomorrow same as yesterday.
Onégin was in the prime of life – no ties,
everywhere brilliant conquests,
every day spent in pleasure.
But was he happy? His rude health,
his heedless way of life, his partying –
were these enough to give him satisfaction?

37   Not so. His feelings soon grew numb.
Society's clamour wore him out.
Attractive women didn't for long
remain the constant topic of his thoughts:
their infidelities exhausted him.
He sickened of friends and friendship;
for he couldn't go on for ever
sprinkling bons mots
and washing down steaks and Strasbourg pâté
in champagne by the bottle,
with a head that kept on aching.
Eventually too,
hot-blooded though he'd been and wild,
he lost his love of quarrels, swords and shot.

38   He gradually fell victim
to the malady (the cause of which
should long ago have been researched)
that's like the English *spleen* –
in short, what we know as depression.
He never thought, thank God, of trying
to shoot himself;
he grew, though, utterly cold to life.
When he appeared in the salons,
he seemed like Childe Harold, morose and listless.
Nothing engaged his interest –
not society scandal, a game of cards,
an affectionate glance, a suggestive sigh.
He noticed nothing.

39–41 ....

42   Причудницы большого света!
Всех прежде вас оставил он;
И правда то, что в наши лета
Довольно скучен высший тон;
Хоть, может быть, иная дама
Толкует Сея и Бентама,
Но вообще их разговор
Несносный, хоть невинный вздор;
К тому ж оне так непорочны,
Так величавы, так умны,
Так благочестия полны,
Так осмотрительны, так точны,
Так неприступны для мужчин,
Что вид их уж рождает сплин.

43   И вы, красотки молодые,
Которых позднею порой
Уносят дрожки удалые
По петербургской мостовой –
И вас покинул мой Евгений.
Отступник бурных наслаждений,
Онегин дома заперся,
Зевая, за перо взялся,
Хотел писать — но труд упорный
Ему был тошен; ничего
Не вышло из пера его,
И не попал он в цех задорный
Людей, о коих не сужу,
Затем, что к ним принадлежу.

44   И снова преданный безделью,
Томясь душевной пустотой,
Уселся он с похвальной целью
Себе присвоить ум чужой;
Отрядом книг уставил полку,
Читал, читал, а всё без толку:
Там скука, там обман и бред;
В том совести, в том смысла нет;
На всех различные вериги;
И устарела старина,
И старым бредит новизна.
Как женщин, он оставил книги,
И полку, с пыльной их семьей,
Задернул траурной тафтой.

42   Those affected high-society women –
they were the first Onégin dropped.
And, undeniably, life in the grandest circles
is these days tiresome enough.
One lady, perhaps,
may talk of Say and Bentham,
but on the whole their conversation
is tedious, if harmless, rubbish.
They're all so pure,
so dignified, so knowing,
so full of piety,
so circumspect, so precious,
so inaccessible to men –
the very sight of them will bring on spleen.

43   Next it was the pretty young girls
he gave up seeing –
the ones who late at night
are driven boldly off in open carriages
along St Petersburg's paved streets.
Forsaking wild pleasures such as these
Onégin shut himself at home
and with a yawn reached for a pen.
He thought he'd take up writing,
but couldn't face the unremitting work,
so the output of his pen was nil,
and he never joined the unruly guild
of folk whom I'll not criticize,
being one of them myself.

44   So Onégin succumbed to indolence once more.
Oppressed by emptiness within,
he settled down, with the estimable aim
of making others' thoughts his own.
He filled a shelf with a platoon of books
and read and read; but all in vain. He found
some boring, some untrue and incoherent;
one work would lack morality; another, reason.
They all showed various cramping limitations:
the ones of past date were outdated,
the new ones were besotted with the past.
Onégin gave up books, as he had women,
and over shelf and dusty occupants
he draped a shroud of taffeta.

45 Условий света свергнув бремя,
  Как он отстав от суеты,
  С ним подружился я в то время.
  Мне нравились его черты,
  Мечтам невольная преданность,
  Неподражательная странность
  И резкий, охлажденный ум.
  Я был озлоблен, он угрюм;
  Страстей игру мы знали оба;
  Томила жизнь обоих нас;
  В обоих сердца жар погас;
  Обоих ожидала злоба
  Слепой Фортуны и людей
  На самом утре наших дней.

46 Кто жил и мыслил, тот не может
  В душе не презирать людей;
  Кто чувствовал, того тревожит
  Призрак невозвратимых дней:
  Тому уж нет очарований,
  Того змия воспоминаний,
  Того раскаянье грызет.
  Всё это часто придает
  Большую прелесть разговору.
  Сперва Онегина язык
  Меня смущал; но я привык
  К его язвительному спору,
  И к шутке, с желчью пополам,
  И злости мрачных эпиграмм.

47 Как часто летнею порою,
  Когда прозрачно и светло
  Ночное небо над Невою
  И вод веселое стекло
  Не отражает лик Дианы,
  Воспомня прежних лет романы,
  Воспомня прежнюю любовь,
  Чувствительны, беспечны вновь,
  Дыханьем ночи благосклонной
  Безмолвно упивались мы!
  Как в лес зеленый из тюрьмы
  Перенесен колодник сонный,
  Так уносились мы мечтой
  К началу жизни молодой.

45   This was the time Onégin and I made friends.
I'd thrown off the burden of society's conventions
and had withdrawn, like him, from its futility.
There was a lot about him that I liked:
his helpless addiction to daydreaming,
his individualism and eccentricity,
his sharp, cold intellect.
I was embittered, he morose.
We'd both known what it was to trifle with emotion;
and we were weary, both of us, with life;
the fire in both our hearts was quenched.
The malice of blind ill fortune and of people,
had lain in wait for both of us
in the very morning of our lives.

46   Anyone who's lived and thought
can't help despising people in their hearts;
and anyone who's sensitive is haunted
by the spectre of days gone never to return.
For them, no more enchantment.
Recollections and remorse
bite them like adders.
Often such feelings
give added zest to conversation.
Onégin's language put me off at first,
but soon I grew accustomed
to his sarcastic repartee,
his jokes half-formed of bitterness,
and the spite of his dark aphorisms.

47   Many a time in summer,
when the night sky above the Nevá
was transparent and bright
and the smiling river's glassy waters
mirrored no image of the moon,
we'd silently drink our fill
of the mild nocturnal air,
remembering romances of past years,
remembering past love,
carefree and sentimental once again.
Like a sleeping prisoner transported in dream
from dungeon to leafy woodland,
so were we borne back in thought
to our first youth.

48   С душою, полной сожалений,
      И опершися на гранит,
      Стоял задумчиво Евгений,
      Как описал себя пиит.
      Всё было тихо; лишь ночные
      Перекликались часовые,
      Да дрожек отдаленный стук
      С Мильонной раздавался вдруг;
      Лишь лодка, веслами махая,
      Плыла по дремлющей реке:
      И нас пленяли вдалеке
      Рожок и песня удалая…
      Но слаще, средь ночных забав,
      Напев Торкватовых октав!

49   Адриатические волны,
      О Брента! нет, увижу вас
      И, вдохновенья снова полный,
      Услышу ваш волшебный глас!
      Он свят для внуков Аполлона;
      По гордой лире Альбиона
      Он мне знаком, он мне родной.
      Ночей Италии златой
      Я негой наслажусь на воле,
      С венецианкою младой,
      То говорливой, то немой,
      Плывя в таинственной гондоле –
      С ней обретут уста мои
      Язык Петрарки и любви.

50   Придет ли час моей свободы?
      Пора, пора! — взываю к ней;
      Брожу над морем, жду погоды,
      Маню ветрила кораблей.
      Под ризой бурь, с волнами споря,
      По вольному распутью моря
      Когда ж начну я вольный бег?
      Пора покинуть скучный брег
      Мне неприязненной стихии
      И средь полуденных зыбей,
      Под небом Африки моей,
      Вздыхать о сумрачной России,
      Где я страдал, где я любил,
      Где сердце я похоронил.

48   Heart full of regrets, Onégin
would stand deep in thought, "arms resting
upon the granite parapet",
as our "bard" described himself.
All would be still. Only the night-watch sentries
would be heard exchanging cries;
and the distant rattle of a carriage
would reach us suddenly from Milyónnaya Street.
Only a boat, with oars a-swinging,
would float down the slumbering river;
and the faraway sound of a horn and a jaunty song
would catch our ears… Delicious moments!
But sweeter still a night out in Venice,
and a boatman singing Torquato's lines!

49   Oh Adriatic waves, oh River Brenta!
Without a doubt I'll see them
and, full once more of inspiration,
I'll hear their magic voice!
That voice is sacred to us poets;
it's known to me through Byron's noble verses;
indeed it's part of me.
Yes, once I'm free, in golden Italy I'll spend
nights of delicious idleness
adrift in a curtained gondola
with a young Venetian girl,
now talkative, now mute;
and in her company my lips will master
the language of Petrarch and of love.

50   Will the hour of freedom ever come for me?
May it come now, yes now, I pray!
I roam the sea cliffs, waiting for the weather,
hailing the sails of passing ships.
When can I start my flight to freedom,
mantled by storms, fighting the waves,
across the open thoroughfare of the sea?
It's time I left the hateful shore
of this unfriendly land –
it's time I sailed the southern swell
beneath the sky of Africa, my home,
lamenting gloomy Russia,
where I have suffered, where I've loved,
and where I've buried my heart.

51 Онегин был готов со мною
    Увидеть чуждые страны;
    Но скоро были мы судьбою
    На долгий срок разведены.
    Отец его тогда скончался.
    Перед Онегиным собрался
    Заимодавцев жадный полк.
    У каждого свой ум и толк:
    Евгений, тяжбы ненавидя,
    Довольный жребием своим,
    Наследство предоставил им,
    Большой потери в том не видя
    Иль предузнав издалека
    Кончину дяди старика.

52 Вдруг получил он в самом деле
    От управителя доклад,
    Что дядя при смерти в постеле
    И с ним проститься был бы рад.
    Прочтя печальное посланье,
    Евгений тотчас на свиданье
    Стремглав по почте поскакал
    И уж заранее зевал,
    Приготовляясь, денег ради,
    На вздохи, скуку и обман
    (И тем я начал мой роман);
    Но, прилетев в деревню дяди,
    Его нашел уж на столе,
    Как дань готовую земле.

53 Нашел он полон двор услуги;
    К покойнику со всех сторон
    Съезжались недруги и други,
    Охотники до похорон.
    Покойника похоронили.
    Попы и гости ели, пили,
    И после важно разошлись,
    Как будто делом занялись.
    Вот наш Онегин сельский житель,
    Заводов, вод, лесов, земель
    Хозяин полный, а досель
    Порядка враг и расточитель,
    И очень рад, что прежний путь
    Переменил на что-нибудь.

51   Onégin was ready to join me
in seeing foreign lands.
But destiny was soon to impose
a lengthy separation on us.
It was now Onégin's father died –
and there confronted him
a greedy horde of moneylenders.
We all have our way of working things out.
Onégin hated lawsuits
and, being contented with his lot,
made over to the creditors his whole inheritance.
Maybe he saw here no great loss;
or maybe he'd a distant inkling
of his old uncle's death.

52   In fact, quite suddenly he did receive
news from the steward
that Uncle was on his deathbed
and wished to take his leave.
On reading these sad tidings,
Onégin without delay drove off post-haste
to visit the old man.
He was already yawning in advance
as he prepared himself, in aid of money,
for sighs and boredom and hypocrisy
(and here it was that I began my novel).
But when he raced up to his uncle's manor,
he found him already laid out on a table,
just like an offering ready for the earth.

53   He found, too, in the forecourt crowds of servants:
the friends – and foes – of the deceased
had ridden in from every side,
keen funeral-goers all.
The dead man's burial took place.
Both priests and guests kept eating, drinking,
then gravely went their ways, as though
they'd been engaged on business.
So there was Onégin, until yesterday
an enemy of good order and a spendthrift,
a country-dweller now, unchallenged owner
of workshops, watercourses, woodlands.
And very pleased he was his earlier path
had changed direction.

54   Два дня ему казались новы
       Уединенные поля,
       Прохлада сумрачной дубровы,
       Журчанье тихого ручья;
       На третий роща, холм и поле
       Его не занимали боле,
       Потом уж наводили сон;
       Потом увидел ясно он,
       Что и в деревне скука та же,
       Хоть нет ни улиц, ни дворцов,
       Ни карт, ни балов, ни стихов.
       Хандра ждала его на страже,
       И бегала за ним она,
       Как тень иль верная жена.

55   Я был рожден для жизни мирной,
       Для деревенской тишины;
       В глуши звучнее голос лирный,
       Живее творческие сны.
       Досугам посвятясь невинным,
       Брожу над озером пустынным,
       И *far niente* мой закон.
       Я каждым утром пробужден
       Для сладкой неги и свободы:
       Читаю мало, много сплю,
       Летучей славы не ловлю.
       Не так ли я в былые годы
       Провел в бездействии, в тени
       Мои счастливейшие дни?

56   Цветы, любовь, деревня, праздность,
       Поля! я предан вам душой.
       Всегда я рад заметить разность
       Между Онегиным и мной,
       Чтобы насмешливый читатель
       Или какой-нибудь издатель
       Замысловатой клеветы,
       Сличая здесь мои черты,
       Не повторял потом безбожно,
       Что намарал я свой портрет,
       Как Байрон, гордости поэт –
       Как будто нам уж невозможно
       Писать поэмы о другом,
       Как только о себе самом.

54   For two days everything seemed fresh –
the lonely countryside,
the trees' cool shade,
the brooklet's quiet murmur.
But on the third day woods, hills, fields
ceased to engage him;
thenceforth they only made him sleepy.
Thenceforth, too, he began to realize
that even in the country,
although there were no streets nor palaces,
no card parties, no balls, no rhyming verses,
boredom was still the same;
depression still kept watch on him,
chasing him like a shadow – or like a faithful wife.

55   For my part, I was born for a life of peace
and rural quietude.
Poetry has more resonance in the wilds,
creative dreams more vividness.
I dedicate myself to harmless pastimes,
I roam by the deserted lake:
far niente is my law.
Each morning I awaken
to pleasant self-indulgence and to freedom.
I don't read much; I sleep a lot;
I don't pursue elusive fame.
Isn't that how in years gone by
I spent my happiest days –
in idleness and anonymity?

56   Flowers, love, leisure, rural life,
the open country – it's these that are near my heart.
I'm always glad to point a difference out
between Onégin and myself.
Then no mocking reader
nor any retailer
of clever slanders
can think they recognize my features here
and spread abroad outrageous tales
that, like that vainest of poets Byron,
I've scribbled down a portrait of myself –
as though we could no longer
write poems about anyone
except ourselves.

57　　Замечу кстати: все поэты —
　　　Любви мечтательной друзья.
　　　Бывало, милые предметы
　　　Мне снились, и душа моя
　　　Их образ тайный сохранила;
　　　Их после муза оживила:
　　　Так я, беспечен, воспевал
　　　И деву гор, мой идеал,
　　　И пленниц берегов Салгира.
　　　Теперь от вас, мои друзья,
　　　Вопрос нередко слышу я:
　　　«О ком твоя вздыхает лира?
　　　Кому, в толпе ревнивых дев,
　　　Ты посвятил ее напев?

58　　Чей взор, волнуя вдохновенье,
　　　Умильной лаской наградил
　　　Твое задумчивое пенье?
　　　Кого твой стих боготворил?»
　　　И, други, никого, ей-богу!
　　　Любви безумную тревогу
　　　Я безотрадно испытал.
　　　Блажен, кто с нею сочетал
　　　Горячку рифм: он тем удвоил
　　　Поэзии священный бред,
　　　Петрарке шествуя вослед,
　　　А муки сердца успокоил,
　　　Поймал и славу между тем;
　　　Но я, любя, был глуп и нем.

59　　Прошла любовь, явилась муза,
　　　И прояснился темный ум.
　　　Свободен, вновь ищу союза
　　　Волшебных звуков, чувств и дум;
　　　Пишу, и сердце не тоскует,
　　　Перо, забывшись, не рисует,
　　　Близ неоконченных стихов,
　　　Ни женских ножек, ни голов;
　　　Погасший пепел уж не вспыхнет,
　　　Я всё грущу; но слез уж нет,
　　　И скоро, скоро бури след
　　　В душе моей совсем утихнет:
　　　Тогда-то я начну писать
　　　Поэму песен в двадцать пять.

57   A passing observation: every poet
enjoys dreaming of love.
Time was when objects of affection
used to appear to me in dreams:
I kept their image
concealed within my heart,
and afterwards my verse brought them to life.
This was how I so easily portrayed
my idealized Caucasian lass
and the girl captives at Bakhchisaráy.
These days my friends quite often ask me:
"Who are these amorous verses of yours about?
All of the girls are jealous –
say who's the dedicatee of this one?...

58   Whose glance stirred your imagination
and won you, for your wistful lyrics,
an affectionate caress?
Who have your lines immortalized?"
My word of honour, friends: it's none of them.
I've not found any relief at all
for love's dementing anguish.
Lucky's the man who's managed to combine
with a love affair the fever of composition!
He's followed Petrarch's footsteps: he'll not only
have doubled poetry's sacred ecstasy,
but he'll have soothed his inner pain as well –
and gained himself a reputation!
But I've been always dull and mute in love.

59   Not till love's passed does inspiration come
and clear the darkness from my mind;
then, free at last, I once more seek to unite
feelings and thoughts with the magical music of words.
I write; my heart's now ceased to ache;
my pen no longer absent-mindedly
clutters the margin of unfinished lines
with drawings of women's heads or dainty feet.
The extinguished embers will flare up no more.
I *am* still sad; but there are no more tears;
and soon, the storm now passed, yes very soon,
deep calm will settle on my soul.
And then I'll begin to write
a twenty-five-canto-long epic!

60   Я думал уж о форме плана
И как героя назову.
Покамест моего романа
Я кончил первую главу;
Пересмотрел всё это строго:
Противоречий очень много,
Но их исправить не хочу.
Цензуре долг свой заплачу
И журналистам на съеденье
Плоды трудов моих отдам:
Иди же к невским берегам,
Новорожденное творенье!
И заслужи мне славы дань —
Кривые толки, шум и брань.

60   Indeed I've started thinking out the plot,
      and what to call the hero…
      but in the meantime I've come to the end
      of my novel's Chapter One.
      I've looked it over with the utmost care:
      contradictions abound;
      I've no mind to correct them, though:
      I'll pay the censor what I owe,
      and serve the fruits of my exertions
      to the reviewers to devour.
      So off you go, my newborn progeny,
      off to St Petersburg,
      and earn me the rewards of fame –
      distortion, uproar and abuse.

ГЛАВА ВТОРАЯ

O rus!..
—Hor.

О Русь!

1. Деревня, где скучал Евгений,
   Была прелестный уголок;
   Там друг невинных наслаждений
   Благословить бы небо мог.
   Господский дом уединенный,
   Горой от ветров огражденный,
   Стоял над речкою. Вдали
   Пред ним пестрели и цвели
   Луга и нивы золотые,
   Мелькали селы здесь и там,
   Стада бродили по лугам,
   И сени расширял густые
   Огромный, запущенный сад,
   Приют задумчивых дриад.

2. Почтенный замок был построен,
   Как замки строиться должны:
   Отменно прочен и спокоен
   Во вкусе умной старины.
   Везде высокие покои,
   В гостиной штофные обои,
   Царей портреты на стенах,
   И печи в пестрых изразцах.
   Всё это ныне обветшало,
   Не знаю, право, почему;
   Да, впрочем, другу моему
   В том нужды было очень мало,
   Затем, что он равно зевал
   Средь модных и старинных зал.

CHAPTER TWO

O countryside!
— Horace

O country, O Russia!

1 The country estate Onégin found so boring
was actually a charming spot.
Anyone fond of innocent pleasures
would have thanked Heaven for it.
The secluded manor house
stood above a river,
sheltered from wind by rising ground.
It looked far out across a luxuriant patchwork
of meadows and golden cornfields;
one glimpsed a village here and there;
in the pastures herds of cattle browsed;
and thick and ample shade was afforded
by a huge neglected park,
likely haunt of pensive wood nymphs.

2 The venerable manor had been built
as manor houses should be built:
exceedingly solid and comfortable,
in the prudent style of a former age –
high-ceilinged rooms throughout,
a parlour hung with damask,
tsars' portraits on the walls,
and stoves with decorated tiles.
All this is quite outdated now,
though indeed I don't know why.
But to my friend, in any case,
it mattered very little:
he yawned in antiquated rooms
as much as in up-to-date ones.

3   Он в том покое поселился,
    Где деревенский старожил
    Лет сорок с ключницей бранился,
    В окно смотрел и мух давил.
    Всё было просто: пол дубовый,
    Два шкафа, стол, диван пуховый,
    Нигде ни пятнышка чернил.
    Онегин шкафы отворил;
    В одном нашел тетрадь расхода,
    В другом наливок целый строй,
    Кувшины с яблочной водой
    И календарь осьмого года:
    Старик, имея много дел,
    В иные книги не глядел.

4   Один среди своих владений,
    Чтоб только время проводить,
    Сперва задумал наш Евгений
    Порядок новый учредить.
    В своей глуши мудрец пустынный,
    Ярем он барщины старинной
    Оброком легким заменил;
    И раб судьбу благословил.
    Зато в углу своем надулся,
    Увидя в этом страшный вред,
    Его расчетливый сосед;
    Другой лукаво улыбнулся,
    И в голос все решили так,
    Что он опаснейший чудак.

5   Сначала все к нему езжали;
    Но так как с заднего крыльца
    Обыкновенно подавали
    Ему донского жеребца,
    Лишь только вдоль большой дороги
    Заслышат их домашни дроги, —
    Поступком оскорбясь таким,
    Все дружбу прекратили с ним.
    «Сосед наш неуч; сумасбродит;
    Он фармазон; он пьет одно
    Стаканом красное вино;
    Он дамам к ручке не подходит;
    Всё *да* да *нет*; не скажет *да-с*
    Иль *нет-с*». Таков был общий глас.

3   Onégin took up residence in the room
where his old rustic predecessor had spent
some forty years quarrelling with the housekeeper,
gazing through the window and swatting flies.
Everything was plain: an oaken floor,
two cupboards, a table, an upholstered couch –
and nowhere the tiniest stain of ink.
Onégin opened up the cupboards.
In one he found a notebook for accounts,
in the other an entire array
of home-made wines, some jars of cider,
and an almanac for year 1808 –
the old man had been far too busy
to look at other books.

4   Onégin had his new domains to himself.
To pass the time (and nothing more),
he began by making plans
to establish a new social order.
A lonely sage in those benighted parts,
he abolished the ancient burden of unpaid work
and charged instead a modest quit-rent.
The serfs blessed Providence.
His thrifty neighbour, on the other hand,
saw dreadful danger here,
and pulled a face behind closed doors;
another neighbour gave a knowing smile;
and everyone united in the view
that here was a maverick and a menace.

5   They'd all paid frequent calls on him at first.
The practice was, though, once the sound was heard
of their home-built carriages on the highway,
that his Don stallion
would be held ready for him
at the rear porch.
They all took umbrage at such conduct
and broke off friendly ties with him.
"This neighbour of ours – he's boorish, raving mad;
he's one of those freethinking masons.
Red wine in tumblerfuls, that's all he drinks.
He never kisses ladies' hands.
It's always 'yes' and 'no'; he won't say 'yes, sir', 'no, sir'."
Such was the universal verdict.

6   В свою деревню в ту же пору
     Помещик новый прискакал
     И столь же строгому разбору
     В соседстве повод подавал:
     По имени Владимир Ленский,
     С душою прямо геттингенской,
     Красавец, в полном цвете лет,
     Поклонник Канта и поэт.
     Он из Германии туманной
     Привез учености плоды:
     Вольнолюбивые мечты,
     Дух пылкий и довольно странный,
     Всегда восторженную речь
     И кудри черные до плеч.

7   От хладного разврата света
     Еще увянуть не успев,
     Его душа была согрета
     Приветом друга, лаской дев;
     Он сердцем милый был невежда,
     Его лелеяла надежда,
     И мира новый блеск и шум
     Еще пленяли юный ум.
     Он забавлял мечтою сладкой
     Сомненья сердца своего;
     Цель жизни нашей для него
     Была заманчивой загадкой,
     Над ней он голову ломал
     И чудеса подозревал.

8   Он верил, что душа родная
     Соединиться с ним должна,
     Что, безотрадно изнывая,
     Его вседневно ждет она;
     Он верил, что друзья готовы
     За честь его приять оковы
     И что не дрогнет их рука
     Разбить сосуд клеветника;
     Что есть избранные судьбами,
     Людей священные друзья;
     Что их бессмертная семья
     Неотразимыми лучами
     Когда-нибудь нас озарит
     И мир блаженством одарит.

6   At this same time another landowner
      Came galloping to his country seat
      and occasioned a scrutiny no less stern
      on the part of the neighbouring gentry.
      Vladímir Lensky was his name,
      true Göttingen alumnus through and through,
      good-looking, in full bloom of life,
      devotee of Kant, and poet.
      Out of the mists of Germany
      he brought the fruits of education:
      fond dreams of freedom,
      a disposition ardent and rather quaint,
      an ever-enthusiastic manner of speech,
      and shoulder-length black curls.

7   Society's chill depravity
      had yet to blight him;
      a friend's kind gesture or a girl's soft touch
      were still enough to warm his heart.
      An amiable innocent in his emotions,
      he was the dupe of hope,
      and the novelty of this world's noise and glitter
      still enthralled his youthful mind.
      He beguiled the doubtings of his heart
      with pleasant fancies.
      The goal of human life
      was for him an intriguing riddle:
      on it he'd rack his brains,
      and inferred supernatural forces.

8   He believed that a kindred soul was destined
      to be made one with him
      and that she languished, unconsoled as yet,
      awaiting him day by day.
      He believed that, in order to defend his honour,
      his friends would submit to be "cast into chains",
      that "their hand would not flinch
      from dashing to pieces the slanderer's cup";
      that there were "beings chosen by destiny
      to be humanity's sacred friends";
      and that their "deathless fellowship"
      would one day "illumine us
      with shafts of overpowering light",
      and "endow the world with bliss".

9 Негодованье, сожаленье,
Ко благу чистая любовь
И славы сладкое мученье
В нем рано волновали кровь.
Он с лирой странствовал на свете;
Под небом Шиллера и Гете
Их поэтическим огнем
Душа воспламенилась в нем;
И муз возвышенных искусства,
Счастливец, он не постыдил:
Он в песнях гордо сохранил
Всегда возвышенные чувства,
Порывы девственной мечты
И прелесть важной простоты.

10 Он пел любовь, любви послушный,
И песнь его была ясна,
Как мысли девы простодушной,
Как сон младенца, как луна
В пустынях неба безмятежных,
Богиня тайн и вздохов нежных.
Он пел разлуку и печаль,
И *нечто*, и *туманну даль*,
И романтические розы;
Он пел те дальные страны,
Где долго в лоно тишины
Лились его живые слезы;
Он пел поблеклый жизни цвет
Без малого в осьмнадцать лет.

11 В пустыне, где один Евгений
Мог оценить его дары,
Господ соседственных селений
Ему не нравились пиры;
Бежал он их беседы шумной.
Их разговор благоразумный
О сенокосе, о вине,
О псарне, о своей родне,
Конечно, не блистал ни чувством,
Ни поэтическим огнем,
Ни остротою, ни умом,
Ни общежития искусством;
Но разговор их милых жен
Гораздо меньше был умен.

9   Indignation, compassion, pure love for what's good,
a sweetly painful longing for renown –
all these were emotions that from an early age
had made his pulse beat faster.
It was in foreign lands he'd sought
his poetry's inspiration. Beneath the German sky
the poetic flame of Schiller and of Goethe
had fired his soul.
He, lucky fellow, never disgraced
the sublimity of his art:
in his verses he proudly kept
to sentiments ever high-minded,
flights of innocent fancy,
and a charm unaffected and grave.

10   He wrote of love, himself love's willing victim;
and his poetry was as serene
as the thoughts of an innocent girl,
as an infant's slumber, or as the moon
in the tranquil deserts of the sky –
that goddess of mysteries and tender sighs.
He wrote of parting and of sorrow,
of a vague "something", of the "misty distance",
and of roses (those romantic flowers!).
He wrote of "yonder far-off lands"
where "his living tears had long been flowing
into the bosom of silence".
He wrote too of "life's faded bloom" –
though still not quite eighteen.

11   In the wilderness where Lensky found himself
there was no one but Onégin to appreciate his gifts.
Lensky disliked the dinners
given by neighbouring gentry,
and he shunned their noisy gatherings.
No surprise that the menfolk's matter-of-fact talk
of haymaking, alcohol, hounds
and homelife
was hardly aglow with feeling,
poetic ardour,
wit, wisdom
or good breeding;
but the prattle of their pretty wives
was even more banal.

12   Богат, хорош собою, Ленский
Везде был принят как жених;
Таков обычай деревенский;
Все дочек прочили своих
За *полурусского соседа*;
Взойдет ли он, тотчас беседа
Заводит слово стороной
О скуке жизни холостой;
Зовут соседа к самовару,
А Дуня разливает чай;
Ей шепчут: «Дуня, примечай!»
Потом приносят и гитару:
И запищит она (Бог мой!):
Приди в чертог ко мне златой!..

13   Но Ленский, не имев, конечно,
Охоты узы брака несть,
С Онегиным желал сердечно
Знакомство покороче свесть.
Они сошлись. Волна и камень,
Стихи и проза, лед и пламень
Не столь различны меж собой.
Сперва взаимной разнотой
Они друг другу были скучны;
Потом понравились; потом
Съезжались каждый день верхом
И скоро стали неразлучны.
Так люди (первый каюсь я)
От *делать нечего* друзья.

14   Но дружбы нет и той меж нами.
Все предрассудки истребя,
Мы почитаем всех нулями,
А единицами — себя.
Мы все глядим в Наполеоны;
Двуногих тварей миллионы
Для нас орудие одно;
Нам чувство дико и смешно.
Сноснее многих был Евгений;
Хоть он людей, конечно, знал
И вообще их презирал,
Но (правил нет без исключений)
Иных он очень отличал
И вчуже чувство уважал.

12   Rich, and in his way good-looking, Lensky
was welcomed everywhere as prospective bridegroom
(such is the country way!).
Everyone marked their daughters out
for the "half-Russian neighbour".
As soon as he dropped in,
the talk would stray
to the tedium of bachelor life.
He's summoned to the samovar –
where Dunya's pouring tea.
They whisper, "Dunya, here's your chance."
Then out the mandolin comes too,
and (heaven help us!) Dunya starts to squeal:
"Come to me in my golden chamber…"

13   Lensky, for sure, had no desire
to wear the chains of matrimony.
He was, though, genuinely keen
to come to know Onégin better;
and so they got acquainted. Water and stone,
poetry and prose, or ice and flame
are not more different.
Their mutual dissimilarity
was irksome to them both at first;
but then they came to like each other; next
they rode together every day;
and soon they were inseparable.
So it is that folk – as I'm the first to admit –
make friends from "having nowt to do".

14   With us even this sort of friendship's absent.
Defying all conventions,
we set everyone at zero
and give a positive value only to ourselves.
We're all would-be Napoleons:
for us, two-legged creatures in their millions
are just a tool;
feelings we find uncivilized and funny.
Onégin was more bearable than most.
Of course, he knew what people are
and generally despised them.
But there's no rule without exceptions,
and he made a handsome exception sometimes,
respecting another's feelings, though numb himself.

15 Он слушал Ленского с улыбкой.
Поэта пылкий разговор,
И ум, еще в сужденьях зыбкий,
И вечно вдохновенный взор —
Онегину всё было ново;
Он охладительное слово
В устах старался удержать
И думал: глупо мне мешать
Его минутному блаженству;
И без меня пора придет;
Пускай покамест он живет
Да верит мира совершенству;
Простим горячке юных лет
И юный жар и юный бред.

16 Меж ними всё рождало споры
И к размышлению влекло:
Племен минувших договоры,
Плоды наук, добро и зло,
И предрассудки вековые,
И гроба тайны роковые,
Судьба и жизнь в свою чреду,
Всё подвергалось их суду.
Поэт в жару своих суждений
Читал, забывшись, между тем
Отрывки северных поэм,
И снисходительный Евгений,
Хоть их не много понимал,
Прилежно юноше внимал.

17 Но чаще занимали страсти
Умы пустынников моих.
Ушед от их мятежной власти,
Онегин говорил об них
С невольным вздохом сожаленья.
Блажен, кто ведал их волненья
И наконец от них отстал;
Блаженней тот, кто их не знал,
Кто охлаждал любовь разлукой,
Вражду злословием; порой
Зевал с друзьями и с женой,
Ревнивой не тревожась мукой,
И дедов верный капитал
Коварной двойке не вверял.

15   He used to listen to Lensky with a smile.
The poet's eager conversation,
his mind unsure still in its views,
his ever rapturous expression –
to Onégin this was wholly new.
He did his best to hold in check
the cynical comments rising to his lips,
thinking, "I'd be a fool to spoil
his momentary bliss –
it'll vanish soon enough without my help.
Meanwhile let him live on in the belief
that the world's a perfect place.
Youth is a kind of fever; we must forgive the young
their fire and their delirium."

16   Everything gave rise to argument between them
and led to deep discussion.
The social contract and its origins,
the benefits of science and the arts,
age-old conventions, good and evil,
the fateful secrets of the grave,
destiny, life itself – each topic
came up for their judicial verdict.
The poet, in the heat of his opinions,
would often so forget himself as to recite
snatches of northern verse;
Onégin understood it little,
but nonetheless indulgently gave the young man
his diligent attention.

17   More often, though, what occupied
the minds of our recluses were the emotions.
Now he'd escaped their arbitrary dominion,
Onégin used to speak of them
with an involuntary murmur of regret.
It's a happy man who's suffered emotional turmoil
and found relief at last.
But happier still is the one who's never known it,
who's used separation to take the warmth from love
and slander to cool down hatred;
who's often yawned when with his friends and wife,
untroubled by pangs of jealousy;
and who's never staked his secure ancestral wealth
upon a perfidious playing card.

18　　Когда прибегнем мы под знамя
　　　Благоразумной тишины,
　　　Когда страстей угаснет пламя,
　　　И нам становятся смешны
　　　Их своевольство иль порывы
　　　И запоздалые отзывы —
　　　Смиренные не без труда,
　　　Мы любим слушать иногда
　　　Страстей чужих язык мятежный,
　　　И нам он сердце шевелит.
　　　Так точно старый инвалид
　　　Охотно клонит слух прилежный
　　　Рассказам юных усачей,
　　　Забытый в хижине своей.

19　　Зато и пламенная младость
　　　Не может ничего скрывать.
　　　Вражду, любовь, печаль и радость
　　　Она готова разболтать.
　　　В любви считаясь инвалидом,
　　　Онегин слушал с важным видом,
　　　Как, сердца исповедь любя,
　　　Поэт высказывал себя;
　　　Свою доверчивую совесть
　　　Он простодушно обнажал.
　　　Евгений без труда узнал
　　　Его любви младую повесть,
　　　Обильный чувствами рассказ,
　　　Давно не новыми для нас.

20　　Ах, он любил, как в наши лета
　　　Уже не любят; как одна
　　　Безумная душа поэта
　　　Еще любить осуждена:
　　　Всегда, везде одно мечтанье,
　　　Одно привычное желанье,
　　　Одна привычная печаль!
　　　Ни охлаждающая даль,
　　　Ни долгие лета разлуки,
　　　Ни музам данные часы,
　　　Ни чужеземные красы,
　　　Ни шум веселий, ни науки
　　　Души не изменили в нем,
　　　Согретой девственным огнем.

18   At length we take our refuge beneath the banner
of common sense and quietude:
at length the flame of our passions dies away,
and their wayward outbursts
and belated reverberations
come to seem laughable to us.
Then, having with a struggle reached tranquillity,
we sometimes like to listen
to the turbulent story of others' emotions
and feel our hearts beat faster,
just as an old war veteran
avidly bends an attentive ear
to the yarns of moustachioed youngsters,
as he sits forgotten in his shack.

19   By contrast, youth in its ardour
finds reticence impossible;
the young are always ready to blurt out
their love and hatred, grief and joy.
Onégin counted himself a veteran in love,
listening with grave demeanour
while Lensky, who liked disclosing what he felt,
talked on about himself;
and as he simple-heartedly laid bare
the aspirations of his trustful nature,
Onégin had no difficulty learning
the still unfolding story of the poet's love –
a narrative abounding in such sentiments
as are far from new to *us*.

20   Yes, Lensky loved as these days
folk love no more –
or as a poet's crazed heart alone
is still condemned to love.
Always and everywhere one single dream,
one constant wish,
one constant sorrow.
Nothing there was, not chilling distance,
not lengthy years of separation,
not hours devoted to the arts,
not sightseeing in foreign lands,
not raucous merriment nor higher studies –
nothing could change his heart,
aflame as it was with love's pure fire.

21 Чуть отрок, Ольгою плененный,
    Сердечных мук еще не знав,
    Он был свидетель умиленный
    Ее младенческих забав;
    В тени хранительной дубравы
    Он разделял ее забавы,
    И детям прочили венцы
    Друзья-соседи, их отцы.
    В глуши, под сению смиренной,
    Невинной прелести полна,
    В глазах родителей, она
    Цвела, как ландыш потаенный,
    Незнаемый в траве глухой
    Ни мотыльками, ни пчелой.

22 Она поэту подарила
    Младых восторгов первый сон,
    И мысль об ней одушевила
    Его цевницы первый стон.
    Простите, игры золотые!
    Он рощи полюбил густые,
    Уединенье, тишину,
    И ночь, и звезды, и луну,
    Луну, небесную лампаду,
    Которой посвящали мы
    Прогулки средь вечерней тьмы,
    И слезы, тайных мук отраду…
    Но нынче видим только в ней
    Замену тусклых фонарей.

23 Всегда скромна, всегда послушна,
    Всегда как утро весела,
    Как жизнь поэта простодушна,
    Как поцелуй любви мила;
    Глаза, как небо, голубые,
    Улыбка, локоны льняные,
    Движенья, голос, легкий стан,
    Всё в Ольге… но любой роман
    Возьмите и найдете верно
    Ее портрет: он очень мил,
    Я прежде сам его любил,
    Но надоел он мне безмерно.
    Позвольте мне, читатель мой,
    Заняться старшею сестрой.

21 Lensky'd taken by Olga when still a boy,
before he knew the pain emotion brings.
He was touched as he watched her
as a toddler at play;
and in the trees' protective shade
he used to share her games.
Their fathers, mutual friends and neighbours,
planned marriage for them.
In her modest home deep in the countryside
Olga had blossomed under her parents' eyes,
full of the charm of innocence,
like a lily of the valley
hidden in thick grass,
unnoticed by the butterflies and bees.

22 It was Olga who gave the poet
the first of his youthful dreams of love;
and it was the thought of her
that inspired his first poetical effusions.
Goodbye to childhood's golden pastimes!
Instead, he came to love dense woodlands,
and solitude and quiet,
the night, the stars, the moon.
(It was to the moon, Heaven's icon lamp,
that we too used to consecrate
those strolls we took through the evening twilight,
those tears that relieved our secret agonies
– though nowadays that moon's no more to us
than a standby for dim street lamps.)

23 Olga... always unassuming, always submissive,
always as cheerful as morning,
as simple-hearted as a poet's soul,
as sweet as a lover's kiss;
eyes blue as heaven,
bright smile, flaxen curls,
graceful movements, pleasant voice and dainty figure –
all this was Olga's. Take any novel,
and you'll be sure to find
her portrait – and very nice it is.
I liked it once myself, but now
I'm sick to death of it.
Allow me, then, dear reader,
to turn to the elder sister.

24   Ее сестра звалась Татьяна…
      Впервые именем таким
      Страницы нежные романа
      Мы своевольно освятим.
      И что ж? оно приятно, звучно;
      Но с ним, я знаю, неразлучно
      Воспоминанье старины
      Иль девичьей. Мы все должны
      Признаться: вкусу очень мало
      У нас и в наших именах
      (Не говорим уж о стихах);
      Нам просвещенье не пристало,
      И нам досталось от него
      Жеманство — больше ничего.

25   Итак, она звалась Татьяной.
      Ни красотой сестры своей,
      Ни свежестью ее румяной
      Не привлекла б она очей.
      Дика, печальна, молчалива,
      Как лань лесная боязлива,
      Она в семье своей родной
      Казалась девочкой чужой.
      Она ласкаться не умела
      К отцу, ни к матери своей;
      Дитя сама, в толпе детей
      Играть и прыгать не хотела,
      И часто, целый день одна,
      Сидела молча у окна.

26   Задумчивость, ее подруга
      От самых колыбельных дней,
      Теченье сельского досуга
      Мечтами украшала ей.
      Ее изнеженные пальцы
      Не знали игл; склонясь на пяльцы,
      Узором шелковым она
      Не оживляла полотна.
      Охоты властвовать примета,
      С послушной куклою дитя
      Приготовляется шутя
      К приличию — закону света,
      И важно повторяет ей
      Уроки маменьки своей.

24   Tatyána was her sister's name…
This is the first time we'll have graced
the delicate pages of a novel
with such a name.
So why this idiosyncratic choice?
Well, it's a pleasing and melodious name.
It is, I know, linked in our minds
inseparably with the ancient past,
or with the housemaids' quarters. But we must
be honest: we show too little taste,
even in the names we choose
(don't mention poetry!).
We haven't taken well to civilization:
it's brought us snobbery, nothing more.

25   Tatyána was her name, then.
Her looks were not as striking as her sister's:
she'd neither Olga's pretty features
nor her complexion, fresh and pink.
She was a lonesome, melancholy, quiet child
as timid as a woodland doe.
Even among her family
she seemed like someone else's little girl.
She didn't have a way of wheedling herself
into her father's or her mother's favour.
As a child she never wanted
to play and prance with lots of other children;
alone all day, she'd often sit
in silence by the window.

26   Her inner thoughts had been her friends,
even from infancy;
and it was the daydreams they brought with them
that brightened up for her
the uneventful course of country life.
Her delicate fingers had never held a needle.
She was never to be found
bent over an embroidering frame,
enlivening tablecloths with silken patterns.
Some children, showing an urge to dominate,
will play with their obedient dolls
at etiquette – society's ritual –
and earnestly repeat to them
the lessons that they've learnt from mummy.

27   Но куклы даже в эти годы
Татьяна в руки не брала;
Про вести города, про моды
Беседы с нею не вела.
И были детские проказы
Ей чужды: страшные рассказы
Зимою в темноте ночей
Пленяли больше сердце ей.
Когда же няня собирала
Для Ольги на широкий луг
Всех маленьких ее подруг,
Она в горелки не играла;
Ей скучен был и звонкий смех,
И шум их ветреных утех.

28   Она любила на балконе
Предупреждать зари восход,
Когда на бледном небосклоне
Звезд исчезает хоровод,
И тихо край земли светлеет,
И, вестник утра, ветер веет,
И всходит постепенно день.
Зимой, когда ночная тень
Полмиром доле обладает,
И доле в праздной тишине
При отуманенной луне
Восток ленивый почивает,
В привычный час пробуждена
Вставала при свечах она.

29   Ей рано нравились романы;
Они ей заменяли всё;
Она влюблялася в обманы
И Ричардсона и Руссо.
Отец ее был добрый малый,
В прошедшем веке запоздалый;
Но в книгах не видал вреда;
Он, не читая никогда,
Их почитал пустой игрушкой
И не заботился о том,
Какой у дочки тайный том
Дремал до утра под подушкой.
Жена ж его была сама
От Ричардсона без ума.

27   But, even as a child, Tatyána
never took dolls up in her arms,
nor did she chat with them
of fashions or the latest news in town.
Childish pranks were alien to her.
What captured her imagination
was reading horror stories
on gloomy winter's nights.
When nurse assembled
all Olga's little friends for her
in the big meadow,
Tatyána never played with them at tag;
she couldn't stand their piercing laughter
and the uproar of their silly games.

28   She loved to go out early
onto her balcony and watch the dawn rise:
the stars in dance formation
would fade from sight on the pale horizon,
the rim of earth would gently glow more brightly,
a breeze would herald the approach of morning,
and little by little day would come.
In winter, when night's shadow
holds longer sway over half the world
and the drowsy east
dozes for longer in idle stillness
beneath a misty moon – even in winter
she'd wake up at her usual hour
and rise by candlelight.

29   Novels had early on engaged Tatyána's fancy.
They took the place of all else in her life.
She took a liking to the fiction
of Richardson and of Rousseau.
Her father, a good-hearted fellow,
was a throwback to the century before;
yet he saw no harm in books.
He never read himself
and thought them useless playthings;
so he never vexed himself
over what secret volume might spend the night
beneath his daughter's pillow.
His wife, for her part,
raved over Richardson.

30   Она любила Ричардсона
      Не потому, чтобы прочла,
      Не потому, чтоб Грандисона
      Она Ловласу предпочла;
      Но в старину княжна Алина,
      Ее московская кузина,
      Твердила часто ей об них.
      В то время был еще жених
      Ее супруг, но по неволе;
      Она вздыхала по другом,
      Который сердцем и умом
      Ей нравился гораздо боле:
      Сей Грандисон был славный франт,
      Игрок и гвардии сержант.

31   Как он, она была одета
      Всегда по моде и к лицу.
      Но, не спросясь ее совета,
      Девицу повезли к венцу;
      И, чтоб ее рассеять горе,
      Разумный муж уехал вскоре
      В свою деревню, где она,
      Бог знает кем окружена,
      Рвалась и плакала сначала,
      С супругом чуть не развелась;
      Потом хозяйством занялась,
      Привыкла и довольна стала.
      Привычка свыше нам дана:
      Замена счастию она.

32   Привычка усладила горе,
      Не отразимое ничем;
      Открытие большое вскоре
      Ее утешило совсем:
      Она меж делом и досугом
      Открыла тайну, как супругом
      Самодержавно управлять,
      И всё тогда пошло на стать.
      Она езжала по работам,
      Солила на зиму грибы,
      Вела расходы, брила лбы,
      Ходила в баню по субботам,
      Служанок била осердясь —
      Всё это мужа не спросясь.

30   The reason she loved Richardson
        was not that she had read him though;
        it wasn't that she'd formed a preference
        for Grandison above Lovelace;
        it was just that in the old days
        Princess Aline, her Moscow cousin,
        had been forever chatting to her about them.
        At that time she and her husband were just engaged –
        and that against her wishes.
        Her heart was set on someone else,
        whose personality and cast of mind
        were much more to her liking.
        This "Grandison" of hers a famous toff,
        gambler and junior officer in the guards.

31   Like him, she always used to dress
        in the smartest, most up-to-date fashion.
        Without being asked her opinion, though,
        she was married off to a husband,
        who, to dispel her distress,
        had the sense to decamp straightaway
        to his country estate. There she,
        surrounded by God knows whom,
        wouldn't stop shaking and sobbing at first,
        and came close to leaving her husband.
        Then she busied herself with the housekeeping,
        adopted a routine, and grew content.
        Routine is Heaven's gift to us:
        it does for happiness.

32   And so the grief that nothing could assuage
        lost bitterness through routine;
        and soon a great discovery
        brought her full consolation.
        In the course of work and leisure
        she grasped the secret of how
        to rule her husband like an autocrat.
        From then on all went as it should.
        She inspected work in the fields,
        pickled mushrooms for winter,
        kept the accounts, chose serfs for soldiers,
        went to the bathhouse Saturdays,
        and beat the maids when she was cross –
        all without asking her husband.

33   Бывало, писывала кровью
Она в альбомы нежных дев,
Звала Полиною Прасковью
И говорила нараспев,
Корсет носила очень узкий,
И русский *Н* как *N* французский
Произносить умела в нос.
Но скоро всё перевелось:
Корсет, альбом, княжну Алину,
Стишков чувствительных тетрадь
Она забыла: стала звать
Акулькой прежнюю Селину
И обновила наконец
На вате шлафор и чепец.

34   Но муж любил ее сердечно,
В ее затеи не входил,
Во всем ей веровал беспечно,
А сам в халате ел и пил;
Покойно жизнь его катилась;
Под вечер иногда сходилась
Соседей добрая семья,
Нецеремонные друзья,
И потужить, и позлословить,
И посмеяться кой о чем.
Проходит время; между тем
Прикажут Ольге чай готовить,
Там ужин, там и спать пора,
И гости едут со двора.

35   Они хранили в жизни мирной
Привычки милой старины;
У них на масленице жирной
Водились русские блины;
Два раза в год они говели;
Любили круглые качели,
Подблюдны песни, хоровод;
В день Троицын, когда народ,
Зевая, слушает молебен,
Умильно на пучок зари
Они роняли слезки три;
Им квас как воздух был потребен,
И за столом у них гостям
Носили блюды по чинам.

33   At one time she'd written entries in blood
in her gentle girlfriends' albums;
she'd swapped "Praskóvya" for French "Pauline";
she'd talked in a sing-song voice;
she'd worn the tightest corsets;
and she'd learnt to pronounce the Russian N
through her nose, like the French one.
But all this quickly changed:
the corsets, albums, Princess Aline,
her notebook, too, of sentimental verses –
she forgot them all; she started
to call Céline "Akúlka" once again;
and in the end she even donned
a quilted dressing gown and mob cap.

34   Her husband loved her fondly though.
He never interfered with her pursuits,
but trustingly left everything to her
and took his meals in his dressing gown.
So, peaceably, his life rolled by.
Sometimes of an evening
a kindly family who lived nearby –
friends they were at their ease with –
dropped in for a little grumble, a little gossip,
a little laughter over this or that.
As the evening passed, they'd order Olga
to make some tea;
then supper time; then time for bed –
and home their visitors would go.

35   Throughout this peaceable existence
they kept up the quaint customs of the past.
At Shrovetide, with the usual rich fare
they served up Russian pancakes.
They kept the church fasts twice a year.
Merry-go-rounds they loved, and country dances,
and songs for telling fortunes.
On Trinity Sunday – when yawning congregations
attend the long thanksgiving service –
they'd shed a couple of repentant tears
onto a bunch of buttercups.
They needed kvass as much as air.
And guests around their table
had dishes served in order of their rank.

36   И так они старели оба.
      И отворились наконец
      Перед супругом двери гроба,
      И новый он приял венец.
      Он умер в час перед обедом,
      Оплаканный своим соседом,
      Детьми и верною женой
      Чистосердечней, чем иной.
      Он был простой и добрый барин,
      И там, где прах его лежит,
      Надгробный памятник гласит:
      СМИРЕННЫЙ ГРЕШНИК, ДМИТРИЙ ЛАРИН
      ГОСПОДНИЙ РАБ И БРИГАДИР
      ПОД КАМНЕМ СИМ ВКУШАЕТ МИР.

37   Своим пенатам возвращенный,
      Владимир Ленский посетил
      Соседа памятник смиренный,
      И вздох он пеплу посвятил;
      И долго сердцу грустно было.
      «*Poor Yorick*! — молвил он уныло. —
      Он на руках меня держал.
      Как часто в детстве я играл
      Его Очаковской медалью!
      Он Ольгу прочил за меня,
      Он говорил: дождусь ли дня?..»
      И, полный искренней печалью,
      Владимир тут же начертал
      Ему надгробный мадригал.

38   И там же надписью печальной
      Отца и матери, в слезах,
      Почтил он прах патриархальный…
      Увы! на жизненных браздах
      Мгновенной жатвой поколенья,
      По тайной воле провиденья,
      Восходят, зреют и падут;
      Другие им вослед идут…
      Так наше ветреное племя
      Растет, волнуется, кипит
      И к гробу прадедов теснит.
      Придет, придет и наше время,
      И наши внуки в добрый час
      Из мира вытеснят и нас!

36   And so the pair grew old together.
At length the gates of death
swung open for the husband,
and he received the "crown that fadeth not".
He died in the hour preceding lunch.
He was lamented,
with more sincerity than most,
by neighbour, children and a faithful wife –
a kindly and unassuming gentleman.
Above the grave where his remains lie buried
the monument declares:
DMITRY LARIN, HUMBLE SINNER,
SERVANT OF THE LORD AND BRIGADIER,
RESTS IN PEACE BENEATH THIS STONE.

37   On returning home
Vladímir Lensky had paid a visit
to his neighbour's simple memorial.
He sighed in sacred remembrance of the deceased,
and his heart was long grief-stricken.
"*Poor Yorick!*" said he despondently.
"He used to hold me in his arms.
So often as a boy I used to play
with the medal he won at Ochákov.
Olga he meant to be my wife.
His words were, 'Shall I see the day?...'"
And Lensky, overwhelmed with heartfelt grief,
sketched out in his honour there and then
a poetic epitaph.

38   In that same graveyard, tears filling his eyes,
he also honoured with a sad inscription
the earthly remains of his own parents...
Alas, the generations of mankind
are like a shortlived corn crop:
they spring up in life's furrows, ripen and fall,
according to the mysterious will of Providence,
and others take their place...
Our heedless generation, true to form,
is growing, heaving, surging,
and pressing its forebears to the grave.
And our day too will come: yes,
in good time *our* grandchildren
will crowd us out in our turn from this world.

39   Покамест упивайтесь ею,
      Сей легкой жизнию, друзья!
      Ее ничтожность разумею
      И мало к ней привязан я;
      Для призраков закрыл я вежды;
      Но отдаленные надежды
      Тревожат сердце иногда:
      Без неприметного следа
      Мне было б грустно мир оставить.
      Живу, пишу не для похвал;
      Но я бы, кажется, желал
      Печальный жребий свой прославить,
      Чтоб обо́ мне, как верный друг,
      Напомнил хоть единый звук.

40   И чье-нибудь он сердце тронет;
      И, сохраненная судьбой,
      Быть может, в Лете не потонет
      Строфа, слагаемая мной;
      Быть может (лестная надежда!),
      Укажет будущий невежда
      На мой прославленный портрет
      И молвит: то-то был поэт!
      Прими ж мои благодаренья,
      Поклонник мирных аонид,
      О ты, чья память сохранит
      Мои летучие творенья,
      Чья благосклонная рука
      Потреплет лавры старика!

39   In the meantime drink your fill, my friends,
of life's weak brew.
I recognize the futility of our existence;
I've little liking for it;
I've closed my eyes to its deluding visions.
But distant hopes
do sometimes stir my soul.
I should be sad to leave this world
without the slightest trace.
Fame's not the purpose of my life and writing;
and yet I feel I'd like to shed
some glory on my wretched lot,
so that at least one phrase of beauty, like a true friend,
may keep my memory alive...

40   and touch the heart of someone.
Fate, maybe, will preserve
this very stanza I'm composing now,
and save it from being drowned in Lethe's waters.
Maybe – oh, flattering hope! –
the common citizen of a future age
will point my celebrated portrait out
and say: "*That* was a poet!"
At all events, my heartfelt thanks
to the devotee of the peaceful arts
whose memory will preserve
what I've created, lightweight though it be,
and whose kind hand will pull back into shape
an old man's crumpled laurels!

ГЛАВА ТРЕТЬЯ

1
«Куда? Уж эти мне поэты!»
— Прощай, Онегин, мне пора.
«Я не держу тебя; но где ты
Свои проводишь вечера?»
— У Лариных. — «Вот это чудно.
Помилуй! и тебе не трудно
Там каждый вечер убивать?»
— Нимало. — «Не могу понять.
Отселе вижу, что такое:
Во-первых (слушай, прав ли я?),
Простая, русская семья,
К гостям усердие большое,
Варенье, вечный разговор
Про дождь, про лен, про скотный двор...»

2
— Я тут еще беды не вижу.
«Да скука, вот беда, мой друг».
— Я модный свет ваш ненавижу;
Милее мне домашний круг,
Где я могу... — «Опять эклога!
Да полно, милый, ради Бога.
Ну что ж? ты едешь: очень жаль.
Ах, слушай, Ленский; да нельзя ль
Увидеть мне Филлиду эту,
Предмет и мыслей, и пера,
И слез, и рифм et cetera?
Представь меня». — Ты шутишь. — «Нету».
— Я рад. — «Когда же?» — Хоть сейчас.
Они с охотой примут нас.

CHAPTER THREE

She was a girl – a girl in love.
– Malfilâtre

1   "Where now? My word! These poets really are—"
     "Goodbye, Onégin. It's time I went."
     "I'm not detaining you, old chap; but where
     do you spend these evenings of yours?"
     "At the Larins' house." "For pity's sake!
     How you amaze me, Lensky! Don't even you
     find it wearisome, killing each evening off there?"
     "Not at all." "I just don't understand it.
     Without shifting from here I can picture the scene.
     In the first place – listen, I'm right, am I not? –
     they're an ordinary Russian family,
     make a great fuss of visitors,
     serve home-made preserves, and chat on for ever
     about rain and flax crop and cow sheds..."

2   "I still don't see what's wrong with that."
     "It's so boring, my friend, that's what's wrong."
     "Well, I loathe that fashionable world of yours.
     To me the family circle means much more,
     where I can—" "Here we go – another idyll!
     Enough, dear fellow, for God's sake!
     You're on your way, then? What a pity!
     But listen, Lensky: aren't I allowed
     to glimpse this shepherdess of yours,
     the target of your thoughts, your letters,
     your tears, your verses, and whatever else?
     So introduce me." "You're joking." "No."
     "Well, I'd be glad to." "Name a time." "What about now?
     They'll welcome us with open arms –

3   Поедем. — Поскакали други,
     Явились; им расточены
     Порой тяжелые услуги
     Гостеприимной старины.
     Обряд известный угощенья:
     Несут на блюдечках варенья,
     На столик ставят вощаной
     Кувшин с брусничною водой.
     . . . .
     . . . .
     . . . .
     . . . .
     . . . .
     . . . .

4   Они дорогой самой краткой
     Домой летят во весь опор.
     Теперь подслушаем украдкой
     Героев наших разговор:
     — Ну что ж, Онегин? ты зеваешь. —
     «Привычка, Ленский». — Но скучаешь
     Ты как-то больше. — «Нет, равно.
     Однако в поле уж темно;
     Скорей! пошел, пошел, Андрюшка!
     Какие глупые места!
     А кстати: Ларина проста,
     Но очень милая старушка;
     Боюсь: брусничная вода
     Мне не наделала б вреда.

5   Скажи: которая Татьяна?»
     — Да та, которая, грустна
     И молчалива как Светлана,
     Вошла и села у окна. —
     «Неужто ты влюблен в меньшую?»
     — А что? — «Я выбрал бы другую,
     Когда б я был, как ты, поэт.
     В чертах у Ольги жизни нет.
     Точь-в-точь в Вандиковой Мадоне:
     Кругла, красна лицом она,
     Как эта глупая луна
     На этом глупом небосклоне».
     Владимир сухо отвечал
     И после во весь путь молчал.

3   "let's go!" The friends drove off at speed,
and soon were there. They were regaled,
to a point that sometimes overwhelmed,
with the attentions of old-time hospitality.
There was the usual ritual of refreshments:
portions of jam were served on little dishes,
and on a small wax-polished table
a jug of cowberry juice was set.

    ....
    ....
    ....
    ....
    ....
    ....

4   The two are speeding homewards now
by the shortest route:
let's eavesdrop
on what they're saying.
"What *is* the matter, Onégin? You keep yawning."
"Just habit, Lensky." "But you seem
somehow more bored than ever." "No, the same...
Well, well, it's dark out there now.
Faster! Get on, Andryúshka! Get along!...
What a stupid place this is!...
And apropos, Mrs Larin's a simple soul,
a very sweet old thing, though...
I'm rather afraid that cowberry juice
may have upset me...

5   "But tell me, which of them's Tatyána?"
"The one that's 'silent
and dejected', like Svetlána;
she came in and sat by the window."
"And it's really the younger girl you're in love with?"
"Why not?" "If I'd been a poet like you,
it's the other one I would have chosen.
Olga's just like a Van Dyck madonna –
no personality at all: she has a
round, pretty face,
like that stupid moon
there in that stupid sky."
Lensky attempted a tart rejoinder,
then held his tongue the whole way home.

6   Меж тем Онегина явленье
       У Лариных произвело
       На всех большое впечатленье
       И всех соседей развлекло.
       Пошла догадка за догадкой.
       Все стали толковать украдкой,
       Шутить, судить не без греха,
       Татьяне прочить жениха;
       Иные даже утверждали,
       Что свадьба слажена совсем,
       Но остановлена затем,
       Что модных колец не достали.
       О свадьбе Ленского давно
       У них уж было решено.

7   Татьяна слушала с досадой
       Такие сплетни; но тайком
       С неизъяснимою отрадой
       Невольно думала о том;
       И в сердце дума заронилась;
       Пора пришла, она влюбилась.
       Так в землю падшее зерно
       Весны огнем оживлено.
       Давно ее воображенье,
       Сгорая негой и тоской,
       Алкало пищи роковой;
       Давно сердечное томленье
       Теснило ей младую грудь;
       Душа ждала… кого-нибудь,

8   И дождалась… Открылись очи;
       Она сказала: это он!
       Увы! теперь и дни и ночи,
       И жаркий одинокий сон,
       Всё полно им; всё деве милой
       Без умолку волшебной силой
       Твердит о нем. Докучны ей
       И звуки ласковых речей,
       И взор заботливой прислуги.
       В уныние погружена,
       Гостей не слушает она
       И проклинает их досуги,
       Их неожиданный приезд
       И продолжительный присест.

6   Meanwhile,
     Onégin's visit to the Larins
     had made a strong impression on the household
     and had intrigued the neighbourhood.
     Conjecture followed on conjecture.
     Everyone started to drop veiled hints,
     crack jokes, voice judgements mischievous at times,
     and name Tatyána's future husband.
     Some even stated as a fact
     that the wedding was all arranged –
     the one delay
     was in finding rings of the latest fashion.
     (Lensky's marriage
     they'd settled long ago.)

7   Tatyána listened with vexation
     to gossip like this; but privately
     she couldn't help thinking of what they said
     with a sense of elation she couldn't explain;
     and the thinking seeped into her heart.
     The time had come; she'd fallen in love.
     It was just like a seed dropping into the earth
     and germinating in the warmth of spring.
     For long now her imagination, consuming itself
     in the furnace of introspective melancholy,
     had been craving deadly food.
     For long now her weary heart
     had ached in her young breast.
     Her soul was waiting for – anyone!

8   And waiting now was over... Her eyes were opened;
     she told herself, "It's him!"
     Poor, affectionate girl! Henceforth her days, her nights,
     her lonely, fevered hours of sleep –
     her very being was obsessed with him.
     Everything unremittingly, with unnatural power,
     kept speaking to her of him. She couldn't bear
     the knowing comments of well-meaning folk
     and the watchful solicitude of servants.
     Plunged as she was in misery,
     she didn't listen to visitors' conversation
     and cursed the time they had to spare,
     their unexpected comings,
     and their interminable stays.

9 Теперь с каким она вниманьем
 Читает сладостный роман,
 С каким живым очарованьем
 Пьет обольстительный обман!
 Счастливой силою мечтанья
 Одушевленные созданья,
 Любовник Юлии Вольмар,
 Малек-Адель и де Линар,
 И Вертер, мученик мятежный,
 И бесподобный Грандисон,
 Который нам наводит сон, —
 Все для мечтательницы нежной
 В единый образ облеклись,
 В одном Онегине слились.

10 Воображаясь героиной
 Своих возлюбленных творцов,
 Кларисой, Юлией, Дельфиной,
 Татьяна в тишине лесов
 Одна с опасной книгой бродит,
 Она в ней ищет и находит
 Свой тайный жар, свои мечты,
 Плоды сердечной полноты,
 Вздыхает и, себе присвоя
 Чужой восторг, чужую грусть,
 В забвенье шепчет наизусть
 Письмо для милого героя…
 Но наш герой, кто б ни был он,
 Уж верно был не Грандисон.

11 Свой слог на важный лад настроя,
 Бывало, пламенный творец
 Являл нам своего героя
 Как совершенства образец.
 Он одарял предмет любимый,
 Всегда неправедно гонимый,
 Душой чувствительной, умом
 И привлекательным лицом.
 Питая жар чистейшей страсти,
 Всегда восторженный герой
 Готов был жертвовать собой,
 И при конце последней части
 Всегда наказан был порок,
 Добру достойный был венок.

9   Still more absorbed did she become
in the sugary romances that she read;
and she imbibed their beguiling falsehoods
with ever keener fascination.
Their heroes, created as they were
under the influence of a fanciful sentimentality –
the lover of Julie Wolmar, for one,
and Malek-Adhel, and de Linar,
and Werther the rebellious martyr,
and peerless Grandison
(who sends us all to sleep) –
to the impressionable dreamer girl
they all took on a single form:
they merged in one Onégin.

10   She pictured herself the heroine
of each of the authors she admired –
Clarissa, Julie, Delphine –
as she wandered alone through the silent woods
clutching each perilous book.
She sought in them, she found in them,
the same secret passion, the very same dreams,
that were maturing in her own pregnant heart.
She'd heave a sigh, and identifying
another's love and another's grief with her own,
unconsciously she'd whisper by heart
the words of a letter to some fond hero or other…
This hero of ours, though, be what he may,
was no Grandison, for sure.

11   In the old days authors were fervently idealistic:
they'd pitch their style in a solemn key,
and present us with a protagonist
who was the model of perfection.
Always wrongfully persecuted,
he'd be lovingly endowed by his creator
with a sensitive nature, intelligence
and handsome features.
Always the dashing hero,
he'd stoke the fire of purest emotion,
and be ever prepared for self-sacrifice.
And at the end of the final chapter
vice was always punished
and virtue received her due reward.

12 А нынче все умы в тумане,
    Мораль на нас наводит сон,
    Порок любезен и в романе,
    И там уж торжествует он.
    Британской музы небылицы
    Тревожат сон отроковицы,
    И стал теперь ее кумир
    Или задумчивый Вампир,
    Или Мельмот, бродяга мрачный,
    Иль Вечный жид, или Корсар,
    Или таинственный Сбогар.
    Лорд Байрон прихотью удачной
    Облек в унылый романтизм
    И безнадежный эгоизм.

13 Друзья мои, что ж толку в этом?
    Быть может, волею небес,
    Я перестану быть поэтом,
    В меня вселится новый бес,
    И, Фебовы презрев угрозы,
    Унижусь до смиренной прозы;
    Тогда роман на старый лад
    Займет веселый мой закат.
    Не муки тайные злодейства
    Я грозно в нем изображу,
    Но просто вам перескажу
    Преданья русского семейства,
    Любви пленительные сны
    Да нравы нашей старины.

14 Перескажу простые речи
    Отца иль дяди-старика,
    Детей условленные встречи
    У старых лип, у ручейка;
    Несчастной ревности мученья,
    Разлуку, слезы примиренья,
    Поссорю вновь, и наконец
    Я поведу их под венец…
    Я вспомню речи неги страстной,
    Слова тоскующей любви,
    Которые в минувши дни
    У ног любовницы прекрасной
    Мне приходили на язык,
    От коих я теперь отвык.

12   These days, though, our standards are all confused.
       Morality sends us to sleep,
       while vice wins admiration, even in novels –
       in novels, indeed, vice actually triumphs.
       It's the fables of British writers
       that now disturb the dreams of teenage girls:
       the characters they idolize
       are either the introverted Vampire,
       or Melmoth the dark wanderer,
       or the Eternal Jew, or the Corsair,
       or the mysterious Sbogár.
       Triumphantly perverse, Lord Byron
       has cloaked in a grim romanticism
       what's just a desperate self-centredness.

13   What nonsense all this is, my friends!
       One day maybe, God willing,
       I'll cease to be a poet;
       some other demon will possess me.
       Maybe, defying Phoebus's threats,
       I'll come down to writing humble prose.
       If so, I'll brighten my declining years
       with work on an olden-style romance.
       I'll not describe in grisly detail there
       the secret torments of a villain;
       I'll just retell to you
       our Russia's household legends
       with their enchanting dreams of love
       and customs sanctified by time.

14   Yes, I'll retell the homely words
       of a father or aged uncle;
       I'll tell of two youngsters' assignations
       beneath old lime trees by a stream,
       of the pain of misunderstanding and jealousy,
       of partings, and tears of reconciliation;
       I'll make them quarrel again, then finally
       I'll lead them both to the altar…
       I'll call to mind those tender and passionate speeches,
       those words of yearning and love,
       that used to come in days gone by
       so readily to my lips,
       as I sat at my loved one's feet…
       though I'm out of practice now.

15   Татьяна, милая Татьяна!
С тобой теперь я слезы лью;
Ты в руки модного тирана
Уж отдала судьбу свою.
Погибнешь, милая; но прежде
Ты в ослепительной надежде
Блаженство темное зовешь,
Ты негу жизни узнаешь,
Ты пьешь волшебный яд желаний,
Тебя преследуют мечты:
Везде воображаешь ты
Приюты счастливых свиданий;
Везде, везде перед тобой
Твой искуситель роковой.

16   Тоска любви Татьяну гонит,
И в сад идет она грустить,
И вдруг недвижны очи клонит,
И лень ей далее ступить.
Приподнялася грудь, ланиты
Мгновенным пламенем покрыты,
Дыханье замерло в устах,
И в слухе шум, и блеск в очах…
Настанет ночь; луна обходит
Дозором дальный свод небес,
И соловей во мгле древес
Напевы звучные заводит.
Татьяна в темноте не спит
И тихо с няней говорит:

17   «Не спится, няня: здесь так душно!
Открой окно, да сядь ко мне».
— Что, Таня, что с тобой? — «Мне скучно,
Поговорим о старине».
— О чем же, Таня? Я, бывало,
Хранила в памяти не мало
Старинных былей, небылиц
Про злых духов и про девиц;
А нынче всё мне тёмно, Таня:
Что знала, то забыла. Да,
Пришла худая череда!
Зашибло… — «Расскажи мне, няня,
Про ваши старые года:
Была ты влюблена тогда?»

15   Tatyána, sweet Tatyána!
You're often in tears – and so am I.
You've now surrendered your future
to the mercy of a socialite used to getting his way.
Your tender heart will surely be broken.
For now, though, you are impatient for the darkness
that, dazzled by hope, you mistake for bliss.
You are tasting life's headiest pleasure
and drinking the magic poison of desire.
Your dreams pursue you constantly:
wherever you are, you picture the spot
as one for a rapturous rendezvous;
wherever you go, wherever you look,
your fateful seducer stands there before your eyes.

16   The pain of love kept harassing Tatyána.
She'd go into the garden to indulge her anguish…
then suddenly she'd look down, her gaze transfixed,
too weak to take a further step,
her bosom heaving, cheeks
glowing with momentary fire,
breath dying on her lips;
sound filled her ears, a glaring light her eyes…
Then came an evening – the moon was on patrol
in heaven's distant vault,
and amid dim trees a nightingale
commenced his melodious song.
Tatyána, wakeful in the darkness,
was talking softly with her nurse:

17   "I can't sleep, nanny: it's so stuffy here.
Open the window, come and sit with me."
"What is it, Tanya? What's the matter?" "I'm so wretched.
Let's talk a bit about the days long past."
"Well, what about them, Tanya? There was a time
when I had lots of tales of long ago
stored in my memory – true ones and make-believe ones,
tales of evil spirits and young lasses.
But now my brain has clouded over, Tanya.
All I knew I've forgotten. Yes,
life's taken a bad turn for me.
I'm fuddled…" "Tell me, nanny,
about your early years:
were you in love then?"

18   — И, полно, Таня! В эти лета
Мы не слыхали про любовь;
А то бы согнала со света
Меня покойница свекровь. —
«Да как же ты венчалась, няня?»
— Так, видно, Бог велел. Мой Ваня
Моложе был меня, мой свет,
А было мне тринадцать лет.
Недели две ходила сваха
К моей родне, и наконец
Благословил меня отец.
Я горько плакала со страха,
Мне с плачем косу расплели
Да с пеньем в церковь повели.

19   И вот ввели в семью чужую…
Да ты не слушаешь меня… —
«Ах, няня, няня, я тоскую,
Мне тошно, милая моя:
Я плакать, я рыдать готова!..»
— Дитя мое, ты нездорова;
Господь помилуй и спаси!
Чего ты хочешь, попроси…
Дай окроплю святой водою,
Ты вся горишь… — «Я не больна:
Я… знаешь, няня… влюблена».
— Дитя мое, господь с тобою! —
И няня девушку с мольбой
Крестила дряхлою рукой.

20   «Я влюблена», — шептала снова
Старушке с горестью она.
— Сердечный друг, ты нездорова.
«Оставь меня: я влюблена».
И между тем луна сияла
И томным светом озаряла
Татьяны бледные красы,
И распущенные власы,
И капли слез, и на скамейке
Пред героиней молодой,
С платком на голове седой,
Старушку в длинной телогрейке;
И всё дремало в тишине
При вдохновительной луне.

18   "Tanya, whatever next! In those times
nobody spoke of love –
or else my mother-in-law (God rest her soul!)
would have chased me out of this world to the next."
"Then how did you get married, nanny?"
"God must have ordained it so, my precious.
Younger than me my Vanya was,
and I was just thirteen.
The go-between – she kept on coming
for a couple of weeks to see my family;
then in the end my father gave me his blessing.
I was in terror and wept bitter tears.
They cried as they undid my plait,
but as they led me to the church they sang,

19   then off to a strange house they took—
But you're not listening to me…"
"Oh nanny, nanny, I'm so wretched.
I don't feel well, nurse dear,
I could cry, could sob my heart out!"
"My child, you're poorly;
May the Lord have mercy and make you better!
What is it you want? Just ask me, dear.
There, let me splash you with holy water,
you're all aflame…" "No, I'm not ill.
I'm… nanny, you surely know… I am in love."
"My child, the Lord be with you!"
And, as she prayed, the nurse with frail hand
gave the girl the sign of the cross.

20   "I'm in love," she said once more
to the little old woman in an anguished whisper.
"My dearest, you're just poorly."
"Oh, leave me alone: I *am* in love."
All the while the moon had been shining;
and with its wan beams it illumined
Tatyána's pale beauty,
her unbound hair,
her teardrops, and on a stool
at the young girl's bedside
the little old nurse in a long quilted dress
with a scarf around her greying head.
All was drowsing in peace
in the moon's evocative light.

21   И сердцем далеко носилась
      Татьяна, смотря на луну…
      Вдруг мысль в уме ее родилась…
      «Поди, оставь меня одну.
      Дай, няня, мне перо, бумагу,
      Да стол подвинь; я скоро лягу;
      Прости». И вот она одна.
      Всё тихо. Светит ей луна.
      Облокотясь, Татьяна пишет,
      И всё Евгений на уме,
      И в необдуманном письме
      Любовь невинной девы дышит.
      Письмо готово, сложено…
      Татьяна! для кого ж оно?

22   Я знал красавиц недоступных,
      Холодных, чистых, как зима,
      Неумолимых, неподкупных,
      Непостижимых для ума;
      Дивился я их спеси модной,
      Их добродетели природной,
      И, признаюсь, от них бежал,
      И, мнится, с ужасом читал
      Над их бровями надпись ада:
      Оставь надежду навсегда.
      Внушать любовь для них беда,
      Пугать людей для них отрада.
      Быть может, на брегах Невы
      Подобных дам видали вы.

23   Среди поклонников послушных
      Других причудниц я видал,
      Самолюбиво равнодушных
      Для вздохов страстных и похвал.
      И что ж нашел я с изумленьем?
      Оне, суровым поведеньем
      Пугая робкую любовь,
      Ее привлечь умели вновь
      По крайней мере сожаленьем,
      По крайней мере звук речей
      Казался иногда нежней,
      И с легковерным ослепленьем
      Опять любовник молодой
      Бежал за милой суетой.

21 As Tatyána watched the moon,
 her thoughts drifted far away…
 All at once an idea came to her mind…
 "Go, nanny; leave me on my own.
 Just give me a pen and paper,
 and move the table across; I'll soon lie down;
 goodnight." And there was Tatyána now alone.
 All was still. The moonlight shone around her.
 Leaning on an elbow, she started writing.
 All the time Onégin filled her mind,
 and the precipitate letter she wrote
 throbbed with the love of an innocent girl.
 At length it was finished, and folded ready…
 Tatyána! Is it really for *him*?

22 I've known lovely women you couldn't approach,
 as cold and pure as winter,
 immune alike to entreaties and gifts,
 beyond man's understanding.
 I used to be taken aback by their voguish hauteur
 and their effortless virtue;
 I confess, they made me run a mile:
 it was as though I'd read above their eyes, with horror,
 the inscription over the gate of hell:
 "Abandon hope for ever…"
 To inspire love is something such women abhor;
 to intimidate others is what they enjoy.
 There, reader, on the banks of the Nevá
 you may have met the likes of these.

23 I've come across other strange women too –
 ones who surround themselves with devoted worshippers,
 but are selfishly indifferent
 to their compliments and outpourings of love.
 And what have I found to my astonishment?
 The very woman
 who was repulsing a timid lover by her harsh demeanour
 was also adept at using the tiniest act of compassion
 to draw him on once again;
 she'd only to make her voice
 sound the tiniest bit more gentle,
 and the lad, blindly credulous in his love,
 would again be pursuing
 that same fond piece of vanity.

24   За что ж виновнее Татьяна?
За то ль, что в милой простоте
Она не ведает обмана
И верит избранной мечте?
За то ль, что любит без искусства,
Послушная влеченью чувства,
Что так доверчива она,
Что от небес одарена
Воображением мятежным,
Умом и волею живой,
И своенравной головой,
И сердцем пламенным и нежным?
Ужели не простите ей
Вы легкомыслия страстей?

25   Кокетка судит хладнокровно,
Татьяна любит не шутя
И предается безусловно
Любви, как милое дитя.
Не говорит она: отложим —
Любви мы цену тем умножим,
Вернее в сети заведем;
Сперва тщеславие кольнем
Надеждой, там недоуменьем
Измучим сердце, а потом
Ревнивым оживим огнем;
А то, скучая наслажденьем,
Невольник хитрый из оков
Всечасно вырваться готов.

26   Еще предвижу затрудненья:
Родной земли спасая честь,
Я должен буду, без сомненья,
Письмо Татьяны перевесть.
Она по-русски плохо знала,
Журналов наших не читала
И выражалася с трудом
На языке своем родном,
Итак, писала по-французски…
Что делать! повторяю вновь:
Доныне дамская любовь
Не изъяснялася по-русски,
Доныне гордый наш язык
К почтовой прозе не привык.

24   How was Tatyána guiltier than these?
Was it that in her fond simplicity
she'd never thought of being deceitful,
but believed in her cherished dream?
Was it that her love was uncontrived
and answered to nothing beyond her true feelings?
Was she too trusting?
Or was it that Heaven had endowed her
with too free an imagination,
with intelligence and a will of her own,
with an impulsive mind
and a warm and tender heart?
No! Rashly she may have given her love,
but surely you'll pardon her that.

25   A flirt will scheme cold-bloodedly;
Tatyána, though, loved in earnest
and surrendered, like an affectionate child,
unreservedly to love.
She would not say: "Let's play for time:
that way we'll increase the asking price of love
and be surer to trap our man.
So let's first prick his vanity
with hope; then we'll exhaust
his heart with doubt, and then
rekindle it with flames of jealousy.
Otherwise, if the prisoner's a clever one,
he'll weary of enjoyment
and be ready any time to break his chains."

26   There's another problem I foresee:
To preserve the honour of my native land,
without a doubt I'll have to give
Tatyána's letter in translation.
She didn't know her Russian well;
she didn't read our Russian journals;
and she found it hard to express herself
in her mother tongue.
And so she wrote in French...
What can be done? I say again:
till now no well-bred lady
has declared her love in Russian;
indeed, till now our noble language
has not had much to do with postal prose.

27   Я знаю: дам хотят заставить
      Читать по-русски. Право, страх!
      Могу ли их себе представить
      С «Благонамеренным» в руках!
      Я шлюсь на вас, мои поэты,
      Не правда ль: милые предметы,
      Которым, за свои грехи,
      Писали втайне вы стихи,
      Которым сердце посвящали,
      Не все ли, русским языком
      Владея слабо и с трудом,
      Его так мило искажали,
      И в их устах язык чужой
      Не обратился ли в родной?

28   Не дай мне Бог сойтись на бале
      Иль при разъезде на крыльце
      С семинаристом в желтой шале
      Иль с академиком в чепце!
      Как уст румяных без улыбки,
      Без грамматической ошибки
      Я русской речи не люблю.
      Быть может, на беду мою,
      Красавиц новых поколенье,
      Журналов вняв молящий глас,
      К грамматике приучит нас;
      Стихи введут в употребленье;
      Но я… какое дело мне?
      Я верен буду старине.

29   Неправильный, небрежный лепет,
      Неточный выговор речей
      По-прежнему сердечный трепет
      Произведут в груди моей;
      Раскаяться во мне нет силы,
      Мне галлицизмы будут милы,
      Как прошлой юности грехи,
      Как Богдановича стихи.
      Но полно. Мне пора заняться
      Письмом красавицы моей;
      Я слово дал, и что ж? ей-ей
      Теперь готов уж отказаться.
      Я знаю: нежного Парни
      Перо не в моде в наши дни.

27 Some people, I know, would force the ladies
to read in Russian. How truly frightful!
I can imagine them holding
that rag *The Well-Intentioned* in their hands!
I appeal to you, my fellow poets,
who (for your sins!) used to write secret verses
to your fond girlfriends
and pledge your hearts to them – isn't it true
that, with their weak and halting command of Russian,
each one of those delightful girls
would savage their native language
in that delightful way of theirs,
although they'd speak a foreign tongue
as if it were their own?

28 May God forbid that at a ball –
even on the steps as guests disperse –
I should ever meet a theology student in a yellow stole,
or an academician in a frilly bonnet!
I hate to hear Russian spoken
without a grammatical mistake –
like a pair of ruby lips without a smile.
Perhaps, to my discomfiture,
a new generation of lovely girls
will listen to the pleadings of the press
and inure our ears to proper grammar
(maybe they'll even read some poetry!)
But I – what's that to me? –
I shall stay loyal to the past.

29 The Russian language,
wrongly pronounced
in a faulty and careless lisp,
will as before make my heart beat faster.
I cannot bring myself to change my mind.
French expressions will still be dear to me,
like the memory of my youthful misdemeanours,
or the verses of Bogdanóvich.
But that's enough. It's time I got on
with my lovely heroine's letter.
I gave my word; but now, to be truthful,
I'm almost ready to break it.
I'm conscious of this: Parny's frank expressions of love
are these days no longer in fashion.

30   Певец Пиров и грусти томной,
Когда б еще ты был со мной,
Я стал бы просьбою нескромной
Тебя тревожить, милый мой:
Чтоб на волшебные напевы
Переложил ты страстной девы
Иноплеменные слова.
Где ты? приди: свои права
Передаю тебе с поклоном…
Но посреди печальных скал,
Отвыкнув сердцем от похвал,
Один, под финским небосклоном,
Он бродит, и душа его
Не слышит горя моего.

31   Письмо Татьяны предо мною;
Его я свято берегу,
Читаю с тайною тоскою
И начитаться не могу.
Кто ей внушал и эту нежность,
И слов любезную небрежность?
Кто ей внушал умильный вздор,
Безумный сердца разговор,
И увлекательный и вредный?
Я не могу понять. Но вот
Неполный, слабый перевод,
С живой картины список бледный
Или разыгранный Фрейшиц
Перстами робких учениц:

Письмо Татьяны к Онегину

Я к вам пишу — чего же боле?
Что я могу еще сказать?
Теперь, я знаю, в вашей воле
Меня презреньем наказать.
Но вы, к моей несчастной доле
Хоть каплю жалости храня,
Вы не оставите меня.

Сначала я молчать хотела;
Поверьте: моего стыда
Вы не узнали б никогда,

30   If only, my dear Baratýnsky,
you were still with me now!
You poet of *Feasts* and aching sadness,
I'd now be pestering you with bold requests
to transpose Tatyána's
passionate French
into magic, melodious rhyme.
Where are you now? If only you'd come, I'd relinquish
the copyright to you with my compliments...
He's forgotten what it means to be praised, though:
he's wandering alone
among gloomy crags under Finnish skies,
quite unaware
of how I miss him.

31   Tatyána's letter lies before me.
I've guarded it religiously.
To read it fills me with inner sadness,
but I can never read it enough.
Who can have taught her to write so tenderly,
so casually, and so endearingly?
Who can have put into her mind such touching nonsense,
such reckless openness about her feelings –
winsome indeed, but dangerous too?
It's beyond my comprehension. Anyhow,
here's my translation, lame, inadequate,
like a pencil sketch of a vivid canvas,
or a piano score of Weber's *Freischütz*
played by a timid girl as an exercise:

Tatyána's Letter to Onégin

I am writing to you... need I say more?
Is there more I can say?
I realize you're free now
to punish me with your contempt.
But you... if you've one drop of pity left
for my unhappy plight,
you'll not abandon me.

    At first I wanted to stay silent.
Believe me, you'd have never
learnt of my guilty secret,

Когда б надежду я имела
Хоть редко, хоть в неделю раз
В деревне нашей видеть вас,
Чтоб только слышать ваши речи,
Вам слово молвить, и потом
Всё думать, думать об одном
И день и ночь до новой встречи.
Но, говорят, вы нелюдим;
В глуши, в деревне всё вам скучно,
А мы... ничем мы не блестим,
Хоть вам и рады простодушно.

Зачем вы посетили нас?
В глуши забытого селенья
Я никогда не знала б вас,
Не знала б горького мученья.
Души неопытной волненья
Смирив со временем (как знать?),
По сердцу я нашла бы друга,
Была бы верная супруга
И добродетельная мать.

Другой!.. Нет, никому на свете
Не отдала бы сердца я!
То в вышнем суждено совете...
То воля неба: я твоя;
Вся жизнь моя была залогом
Свиданья верного с тобой;
Я знаю, ты мне послан Богом,
До гроба ты хранитель мой...
Ты в сновиденьях мне являлся,
Незримый, ты мне был уж мил,
Твой чудный взгляд меня томил,
В душе твой голос раздавался
Давно... нет, это был не сон!
Ты чуть вошел, я вмиг узнала,
Вся обомлела, запылала
И в мыслях молвила: вот он!
Не правда ль? я тебя слыхала:
Ты говорил со мной в тиши,
Когда я бедным помогала
Или молитвой услаждала
Тоску волнуемой души?
И в это самое мгновенье
Не ты ли, милое виденье,

if I'd had any hope
of seeing you at our place
even occasionally, even once a week –
so that I could have heard you talk,
uttered a word to you myself, and then been able
to think and think of that and only that
both night and day, until we met again.
But they say you don't like company,
that everything bores you here in the depths of the country.
And we... we have no claim on your attention –
but for the simple pleasure your presence gives us.

Why did you come to visit us?
Buried away in this forgotten hamlet
I'd never have known of your existence,
never have known this agony, this torture.
I might in time (who knows?)
have quelled the turmoil of these feelings I can't control,
have found in someone else a soulmate,
become a loyal wife,
devoted mother...

Did I say "someone else"? No, no, there's no one,
no one on earth to whom I'd have given my heart.
The powers on high have preordained it,
Heaven has willed it: Eugene, I am yours.
My whole life up to now has been a prelude
to our predestined meeting.
I know that you are sent to me by God.
You are to be my guardian until death...
You used to appear to me in dreams:
I was already fond of you before I met you;
those wonderful eyes of yours had haunted me;
your voice I'd heard beforehand in my heart
long, long ago... No, those were not just dreams!
I knew you the very moment you came in;
I felt all faint, on fire,
and told myself: "He's come!"
Isn't it true I used to hear your voice?
Did you not often speak to me in the silence,
when I was caring for the poor
or trying to relieve
the anguish of my troubled heart in prayer?
And at this very moment didn't I
just catch a precious glimpse of you,

В прозрачной темноте мелькнул,
Приникнул тихо к изголовью?
Не ты ль, с отрадой и любовью,
Слова надежды мне шепнул?
Кто ты, мой ангел ли хранитель,
Или коварный искуситель:
Мои сомненья разреши.
Быть может, это всё пустое,
Обман неопытной души!
И суждено совсем иное...
Но так и быть! Судьбу мою
Отныне я тебе вручаю,
Перед тобою слезы лью,
Твоей защиты умоляю...
Вообрази: я здесь одна,
Никто меня не понимает,
Рассудок мой изнемогает,
И молча гибнуть я должна.
Я жду тебя: единым взором
Надежды сердца оживи
Иль сон тяжелый перерви,
Увы, заслуженным укором!

Кончаю! Страшно перечесть...
Стыдом и страхом замираю...
Но мне порукой ваша честь,
И смело ей себя вверяю...

32   Татьяна то вздохнет, то охнет;
Письмо дрожит в ее руке;
Облатка розовая сохнет
На воспаленном языке.
К плечу головушкой склонилась,
Сорочка легкая спустилась
С ее прелестного плеча...
Но вот уж лунного луча
Сиянье гаснет. Там долина
Сквозь пар яснеет. Там поток
Засеребрился; там рожок
Пастуший будит селянина.
Вот утро: встали все давно,
Моей Татьяне всё равно.

as you darted through the twilight of my room,
stooped gently down towards my pillow,
and whispered words of comfort and of love
to give me hope?
Who are you, Eugene – are you my guardian angel?
or a philanderer not to be trusted?
Resolve my doubts.
Maybe all this is nothing after all –
just the illusion of a naive girl's heart,
and fate holds quite a different future for me.
If so, so be it: I am placing
my destiny from now on in your hands;
with tears I beg you,
I implore you, to protect me...
Picture me – on my own here
with no one to understand me,
my reason failing,
and nothing left me but to die in silence.
I'm waiting for you. With a single glance
now bring my inner hopes to life –
or else cut short this stifling dream of mine
with the rebuke that, sadly, I deserve.

    That's all! I'm too afraid to read it over...
I'm faint with shame and fear...
Your sense of honour, sir, is my one safeguard;
in it I boldly place my trust...

32   Tatyána's breathing was heavy and uneven;
the letter trembled in her hand;
her burning tongue was parched and couldn't stick
the pink disc to the folded paper.
And then her head dropped sideways,
and the flimsy nightdress
slipped down from off her lovely shoulder...
But the rays of moonlight
were already waning; the valley
was showing through the mist; the river
glistened like silver; and the sound of a herdsman's pipe
was wakening the villagers from their sleep.
The morning came, and folk had long been up,
but Tatyána was still past caring.

33   Она зари не замечает,
Сидит с поникшею главой
И на письмо не напирает
Своей печати вырезной.
Но, дверь тихонько отпирая,
Уж ей Филатьевна седая
Приносит на подносе чай.
«Пора, дитя мое, вставай:
Да ты, красавица, готова!
О пташка ранняя моя!
Вечор уж как боялась я!
Да, слава Богу, ты здорова!
Тоски ночной и следу нет,
Лицо твое как маков цвет».

34   — Ах! няня, сделай одолженье. —
«Изволь, родная, прикажи».
— Не думай… право… подозренье…
Но видишь… ах! не откажи. —
«Мой друг, вот Бог тебе порука».
— Итак, пошли тихонько внука
С запиской этой к О… к тому…
К соседу… да велеть ему,
Чтоб он не говорил ни слова,
Чтоб он не называл меня… —
«Кому же, милая моя?
Я нынче стала бестолкова.
Кругом соседей много есть;
Куда мне их и перечесть».

35   — Как недогадлива ты, няня! —
«Сердечный друг, уж я стара,
Стара; тупеет разум, Таня;
А то, бывало, я востра,
Бывало, слово барской воли…»
— Ах, няня, няня! до того ли?
Что нужды мне в твоем уме?
Ты видишь, дело о письме
К Онегину. — «Ну, дело, дело.
Не гневайся, душа моя,
Ты знаешь, непонятна я…
Да что ж ты снова побледнела?»
— Так, няня, право ничего.
Пошли же внука своего.

33 She'd not observed the rising sun,
but sat on there with lowered head,
without impressing her graven seal
onto the letter.
Eventually the door swung open softly:
grey-haired Filátyevna
was bringing her a tray of tea.
"It's time, my child – up you get…
But you're already up, my pretty one!
Oh, aren't you an early bird!
I was so frightened for you yester-evening;
but now, praise God, you're well again.
There's not a trace of last night's trouble,
your face is like a poppy bloom!"

34 "Oh, nanny, will you do a favour?"
"Of course, my darling. Ask away."
"Don't think… No, truly… Any suspicion…
But do you see?… Oh, nanny, don't refuse!"
"My dear, I promise in God's name."
"Well, get your grandson quietly
to take this note to Mr O… to that…
that neighbour; and tell the boy
that he is not to speak a word
or say my name…"
"But who is it you mean, my sweet?
My mind's no good these days.
We've such a lot of neighbours all around.
You'll have to read to me which one it is."

35 "Oh, nanny, you're so dense!"
"I'm old now, dearest child,
I'm old. Wits lose their sharpness, Tanya.
There was a time I was alert;
yes, once at a word of my mistress's bidding…"
"Oh nanny, nanny! Don't waste time!
Why do I need to hear about your wits?
Just look – I'm talking about this letter
to Mr Onégin." "Ah now, there, that's better…
Don't be annoyed, dear heart,
you know how hard I am of understanding…
But why have you gone pale again?"
"It's all right, nanny. It's nothing, truly.
Just go and send your grandson on his errand."

36   Но день протек, и нет ответа.
Другой настал: всё нет как нет.
Бледна, как тень, с утра одета,
Татьяна ждет: когда ж ответ?
Приехал Ольгин обожатель.
«Скажите: где же ваш приятель? —
Ему вопрос хозяйки был. —
Он что-то нас совсем забыл».
Татьяна, вспыхнув, задрожала.
— Сегодня быть он обещал, —
Старушке Ленский отвечал, —
Да, видно, почта задержала. —
Татьяна потупила взор,
Как будто слыша злой укор.

37   Смеркалось; на столе, блистая,
Шипел вечерний самовар,
Китайский чайник нагревая;
Под ним клубился легкий пар.
Разлитый Ольгиной рукою,
По чашкам темною струею
Уже душистый чай бежал,
И сливки мальчик подавал;
Татьяна пред окном стояла,
На стекла хладные дыша,
Задумавшись, моя душа,
Прелестным пальчиком писала
На отуманенном стекле
Заветный вензель *О* да *Е*.

38   И между тем душа в ней ныла,
И слез был полон томный взор.
Вдруг топот!.. кровь ее застыла.
Вот ближе! скачут… и на двор
Евгений! «Ах!» — и легче тени
Татьяна прыг в другие сени,
С крыльца на двор, и прямо в сад;
Летит, летит; взглянуть назад
Не смеет; мигом обежала
Куртины, мостики, лужок,
Аллею к озеру, лесок,
Кусты сирень переломала,
По цветникам летя к ручью.
И, задыхаясь, на скамью

36   The day passed; there was no reply.
The next day came; still not a word.
Pale as a ghost, and dressed since morning
for visitors, Tatyána waited. When would an answer come?
Lensky arrived to see the girl he worshipped.
"Tell me, wherever is your friend?"
was Mrs Larin's opening question.
"He seems to have quite forgotten us."
Tatyána flushed and started trembling.
"He promised to be here today,"
said Lensky to the older lady.
"His mail's delayed him, I suppose."
Tatyána looked down at the floor,
as though she'd heard a snide rebuke.

37   Evening was drawing in; the light was fading.
On the table simmered a gleaming samovar,
warming the Chinese teapot
in spiralling wisps of steam.
Olga poured tea,
and it gave off a lovely fragrance
as the dark stream filled each cup.
A house boy served the cream.
Tatyána, my poor darling, stood by the window
engrossed in thought.
There, breathing on the chilly glass
she wrote with a dainty finger
on a misted pane
the sacred monogram – *E.O.*

38   And all the time her heart was aching
and her weary eyes were full of tears.
Then, clattering hooves! Her blood ran cold.
Now closer, at a gallop... and there outside
was Eugene! "Aah!" Tatyána lighter than a shadow
leapt to the other porch,
down steps to yard, then straight into the garden.
On, on she flew, not daring
to look back. She ran like lightning
across low walls, raised walkways, lawn,
the lakeward avenue, the copse,
breaking off lilacs as she dashed
between the flowering shrubs towards the stream –
till, gasping, onto a bench

39   Упала… «Здесь он! здесь Евгений!
О боже! что подумал он!»
В ней сердце, полное мучений,
Хранит надежды темный сон;
Она дрожит и жаром пышет,
И ждет: нейдет ли? Но не слышит.
В саду служанки, на грядах,
Сбирали ягоду в кустах
И хором по наказу пели
(Наказ, основанный на том,
Чтоб барской ягоды тайком
Уста лукавые не ели
И пеньем были заняты:
Затея сельской остроты!)

Песня девушек

Девицы, красавицы,
Душеньки, подруженьки,
Разыграйтесь девицы,
Разгуляйтесь, милые!
Затяните песенку,
Песенку заветную,
Заманите молодца
К хороводу нашему.
Как заманим молодца,
Как завидим издали,
Разбежимтесь, милые,
Закидаем вишеньем,
Вишеньем, малиною,
Красною смородиной.
Не ходи подслушивать
Песенки заветные,
Не ходи подсматривать
Игры наши девичьи.

39   she slumped. "He's here! Eugene is here!
Oh God, what has he thought?"
Her anguished heart still clung
to its dim dream of hope.
Though feeling hot and flushed, she trembled,
waiting expectantly, but couldn't hear him.
In the kitchen garden servant girls
were picking fruit among the rows of bushes,
singing in chorus, as instructed.
(The thought behind the instruction was
that greedy mouths
engaged in singing
wouldn't eat the squire's fruit on the sly –
a ploy that shows the wit of country folk!)

Song of the Peasant Girls

    Come, dear friends; come, girls, and play!
Up, pretty ones, let's have a merry day!
    Start the song, our secret song,
and to our dance let's lure a lad along.
    Then, girls, once we've lured the boy
and glimpsed him yonder, fooled by our decoy –
    then let's break, sweet friends, and run.
Quick, pelt him hard with cherries, everyone!
    When our cherries we have shed,
raspberries we'll throw at him, and currants red.
    That will teach the lad it's wrong
to come and eavesdrop on our secret song.
    Mark the lesson: keep away,
don't spy upon us girls when we're at play!

40   Оне поют, и с небреженьем
       Внимая звонкий голос их,
       Ждала Татьяна с нетерпеньем,
       Чтоб трепет сердца в ней затих,
       Чтобы прошло ланит пыланье.
       Но в персях то же трепетанье,
       И не проходит жар ланит,
       Но ярче, ярче лишь горит…
       Так бедный мотылек и блещет
       И бьется радужным крылом,
       Плененный школьным шалуном;
       Так зайчик в озими трепещет,
       Увидя вдруг издалека
       В кусты припадшего стрелка.

41   Но наконец она вздохнула
       И встала со скамьи своей;
       Пошла, но только повернула
       В аллею – прямо перед ней,
       Блистая взорами, Евгений
       Стоит подобно грозной тени,
       И, как огнем обожжена,
       Остановилася она.
       Но следствия нежданной встречи
       Сегодня, милые друзья,
       Пересказать не в силах я;
       Мне должно после долгой речи
       И погулять и отдохнуть:
       Докончу после как-нибудь.

40   As they sang on, Tatyána absently
half-listened to their ringing voices
and waited with impatience
for her heart to stop its pounding
and her cheeks to lose their burning.
But the pounding in her breast went on,
and the fire in her cheeks would not die down,
but just blazed fiercer, fiercer.
Just so a helpless butterfly,
captured by a schoolboy for a prank,
flickers and flutters its iridescent wings;
or a young hare waits quivering in the winter corn,
despite the distant glimpse he's caught
of a marksman taking cover in the bushes.

41   At length Tatyána gave a sigh,
arose from her bench
and began to walk; but she'd no sooner
turned into the avenue than straight ahead
she saw Eugene, eyes flashing,
standing like a looming thundercloud.
Tatyána, as though scorched by fire,
stopped dead.
But today, dear friends,
I'm too exhausted to relate
the sequel to this unlooked-for meeting.
After so long a narrative I must
go for a stroll and have a rest.
I'll finish off my story later, somehow.

ГЛАВА ЧЕТВЕРТАЯ

La morale est dans la nature des choses.
—Necker

1–6   . . . .

7   Чем меньше женщину мы любим,
Тем легче нравимся мы ей
И тем ее вернее губим
Средь обольстительных сетей.
Разврат, бывало, хладнокровный
Наукой славился любовной,
Сам о себе везде трубя
И наслаждаясь не любя.
Но эта важная забава
Достойна старых обезьян
Хваленых дедовских времян:
Ловласов обветшала слава
Со славой красных каблуков
И величавых париков.

8   Кому не скучно лицемерить,
Различно повторять одно,
Стараться важно в том уверить,
В чем все уверены давно,
Всё те же слышать возраженья,
Уничтожать предрассужденья,
Которых не было и нет
У девочки в тринадцать лет!
Кого не утомят угрозы,
Моленья, клятвы, мнимый страх,
Записки на шести листах,
Обманы, сплетни, кольца, слезы,
Надзоры теток, матерей
И дружба тяжкая мужей!

110

CHAPTER FOUR

Morality is in the nature of things.
– Necker

1–6 ....

7 The less we love a woman
the more readily we attract her,
and the surer we are of luring her
into a ruinous entanglement.
Cold-blooded sensuality of this kind
used once to be celebrated as the "art of love":
men were forever boasting of their skill,
though love it wasn't, just self-gratification.
This pastime that men took so seriously
is much what you'd expect of the old baboons
of our grandfathers' glorious days:
the kudos such Lovelaces earned is passé now,
along with the fashion for red-heeled shoes
and grandiose wigs.

8 Today we're all impatient of such play-acting –
of repeating one idea in different words;
of trying to give earnest reassurance
of something folk were sure of long ago;
of always listening to the same objections;
of always refuting prejudices –
as if a thirteen-year-old girl
ever had prejudices in the first place!
Now everybody's tired of threats,
entreaties, vows and feigned anxiety;
of "notes" six pages long;
of lies and gossip, rings and tears;
of vigilance from aunts and mothers –
and of the burdensome companionship of husbands.

9   Так точно думал мой Евгений.
     Он в первой юности своей
     Был жертвой бурных заблуждений
     И необузданных страстей.
     Привычкой жизни избалован,
     Одним на время очарован,
     Разочарованный другим,
     Желаньем медленно томим,
     Томим и ветреным успехом,
     Внимая в шуме и в тиши
     Роптанье вечное души,
     Зевоту подавляя смехом:
     Вот как убил он восемь лет,
     Утратя жизни лучший цвет.

10   В красавиц он уж не влюблялся,
     А волочился как-нибудь;
     Откажут — мигом утешался;
     Изменят — рад был отдохнуть.
     Он их искал без упоенья,
     А оставлял без сожаленья,
     Чуть помня их любовь и злость.
     Так точно равнодушный гость
     На *вист* вечерний приезжает,
     Садится; кончилась игра:
     Он уезжает со двора,
     Спокойно дома засыпает
     И сам не знает поутру,
     Куда поедет ввечеру.

11   Но, получив посланье Тани,
     Онегин живо тронут был:
     Язык девических мечтаний
     В нем думы роем возмутил;
     И вспомнил он Татьяны милой
     И бледный цвет и вид унылый;
     И в сладостный, безгрешный сон
     Душою погрузился он.
     Быть может, чувствий пыл старинный
     Им на минуту овладел;
     Но обмануть он не хотел
     Доверчивость души невинной.
     Теперь мы в сад перелетим,
     Где встретилась Татьяна с ним.

9   This was Onégin's attitude exactly.
As a young adolescent,
he'd been prey
to bouts of unruliness and lechery.
That self-indulgent life had spoilt him:
enchanted first, then disenchanted
by one thing and another in succession,
gradually wearied by desire
and wearied too by the transience of its achievement,
conscious in din and quietude alike
of the perpetual grumbling of his soul,
suppressing yawns with laughter –
that's how he'd killed eight years of life
and wasted its finest flowering.

10   He no longer fell in love with attractive women,
but trailed behind them casually.
If women repulsed him, that was fine by him;
if they deserted him, that was a welcome respite;
he sought them without enthusiasm
and left them without regret,
with scarcely a memory of their love or malice.
In just this way a nonchalant visitor
might call and take his seat for an evening's whist.
Once the game is over,
he drives away,
falls peacefully asleep at home,
and on the morrow has no idea
whom he'll be visiting that night.

11   On receiving Tatyána's letter, nonetheless,
Onégin was deeply moved.
The language of her girlish dreams
stirred up a swarm of thoughts within him;
he recalled how he'd been charmed by Tatyána's
wan complexion and downcast eyes,
and he sank into a reverie
both blameless and delightful.
Maybe for a moment he succumbed
to the feverishness of his old sensuality;
but he was disinclined to take advantage
of the trustfulness of such a guileless soul.
Now, though, we'd better hurry to the park,
where he and Tatyána had come face to face.

12 Минуты две они молчали,
    Но к ней Онегин подошел
    И молвил: «Вы ко мне писали,
    Не отпирайтесь. Я прочел
    Души доверчивой признанья,
    Любви невинной излиянья;
    Мне ваша искренность мила;
    Она в волненье привела
    Давно умолкнувшие чувства;
    Но вас хвалить я не хочу;
    Я за нее вам отплачу
    Признаньем также без искусства;
    Примите исповедь мою:
    Себя на суд вам отдаю.

13 Когда бы жизнь домашним кругом
    Я ограничить захотел;
    Когда б мне быть отцом, супругом
    Приятный жребий повелел;
    Когда б семейственной картиной
    Пленился я хоть миг единый, —
    То, верно б, кроме вас одной
    Невесты не искал иной.
    Скажу без блесток мадригальных:
    Нашед мой прежний идеал,
    Я верно б вас одну избрал
    В подруги дней моих печальных,
    Всего прекрасного в залог,
    И был бы счастлив… сколько мог!

14 Но я не создан для блаженства;
    Ему чужда душа моя;
    Напрасны ваши совершенства:
    Их вовсе недостоин я.
    Поверьте (совесть в том порукой),
    Супружество нам будет мукой.
    Я, сколько ни любил бы вас,
    Привыкнув, разлюблю тотчас;
    Начнете плакать: ваши слезы
    Не тронут сердца моего,
    А будут лишь бесить его.
    Судите ж вы, какие розы
    Нам заготовит Гименей
    И, может быть, на много дней.

12   For a minute or two they stood in silence.
Then Onégin walked across to her
and spoke: "You wrote to me –
don't try to take it back. I've read
those admissions of a trusting heart,
those outpourings of innocent love.
Your sincerity has touched me,
stirring within me
emotions that had long lain still.
It's not that I mean to flatter you;
but in return for this sincerity I'll pay you
the compliment of an admission just as frank.
So listen to the confession that I'm making;
then reach your verdict – I submit to that.

13   "If I had wanted to confine
my life to the domestic sphere,
if it had been my happy destiny
to be a husband and a father,
if I'd been for a single moment tempted
by the prospect of a family,
then truly I'd have sought
no bride but you alone.
I'm telling you as plainly as I can:
if life had turned out as I once had dreamt,
it's you alone, for certain, I'd have chosen
to be my friend in times of sorrow
and to assure me that the world was good;
and I'd have been happy – were that possible!

14   "But I wasn't made for happiness;
it's something foreign to my nature.
Your admirable qualities are lost on me –
I'm quite unworthy of them.
Believe me – my conscience vouches for it –
marriage for us would be a torment.
However much I loved you at the outset,
once I got used to you my love would fail.
You'd start to cry, but no amount of tears
would stir me to pity –
they'd only madden me.
Judge for yourself, then, what thorny roses
marriage would bring us –
maybe for a lifetime.

115

15   Что может быть на свете хуже
Семьи, где бедная жена
Грустит о недостойном муже,
И днем и вечером одна;
Где скучный муж, ей цену зная
(Судьбу, однако ж, проклиная),
Всегда нахмурен, молчалив,
Сердит и холодно-ревнив!
Таков я. И того ль искали
Вы чистой, пламенной душой,
Когда с такою простотой,
С таким умом ко мне писали?
Ужели жребий вам такой
Назначен строгою судьбой?

16   Мечтам и годам нет возврата;
Не обновлю души моей…
Я вас люблю любовью брата
И, может быть, еще нежней.
Послушайте ж меня без гнева:
Сменит не раз младая дева
Мечтами легкие мечты;
Так деревцо свои листы
Меняет с каждою весною.
Так видно небом суждено.
Полюбите вы снова: но…
Учитесь властвовать собою;
Не всякий вас, как я, поймет;
К беде неопытность ведет».

17   Так проповедывал Евгений.
Сквозь слез не видя ничего,
Едва дыша, без возражений,
Татьяна слушала его.
Он подал руку ей. Печально
(Как говорится, *машинально*)
Татьяна молча оперлась,
Головкой томною склонясь;
Пошли домой вкруг огорода;
Явились вместе, и никто
Не вздумал им пенять на то.
Имеет сельская свобода
Свои счастливые права,
Как и надменная Москва.

15   "What in the world, I ask you, could be worse
than a family in which the wife, poor woman,
spends day and night alone
grieving for her unworthy husband,
while he, the wretch, knowing her worth
yet cursing the fate that had united them,
is ever scowling, silent,
morose and coldly jealous.
This is the sort of man I am. And is this what,
pure and ardent as you are, you sought
when you wrote me that open-hearted
and thoughtful letter?
Surely fate cannot be so harsh
as to have marked you out for such a future.

16   "We can't have back our dreams or youth, you know;
I cannot give myself another soul.
I love you with the love a brother feels –
and perhaps more tenderly than that.
Listen, and don't be angry at what I say.
A young girl has a nimble imagination:
she'll change her fancies more than once,
just as a sapling has a change of leaves
with each succeeding springtime.
That's clearly how it's meant to be.
You'll fall in love again; even so…
you must learn self-control –
not all will understand you as I do.
Yes, inexperience can lead to trouble."

17   Such was Onégin's sermon.
Tatyána, scarcely breathing,
blinded by tears,
heard him without rejoinder.
He offered her his arm; and mournfully –
mechanically, as they say –
she leant on it in silence,
her poor head drooping wearily.
They walked back home around the kitchen garden.
They were seen together; no one, though,
thought any the worse of them for that:
our country folk are easy-going, they've
their own benevolent standards of right and wrong –
as supercilious Moscow has as well.

18   Вы согласитесь, мой читатель,
        Что очень мило поступил
        С печальной Таней наш приятель;
        Не в первый раз он тут явил
        Души прямое благородство,
        Хотя людей недоброхотство
        В нем не щадило ничего:
        Враги его, друзья его
        (Что, может быть, одно и то же)
        Его честили так и сяк.
        Врагов имеет в мире всяк,
        Но от друзей спаси нас, боже!
        Уж эти мне друзья, друзья!
        Об них недаром вспомнил я.

19   А что? Да так. Я усыпляю
        Пустые, черные мечты;
        Я только *в скобках* замечаю,
        Что нет презренной клеветы,
        На чердаке вралем рожденной
        И светской чернью ободренной,
        Что нет нелепицы такой,
        Ни эпиграммы площадной,
        Которой бы ваш друг с улыбкой,
        В кругу порядочных людей,
        Без всякой злобы и затей,
        Не повторил стократ ошибкой;
        А впрочем, он за вас горой:
        Он вас так любит... как родной!

20   Гм! гм! Читатель благородный,
        Здорова ль ваша вся родня?
        Позвольте: может быть, угодно
        Теперь узнать вам от меня,
        Что значат именно *родные*.
        Родные люди вот какие:
        Мы их обязаны ласкать,
        Любить, душевно уважать
        И, по обычаю народа,
        О Рождестве их навещать
        Или по почте поздравлять,
        Чтоб остальное время года
        Не думали о нас они...
        Итак, дай Бог им долги дни!

18   My readers, you'll agree that our Onégin
behaved extremely decently
towards Tatyána in her distress.
This wasn't the first time that he'd demonstrated
a true nobility of character, despite the unsparing malice
he'd suffered from other people –
for enemies and friends alike
had never missed a chance
of running him down, this way or that.
Perhaps, indeed, our enemies and friends
are one and the same. We all have enemies –
but God preserve us from our friends!
I've had enough of friends, my friends:
I've good cause to remember them.

19   What's that I said? Oh, nothing. I'm just stifling
some dark and purposeless reflections.
I make (in brackets) just one comment:
there is no slander, despicable as may be,
hatched in a garret by some rumour-monger
and nurtured by society's scum,
there's no coarse jibe,
no indiscretion,
that your dear friend won't smilingly,
with no ulterior motive or ill will,
quite absent-mindedly repeat a hundred times
in the most honourable company.
For the rest, though, he's a rock in your defence –
he loves you after all, like... family!

20   Ah, talking of family...
my honoured reader,
how are all your relations? Are they well?
Allow me – perhaps you'd like me to inform you
just what this word "relations" means?
"Relations" means those characters
that we're obliged to make a fuss of,
to love, to hold in deep respect,
and – such is the popular convention –
to call upon at Christmastide
or send our greetings to by post,
so that, for the remainder of the year,
they needn't give a thought to us...
Quite so. God grant them length of days!

21   Зато любовь красавиц нежных
Надежней дружбы и родства:
Над нею и средь бурь мятежных
Вы сохраняете права.
Конечно так. Но вихорь моды,
Но своенравие природы,
Но мненья светского поток…
А милый пол, как пух, легок.
К тому ж и мнения супруга
Для добродетельной жены
Всегда почтенны быть должны;
Так ваша верная подруга
Бывает вмиг увлечена:
Любовью шутит сатана.

22   Кого ж любить? Кому же верить?
Кто не изменит нам один?
Кто все дела, все речи мерит
Услужливо на наш аршин?
Кто клеветы про нас не сеет?
Кто нас заботливо лелеет?
Кому порок наш не беда?
Кто не наскучит никогда?
Призрака суетный искатель,
Трудов напрасно не губя,
Любите самого себя,
Достопочтенный мой читатель!
Предмет достойный: ничего
Любезней, верно, нет его.

23   Что было следствием свиданья?
Увы, не трудно угадать!
Любви безумные страданья
Не перестали волновать
Младой души, печали жадной;
Нет, пуще страстью безотрадной
Татьяна бедная горит;
Ее постели сон бежит;
Здоровье, жизни цвет и сладость,
Улыбка, девственный покой,
Пропало всё, что звук пустой,
И меркнет милой Тани младость:
Так одевает бури тень
Едва рождающийся день.

21   The love of a sweet and pretty girl, by contrast,
is firmer than friendship or family ties.
Your girlfriend's allegiance you'll retain
throughout life's fiercest storms – of course, of course...
There's the whirlwind, though, of fashion,
the waywardness of human nature,
the strong tide of society's opinion...
the charming sex, in any case, is light as fluff!
What's more, a husband's high regard
for a wife's virtue
must always be respected.
So, you see, your "devoted" girlfriend
is lost to you in a trice:
love is the Devil's toy.

22   Who is there, then, to love? Whom can we trust?
Is there one person who won't turn against us,
who'll obligingly take our part
in all they do and say,
who'll not spread calumnies about us,
who'll use all openings to flatter us,
who'll not be put off by our faults,
who'll never ever be a nuisance?
You'll search in vain. Don't waste
your efforts in chasing phantoms –
just love yourself: that's my advice.
A worthy chap you are, dear reader,
a worthy object of your love. Yes truly,
there's nothing that's more lovable than you!

23   But what was the sequel to that meeting?
Alas, not hard to guess! Tatyána remained
tormented to distraction by her love;
her youthful sensibilities thrived on anguish,
and there was no respite to their turmoil.
No, poor girl, she was the more consumed by passion
as it lost its prospect of fulfilment.
She couldn't sleep at night.
Her health, her sense of beauty and enjoyment,
her smile, her innocent serenity –
all faded like an empty sound.
A shadow dimmed her youth and hid its charm;
as when a storm cloud veils
a new day's very dawning.

24   Увы, Татьяна увядает,
      Бледнеет, гаснет и молчит!
      Ничто ее не занимает,
      Ее души не шевелит.
      Качая важно головою,
      Соседи шепчут меж собою:
      Пора, пора бы замуж ей!..
      Но полно. Надо мне скорей
      Развеселить воображенье
      Картиной счастливой любви.
      Невольно, милые мои,
      Меня стесняет сожаленье;
      Простите мне: я так люблю
      Татьяну милую мою!

25   Час от часу плененный боле
      Красами Ольги молодой,
      Владимир сладостной неволе
      Предался полною душой.
      Он вечно с ней. В ее покое
      Они сидят в потемках двое;
      Они в саду, рука с рукой,
      Гуляют утренней порой;
      И что ж? Любовью упоенный,
      В смятенье нежного стыда,
      Он только смеет иногда,
      Улыбкой Ольги ободренный,
      Развитым локоном играть
      Иль край одежды целовать.

26   Он иногда читает Оле
      Нравоучительный роман,
      В котором автор знает боле
      Природу, чем Шатобриан,
      А между тем две, три страницы
      (Пустые бредни, небылицы,
      Опасные для сердца дев)
      Он пропускает, покраснев.
      Уединясь от всех далеко,
      Они над шахматной доской,
      На стол облокотясь, порой
      Сидят, задумавшись глубоко,
      И Ленский пешкою ладью
      Берет в рассеянье свою.

24   It was sad how Tatyána wilted,
grew pallid, dispirited and silent.
Nothing engaged
her interest or emotions.
The neighbours gravely shook their heads
and whispered among themselves:
"It's high time she was married!..."
But enough! I must hurry on
to brighten my mind's eye
with a portrayal of happy love –
though I admit, dear friends,
that I have to fight back my regrets.
Forgive me: I'm so fond
of my dear Tatyána.

25   Vladímir Lensky was hourly growing more enthralled
by Olga's youthful charms,
and he surrendered himself wholeheartedly
to their delightful bondage.
He was forever in her company:
they'd sit together in the darkness of her room;
they'd walk in the grounds of a morning hand in hand.
And – would you imagine? – even when Lensky
was in an ecstasy of love,
he suffered such agonies of shyness that only sometimes –
if she emboldened him with a smile –
could he pluck up the courage
to play with a loose lock of her hair
or kiss the hem of her dress.

26   He'd sometimes read to Olga
a moralizing novel, in which he felt
the author showed a better knowledge
of the "nature of things" than Chateaubriand;
but in the middle, with a blush,
he'd skip a couple of pages –
silly, far-fetched nonsense,
too unsettling to a young girl's feelings.
Or the two of them would escape from everyone
and sit there, over a chessboard,
elbows resting on the table,
deep in thought;
then Lensky absent-mindedly would move
a pawn to take a castle of his own.

27 Поедет ли домой, и дома
    Он занят Ольгою своей.
    Летучие листки альбома
    Прилежно украшает ей:
    То в них рисует сельски виды,
    Надгробный камень, храм Киприды,
    Или на лире голубка
    Пером и красками слегка;
    То на листках воспоминанья
    Пониже подписи других
    Он оставляет нежный стих,
    Безмолвный памятник мечтанья,
    Мгновенной думы легкий след,
    Всё тот же после многих лет.

28 Конечно, вы не раз видали
    Уездной барышни альбом,
    Что все подружки измарали
    С конца, с начала и кругом.
    Сюда, назло правописанью,
    Стихи без меры по преданью
    В знак дружбы верной внесены,
    Уменьшены, продолжены.
    На первом листике встречаешь
    Qu'écrirez-vous sur ces tablettes,
    И подпись: *t. à v. Annette*;
    А на последнем прочитаешь:
    «*Кто любит более тебя,*
    Пусть пишет далее меня».

29 Тут непременно вы найдете
    Два сердца, факел и цветки;
    Тут верно клятвы вы прочтете
    В любви до гробовой доски;
    Какой-нибудь *пиит* армейский
    Тут подмахнул стишок злодейский.
    В такой альбом, мои друзья,
    Признаться, рад писать и я,
    Уверен будучи душою,
    Что всякий мой усердный вздор
    Заслужит благосклонный взор,
    И что потом с улыбкой злою
    Не станут важно разбирать,
    Остро иль нет я мог соврать.

27   When he rode home, there too
Olga was his preoccupation.
Painstakingly he'd beautify
her album's fluttering pages.
Sometimes he'd do pen drawings of rustic scenes,
a tombstone, a shrine of Venus,
or of a dove upon a lyre,
and paint them in with pastel tints.
Or he might write a touching verse
on one of the commemorative pages
beneath the signature of someone else –
the silent memento of a reverie,
light imprint of a momentary thought,
fixed there for many years to come.

28   Reader, no doubt you'll more than once have seen
the album of some country miss,
smudged front and back and everywhere
by all of her young friends.
In it, in token of undying friendship –
and in defiance of the rules of spelling –
they'll have copied, shortened or enlarged upon
the unmetrical verses called for by tradition.
On the first page of all you'll find:
"Qu'écrirez-vous sur ces tablettes?"
– signed: *"toute à vous, Annette"*;
and on the final one you'll read:
*"Let any who love you more than I
sign farther on – just let them try!"*

29   You're sure to find in albums such as these
a pair of hearts, a flambeau, floral sketches;
you'll certainly read vows
of "love that will endure unto the grave";
and some barrack-room "bard"
will have put his name to a wicked epigram.
To tell the truth, my friends,
I enjoy inscribing albums like this myself,
for I know at bottom that here at least
all the fond rubbish that I write
will win a kindly glance;
people won't later smirk and sneer
and start discussing pompously
the wittiness or otherwise of my banter.

30   Но вы, разрозненные томы
Из библиотеки чертей,
Великолепные альбомы,
Мученье модных рифмачей,
Вы, украшенные проворно
Толстого кистью чудотворной
Иль Баратынского пером,
Пускай сожжет вас Божий гром!
Когда блистательная дама
Мне свой in-quarto подает,
И дрожь и злость меня берет,
И шевелится эпиграмма
Во глубине моей души,
А мадригалы им пиши!

31   Не мадригалы Ленский пишет
В альбоме Ольги молодой;
Его перо любовью дышит,
Не хладно блещет остротой;
Что ни заметит, ни услышит
Об Ольге, он про то и пишет:
И, полны истины живой,
Текут элегии рекой.
Так ты, Языков вдохновенный,
В порывах сердца своего,
Поешь Бог ведает кого,
И свод элегий драгоценный
Представит некогда тебе
Всю повесть о твоей судьбе.

32   Но тише! Слышишь? Критик строгий
Повелевает сбросить нам
Элегии венок убогий,
И нашей братье рифмачам
Кричит: «Да перестаньте плакать,
И всё одно и то же квакать,
Жалеть *о прежнем, о былом*:
Довольно, пойте о другом!»
— Ты прав, и верно нам укажешь
Трубу, личину и кинжал,
И мыслей мертвый капитал
Отвсюду воскресить прикажешь:
Не так ли, друг? — «Ничуть. Куда!
Пишите оды, господа,

30   Quite different are those albums meant for show,
so deftly adorned
by the wonder-working paintbrush of Tolstóy
or Baratýnsky's pen –
a voguish versifier's bed of nails,
stray volumes
from the Devil's library!
I dearly wish a thunderbolt from God
would incinerate the lot! When a lady of high standing
offers me her quarto-sized edition
I start to shake with mischievous excitement
as I feel a witty jibe
stirring deep down within me.
But all they want's a pretty verse!

31   It wasn't pretty verses Lensky wrote
in his young Olga's album;
nor did his words have the cold gleam of wit:
they throbbed with love.
He wrote of everything he saw in Olga,
of everything he heard about her.
A flood of elegies poured forth,
brimming with ardour and sincerity.
(Yazýkov, it's the same with you:
whoever you celebrate in the inspired verse you write,
you're carried away so much by your emotions
that the precious collection of your elegies
will one day give in full
the story of your life.)

32   But hush! I seem to hear one of our sterner critics
telling us to fling away
the tattered garland of elegiac verse.
"Can't you stop being so woesome?" he cries
to rhymesters of our persuasion.
"You're always croaking the same old tune,
bemoaning 'time past' and 'days of yore'.
Enough! Write verses about something else."
"All right then. You'll no doubt prescribe for us
the classical trumpet, mask and dagger;
you'll have us striving to reactivate
a fund of ideas written off long ago.
Isn't that so, my friend?" "Not in the least. What next!
It's odes you gentlemen should write –

33   Как их писали в мощны годы,
Как было встарь заведено…»
— Одне торжественные оды!
И, полно, друг; не всё ль равно?
Припомни, что сказал сатирик!
«Чужого толка» хитрый лирик
Ужели для тебя сносней
Унылых наших рифмачей? —
«Но всё в элегии ничтожно;
Пустая цель ее жалка;
Меж тем цель оды высока
И благородна…» Тут бы можно
Поспорить нам, но я молчу:
Два века ссорить не хочу.

34   Поклонник славы и свободы,
В волненьи бурных дум своих
Владимир и писал бы оды,
Да Ольга не читала их.
Случалось ли поэтам слезным
Читать в глаза своим любезным
Свои творенья? Говорят,
Что в мире выше нет наград.
И впрямь, блажен любовник скромный,
Читающий мечты свои
Предмету песен и любви,
Красавице приятно-томной!
Блажен… хоть, может быть, она
Совсем иным развлечена.

35   Но я плоды моих мечтаний
И гармонических затей
Читаю только старой няне,
Подруге юности моей;
Да после скучного обеда
Ко мне забредшего соседа,
Поймав нежданно за полу,
Душу трагедией в углу;
Или (но это кроме шуток),
Тоской и рифмами томим,
Бродя над озером моим,
Пугаю стадо диких уток:
Вняв пенью сладкозвучных строф,
Оне слетают с берегов.

33   odes like they used to write in the brave old days;
odes are an institution dating back…"
"So it's ceremonial odes and nothing else!
Come off it, old friend; how's that any better?
Remember Dmítriev's lampoon:
you surely don't find his crafy odester
more easy to stomach
than our despondent elegists?"
"But there's no substance to an elegy.
They're pointless and pathetic,
while odes have a purpose that's sublime
and noble…" We could have
quite a quarrel over this, but I'll keep quiet –
I don't want to set two centuries at odds!

34   Ardent idealist and liberal as he was,
Lensky could very easily have been stirred
by the vehemence of his convictions to write odes –
only Olga never read them.
Some poets may have had the chance
tearfully to recite their compositions
to their loved ones face to face – one hears
that there's nothing so rewarding in the world.
Indeed, I envy the bashful lover
reciting his flights of fancy
to the object of his verses and his love,
some beautiful languid creature.
I envy him… But how do we actually know
that her attention's not engaged elsewhere?

35   As for me, it's only to my old nurse,
my friend since childhood,
that I read out the product of my daydreams
and of my experiments with word music.
Or, after a tedious dinner,
should a neighbour stroll in to see me,
I seize him abruptly by his coat lapel
and smother him with a tragedy in the corner.
Or else (and I'm not joking now),
worn out with rhymes and heartache,
I wander by my lake
and scare a flock of ducks –
when they hear the melodious music of my stanzas,
the birds take wing from the bank and fly away.

36 . . . .

37   А что ж Онегин? Кстати, братья!
Терпенья вашего прошу:
Его вседневные занятья
Я вам подробно опишу.
Онегин жил анахоретом:
В седьмом часу вставал он летом
И отправлялся налегке
К бегущей под горой реке;
Певцу Гюльнары подражая,
Сей Геллеспонт переплывал,
Потом свой кофе выпивал,
Плохой журнал перебирая,
И одевался. . . . .
. . . .

38 . . . .

39   Прогулки, чтенье, сон глубокий,
Лесная тень, журчанье струй,
Порой белянки черноокой
Младой и свежий поцелуй,
Узде послушный конь ретивый,
Обед довольно прихотливый,
Бутылка светлого вина,
Уединенье, тишина:
Вот жизнь Онегина святая;
И нечувствительно он ей
Предался, красных летних дней
В беспечной неге не считая,
Забыв и город, и друзей,
И скуку праздничных затей.

40   Но наше северное лето,
Карикатура южных зим,
Мелькнет и нет: известно это,
Хоть мы признаться не хотим.
Уж небо осенью дышало,
Уж реже солнышко блистало,
Короче становился день,
Лесов таинственная сень
С печальным шумом обнажалась,
Ложился на поля туман,
Гусей крикливых караван
Тянулся к югу: приближалась
Довольно скучная пора;
Стоял ноябрь уж у двора.

36   ....

37   "But what about Onégin?"
        All in good time, friends – please be patient:
        I'm about to describe for you
        the details of his day-to-day routine.
        Onégin lived a hermit's life.
        In summer he'd get up by seven
        and, just as he was, go off
        to the river below the hill
        for a swim to the other side and back –
        in the tradition of Byron swimming the Hellespont.
        He'd drink his coffee next,
        while flicking through some paltry magazine,
        and then get dressed......
        ....

38   ....

39   Walks, reading, deep sleep,
        woodland shade and murmuring streams;
        now and again a young, fresh kiss
        from a fair-skinned, dark-eyed girl;
        a spirited horse obedient to the reins;
        an evening meal of what he fancied;
        a bottle of sparkling wine;
        and solitude and tranquillity –
        this was Onégin's holy-hermit lifestyle,
        to which, unconsciously, he yielded himself.
        So carefree and relaxed did he become
        that he ceased to count the lovely summer days;
        he forgot the city and his friends,
        and the tedium of their contrived festivities.

40   Our northern summer, though,
        is but a caricature of southern winters:
        it gleams for a moment and is gone.
        We know this well, although we're loath to admit it.
        Too soon a whiff of autumn filled the air,
        the feeble sunshine glimmered ever more rarely,
        the days grew shorter,
        and with a mournful rustling the woods
        were losing the canopy that hid their secrets.
        Mist often settled on the meadows;
        and a clamouring caravan of wild geese
        reached south across the sky.
        A trying time of year drew near:
        November mounted guard outside.

41   Встает заря во мгле холодной;
      На нивах шум работ умолк;
      С своей волчихою голодной
      Выходит на дорогу волк;
      Его почуя, конь дорожный
      Храпит — и путник осторожный
      Несется в гору во весь дух;
      На утренней заре пастух
      Не гонит уж коров из хлева,
      И в час полуденный в кружок
      Их не зовет его рожок;
      В избушке распевая, дева
      Прядет, и, зимних друг ночей,
      Трещит лучинка перед ней.

42   И вот уже трещат морозы
      И серебрятся средь полей…
      (Читатель ждет уж рифмы *розы*:
      На, вот возьми ее скорей!)
      Опрятней модного паркета
      Блистает речка, льдом одета.
      Мальчишек радостный народ
      Коньками звучно режет лед;
      На красных лапках гусь тяжелый,
      Задумав плыть по лону вод,
      Ступает бережно на лед,
      Скользит и падает; веселый
      Мелькает, вьется первый снег,
      Звездами падая на брег.

43   В глуши что делать в эту пору?
      Гулять? Деревня той порой
      Невольно докучает взору
      Однообразной наготой.
      Скакать верхом в степи суровой?
      Но конь, притупленной подковой
      Неверный зацепляя лед,
      Того и жди, что упадет.
      Сиди под кровлею пустынной,
      Читай: вот Прадт, вот W. Scott.
      Не хочешь? — поверяй расход,
      Сердись иль пей, и вечер длинный
      Кой-как пройдет, а завтра тож,
      И славно зиму проведешь.

41   A chilly fog veiled each sunrise now.
The noise of farm work in the fields had ceased.
Wolves ventured out onto the highway
in hungry pairs;
a passing horse would scent them
and snort, and the anxious rider
would gallop fast uphill.
No longer did the herdsman drive his cows
out of their shed at daybreak,
or call them together at midday with his horn.
In her cottage home a young girl hummed a song
as she did her spinning, while in front of her
crackled the little torch of flaming pinewood
that kept her company on winter nights.

42   Outside, frosts crackled too
and glittered like silver on the fields.
(If you're expecting "a rose" to rhyme with "froze",
there! – take it, reader, quick!)
The stream, arrayed in ice,
gleamed brighter than the latest parquet floor.
Young boys in happy crowds began to skate,
grooving the frozen surface crisply.
The farmyard gander, heavy on pink feet,
meaning to swim across the water,
stepped gingerly out onto the ice,
slithered, and fell.
The first snow sparkled gaily, swirled
and settled like stardust on the bank.

43   What's there to do in the backwoods at this season?
Take walks? But the landscape
inevitably wearies the eye
with its uniform bareness.
Gallop on horseback across the uneven steppe?
But your horse at any moment
may catch some treacherous ice
with a slippery horseshoe and give you a fall.
So sit at home by yourself,
and read – there's Pradt, or Walter Scott.
Not to your taste? Then check the accounts,
lose your temper, or drink – the evening's long,
but somehow will pass, and tomorrow the same...
and you'll have a magnificent winter!

44 Прямым Онегин Чильд-Гарольдом
Вдался в задумчивую лень:
Со сна садится в ванну со льдом,
И после, дома целый день,
Один, в расчеты погруженный,
Тупым кием вооруженный,
Он на бильярде в два шара
Играет с самого утра.
Настанет вечер деревенский:
Бильярд оставлен, кий забыт,
Перед камином стол накрыт,
Евгений ждет: вот едет Ленский
На тройке чалых лошадей;
Давай обедать поскорей!

45 Вдовы Клико или Моэта
Благословенное вино
В бутылке мерзлой для поэта
На стол тотчас принесено.
Оно сверкает Ипокреной;
Оно своей игрой и пеной
(Подобием того-сего)
Меня пленяло: за него
Последний бедный лепт, бывало,
Давал я, помните ль, друзья?
Его волшебная струя
Рождала глупостей не мало,
А сколько шуток и стихов,
И споров, и веселых снов!

46 Но изменяет пеной шумной
Оно желудку моему,
И я *Бордо* благоразумный
Уж нынче предпочел ему.
К *Аи* я больше не способен;
Аи любовнице подобен
Блестящей, ветреной, живой,
И своенравной, и пустой…
Но ты, *Бордо*, подобен другу,
Который, в горе и в беде,
Товарищ завсегда, везде,
Готов нам оказать услугу
Иль тихий разделить досуг.
Да здравствует *Бордо*, наш друг!

44   Like a true Childe Harold, Onégin
surrendered himself to reflective inertia:
he rose from bed to sit straight in an ice bath,
then spent the whole day at home alone.
Engrossed in calculations
and armed with a flat-ended cue
he'd play at billiards with two balls
from dawn to dusk.
When the landscape grew dark outside,
he dropped his cue, abandoned billiards,
had the table laid in front of the fire
and waited... Now here comes Lensky
in his sleigh behind three roan horses...
"Serve supper straight away!"

45   Immediately he'd have a well-chilled bottle
of Veuve Clicquot or of Moët
fetched to the table in the poet's honour.
A heavenly wine, champagne!
It sparkles like a sacred spring.
It used to entrance me
with its bubbling and foaming,
and with its resemblance to... this or that.
In times gone by – you remember, my friends? –
I've given my "last poor farthing" for a glass.
Its magic potency
caused a lot of tomfoolery –
but plenty of laughter and poetry, too,
and banter and happy dreams.

46   But its fizzing froth
plays my stomach false;
and these days I've come to prefer
a more steady Bordeaux.
I'm no longer up to champagne from Ay;
it resembles a mistress:
sparkling, flighty, vivacious,
wayward – and not to be trusted.
But Bordeaux's like a friend
who in times of grief and misfortune
stands by us wherever, for ever,
ready to give us help
or just to share our quiet leisure.
So raise your glasses – to our friend Bordeaux!

47 Огонь потух; едва золою
    Подернут уголь золотой;
    Едва заметною струею
    Виется пар, и теплотой
    Камин чуть дышит. Дым из трубок
    В трубу уходит. Светлый кубок
    Еще шипит среди стола.
    Вечерняя находит мгла…
    (Люблю я дружеские враки
    И дружеский бокал вина
    Порою той, что названа
    Пора меж волка и собаки,
    А почему, не вижу я.)
    Теперь беседуют друзья:

48 «Ну, что соседки? Что Татьяна?
    Что Ольга резвая твоя?»
    — Налей еще мне полстакана…
    Довольно, милый… Вся семья
    Здорова; кланяться велели.
    Ах, милый, как похорошели
    У Ольги плечи, что за грудь!
    Что за душа!.. Когда-нибудь
    Заедем к ним; ты их обяжешь;
    А то, мой друг, суди ты сам:
    Два раза заглянул, а там
    Уж к ним и носу не покажешь.
    Да вот… какой же я болван!
    Ты к ним на той неделе зван.

49 «Я?» — Да, Татьяны именины
    В субботу. Оленька и мать
    Велели звать, и нет причины
    Тебе на зов не приезжать. —
    «Но куча будет там народу
    И всякого такого сброду…»
    — И, никого, уверен я!
    Кто будет там? своя семья.
    Поедем, сделай одолженье!
    Ну, что ж? — «Согласен». — Как ты мил! —
    При сих словах он осушил
    Стакан, соседке приношенье,
    Потом разговорился вновь
    Про Ольгу: такова любовь!

47   One evening the fire'd gone out; there was scarcely
a glowing ember left in the ash;
the smoke had dwindled
to a tenuous spiral; and the grate
hardly gave any warmth. Pipe smoke was drifting
up the chimney pipe. On the table
a wine glass still frothed and sparkled.
Outside an evening mist was closing in…
(I love a friendly gossip
and a friendly glass of wine
during the evening – the time they call,
for some unaccountable reason,
"'twixt dog and wolf".)
Now the two friends are talking:

48   "Well, what of our fair neighbours? How's Tatyána?
And how's that skittish Olga of yours?"
"Just pour me another half-glass…
Enough, old chap… All the family
are well; they send their greetings.
My dear chap, how lovely
are Olga's shoulders now! What breasts she has!
What depth of character!… Some time
let's pay them a visit together; they'll be so glad to see you.
After all, old friend, just think:
you looked in on them twice, and since that time
you haven't so much as shown your nose there.
But I've just remembered – what a blockhead I am! –
they've invited you over next week."

49   "Me?" "Yes; the Saturday's
Tatyána's name day. My little Olga and her mother
asked me to invite you, and you really haven't
any excuse for not coming."
"But there'll be a load of people there,
all sorts of riff-raff, the kind that—"
"Oh, no; there'll be no one, I'm sure.
Just her family – that'll be all.
Do let's go, as a favour to me…
What about it?" "All right." "Good fellow!"
And with that he drained his glass,
a toast to their "fair neighbour".
Then on he went talking again
about Olga. Such is love!

50 Он весел был. Чрез две недели
   Назначен был счастливый срок.
   И тайна брачныя постели,
   И сладостной любви венок
   Его восторгов ожидали.
   Гимена хлопоты, печали,
   Зевоты хладная чреда
   Ему не снились никогда.
   Меж тем как мы, враги Гимена,
   В домашней жизни зрим один
   Ряд утомительных картин,
   Роман во вкусе Лафонтена…
   Мой бедный Ленский, сердцем он
   Для оной жизни был рожден.

51 Он был любим… по крайней мере
   Так думал он, и был счастлив.
   Стократ блажен, кто предан вере,
   Кто, хладный ум угомонив,
   Покоится в сердечной неге,
   Как пьяный путник на ночлеге,
   Или, нежней, как мотылек,
   В весенний впившийся цветок;
   Но жалок тот, кто всё предвидит,
   Чья не кружится голова,
   Кто все движенья, все слова
   В их переводе ненавидит,
   Чье сердце опыт остудил
   И забываться запретил!

50   Lensky was overjoyed. The happy day
had been fixed for two weeks thence;
he'd be initiated then into the mystery of wedlock;
his love would be crowned with delight;
he'd have achieved the object of his desires.
The vexations of married life, its sorrows,
its boring and chilling routine
never entered his mind –
even though foes of marriage like me,
see nothing in domesticity
but a succession of wearisome scenes,
like a novel by Lafontaine.
Poor Lensky! That's the sort of life
that, emotionally, he was born for.

51   Lensky had someone that loved him – at least,
so he thought, and it made him happy.
A hundred times blessed is the man who's committed
to what he believes, who's stifled his mental detachment
and can luxuriate in his affections –
like a tipsy traveller bedded down at an inn,
or – more delicately – a butterfly
regaling itself on a flower in spring.
But others there are who see everything coming,
whose heads never whirl,
who interpret cynically each act and word,
and whose hearts are so chilled by experience
that they can't lose awareness of themselves –
oh, pity such!

ГЛАВА ПЯТАЯ

1   В тот год осенняя погода
Стояла долго на дворе,
Зимы ждала, ждала природа.
Снег выпал только в январе
На третье в ночь. Проснувшись рано,
В окно увидела Татьяна
Поутру побелевший двор,
Куртины, кровли и забор,
На стеклах легкие узоры,
Деревья в зимнем серебре,
Сорок веселых на дворе
И мягко устланные горы
Зимы блистательным ковром.
Всё ярко, всё бело кругом.

2   Зима!.. Крестьянин, торжествуя,
На дровнях обновляет путь;
Его лошадка, снег почуя,
Плетется рысью как-нибудь;
Бразды пушистые взрывая,
Летит кибитка удалая;
Ямщик сидит на облучке
В тулупе, в красном кушаке.
Вот бегает дворовый мальчик,
В салазки *жучку* посадив,
Себя в коня преобразив;
Шалун уж заморозил пальчик:
Ему и больно и смешно,
А мать грозит ему в окно…

CHAPTER FIVE

My Svetlána, be you spared
all such dreadful nightmares...
– Zhukóvsky

1   That year the autumn weather
had lingered long outside,
while nature waited, waited, for winter to come.
Snow only fell on January the third,
in the small hours. Awake next morning early,
Tatyána through the window saw the grounds –
flower beds, roofs and fences –
transformed to white;
on the glass were delicate patterns;
outside, pert magpies,
trees in their seasonal finery of silver,
and the hills beyond softly overspread
with winter's glistening carpet.
Everywhere all was brilliant, all was white.

2   Yes, winter!... A jubilant peasant
pioneered a path on his sledge,
while his poor old nag, sniffing the snow,
struggled on at an unsteady trot.
A covered sleigh flew boldly by,
churning up powdery furrows,
the coachman seated on the box
in sheepskin coat with sash of red.
The kitchen boy had sat the house dog, Smut,
on a toboggan and had been running with him,
pretending to be the horse;
the scamp had got his finger frozen
and didn't know whether to laugh or cry,
as mother scolded him through the window...

3   Но, может быть, такого рода
Картины вас не привлекут:
Всё это низкая природа;
Изящного не много тут.
Согретый вдохновенья богом,
Другой поэт роскошным слогом
Живописал нам первый снег
И все оттенки зимних нег;
Он вас пленит, я в том уверен,
Рисуя в пламенных стихах
Прогулки тайные в санях;
Но я бороться не намерен
Ни с ним покамест, ни с тобой,
Певец финляндки молодой!

4   Татьяна (русская душою,
Сама не зная почему)
С ее холодною красою
Любила русскую зиму,
На солнце иний в день морозный,
И сани, и зарею поздной
Сиянье розовых снегов,
И мглу крещенских вечеров.
По старине торжествовали
В их доме эти вечера:
Служанки со всего двора
Про барышень своих гадали
И им сулили каждый год
Мужьев военных и поход.

5   Татьяна верила преданьям
Простонародной старины,
И снам, и карточным гаданьям,
И предсказаниям луны.
Ее тревожили приметы;
Таинственно ей все предметы
Провозглашали что-нибудь,
Предчувствия теснили грудь.
Жеманный кот, на печке сидя,
Мурлыча, лапкой рыльце мыл:
То несомненный знак ей был,
Что едут гости. Вдруг увидя
Младой двурогий лик луны
На небе с левой стороны,

3 But, readers, perhaps you won't be attracted
by scenes like this –
it's all rather lowbrow;
little elegance here.
Another poet, aglow with sublime inspiration,
has painted a lavish picture for us
of the "first snow",
employing a full range of colours for winter's delights.
He'll entrance you, I know,
with his ardent description in verse
of intimate sleigh rides.
But don't intend to compete with him
nor, my dear Baratýnsky, with you
and your tale of a young Finnish girl.

4 Tatyána was Russian through and through;
and – though herself not knowing why –
she loved the Russian winter
in all its frozen beauty:
she loved the sunlit hoar frost on icy days,
she loved sleigh rides, she loved the rose-pink light
on the snow as the late sun rose,
and she loved the misty evenings around Epiphany.
At the Larins' they still marked
Epiphanytide evenings in the old way:
the maidservants would gather from the whole estate
to tell their young mistresses' fortunes
and promise the two of them year after year
a soldier husband and a war.

5 Tatyána believed
in the simple folklore of olden days,
in dreams, in fortunes told from cards,
and in predictions by the moon.
Omens alarmed her;
every incident had for her
a secret significance of some kind
and made her breathless with foreboding.
If their cat, complacent creature, sat purring on the stove,
washing his face with a paw,
that was to her a certain sign
that visitors were on their way. If all at once
she noticed a young moon's horns
in the sky to her left…

6   Она дрожала и бледнела.
Когда ж падучая звезда
По небу темному летела
И рассыпалася, тогда
В смятенье Таня торопилась,
Пока звезда еще катилась,
Желанье сердца ей шепнуть.
Когда случалось где-нибудь
Ей встретить черного монаха
Иль быстрый заяц меж полей
Перебегал дорогу ей,
Не зная, что начать со страха,
Предчувствий горестных полна,
Ждала несчастья уж она.

7   Что ж? Тайну прелесть находила
И в самом ужасе она:
Так нас природа сотворила,
К противуречию склонна.
Настали святки. То-то радость!
Гадает ветреная младость,
Которой ничего не жаль,
Перед которой жизни даль
Лежит светла, необозрима;
Гадает старость сквозь очки
У гробовой своей доски,
Всё потеряв невозвратимо;
И всё равно: надежда им
Лжет детским лепетом своим.

8   Татьяна любопытным взором
На воск потопленный глядит:
Он чудно-вылитым узором
Ей что-то чудное гласит;
Из блюда, полного водою,
Выходят кольца чередою;
И вынулось колечко ей
Под песенку старинных дней:
«*Там мужички-то всё богаты,*
Гребут лопатой серебро;
Кому поем, тому добро
И слава!» Но сулит утраты
Сей песни жалостный напев;
Милей *кошурка* сердцу дев.

6 ...she'd shudder and turn pale.
And if a meteorite
should dart across the darkened sky
disintegrating, then in consternation
she'd hurriedly whisper
her secret wish
while it yet fell.
If anywhere she chanced to meet
a black-robed monk, or if a hare
raced swiftly across her path in the fields,
she'd be so frightened
she'd not know what to do next;
full of the direst premonitions,
she'd await an imminent disaster.

7 Strange to say, the very terror
gave her a secret thrill.
That's how Mother Nature has made us,
with her fondness for paradox.
So when Epiphany drew near, imagine the excitement!
All had their fortunes told.
The light-hearted youngsters had no regrets
and saw life's vistas
stretching before them bright and boundless.
The old, for their part, by their gravestone
still peered through spectacles to see the future,
though all was lost beyond recall.
Young or old – no matter: in her childish lisp
Hope lied to each and every one.

8 As for Tatyána, she anxiously watched
the melted wax:
as it formed strange shapes underwater,
it warned her of strange events.
Then the girls' rings were drawn in turn
from a brimming bowl:
Tatyána's came out
to the sound of the old song that goes:
There silver's always plentiful:
folk scoop it by the shovelful.
The one to whom we sing this song –
to her shall wealth and fame belong!
– but the mournful tune foretold a loss.
Young girls prefer the "she-puss" song.

9 Морозна ночь, всё небо ясно;
  Светил небесных дивный хор
  Течет так тихо, так согласно…
  Татьяна на широкой двор
  В открытом платьице выходит,
  На месяц зеркало наводит;
  Но в темном зеркале одна
  Дрожит печальная луна…
  Чу… снег хрустит… прохожий; дева
  К нему на цыпочках летит,
  И голосок ее звучит
  Нежней свирельного напева:
  Как ваше имя? Смотрит он
  И отвечает: Агафон.

10 Татьяна, по совету няни
  Сбираясь ночью ворожить,
  Тихонько приказала в бане
  На два прибора стол накрыть;
  Но стало страшно вдруг Татьяне…
  И я — при мысли о Светлане
  Мне стало страшно — так и быть…
  С Татьяной нам не ворожить.
  Татьяна поясок шелковый
  Сняла, разделась и в постель
  Легла. Над нею вьется Лель,
  А под подушкою пуховой
  Девичье зеркало лежит.
  Утихло всё. Татьяна спит.

11 И снится чудный сон Татьяне.
  Ей снится, будто бы она
  Идет по снеговой поляне,
  Печальной мглой окружена;
  В сугробах снежных перед нею
  Шумит, клубит волной своею
  Кипучий, темный и седой
  Поток, не скованный зимой;
  Две жердочки, склеены льдиной,
  Дрожащий, гибельный мосток,
  Положены через поток;
  И пред шумящею пучиной,
  Недоумения полна,
  Остановилася она.

9   It was frosty that night; the whole sky was clear;
the stars in their ethereal dance
were wheeling around in unison, serene.
Tatyána went out into the open courtyard
in a flimsy low-cut dress.
She held out a mirror to catch the moon,
but all she saw was its mournful face
trembling in the darkened glass...
Suddenly, a sound! – a crunch of snow;
someone was coming. She ran up on tiptoe
and asked him in tones
softer than a reed pipe's:
"What's your name?" He stared,
and replied, "Agafón."

10   On her nurse's advice, Tatyána
decided to conjure that night:
so she gave secret orders for a table
to be laid in the bathhouse for two.
But she took fright all of a sudden –
and so did I when I remembered
what happened to Svetlána. So, just as well:
we'll not after all be joining Tatyána's seance.
Instead, she took off her silken girdle,
undressed, and into bed
she climbed. Above her hung a love charm,
and beneath the downy pillow
her vanity mirror lay.
All fell still; Tatyána slept...

11   and, as she slept, she had a fateful dream.
She dreamt that she was walking
across an expanse of snow,
encircled in a dismal fog.
In front, amidst the snowdrifts,
there roared and swirled a seething torrent,
whose dark and foam-flecked waters
were not yet clamped in winter's chains.
Two sticks held together with ice
had been laid across the stream
to form an unsteady and perilous footbridge.
Confronted by this thundering chasm,
Tatyána stopped short
in utter bafflement.

12   Как на досадную разлуку,
Татьяна ропщет на ручей;
Не видит никого, кто руку
С той стороны подал бы ей;
Но вдруг сугроб зашевелился.
И кто ж из-под него явился?
Большой, взъерошенный медведь;
Татьяна *ах!* а он реветь,
И лапу с острыми когтями
Ей протянул; она скрепясь
Дрожащей ручкой оперлась
И боязливыми шагами
Перебралась через ручей;
Пошла — и что ж? медведь за ней!

13   Она, взглянуть назад не смея,
Поспешный ускоряет шаг;
Но от косматого лакея
Не может убежать никак;
Кряхтя, валит медведь несносный;
Пред ними лес; недвижны сосны
В своей нахмуренной красе;
Отягчены их ветви все
Клоками снега; сквозь вершины
Осин, берёз и лип нагих
Сияет луч светил ночных;
Дороги нет; кусты, стремнины
Метелью все занесены,
Глубоко в снег погружены.

14   Татьяна в лес; медведь за нею;
Снег рыхлый по колено ей;
То длинный сук её за шею
Зацепит вдруг, то из ушей
Златые серьги вырвет силой;
То в хрупком снеге с ножки милой
Увязнет мокрый башмачок;
То выронит она платок;
Поднять ей некогда; боится,
Медведя слышит за собой,
И даже трепетной рукой
Одежды край поднять стыдится;
Она бежит, он всё вослед,
И сил уже бежать ей нет.

12   She muttered protests at the river,
as though at some vexatious obstacle.
At first there was no one she could see
to offer a hand from the other side,
but suddenly a snowdrift heaved,
and what should emerge from beneath it
but a great bristling bear.
Tatyána shrieked; the bear for its part growled
and extended to her
a sharp-clawed paw.
So she summoned her courage
and, steadying herself with trembling hand,
stepped gingerly across the torrent.
Then she set off – the bear behind!

13   Not daring to look back,
she quickened her pace;
but, try as she might, she failed
to rid herself of her shaggy escort:
the insufferable beast lumbered on, grunting.
In front was a forest: motionless pines stood
stern in their beauty,
each bough weighed down
with clumps of snow; through the tops
of bare aspens, birches and limes
the nocturnal starlight shone.
There was no path; the bushes, the rough terrain
were all overlaid with snow,
choked with deep drifts.

14   Tatyána entered the forest, the bear behind her.
The soft snow reached her knees.
Now a long branch abruptly
caught round her neck; now twigs
wrenched golden earrings from her ears;
next a wet shoe stuck in the crumbling snow
coming loose from her slim foot;
then she dropped a handkerchief,
but couldn't pause to pick it up. She was frightened;
the bear she could hear behind her;
but, trembling though she was,
her modesty stopped her from lifting the edge of her dress.
She ran on, chased still by the bear,
till she'd no more strength to run.

149

15   Упала в снег; медведь проворно
      Ее хватает и несет;
      Она бесчувственно-покорна,
      Не шевельнется, не дохнет;
      Он мчит ее лесной дорогой;
      Вдруг меж дерев шалаш убогий;
      Кругом всё глушь; отвсюду он
      Пустынным снегом занесен,
      И ярко светится окошко,
      И в шалаше и крик и шум;
      Медведь промолвил: «Здесь мой кум:
      Погрейся у него немножко!»
      И в сени прямо он идет
      И на порог ее кладет.

16   Опомнилась, глядит Татьяна:
      Медведя нет; она в сенях;
      За дверью крик и звон стакана,
      Как на больших похоронах;
      Не видя тут ни капли толку,
      Глядит она тихонько в щелку,
      И что же видит?.. за столом
      Сидят чудовища кругом:
      Один в рогах с собачьей мордой,
      Другой с петушьей головой,
      Здесь ведьма с козьей бородой,
      Тут остов чопорный и гордый,
      Там карла с хвостиком, а вот
      Полужуравль и полукот.

17   Еще страшней, еще чуднее:
      Вот рак верхом на пауке,
      Вот череп на гусиной шее
      Вертится в красном колпаке,
      Вот мельница вприсядку пляшет
      И крыльями трещит и машет;
      Лай, хохот, пенье, свист и хлоп,
      Людская молвь и конский топ!
      Но что подумала Татьяна,
      Когда узнала меж гостей
      Того, кто мил и страшен ей,
      Героя нашего романа!
      Онегин за столом сидит
      И в дверь украдкою глядит.

15   She collapsed in the snow – and promptly the bear
seized her and carried her off.
Numb and inert,
she neither stirred nor breathed.
The bear bore her briskly by a woodland pathway,
till all at once they came through the trees
to a ramshackle cabin, encircled in forest,
half-buried in desolate snowdrifts on every side.
A light shone brightly through a little window,
and from within came shouts and uproar.
The bear spoke: "Here's where my pal lives:
warm yourself up a bit at his place."
Then straight into the porch he went
and put her down in the doorway.

16   When Tatyána came to herself she looked around.
She was in the porch. No bear.
Through the door came shouts and the clink of glasses,
as at some great funeral.
Tatyána could make no sense of it at all,
so she quietly peeped through a chink.
She couldn't believe what she saw. Round a table
was seated a circle of monsters.
One had horns and the muzzle of a dog,
another the head of a cockerel;
in one place was a witch with the beard of a goat,
in another a skeleton, fastidious and haughty;
elsewhere was a stub-tailed dwarf,
and a creature half-crane and half-cat.

17   More horrific and weirder still
were a crayfish astride a spider,
a skull in a scarlet nightcap
that turned on a goose's neck,
and a windmill dancing on its haunches
as it rattled and waved its sails.
There was barking, chortling, warbling, whistling, clapping,
there was human speech, and stamp of hooves.
But imagine Tatyána's amazement
when she recognized among the company
the man she both loved and dreaded,
our novel's hero!
Onégin was sitting at the table,
and stealthily scanning the doorway.

18   Он знак подаст — и все хлопочут;
      Он пьет — все пьют и все кричат;
      Он засмеется — все хохочут;
      Нахмурит брови — все молчат;
      Он там хозяин, это ясно:
      И Тане уж не так ужасно,
      И любопытная теперь
      Немного растворила дверь…
      Вдруг ветер дунул, загашая
      Огонь светильников ночных;
      Смутилась шайка домовых;
      Онегин, взорами сверкая,
      Из-за стола гремя встает;
      Все встали: он к дверям идет.

19   И страшно ей; и торопливо
      Татьяна силится бежать:
      Нельзя никак; нетерпеливо
      Метаясь, хочет закричать:
      Не может; дверь толкнул Евгений:
      И взорам адских привидений
      Явилась дева; ярый смех
      Раздался дико; очи всех,
      Копыты, хоботы кривые,
      Хвосты хохлатые, клыки,
      Усы, кровавы языки,
      Рога и пальцы костяные,
      Всё указует на нее,
      И все кричат: мое! мое!

20   *Мое!* — сказал Евгений грозно,
      И шайка вся сокрылась вдруг;
      Осталася во тьме морозной
      Младая дева с ним сам-друг;
      Онегин тихо увлекает
      Татьяну в угол и слагает
      Ее на шаткую скамью
      И клонит голову свою
      К ней на плечо; вдруг Ольга входит,
      За нею Ленский; свет блеснул;
      Онегин руку замахнул,
      И дико он очами бродит,
      И незваных гостей бранит;
      Татьяна чуть жива лежит.

18   When he gave a sign, they all grew excited;
when he drank, they all drank too and shouted;
when he laughed, they all broke into guffaws;
and when he frowned, they all fell mute.
He was master there, that was clear;
and this reassured Tatyána somewhat.
Inquisitive now,
she eased the door ajar...
but at once a gust of wind blew out
the lamp flames (it was night)
and plunged the gang of demons into confusion.
Eyes flashing, Onégin
rose from the table with a clatter.
Everyone stood; he strode towards the door.

19   Tatyána was terrified; in panic
she tried to run away,
but struggle as she might she had no strength.
Desperately she strove with herself, wanted to scream,
but could not. Onégin pushed at the door,
and there was the girl exposed
to the gaze of those hellish spectres. They burst
into wild and frenzied laughter; all their eyes,
hooves, curving snouts,
tufted tails, tusks,
feelers, bloody tongues,
horns, bony fingers –
everything pointed at her;
they all cried out: "Mine! Mine!"

20   "No, mine!" said Onégin grimly.
And the whole pack vanished at once.
Tatyána was left in the frosty darkness
with Onégin, the two alone.
He drew her gently
into a corner and laid her on a shaky bench;
then, leaning over,
he rested his head on her shoulder.
Suddenly Olga came in,
followed by Lensky. A light shone.
Onégin raised his arm,
gazed wildly around,
and berated the two intruders.
Tatyána lay there, more dead than alive.

21   Спор громче, громче; вдруг Евгений
Хватает длинный нож, и вмиг
Повержен Ленский; страшно тени
Сгустились; нестерпимый крик
Раздался… хижина шатнулась…
И Таня в ужасе проснулась…
Глядит, уж в комнате светло;
В окне сквозь мерзлое стекло
Зари багряный луч играет;
Дверь отворилась. Ольга к ней,
Авроры северной алей
И легче ласточки, влетает;
«Ну, говорит, скажи ж ты мне,
Кого ты видела во сне?»

22   Но та, сестры не замечая,
В постеле с книгою лежит,
За листом лист перебирая,
И ничего не говорит.
Хоть не являла книга эта
Ни сладких вымыслов поэта,
Ни мудрых истин, ни картин,
Но ни Виргилий, ни Расин,
Ни Скотт, ни Байрон, ни Сенека,
Ни даже Дамских Мод Журнал
Так никого не занимал:
То был, друзья, Мартын Задека,
Глава халдейских мудрецов,
Гадатель, толкователь снов.

23   Сие глубокое творенье
Завез кочующий купец
Однажды к ним в уединенье
И для Татьяны наконец
Его с разрозненной «Мальвиной»
Он уступил за три с полтиной,
В придачу взяв еще за них
Собранье басен площадных,
Грамматику, две Петриады
Да Мармонтеля третий том.
Мартын Задека стал потом
Любимец Тани… Он отрады
Во всех печалях ей дарит
И безотлучно с нею спит.

21   The quarrel grew louder and louder, till all at once
Onégin seized a long knife: a moment later
Lensky had slumped to the ground; the shadows
grew thick and menacing; a hideous scream
rang out; the cabin began to reel –
and Tatyána awoke in terror…
She opened her eyes. The room was already light:
dawn's crimson rays were sparkling
through the frost on the window pane.
The door swung open, and Olga,
rosier than the Northern Lights
and daintier than a swallow, darted in to find her.
"Well," she said, "do tell me,
who did you see in your dream?"

22   But Tatyána ignored her sister:
she lay on the bed with a book,
turning the pages in quick succession,
and saying nothing.
It didn't look
like a book of nice poetry,
wise maxims, or pretty pictures –
but no one could have been that engrossed
in Virgil or Racine
or Scott or Byron or Seneca,
or even the *Journal of Ladies' Fashions*.
No, the book, my friends, was *Martin Zadeck*,
leading astrologer, fortune-teller
and interpreter of dreams.

23   This profound composition
had been brought to their out-of-the-way house
long ago by an itinerant salesman;
he'd finally parted with it to Tatyána,
along with an incomplete *Malvina*,
for three roubles and a half,
taking a collection
of popular tales,
a grammar book, two epics on Peter the Great,
and Marmontel's Volume Three into the bargain.
Martin Zadeck thereafter became
Tatyána's favourite: he gave her
comfort in all her sorrows,
and always slept close by her.

24   Ее тревожит сновиденье.
      Не зная, как его понять,
      Мечтанья страшного значенье
      Татьяна хочет отыскать.
      Татьяна в оглавленьи кратком
      Находит азбучным порядком
      Слова: бор, буря, ведьма, ель,
      Еж, мрак, мосток, медведь, метель
      И прочая. Ее сомнений
      Мартын Задека не решит;
      Но сон зловещий ей сулит
      Печальных много приключений.
      Дней несколько она потом
      Всё беспокоилась о том.

25   Но вот багряною рукою
      Заря от утренних долин
      Выводит с солнцем за собою
      Веселый праздник именин.
      С утра дом Лариной гостями
      Весь полон; целыми семьями
      Соседи съехались в возках,
      В кибитках, в бричках и в санях.
      В передней толкотня, тревога;
      В гостиной встреча новых лиц,
      Лай мосек, чмоканье девиц,
      Шум, хохот, давка у порога,
      Поклоны, шарканье гостей,
      Кормилиц крик и плач детей.

26   С своей супругою дородной
      Приехал толстый Пустяков;
      Гвоздин, хозяин превосходный,
      Владелец нищих мужиков;
      Скотинины, чета седая,
      С детьми всех возрастов, считая
      От тридцати до двух годов;
      Уездный франтик Петушков,
      Мой брат двоюродный, Буянов,
      В пуху, в картузе с козырьком
      (Как вам, конечно, он знаком),
      И отставной советник Флянов,
      Тяжелый сплетник, старый плут,
      Обжора, взяточник и шут.

24   Tatyána was vexed by her dream.
She couldn't make it out;
but, frightening though it was,
she was anxious to learn its meaning.
In the book's brief index
she looked up alphabetically the words:
bear, blizzard, bridge, fir,
gale, gloom, hedgehog, pinewood, raven,
and so on. In the event, *Martin Zadeck*
failed to resolve her queries;
but she was sure her sinister dream
portended numerous dire events.
For several days more
it still distressed her.

25   But then "with crimson hand
Dawn ushers from the plains of morning
the sun, and with the sun" –
the jolly name-day celebration.
From morning onwards Mrs Larin's house
was crammed with visitors. Whole families
of neighbours had descended
in covered sleighs, in open sleighs, in carts and carriages.
In the entrance hall was jostle and confusion;
in the drawing room were strangers meeting,
pug dogs barking, girls a-kissing,
people shouting, chortling, squeezing through the door,
bows and curtseys between guests,
scolding nursemaids, squalling kids.

26   Stout Pustyakóv drove up
with his huge wife;
so did Gvozdín (who managed his estates so well
that his serfs were poor as beggars).
The Skotínins came (a grey-haired couple
with children of all ages
from thirty down to two);
and Petushkóv, the local man-of-fashion;
my cousin, too, Buyánov
(his clothes all fluff,
and wearing that peaked cap we know him by);
and the retired councillor Flyánov
(wearisome scandal-monger, rogue of long standing,
glutton, grafter and buffoon).

27 С семьей Панфила Харликова
Приехал и мосье Трике,
Остряк, недавно из Тамбова,
В очках и в рыжем парике.
Как истинный француз, в кармане
Трике привез куплет Татьяне
На голос, знаемый детьми:
Réveillez vous, belle endormie.
Меж ветхих песен альманаха
Был напечатан сей куплет;
Трике, догадливый поэт,
Его на свет явил из праха,
И смело вместо *belle Nina*
Поставил *belle Tatiana.*

28 И вот из ближнего посада
Созревших барышень кумир,
Уездных матушек отрада,
Приехал ротный командир;
Вошел… Ах, новость, да какая!
Музыка будет полковая!
Полковник сам ее послал.
Какая радость: будет бал!
Девчонки прыгают заране;
Но кушать подали. Четой
Идут за стол рука с рукой.
Теснятся барышни к Татьяне;
Мужчины против; и, крестясь,
Толпа жужжит, за стол садясь.

29 На миг умолкли разговоры;
Уста жуют. Со всех сторон
Гремят тарелки и приборы
Да рюмок раздается звон.
Но вскоре гости понемногу
Подъемлют общую тревогу.
Никто не слушает, кричат,
Смеются, спорят и пищат.
Вдруг двери настежь. Ленский входит,
И с ним Онегин. «Ах, творец! —
Кричит хозяйка: — наконец!»
Теснятся гости, всяк отводит
Приборы, стулья поскорей;
Зовут, сажают двух друзей.

27   Along with Panfíl Harlikóv's folk
there arrived, in spectacles and ginger wig,
Monsieur Triquet as well,
a witty man, come lately from Tambóv.
True Frenchman, he'd brought in his pocket
a verse in honour of Tatyána
set to the well-known children's tune
'*Réveillez-vous, belle endormie*'.
The text was one he'd found in print
in an album of outdated songs.
Triquet, resourceful poet that he was,
had brought the dusty pages back to light
and, daringly, for "*belle Niná*",
had substituted "*belle Tatianá*".

28   Next to drive up was the company-commander
from the neighbouring town –
the joy of local mothers
and idol of their eligible daughters.
He entered with tremendous news:
the regimental band was coming –
"sent by the colonel personally".
What fun – there'd be a ball!
The local lasses hopped in expectation.
But first, dinner was served. In couples, arm in arm,
they all moved to their places at the table.
The misses squeezed in by Tatyána;
the men stood opposite. The company
crossed themselves, buzzing, and took their seats.

29   For a moment chatter abated:
mouths chewed. On every side
was the clatter of cutlery and plates,
and the tinkle of glasses.
But soon the party started to resume
its general animation:
no one listened, all were shouting,
laughing, arguing and squealing.
The doors all at once flew open. Lensky entered,
and with him Onégin. "God above! The poet!"
exclaimed Mrs Larin. "At long last!"
The guests squeezed up, each hurriedly shifting
their chairs and place settings sideways.
The pair of friends were summoned and given seats

30   Сажают прямо против Тани,
      И, утренней луны бледней
      И трепетней гонимой лани,
      Она темнеющих очей
      Не подымает: пышет бурно
      В ней страстный жар; ей душно, дурно;
      Она приветствий двух друзей
      Не слышит, слезы из очей
      Хотят уж капать; уж готова
      Бедняжка в обморок упасть;
      Но воля и рассудка власть
      Превозмогли. Она два слова
      Сквозь зубы молвила тишком
      И усидела за столом.

31   Траги-нервичсских явлений,
      Девичьих обмороков, слез
      Давно терпеть не мог Евгений:
      Довольно их он перенес.
      Чудак, попав на пир огромный,
      Уж был сердит. Но девы томной
      Заметя трепетный порыв,
      С досады взоры опустив,
      Надулся он и, негодуя,
      Поклялся Ленского взбесить
      И уж порядком отомстить.
      Теперь, заране торжествуя,
      Он стал чертить в душе своей
      Карикатуры всех гостей.

32   Конечно, не один Евгений
      Смятенье Тани видеть мог;
      Но целью взоров и суждений
      В то время жирный был пирог
      (К несчастию, пересоленный);
      Да вот в бутылке засмоленной,
      Между жарким и блан-манже,
      Цимлянское несут уже;
      За ним строй рюмок узких, длинных,
      Подобно талии твоей,
      Зизи, кристалл души моей,
      Предмет стихов моих невинных,
      Любви приманчивый фиал,
      Ты, от кого я пьян бывал!

30   right opposite Tatyána.
Paler than the moon at dawn,
more tremulous than a hunted doe,
she dared not raise
her dimming eyes. Her passion flared within her
like a violent fever. She felt breathless and faint;
the two friends' greetings
she didn't hear. Tears were about to trickle
down from her eyes, and she was ready,
poor girl, to swoon away;
but willpower and common sense
prevailed: she mumbled
a couple of words between her teeth,
and kept her seat at table.

31   Onégin had long been unable to endure
theatrical manifestations of emotion,
like girlish swoons and tears:
he'd been through quite enough of that.
Despising convention as he did, he was now angry
to find himself at such an enormous party.
But observing Tatyána in a trembling fit
and near to fainting, he looked down in annoyance,
pouted his lips, and in exasperation
vowed to take due revenge
by baiting Lensky in return.
Then, in anticipation of his triumph,
he started mentally to draw
caricatures of all the guests.

32   Of course, Onégin wasn't the only one
who might have observed Tatyána's agitation;
but it so happened that at that very moment
all looks and comments were directed to
a rich meat pie (regrettably, too salty).
Between the roast course and the *blancmanger*,
pitch-sealed bottles of sparkling Russian wine
were carried in, and after them
an array of glasses –
long slender ones, just like your waist, Zizí.
(I once wrote innocent verses
about Zizí: she's like a piece of lovely crystal,
a fascinating goblet of love,
who used to make me tipsy!)

33 Освободясь от пробки влажной,
Бутылка хлопнула; вино
Шипит; и вот с осанкой важной,
Куплетом мучимый давно,
Трике встает; пред ним собранье
Хранит глубокое молчанье.
Татьяна чуть жива; Трике,
К ней обратясь с листком в руке,
Запел, фальшивя. Плески, клики
Его приветствуют. Она
Певцу присесть принуждена;
Поэт же скромный, хоть великий,
Ее здоровье первый пьет
И ей куплет передает.

34 Пошли приветы, поздравленья;
Татьяна всех благодарит.
Когда же дело до Евгенья
Дошло, то девы томный вид,
Ее смущение, усталость
В его душе родили жалость:
Он молча поклонился ей,
Но как-то взор его очей
Был чудно нежен. Оттого ли,
Что он и вправду тронут был,
Иль он, кокетствуя, шалил,
Невольно ль, иль из доброй воли,
Но взор сей нежность изъявил:
Он сердце Тани оживил.

35 Гремят отдвинутые стулья;
Толпа в гостиную валит:
Так пчел из лакомого улья
На ниву шумный рой летит.
Довольный праздничным обедом,
Сосед сопит перед соседом;
Подсели дамы к камельку;
Девицы шепчут в уголку;
Столы зеленые раскрыты:
Зовут задорных игроков
Бостон и ломбер стариков,
И вист, доныне знаменитый,
Однообразная семья,
Все жадной скуки сыновья.

33   Moist corks popped free
from bottles; wine
frothed over. Now Triquet,
who'd long been itching to perform his song,
stood up with an important air. The company in response
fell solemnly silent.
Tatyána nearly died. Triquet,
holding his sheet of paper, turned towards her
and started to sing – off-key. His act
was greeted with applause and cheers. Tatyána
was obliged to curtsey to the singer;
and he, for all his eminence as a poet,
modestly proposed the toast to Tatyána's health,
donating her the verse.

34   There followed compliments and congratulations.
Tatyána thanked each guest.
When it came to Onégin's turn,
her strained expression,
distress and obvious fatigue
moved him to pity.
He bowed to her in silence,
but the look in his eyes was somehow
strangely tender. Whether
he'd really been moved,
or was flirting for amusement;
whether unconsciously, or from deliberate kindness –
however it was, his look showed tenderness;
and it gave Tatyána's heart new life.

35   Chairs were pushed backwards with a clatter,
and the company streamed into the drawing room,
like a noisy swarm of bees
leaving their honey-sweet hive to fly to the open fields.
Neighbour expressed to neighbour
a grunted appreciation of the festive dinner;
the ladies sat down near the fire;
and the girls gathered whispering in a corner.
Green baize-covered tables were set up,
and eager card-players answered the call
for Boston, or for ombre (the old folks' favourite),
or for still-popular whist.
(These games have a family likeness –
insatiable boredom's offspring, every one!)

36 Уж восемь робертов сыграли
Герои виста; восемь раз
Они места переменяли;
И чай несут. Люблю я час
Определять обедом, чаем
И ужином. Мы время знаем
В деревне без больших сует:
Желудок — верный наш брегет;
И кстати я замечу в скобках,
Что речь веду в моих строфах
Я столь же часто о пирах,
О разных кушаньях и пробках,
Как ты, божественный Омир,
Ты, тридцати веков кумир!

37, 38 . . . .

39 Но чай несут; девицы чинно
Едва за блюдечки взялись,
Вдруг из-за двери в зале длинной
Фагот и флейта раздались.
Обрадован музыки громом,
Оставя чашку чаю с ромом,
Парис окружных городков,
Подходит к Ольге Петушков,
К Татьяне Ленский; Харликову,
Невесту переспелых лет,
Берет тамбовский мой поэт;
Умчал Буянов Пустякову;
И в залу высыпали все,
И бал блестит во всей красе.

40 В начале моего романа
(Смотрите первую тетрадь)
Хотелось вроде мне Альбана
Бал петербургский описать;
Но, развлечен пустым мечтаньем,
Я занялся воспоминаньем
О ножках мне знакомых дам.
По вашим узеньким следам,
О ножки, полно заблуждаться!
С изменой юности моей
Пора мне сделаться умней,
В делах и в слоге поправляться,
И эту пятую тетрадь
От отступлений очищать.

36   Whist's champions had already played
eight rubbers, and for the eighth time
were changing places,
when tea was served. I like to identify
the time by reference to "dinner", "tea"
or "supper". In the country
we've no great problem in knowing the time of day:
our stomachs are our chiming watches – good ones!
And, talking of meals, I'll mention here, in brackets,
that, in describing feasts
and various foods and beverages
so often in these stanzas,
I'm following *your* inspired example, Homer,
celebrity author for three thousand years...

37, 38 ....

39   Well, tea was being served. The girls had scarcely
taken a decorous hold of their saucers,
when behind the door to the long ballroom
all at once bassoons and flutes struck up.
Petushkóv, the local small-town heart-throb,
was overjoyed by the music's blare;
abandoning his cup of rum-laced tea,
he went across to Olga.
Lensky approached Tatyána;
Miss Harlikóv, a girl overripe for marriage,
was taken by my poet from Tambóv;
and Buyánov swept Mrs Pustyakóv away.
They all spilt through into the ballroom,
and the ball soon glittered in all its glamour.

40   At the start of my novel
(see Chapter One)
I meant to depict a St Petersburg ball
in the manner of Albani;
but I was distracted by a silly train of thought
and spent the time reminiscing
about the dainty feet of ladies that I'd known.
I mustn't let those slender little footsteps
lead me astray again –
it's time I learnt the lesson
of youthful disappointments
and reformed my behaviour and my style,
keeping the draft of this fifth chapter
clear of digressions.

41   Однообразный и безумный,
Как вихорь жизни молодой,
Кружится вальса вихорь шумный;
Чета мелькает за четой.
К минуте мщенья приближаясь,
Онегин, втайне усмехаясь,
Подходит к Ольге. Быстро с ней
Вертится около гостей,
Потом на стул ее сажает,
Заводит речь о том о сем;
Спустя минуты две потом
Вновь с нею вальс он продолжает;
Все в изумленье. Ленский сам
Не верит собственным глазам.

42   Мазурка раздалась. Бывало,
Когда гремел мазурки гром,
В огромной зале всё дрожало,
Паркет трещал под каблуком,
Тряслися, дребезжали рамы;
Теперь не то: и мы, как дамы,
Скользим по лаковым доскам.
Но в городах, по деревням,
Еще мазурка сохранила
Первоначальные красы:
Припрыжки, каблуки, усы
Всё те же: их не изменила
Лихая мода, наш тиран,
Недуг новейших россиян.

43   . . . .

44   Буянов, братец мой задорный,
К герою нашему подвел
Татьяну с Ольгою; проворно
Онегин с Ольгою пошел;
Ведет ее, скользя небрежно,
И, наклонясь, ей шепчет нежно
Какой-то пошлый мадригал,
И руку жмет — и запылал
В ее лице самолюбивом
Румянец ярче. Ленский мой
Всё видел: вспыхнул, сам не свой;
В негодовании ревнивом
Поэт конца мазурки ждет
И в котильон ее зовет.

41   A waltz was whirling noisily around –
monotonous and frenzied,
like the whirl of life when one is young.
Couples flashed by in quick succession.
Onégin's moment of revenge drew near:
hiding a smirk,
he went to Olga and very soon
was twirling with her among the guests.
Then he escorted her to a chair
and started chatting about this and that.
After another couple of minutes
they were waltzing again.
All were astonished; and, as for Lensky,
he couldn't believe his eyes.

42   The band struck up a mazurka. (At one time,
when a mazurka thundered out,
the whole vast ballroom would vibrate,
the parquet would crack to the dancers' heels,
and window frames would shake and rattle.
It's different now; we copy the ladies
in the way we glide over the lacquered blocks.
Even so, in the provinces – town and country –
the mazurka's kept
its old, original delights:
the leaps, the heel-beats, the mustachios –
still just the same,
unchanged by Fashion, our malevolent despot,
that scourge of the young Russians of today.)

43   . . . .

44   My impetuous cousin Buyánov
conducted Tatyána and her sister
over to Onégin, who without ado
walked off with Olga.
He partnered her with carelessly sliding steps,
and kept bending towards her, whispering
sweet nothings softly in her ear
and squeezing her hand. The pink complexion
in Olga's complacent face
flushed redder and redder. Lensky
saw everything: beside himself, and seething within,
he waited in a jealous rage
for the mazurka to end,
then asked her for the cotillion.

45 Но ей нельзя. Нельзя? Но что же?
Да Ольга слово уж дала
Онегину. О Боже, Боже!
Что слышит он? Она могла…
Возможно ль? Чуть лишь из пеленок,
Кокетка, ветреный ребенок!
Уж хитрость ведает она,
Уж изменять научена!
Не в силах Ленский снесть удара;
Проказы женские кляня,
Выходит, требует коня
И скачет. Пистолетов пара,
Две пули — больше ничего —
Вдруг разрешат судьбу его.

45   But no, she couldn't. – "No? Why not?"
She'd promised it already
to Onégin. – "God, O God!
What's this he's hearing? That she could!…
Can it be so? Not long out of baby clothes,
and now a flirt, the fickle child!
So she's already versed in trickery,
already practised in deceit!"
Lensky could not sustain the blow.
Cursing a woman's antics,
he strode outside, called for a horse,
and galloped off. Now suddenly
his fate was to be settled
by a brace of pistols, two lead balls, that's all.

ГЛАВА ШЕСТАЯ

Là sotto i giorni nubilosi e brevi,
Nasce una gente a cui 'l morir non dole.
— *Petr.*

1   Заметив, что Владимир скрылся,
Онегин, скукой вновь гоним,
Близ Ольги в думу погрузился,
Довольный мщением своим.
За ним и Оленька зевала,
Глазами Ленского искала,
И бесконечный котильон
Ее томил, как тяжкий сон.
Но кончен он. Идут за ужин.
Постели стелют; для гостей
Ночлег отводят от сеней
До самой девичьи. Всем нужен
Покойный сон. Онегин мой
Один уехал спать домой.

2   Всё успокоилось: в гостиной
Храпит тяжелый Пустяков
С своей тяжелой половиной.
Гвоздин, Буянов, Петушков
И Флянов, не совсем здоровый,
На стульях улеглись в столовой,
А на полу мосье Трике,
В фуфайке, в старом колпаке.
Девицы в комнатах Татьяны
И Ольги все объяты сном.
Одна, печальна под окном
Озарена лучом Дианы,
Татьяна бедная не спит
И в поле темное глядит.

CHAPTER SIX

Where skies are overcast and days are short
a race is born that feels no pain in death.
— Petrarch

1   When he noticed Lensky had disappeared,
Onégin succumbed again to boredom
and, as he danced with Olga, sank
into a smug contemplation of his revenge.
Olga caught his mood and herself began to yawn.
She kept looking round for Lensky.
The endless cotillion was wearying her,
like an oppressive dream.
At last it was over, and everyone went to supper.
Beds were made up, and guests
were allotted space for the night from entrance hall
to maid's room: all were in need
of a quiet sleep. Onégin alone
drove home to bed.

2   The house grew still. In the parlour
the ponderous Pustyakóv was snoring
beside his ponderous spouse.
In the dining room Gvozdín, Buyánov,
Petushkóv, and Flyánov (feeling less than well)
had stretched themselves out on chairs,
while Monsieur Triquet lay on the floor
in flannel vest and ancient nightcap.
All of the girls were fast asleep
in Tatyána's and Olga's rooms.
Only Tatyána, poor thing, was still awake:
the moon shone on her as she lay
pensively by the window, gazing out
into the darkened countryside.

171

3   Его нежданным появленьем,
       Мгновенной нежностью очей
       И странным с Ольгой поведеньем
       До глубины души своей
       Она проникнута; не может
       Никак понять его; тревожит
       Ее ревнивая тоска,
       Как будто хладная рука
       Ей сердце жмет, как будто бездна
       Под ней чернеет и шумит…
       «Погибну, — Таня говорит, —
       Но гибель от него любезна.
       Я не ропщу: зачем роптать?
       Не может он мне счастья дать».

4   Вперед, вперед, моя исторья!
       Лицо нас новое зовет.
       В пяти верстах от Красногорья,
       Деревни Ленского, живет
       И здравствует еще доныне
       В философической пустыне
       Зарецкий, некогда буян,
       Картежной шайки атаман,
       Глава повес, трибун трактирный,
       Теперь же добрый и простой
       Отец семейства холостой,
       Надежный друг, помещик мирный
       И даже честный человек:
       Так исправляется наш век!

5   Бывало, льстивый голос света
       В нем злую храбрость выхвалял:
       Он, правда, в туз из пистолета
       В пяти саженях попадал,
       И то сказать, что и в сраженьи
       Раз в настоящем упоеньи
       Он отличился, смело в грязь
       С коня калмыцкого свалясь,
       Как зюзя пьяный, и французам
       Достался в плен: драгой залог!
       Новейший Регул, чести бог,
       Готовый вновь предаться узам,
       Чтоб каждым утром у Вери
       В долг осушать бутылки три.

3   Onégin's unexpected appearance,
that momentary look of tenderness in his eyes,
and the strange way that he'd behaved with Olga
had pierced her to her very soul.
She found it quite impossible
to make him out. A sickening feeling
of jealousy afflicted her,
as though an ice-cold hand
were squeezing her heart, or as though a black
and thunderous abyss were yawning at her feet.
"I'll die," she said,
"but dying because of him will be a joy.
I don't complain – what good's complaining?
He cannot give me happiness."

4   But we must spur my story on,
for there's a new character summoning us.
Three miles from Krasnogórye,
Lensky's estate, lived one Zarétsky,
and flourishes there still
in philosophical solitude.
He'd been a ruffian in the past –
chief of a gambling gang, prime ne'er-do-well,
and demagogue of drinking houses –
but now he'd become (though bachelor) a family man,
benevolent, plain-living,
a peaceable landowner, trusty friend,
and even man of honour.
Thus our contemporaries mend their ways!

5   In the old days society's flattering voice
had commended his mischievous bravado:
true, he could hit an ace
with a pistol at a dozen yards;
in battle too, for that matter,
he was once so utterly carried away
that he quite distinguished himself, fearlessly toppling
from his Kalmuk stallion into the mud
(dead drunk, of course), and got himself
captured by the French – a priceless hostage!
This latterday Regulus, this paragon of honour,
was ready, once set free, to enter captivity again –
if only, back in Paris, to drain three bottles a morning
on credit at Véry's.

6 Бывало, он трунил забавно,
Умел морочить дурака
И умного дурачить славно,
Иль явно, иль исподтишка,
Хоть и ему иные штуки
Не проходили без науки,
Хоть иногда и сам впросак
Он попадался, как простак.
Умел он весело поспорить,
Остро и тупо отвечать,
Порой расчетливо смолчать,
Порой расчетливо повздорить,
Друзей поссорить молодых
И на барьер поставить их,

7 Иль помириться их заставить,
Дабы позавтракать втроем,
И после тайно обесславить
Веселой шуткою, враньем.
Sed alia tempora! Удалость
(Как сон любви, другая шалость)
Проходит с юностью живой.
Как я сказал, Зарецкий мой,
Под сень черемух и акаций
От бурь укрывшись наконец,
Живет, как истинный мудрец,
Капусту садит, как Гораций,
Разводит уток и гусей
И учит азбуке детей.

8 Он был не глуп; и мой Евгений,
Не уважая сердца в нем,
Любил и дух его суждений,
И здравый толк о том о сем.
Он с удовольствием, бывало,
Видался с ним, и так нимало
Поутру не был удивлен,
Когда его увидел он.
Тот после первого привета,
Прервав начатый разговор,
Онегину, осклабя взор,
Вручил записку от поэта.
К окну Онегин подошел
И про себя ее прочел.

6   Yes, in the old days Zarétsky'd been an engaging wag.
He was good at playing pranks on fools,
and brilliant at making fools of clever men,
whether openly or without their knowledge.
But even he didn't get away unscathed
with all his tricks: at times
he was made to look a booby himself
by falling into others' traps.
He was adept at arguing good-humouredly
and at giving rejoinders sharp or smooth;
to achieve his ends he could hold his peace
or pick a quarrel, as the case required.
He could make trouble between young friends
and bring them to a duel –

7   or he could get them to make it up
and have the two of them to breakfast,
and then defame them with a witty jibe
or calumny behind their backs.
Things change with time, though. Daredevilry
(like dreaming of love – another folly)
passes with youthful high spirits.
As I've said, friend Zarétsky
at length took refuge from life's storms
"in the shelter of his bird cherries and laburnums".
He lives now a true philosopher's life,
planting cabbages like Horace,
breeding ducks and geese,
and teaching children their ABC.

8   Zarétsky was no fool; and my friend Onégin,
though mistrusting his integrity,
admired his cast of mind
and his robust good sense on this and that.
In the past he'd found Zarétsky's company
agreeable, and so
was not in the least surprised
to see him that morning.
After an initial greeting, Zarétsky
cut short the incipient pleasantries,
and with a sly gleam in his eye
handed Onégin a note from Lensky.
Onégin moved towards the window
and read it over to himself.

9 То был приятный, благородный,
Короткий вызов, иль *картель*:
Учтиво, с ясностью холодной
Звал друга Ленский на дуэль.
Онегин с первого движенья,
К послу такого порученья
Оборотясь, без лишних слов
Сказал, что он *всегда готов.*
Зарецкий встал без объяснений;
Остаться доле не хотел,
Имея дома много дел,
И тотчас вышел; но Евгений
Наедине с своей душой
Был недоволен сам собой.

10 И поделом: в разборе строгом,
На тайный суд себя призвав,
Он обвинял себя во многом:
Во-первых, он уж был неправ,
Что над любовью робкой, нежной
Так подшутил вечор небрежно.
А во-вторых: пускай поэт
Дурачится; в осьмнадцать лет
Оно простительно. Евгений,
Всем сердцем юношу любя,
Был должен оказать себя
Не мячиком предрассуждений,
Не пылким мальчиком, бойцом,
Но мужем с честью и с умом.

11 Он мог бы чувства обнаружить,
А не щетиниться, как зверь;
Он должен был обезоружить
Младое сердце. «Но теперь
Уж поздно; время улетело…
К тому ж — он мыслит — в это дело
Вмешался старый дуэлист;
Он зол, он сплетник, он речист…
Конечно, быть должно презренье
Ценой его забавных слов,
Но шепот, хохотня глупцов…»
И вот общественное мненье –
Пружина чести, наш кумир!
И вот на чем вертится мир!

9   It was a *cartel*, a challenge,
civil, dignified and brief:
politely, and with chilling lucidity,
Lensky was calling his friend out to a duel.
Onégin, obeying his first impulse,
turned to the bearer of the message
and said, without unnecessary words,
that he was "ready at any time".
Zarétsky rose without a comment –
he didn't want to stay,
as he'd a lot to do at home –
and left the house at once. Onégin,
alone with his thoughts,
felt less than happy with himself – and rightly so.

10   He summoned himself mentally to court
and after a stern interrogation
found himself guilty on several counts.
First, he'd been wrong the night before
so thoughtlessly to trifle
with a lover's shy and tender feelings.
And secondly, granted that Lensky
was making a fool of himself, at eighteen
that was excusable. Then again, Onégin
was genuinely fond of the younger man:
he ought to have shown himself
more than a plaything of conventional prejudice,
more than a hot-headed, trigger-happy boy –
but, rather, a man of intelligence and honour.

11   He could have laid bare his real feelings,
not bristled like a wild beast.
He ought to have calmed
the touchy youngster down. "But now
it's too late; the time has passed…
Besides," he thought, "that veteran duellist
is mixed up in it now;
and he's a talker, scandal-monger, troublemaker…
Of course I should have repaid
his silly message with the scorn it deserved;
but people would whisper and snigger – idiots!…"
So there is public opinion for you! – the mainspring
that keeps honour ticking, the idol we worship,
the axis on which our world revolves!

12   Кипя враждой нетерпеливой,
Ответа дома ждет поэт;
И вот сосед велеречивый
Привез торжественно ответ.
Теперь ревнивцу то-то праздник!
Он всё боялся, чтоб проказник
Не отшутился как-нибудь,
Уловку выдумав и грудь
Отворотив от пистолета.
Теперь сомненья решены:
Они на мельницу должны
Приехать завтра до рассвета,
Взвести друг на друга курок
И метить в ляжку иль в висок.

13   Решась кокетку ненавидеть,
Кипящий Ленский не хотел
Пред поединком Ольгу видеть;
На солнце, на часы смотрел,
Махнул рукою напоследок —
И очутился у соседок.
Он думал Оленьку смутить,
Своим приездом поразить;
Не тут-то было: как и прежде,
На встречу бедного певца
Прыгнула Оленька с крыльца,
Подобна ветреной надежде,
Резва, беспечна, весела,
Ну точно та же, как была.

14   «Зачем вечор так рано скрылись?»
Был первый Оленькин вопрос.
Все чувства в Ленском помутились,
И молча он повесил нос.
Исчезла ревность и досада
Пред этой ясностию взгляда,
Пред этой нежной простотой,
Пред этой резвою душой! ..
Он смотрит в сладком умиленье;
Он видит: он еще любим;
Уж он, раскаяньем томим,
Готов просить у ней прощенье,
Трепещет, не находит слов,
Он счастлив, он почти здоров…

12   Lensky was seething with impatient hatred
as he waited at home for an answer.
Then up rode his pompous neighbour,
triumphantly bearing the response –
one to delight the jealous chap!
He'd been afraid that Onégin, the bounder,
would somehow joke his way out,
that he'd think up a ruse
to place himself out of firing range.
Now all was settled.
Tomorrow, by daybreak,
they were to ride to the mill,
cock their pistols, point them at each other,
and take their aim at thigh – or head.

13   Lensky had decided, in his rage,
to hate the flirt in Olga and hadn't meant
to see her before the duel.
Now he kept looking at sun and clock,
then finally gave a wave of the arm –
and turned up at the Larins'.
He'd thought to take young Olga aback,
to stun her with his arrival.
But not in the least: as the wretched poet
rode up to the house,
down the steps leapt Olga to meet him as usual;
she was like our giddiest hopes –
playful, exuberant, carefree,
exactly as she'd always been.

14   "Why did you vanish so early last night?"
was Olga's first question.
All Lensky's feelings were thrown in confusion.
In silence he hung his head;
his jealousy and vexation vanished
before the brightness of that glance,
before that mildness and simplicity,
before that playful nature of hers.
He looked with sentiment and affection
and saw that, yes, he was still loved.
Overcome with regret,
he was ready to beg her forgiveness;
he trembled, but couldn't find the right words;
he was happy, almost his old self.

15, 16 ....

17   И вновь задумчивый, унылый
Пред милой Ольгою своей,
Владимир не имеет силы
Вчерашний день напомнить ей;
Он мыслит: «Буду ей спаситель.
Не потерплю, чтоб развратитель
Огнем и вздохов и похвал
Младое сердце искушал;
Чтоб червь презренный, ядовитый
Точил лилеи стебелек;
Чтобы двухутренний цветок
Увял еще полураскрытый».
Всё это значило, друзья:
С приятелем стреляюсь я.

18   Когда б он знал, какая рана
Моей Татьяны сердце жгла!
Когда бы ведала Татьяна,
Когда бы знать она могла,
Что завтра Ленский и Евгений
Заспорят о могильной сени;
Ах, может быть, ее любовь
Друзей соединила б вновь!
Но этой страсти и случайно
Еще никто не открывал.
Онегин обо всем молчал;
Татьяна изнывала тайно;
Одна бы няня знать могла,
Да недогадлива была.

19   Весь вечер Ленский был рассеян,
То молчалив, то весел вновь;
Но тот, кто музою взлелеян,
Всегда таков: нахмуря бровь,
Садился он за клавикорды
И брал на них одни аккорды,
То, к Ольге взоры устремив,
Шептал: не правда ль? я счастлив.
Но поздно; время ехать. Сжалось
В нем сердце, полное тоской;
Прощаясь с девой молодой,
Оно как будто разрывалось.
Она глядит ему в лицо.
«Что с вами?» — Так. — И на крыльцо.

15, 16 ....

17   Then he began once more to brood; the presence
of his dear Olga dispirited him anew,
and he couldn't summon up the strength
to remind her of the day before.
He thought: "I'll be her saviour.
I will not suffer that seducer
to lead her young heart astray
with ardent flattery and protestations.
I'll not permit that vile and poisonous worm
to go on gnawing the lily's tender stem;
the little flower is but two mornings old,
still just half-open: it mustn't wither yet."
(All of which, friends, meant simply this:
"I'm going to have a shoot-out with my chum.")

18   If only Lensky had known the wound
that smarted in poor Tatyána's heart!
If only Tatyána had been aware,
if only she could have discovered,
that next day Lensky and Onégin
would fight each other to the death!...
Ah, then perhaps her love
might have brought the friends back together.
But no one as yet had learnt of her infatuation,
even by accident:
Onégin had kept it all to himself;
Tatyána still pined in secret;
only the nurse might have realized –
if she'd not been so slow-witted.

19   All evening Lensky couldn't concentrate.
He was taciturn and jovial by turns –
but those who fancy themselves as artists
are commonly like that. He kept sitting down
at the clavichord, frowning,
and just played chords.
And then he'd fix his eyes on Olga and murmur:
"Yes, surely I've good reason to be happy."
But it grew late, time to depart. His heart
was so full of sadness it felt quite tight within him;
and as he said goodbye to the girl
it seemed that it would burst.
She looked him in the face: "What's up with you?"
"Oh, nothing," he said, and went off down the steps.

20   Домой приехав, пистолеты
      Он осмотрел, потом вложил
      Опять их в ящик и, раздетый,
      При свечке, Шиллера открыл;
      Но мысль одна его объемлет;
      В нем сердце грустное не дремлет:
      С неизъяснимою красой
      Он видит Ольгу пред собой.
      Владимир книгу закрывает,
      Берет перо; его стихи,
      Полны любовной чепухи,
      Звучат и льются. Их читает
      Он вслух, в лирическом жару,
      Как Дельвиг пьяный на пиру.

21   Стихи на случай сохранились;
      Я их имею; вот они:
      «Куда, куда вы удалились,
      Весны моей златые дни?
      Что день грядущий мне готовит?
      Его мой взор напрасно ловит,
      В глубокой мгле таится он.
      Нет нужды; прав судьбы закон.
      Паду ли я, стрелой пронзенный,
      Иль мимо пролетит она,
      Всё благо: бдения и сна
      Приходит час определенный;
      Благословен и день забот,
      Благословен и тьмы приход!

22   *Блеснет заутра луч денницы*
      И заиграет яркий день;
      А я, быть может, я гробницы
      Сойду в таинственную сень,
      И память юного поэта
      Поглотит медленная Лета,
      Забудет мир меня; но ты
      Придешь ли, дева красоты,
      Слезу пролить над ранней урной
      И думать: он меня любил,
      Он мне единой посвятил
      Рассвет печальный жизни бурной!..
      Сердечный друг, желанный друг,
      Приди, приди: я твой супруг!..»

20   On reaching home, Lensky
      inspected his pistols and put them back
      into their case. Then he undressed,
      and by candlelight opened his Schiller.
      But one thought gripped his mind
      and left his heart no respite from its anguish:
      an inexpressibly lovely vision
      of Olga hung before his eyes.
      He shut the book
      and picked up his pen; his verses
      came in a melodious torrent,
      full of amorous nonsense. Then he read them
      aloud – with that same lyrical fervour
      as Delvig displays when tipsy at a party.

21   By chance those verses have survived;
      they're now in my possession. Here they are:
      "*My springtime's golden days – oh where,*
      where have you fled? The coming day,
      what will it hold in store for me?
      I look in vain for dawn's first glow;
      it lurks still in the darkest gloom.
      No matter: Fate's decrees are just.
      If I should fall, pierced through by the arrow,
      or if that arrow pass me by,
      all's for the best: both sleep and waking
      come at their predetermined time.
      God-given is our day of cares,
      God-given too the gathering dusk.

22   "*The day star's beam will soon shine forth*
      to usher in a bright new day;
      while I perhaps go down to take
      an eerie refuge in the tomb.
      Oblivion's sluggish stream will soon
      engulf this youthful poet's name;
      all will forget me – or will you,
      my maid of beauty, come to shed
      a tear at my untimely grave?
      And will you think: 'He used to love me;
      he pledged to me, to me alone,
      the sad dawn of his stormy life'?…
      Dear friend, dear love, for you I long:
      come to me, come to your betrothed!…"

23   Так он писал *темно* и *вяло*
(Что романтизмом мы зовем,
Хоть романтизма тут нимало
Не вижу я; да что нам в том?)
И наконец перед зарею,
Склонясь усталой головою,
На модном слове *идеал*
Тихонько Ленский задремал;
Но только сонным обаяньем
Он позабылся, уж сосед
В безмолвный входит кабинет
И будит Ленского воззваньем:
«Пора вставать: седьмой уж час.
Онегин верно ждет уж нас».

24   Но ошибался он: Евгений
Спал в это время мертвым сном.
Уже редеют ночи тени
И встречен Веспер петухом;
Онегин спит себе глубоко.
Уж солнце катится высоко,
И перелетная метель
Блестит и вьется; но постель
Еще Евгений не покинул,
Еще над ним летает сон.
Вот наконец проснулся он
И полы завеса раздвинул;
Глядит — и видит, что пора
Давно уж ехать со двора.

25   Он поскорей звонит. Вбегает
К нему слуга француз Гильо,
Халат и туфли предлагает
И подает ему белье.
Спешит Онегин одеваться,
Слуге велит приготовляться
С ним вместе ехать и с собой
Взять также ящик боевой.
Готовы санки беговые.
Он сел, на мельницу летит.
Примчались. Он слуге велит
Лепажа стволы роковые
Нести за ним, а лошадям
Отъехать в поле к двум дубкам.

23   On he wrote like this in the style, obscure and limp,
that we call "romanticism" (though I myself
see nothing at all romantic in it –
but let's not go into that).
Then finally, just before dawn,
his weary head began to droop,
and over that modish word "ideal"
he quietly dozed off.
But no sooner had he lost his self-awareness
under sleep's magic spell than Zarétsky
entered the silent study
and woke him with the summons:
"Time to be up! It's already after six.
Onégin's sure to be waiting for us by now."

24   But he was wrong: Onégin
was even then still dead to the world.
The shadows of night were starting to disperse,
and a cock crowed greetings to the morning star;
but Onégin lay on deep in slumber.
Even when the sun had climbed up high,
and a transient shower of snow
whirled and glittered outside,
he was still there in bed,
sleep still hovering above him.
At length he did wake up,
pulled the curtains aside,
looked out – and saw it was long past time
for him to be up and away.

25   He rang the bell at once. Guillot,
his French valet, rushed in,
offered him dressing gown and slippers
and handed him underwear.
Onégin dressed in a hurry;
he told the valet to prepare
to drive out with him, and to bring
the case of pistols too.
As soon as the racing sleigh was ready,
Onégin took his seat, and off they flew to the mill.
They arrived at speed. Onégin gave instructions
for the valet to follow on behind him
with Lepage's deadly firearms, and for the horses
to be driven off to a field to two young oaks.

185

26   Опершись на плотину, Ленский
Давно нетерпеливо ждал;
Меж тем, механик деревенский,
Зарецкий жернов осуждал.
Идет Онегин с извиненьем.
«Но где же, — молвил с изумленьем
Зарецкий, — где ваш секундант?»
В дуэлях классик и педант,
Любил методу он из чувства,
И человека растянуть
Он позволял не как-нибудь,
Но в строгих правилах искусства,
По всем преданьям старины
(Что похвалить мы в нем должны).

27   «Мой секундант? — сказал Евгений, —
Вот он: мой друг, *monsieur* Guillot.
Я не предвижу возражений
На представление мое:
Хоть человек он неизвестный,
Но уж конечно малый честный».
Зарецкий губу закусил.
Онегин Ленского спросил:
«Что ж, начинать?» — Начнем, пожалуй, —
Сказал Владимир. И пошли
За мельницу. Пока вдали
Зарецкий наш и *честный малый*
Вступили в важный договор,
Враги стоят, потупя взор.

28   Враги! Давно ли друг от друга
Их жажда крови отвела?
Давно ль они часы досуга,
Трапезу, мысли и дела
Делили дружно? Ныне злобно,
Врагам наследственным подобно,
Как в страшном, непонятном сне,
Они друг другу в тишине
Готовят гибель хладнокровно…
Не засмеяться ль им, пока
Не обагрилась их рука,
Не разойтиться ль полюбовно?..
Но дико светская вражда
Боится ложного стыда.

26   Lensky had long been leaning
on the parapet of the dam, impatiently waiting.
Meanwhile that rustic engineer Zarétsky
had been finding fault with the millstones.
Onégin came over with apologies.
"But where's…" Zarétsky asked
in astonishment, "where's your second?"
Past-master in the etiquette of duels,
by temperament too he liked things done just so;
he wouldn't therefore have a man
laid out any old how;
it had to be done by the strictest professional standards,
in line with time-honoured traditions –
a trait of his we must commend.

27   "My second?" said Onégin.
"He's here – my friend Monsieur Guillot.
I don't foresee objections
to my choice of representative;
he's not well-known;
but he's a decent chap, no question."
Zarétsky bit his lip. Onégin
turned towards Lensky and enquired:
 "Well, shall we start?" "All right, let's start,"
Lensky replied. And off they strode
beyond the mill. Keeping their distance,
Zarétsky and the "decent chap"
solemnly agreed the match's rules,
while the enemies stood avoiding each other's gaze.

28   Yes, enemies! Yet surely it wasn't long
since bloodlust had drawn the two of them apart,
surely it wasn't long
since as friends they'd still been sharing
leisure hours, meals, thoughts and activities? Now, though,
as if in an incoherent nightmare,
with the hatred shown by hereditary foes,
in silence, in cold blood,
each was preparing the other's destruction.
Wasn't there time even now,
before blood stained their hands,
to laugh it off, to part in amity?
No: gentlemanly foes are scared to death
of what they misinterpret as disgrace.

29 Вот пистолеты уж блеснули,
Гремит о шомпол молоток.
В граненый ствол уходят пули,
И щелкнул в первый раз курок.
Вот порох струйкой сероватой
На полку сыплется. Зубчатый,
Надежно ввинченный кремень
Взведен еще. За ближний пень
Становится Гильо смущенный.
Плащи бросают два врага.
Зарецкий тридцать два шага
Отмерил с точностью отменной,
Друзей развел по крайний след,
И каждый взял свой пистолет.

30 «Теперь сходитесь». Хладнокровно,
Еще не целя, два врага
Походкой твердой, тихо, ровно
Четыре перешли шага,
Четыре смертные ступени.
Свой пистолет тогда Евгений,
Не преставая наступать,
Стал первый тихо подымать.
Вот пять шагов еще ступили,
И Ленский, жмуря левый глаз,
Стал также целить — но как раз
Онегин выстрелил... Пробили
Часы урочные: поэт
Роняет молча пистолет,

31 На грудь кладет тихонько руку
И падает. Туманный взор
Изображает смерть, не муку.
Так медленно по скату гор,
На солнце искрами блистая,
Спадает глыба снеговая.
Мгновенным холодом облит,
Онегин к юноше спешит,
Глядит, зовет его... напрасно:
Его уж нет. Младой певец
Нашел безвременный конец!
Дохнула буря, цвет прекрасный
Увял на утренней заре,
Потух огонь на алтаре!..

29   You could see the pistols glinting,
         you could hear the ring of hammer on ramrod.
         Into each faceted barrel the lead balls dropped;
         each gun was half-cocked with a click;
         then onto each pan there trickled
         a stream of greyish powder. Jagged flints,
         screwed firmly into place,
         were primed for use. Behind a nearby tree trunk
         Guillot took up position, overawed.
         The two opponents threw their cloaks to the ground.
         Zarétsky, with impeccable precision,
         measured out thirty-two paces
         and led the friends apart to the outermost marks.
         Then each one took his weapon.

30   "Advance now!" The pair of combatants,
         without yet taking aim, coolly
         and with a relentlessly calm and even gait
         took four steps forward,
         four deadly paces.
         Then first Onégin,
         advancing still,
         quietly began to raise his gun.
         When they'd covered five paces more,
         Lensky too closed his left eye
         and began to take aim. But at that very moment
         Onégin fired... The appointed hour
         had struck. The poet
         in silence dropped his pistol,

31   quietly placed his hand on his chest,
         and fell. The message
         in his misty eyes was death, not pain.
         Just so will a mass of snow,
         sparkling in sunlight,
         topple slowly down a mountain crag.
         Onégin broke into a cold sweat at once.
         He rushed to the youngster,
         stared at him, called him by name – in vain:
         he was already gone. The youthful poet
         had met his untimely end.
         The storm had done its worst; a lovely flower
         had wilted in the morning's early glow;
         the fire on the altar was extinguished.

32   Недвижим он лежал, и странен
Был томный мир его чела.
Под грудь он был навылет ранен;
Дымясь из раны кровь текла.
Тому назад одно мгновенье
В сем сердце билось вдохновенье,
Вражда, надежда и любовь,
Играла жизнь, кипела кровь:
Теперь, как в доме опустелом,
Всё в нем и тихо и темно;
Замолкло навсегда оно.
Закрыты ставни, окны мелом
Забелены. Хозяйки нет.
А где, Бог весть. Пропал и след.

33   Приятно дерзкой эпиграммой
Взбесить оплошного врага;
Приятно зреть, как он, упрямо
Склонив бодливые рога,
Невольно в зеркало глядится
И узнавать себя стыдится;
Приятней, если он, друзья,
Завоет сдуру: это я!
Еще приятнее в молчанье
Ему готовить честный гроб
И тихо целить в бледный лоб
На благородном расстоянье;
Но отослать его к отцам
Едва ль приятно будет вам.

34   Что ж, если вашим пистолетом
Сражен приятель молодой,
Нескромным взглядом, иль ответом,
Или безделицей иной
Вас оскорбивший за бутылкой,
Иль даже сам в досаде пылкой
Вас гордо вызвавший на бой –
Скажите: вашею душой
Какое чувство овладеет,
Когда недвижим, на земле
Пред вами с смертью на челе,
Он постепенно костенеет,
Когда он глух и молчалив
На ваш отчаянный призыв?

32   He lay there motionless. His brow
      wore a strange look of tired tranquillity.
      The shot had passed right through below the breast;
      blood trickled, steaming, from the wound.
      Only a moment earlier
      this heart had been beating with inspiration,
      with hatred, hope and love;
      it had throbbed with life and pulsed with blood.
      Now, like a derelict house,
      it was utterly still and dark;
      it had fallen silent for ever.
      The shutters were closed, the windows
      were whitewashed over. The lady of the house was gone,
      God alone knew where. All trace had vanished.

33   It's fun to catch an enemy off guard
      and sting him to fury with a daring quip.
      And when the headstrong fellow
      lowers his horns for the charge,
      it's fun to see him looking, against his will,
      into a mirror, ashamed to acknowledge himself.
      And, friends, it's even funnier
      if he's then fool enough to bellow out "That's me!"
      Better fun still is privately
      to plan for him an honourable death,
      taking mental aim at his wan forehead,
      from a decent range. But actually
      to dispatch him to his forebears –
      you're hardly likely to find fun in that.

34   Imagine that you've shot dead
      a young friend of your own,
      because after a drink he offended you
      with an impudent look or remark
      or in some other trifling way –
      or perhaps, his own honour slighted, in a blaze of anger
      he challenged *you* to a duel.
      Just imagine him lying on the ground before you
      motionless, death spelt out on his brow,
      his body slowly rigidifying:
      desperately though you call him
      he neither hears nor answers...
      Tell me: what feeling now
      will overwhelm your heart?

35   В тоске сердечных угрызений,
     Рукою стиснув пистолет,
     Глядит на Ленского Евгений.
     «Ну, что ж? убит», — решил сосед.
     Убит!.. Сим страшным восклицаньем
     Сражен, Онегин с содроганьем
     Отходит и людей зовет.
     Зарецкий бережно кладет
     На сани труп оледенелый;
     Домой везет он страшный клад.
     Почуя мертвого, храпят
     И бьются кони, пеной белой
     Стальные мочат удила,
     И полетели как стрела.

36   Друзья мои, вам жаль поэта:
     Во цвете радостных надежд,
     Их не свершив еще для света,
     Чуть из младенческих одежд,
     Увял! Где жаркое волненье,
     Где благородное стремленье
     И чувств и мыслей молодых,
     Высоких, нежных, удалых?
     Где бурные любви желанья,
     И жажда знаний и труда,
     И страх порока и стыда,
     И вы, заветные мечтанья,
     Вы, призрак жизни неземной,
     Вы, сны поэзии святой!

37   Быть может, он для блага мира
     Иль хоть для славы был рожден;
     Его умолкнувшая лира
     Гремучий, непрерывный звон
     В веках поднять могла. Поэта,
     Быть может, на ступенях света
     Ждала высокая ступень.
     Его страдальческая тень,
     Быть может, унесла с собою
     Святую тайну, и для нас
     Погиб животворящий глас,
     И за могильною чертою
     К ней не домчится гимн времен,
     Благословение племен.

35   Onégin was watching Lensky,
pistol clenched tight in hand,
in agonies of heartfelt remorse.
"Let's see, then... Shot dead," came Zarétsky's verdict.
Shot dead!... Onégin, shattered
by these appalling words, shuddered
and walked away to call his men.
Zarétsky carefully laid
the frozen body onto his sleigh
and prepared to drive home with his fearful prize.
The horses, scenting the corpse,
grew restive and snorted,
their steel bits moist with white foam.
Then, like an arrow, off they flew.

36   My friends, you'll feel sorry for Lensky.
He'd barely grown out of his boy's clothes,
when in the bloom of his eager hopes
he wilted away, robbing the world of their fruition.
Gone were the tumultuous fervour
and noble aspiration
of his young thoughts and emotions,
so lofty, tender and courageous.
Gone were the turbulent craving for love,
the zeal for knowledge and work,
the dread of wrongdoing and disgrace.
And those mystical visions,
those intimations of life in a world beyond,
those sacred poetical dreams – they too were gone.

37   Maybe he'd been born as a boon to mankind,
or at least to be famous.
Maybe the music of his poetry, now hushed,
would have resounded loud and unbroken
down through the ages. As a poet, maybe,
he'd have risen high
in society's ranking.
Maybe his martyred spirit
carried off still undisclosed
a heaven-sent message, silencing for us
a voice whose words breathed life,
and forfeiting the grateful acclaim
of future generations that might otherwise
have reached it beyond death's frontier.

38   ·

39   А может быть и то: поэта
Обыкновенный ждал удел.
Прошли бы юношества лета:
В нем пыл души бы охладел.
Во многом он бы изменился,
Расстался б с музами, женился,
В деревне, счастлив и рогат,
Носил бы стеганый халат;
Узнал бы жизнь на самом деле,
Подагру б в сорок лет имел,
Пил, ел, скучал, толстел, хирел,
И наконец в своей постеле
Скончался б посреди детей,
Плаксивых баб и лекарей.

40   Но что бы ни было, читатель,
Увы, любовник молодой,
Поэт, задумчивый мечтатель,
Убит приятельской рукой!
Есть место: влево от селенья,
Где жил питомец вдохновенья,
Две сосны корнями срослись;
Под ними струйки извились
Ручья соседственной долины.
Там пахарь любит отдыхать,
И жницы в волны погружать
Приходят звонкие кувшины;
Там у ручья в тени густой
Поставлен памятник простой.

41   Под ним (как начинает капать
Весенний дождь на злак полей)
Пастух, плетя свой пестрый лапоть,
Поет про волжских рыбарей;
И горожанка молодая,
В деревне лето провождая,
Когда стремглав верхом она
Несется по полям одна,
Коня пред ним остановляет,
Ремянный повод натянув,
И, флер от шляпы отвернув,
Глазами беглыми читает
Простую надпись — и слеза
Туманит нежные глаза.

38   ....

39   But there's another possibility:
a more conventional future could have awaited Lensky.
The years of youthfulness would have passed,
the fire in his nature grown cold.
He'd have changed in many a way:
he'd have taken leave of poetry, got married,
and stayed in the country, robed in a quilted dressing gown,
his contentment unspoilt by his wife's escapades.
He'd have recognized life for what it is:
gout at forty, eating, drinking,
growing tired, fat and feeble;
and at length he'd have ended his days in bed,
surrounded by children,
tearful old women and doctors.

40   But, reader, whatever *might* have been,
the sad reality was this: Lensky, young lover,
poet and wistful daydreamer,
was dead, shot by his friend.
There's a spot on the left, as you leave the village
in which the budding poet used to live;
two pines there have grown together at the roots.
Beneath them meander rivulets
of the stream that flows through the neighbouring valley.
It's a place where ploughmen love to rest,
and where the women come from reaping
to dip their echoing pitchers in the swirling water.
There in deep shade beside the stream
a simple memorial stone now stands.

41   At its foot, as the springtime rains
start to fall on the grassy meadows,
a shepherd will sometimes sit singing of Volga fisherfolk
and plaiting strips of lime bark into a chequered sandal.
And a girl from the city,
spending summer in the country,
will come galloping recklessly
over the fields alone.
Picture her as she reins in her stallion
and brings him to a halt by the memorial;
turning back the light veil on her hat,
she eagerly scans
the simple inscription – and her gentle eyes
grow dim with tears.

42 И шагом едет в чистом поле,
    В мечтанья погрузясь, она;
    Душа в ней долго поневоле
    Судьбою Ленского полна;
    И мыслит: «Что-то с Ольгой стало?
    В ней сердце долго ли страдало,
    Иль скоро слез прошла пора?
    И где теперь ее сестра?
    И где ж беглец людей и света,
    Красавиц модных модный враг,
    Где этот пасмурный чудак,
    Убийца юного поэта?»
    Со временем отчет я вам
    Подробно обо всем отдам,

43 Но не теперь. Хоть я сердечно
    Люблю героя моего,
    Хоть возвращусь к нему, конечно,
    Но мне теперь не до него.
    Лета к суровой прозе клонят,
    Лета шалунью рифму гонят,
    И я — со вздохом признаюсь —
    За ней ленивей волочусь.
    Перу старинной нет охоты
    Марать летучие листы;
    Другие, хладные мечты,
    Другие, строгие заботы
    И в шуме света и в тиши
    Тревожат сон моей души.

44 Познал я глас иных желаний,
    Познал я новую печаль;
    Для первых нет мне упований,
    А старой мне печали жаль.
    Мечты, мечты! где ваша сладость?
    Где, вечная к ней рифма, *младость*?
    Ужель и вправду наконец
    Увял, увял ее венец?
    Ужель и впрям и в самом деле
    Без элегических затей
    Весна моих промчалась дней
    (Что я шутя твердил доселе)?
    И ей ужель возврата нет?
    Ужель мне скоро тридцать лет?

42   She rides on, slowly now, over the open fields
deep in a reverie.
For long she can think of nothing
but Lensky and his story.
"What has become of Olga?" she wonders.
"Did she stay heartbroken for long,
or did her tears soon pass?
Where is her sister now?
And wherever's that fugitive from human society,
that fashionable menace to ladies of fashion? –
yes, where is that gloomy maverick
who took the young poet's life?"
In good time I'll give you
a detailed account of all this,

43   but not at this moment. I'm genuinely
fond of my hero,
and I'll come back to him, of course;
but I'm not in the mood for him now.
The years draw me closer to the austere art of prose
and drive frivolous rhyme far away;
indeed regretfully I must confess
that I'm getting too lazy in courting rhyme.
My pen doesn't have its old urge
to cover page after page with scribble.
In the uproar of society and in silence alike
the slumber of my inner being
is troubled by different, chillier dreams,
by different, harsher anxieties.

44   I've got to know the voice of new desires,
I've got to know new sorrows too.
But these desires are unaccompanied by hope;
and – how I miss my former sorrows!
My dreams, my dreams! What's become of their sweetness?
Indeed what's become of my youth?
Can it be that its garland of flowers
has wilted, has really wilted at last?
Can it be that poetic fancy
has given way to hard fact,
and the springtime of my life has really slipped past –
as in jest I've maintained up to now?
And is it never to return?...
And will I really soon be thirty?

45   Так, полдень мой настал, и нужно
      Мне в том сознаться, вижу я.
      Но так и быть: простимся дружно,
      О юность легкая моя!
      Благодарю за наслажденья,
      За грусть, за милые мученья,
      За шум, за бури, за пиры,
      За все, за все твои дары;
      Благодарю тебя. Тобою,
      Среди тревог и в тишине,
      Я насладился… и вполне;
      Довольно! С ясною душою
      Пускаюсь ныне в новый путь
      От жизни прошлой отдохнуть.

46   Дай оглянусь. Простите ж, сени,
      Где дни мои текли в глуши,
      Исполнены страстей и лени
      И снов задумчивой души.
      А ты, младое вдохновенье,
      Волнуй мое воображенье,
      Дремоту сердца оживляй,
      В мой угол чаще прилетай,
      Не дай остыть душе поэта,
      Ожесточиться, очерстветь,
      И наконец окаменеть
      В мертвящем упоенье света,
      В сем омуте, где с вами я
      Купаюсь, милые друзья!

45   Yes, life has reached its noontide, and I see
that I'd better face up to that.
But never mind. My youth,
my carefree youth and I must part as friends.
I'm grateful for its delights,
its sadness, its fond agonies,
its noise, its tempests, its festivities;
my thanks for all its gifts –
yes, all of them.
Hectic or tranquil, I've enjoyed it all,
enjoyed it to the full.
Enough, then. With a heart unclouded by regrets
I'll now embark on a fresh journey,
to recuperate from the life I leave behind…

46   One last look back – to say goodbye to the sheltered spots
where in seclusion day after day
I used to indulge my emotions, indolence
and wistful dreams…
But my youthful inspiration – please not "goodbye" to that!
May it wing its way more often to my corner,
to stir my imagination
and enliven the musings of my soul,
so that my poet's heart may not grow cold
and hard and stale,
and not be turned at last to stone
in society's lethal frenzy,
in this morass, friends, where we're all
wallowing together, you and I!

ГЛАВА СЕДЬМАЯ

1   Гонимы вешними лучами,
       С окрестных гор уже снега
       Сбежали мутными ручьями
       На потопленные луга.
       Улыбкой ясною природа
       Сквозь сон встречает утро года;
       Синея, блещут небеса.
       Еще прозрачные, леса
       Как будто пухом зеленеют.
       Пчела за данью полевой
       Летит из кельи восковой.
       Долины сохнут и пестреют;
       Стада шумят, и соловей
       Уж пел в безмолвии ночей.

2   Как грустно мне твое явленье,
       Весна, весна! пора любви!
       Какое томное волненье
       В моей душе, в моей крови!
       С каким тяжелым умиленьем
       Я наслаждаюсь дуновеньем
       В лицо мне веющей весны
       На лоне сельской тишины!
       Или мне чуждо наслажденье,
       И всё, что радует, живит,
       Всё, что ликует и блестит,
       Наводит скуку и томленье
       На душу мертвую давно,
       И всё ей кажется темно?

CHAPTER SEVEN

Moscow, Russia's favourite daughter –
Where's your equal to be found?
*   – Dmítriev*

I cannot but love my native Moscow.
*   – Baratýnsky*

– Disparage Moscow! What it is to know
the world! Just tell me somewhere better.
– Where there's none of us.
*   – Griboyédov*

1 Chased by spring sunshine
off the surrounding hills, the snows
were coursing now in turbid streams
down to the flooded meadows.
Nature, still half-asleep,
smiled a bright greeting to the year's morning.
The skies gleamed deeper blue.
The still-transparent woods
sprouted a down of green.
Bees flew from their waxen cells
to collect their dues from the fields.
The water meadows, drying, gleamed with colour.
Cattle were lowing; and in the nocturnal stillness
a nightingale now sang.

2 We call spring "season of love" –
but for me spring's coming holds such sadness:
in body and soul alike
I'm so oppressed and so unsettled;
when I'm relaxing in the peaceful countryside,
my delight as the breath of spring
blows in my face
is mingled with such heaviness of heart.
So why does all that offers joy and life,
all that is jubilant and bright,
cause me distaste and weariness
and wear for me a sombre hue?
Is it that delight and I are strangers?
Is it that my soul has long been dead?

3   Или, не радуясь возврату
Погибших осенью листов,
Мы помним горькую утрату,
Внимая новый шум лесов;
Или с природой оживленной
Сближаем думою смущенной
Мы увяданье наших лет,
Которым возрожденья нет?
Быть может, в мысли нам приходит
Средь поэтического сна
Иная, старая весна
И в трепет сердце нам приводит
Мечтой о дальной стороне,
О чудной ночи, о луне…

4   Вот время: добрые ленивцы,
Эпикурейцы-мудрецы,
Вы, равнодушные счастливцы,
Вы, школы Левшина птенцы,
Вы, деревенские Приамы,
И вы, чувствительные дамы,
Весна в деревню вас зовет,
Пора тепла, цветов, работ,
Пора гуляний вдохновенных
И соблазнительных ночей.
В поля, друзья! скорей, скорей,
В каретах, тяжко нагруженных,
На долгих иль на почтовых
Тянитесь из застав градских.

5   И вы, читатель благосклонный,
В своей коляске выписной
Оставьте град неугомонный,
Где веселились вы зимой;
С моею музой своенравной
Пойдемте слушать шум дубравный
Над безыменною рекой
В деревне, где Евгений мой,
Отшельник праздный и унылый,
Еще недавно жил зимой
В соседстве Тани молодой,
Моей мечтательницы милой,
Но где его теперь уж нет…
Где грустный он оставил след.

3   Or, as we listen to the woods' fresh rustling,
maybe we don't rejoice in the return
of leaves that died last autumn
because we recall that bitter loss.
Or do our disordered thoughts
link nature's revival with the withering
of our own blighted lives –
lives that will have no rebirth?
Or maybe there comes to mind,
in our poetical reflections,
another spring of long ago,
prompting our heart to throb
as we recall some far-off place,
a wondrous night, a moon…

4   Spring's here, then: and you, gentle idlers –
you, enlightened Epicureans –
you, apathetic plutocrats –
you, armchair agriculturalists –
and you, prolific squires
and sentimental ladies –
spring's summoning you to the country.
The weather's warm – it's time for flowers,
for farm work, for exhilarating walks
and for seductive nights.
To the country, then, friends, quick, be quick!
In your well-laden carriages,
drawn by your own slow nags or fast post horses,
stream out from the city gates!

5   You too, kind reader, must bring out
that open carriage that you purchased from abroad,
and leave the hectic city
where you've spent a jolly winter.
Let's rejoin the wayward goddess who inspires me;
let's go together and listen to the whispering trees
above that nameless brook,
there in the country where my friend Eugene
was only last winter dwelling still,
an idle and disconsolate recluse,
not far from my Tatyána's home,
that sweet young dreamer of dreams.
Eugene's no longer there now…
but he's left a grim memento of his stay.

6   Меж гор, лежащих полукругом,
    Пойдем туда, где ручеек,
    Виясь, бежит зеленым лугом
    К реке сквозь липовый лесок.
    Там соловей, весны любовник,
    Всю ночь поет; цветет шиповник,
    И слышен говор ключевой, —
    Там виден камень гробовой
    В тени двух сосен устарелых.
    Пришельцу надпись говорит:
    ВЛАДИМИР ЛЕНСКИЙ ЗДЕСЬ ЛЕЖИТ,
    ПОГИБШИЙ РАНО СМЕРТЬЮ СМЕЛЫХ,
    (В такой-то год, таких-то лет).
    ПОКОЙСЯ, ЮНОША-ПОЭТ!

7   На ветви сосны преклоненной,
    Бывало, ранний ветерок
    Над этой урною смиренной
    Качал таинственный венок.
    Бывало, в поздние досуги
    Сюда ходили две подруги,
    И на могиле при луне,
    Обнявшись, плакали оне.
    Но ныне… памятник унылый
    Забыт. К нему привычный след
    Заглох. Венка на ветви нет;
    Один, под ним, седой и хилый
    Пастух по-прежнему поет
    И обувь бедную плетет.

8–9   . . . .

10   Мой бедный Ленский! изнывая,
    Не долго плакала она.
    Увы! невеста молодая
    Своей печали неверна.
    Другой увлек ее вниманье,
    Другой успел ее страданье
    Любовной лестью усыпить,
    Улан умел ее пленить,
    Улан любим ее душою…
    И вот уж с ним пред алтарем
    Она стыдливо под венцом
    Стоит с поникшей головою,
    С огнем в потупленных очах,
    С улыбкой легкой на устах.

6   Let's go to the spot,
in a crescent of hills, where the brook
winds its course through green meadows
and runs through a thicket of limes to the river.
Spring's suitor, the nightingale,
sings there all night; there's sweetbriar in bloom,
and the chattering sound of fresh water.
There, in the shade of two gnarled pines,
you'll see the gravestone.
To the passer-by an epitaph announces:
HERE LIES VLADIMIR LENSKY
WHO DIED THE EARLY DEATH OF THE BRAVE
(year such-and-such, aged so-and-so).
BOY POET, REST IN PEACE.

7   A wreath once used to hang, half-hidden,
on a drooping pine bough
above this humble resting place,
swaying in the morning breeze.
Two girls would come here together
when free of an evening;
they'd embrace in the moonlight
and weep by the grave.
But now... the memorial stands forlorn,
forgotten. The once well-trodden path that leads there
is overgrown. There's no wreath on the bough.
Only the shepherd, grey-haired and frail,
sits at its foot, singing as always,
and plaiting his primitive footgear.

8, 9   ....

10   Poor Lensky! It didn't take Olga long
to get over her tears and grief.
Still young and marriageable,
she was, alas, disloyal to her sorrow.
Another man caught her attention
and successfully deployed his charm as lover
to soothe her heartache.
A lancer in the cavalry, he knew how best to woo her,
and he won her heart...
Soon there she was by the altar
beneath her bridal crown,
standing shyly beside him,
head bowed, her lowered eyes aflame,
faint smile upon her lips.

11   Мой бедный Ленский! за могилой
    В пределах вечности глухой
    Смутился ли, певец унылый,
    Измены вестью роковой,
    Или над Летой усыпленный
    Поэт, бесчувствием блаженный,
    Уж не смущается ничем,
    И мир ему закрыт и нем?..
    Так! равнодушное забвенье
    За гробом ожидает нас.
    Врагов, друзей, любовниц глас
    Вдруг молкнет. Про одно именье
    Наследников сердитый хор
    Заводит непристойный спор.

12   И скоро звонкий голос Оли
    В семействе Лариных умолк.
    Улан, своей невольник доли,
    Был должен ехать с нею в полк.
    Слезами горько обливаясь,
    Старушка, с дочерью прощаясь,
    Казалось, чуть жива была,
    Но Таня плакать не могла;
    Лишь смертной бледностью покрылось
    Ее печальное лицо.
    Когда все вышли на крыльцо,
    И всё, прощаясь, суетилось
    Вокруг кареты молодых,
    Татьяна проводила их.

13   И долго, будто сквозь тумана,
    Она глядела им вослед…
    И вот одна, одна Татьяна!
    Увы! подруга стольких лет,
    Ее голубка молодая,
    Ее наперсница родная,
    Судьбою вдаль занесена,
    С ней навсегда разлучена.
    Как тень она без цели бродит,
    То смотрит в опустелый сад…
    Нигде, ни в чем ей нет отрад,
    И облегченья не находит
    Она подавленным слезам,
    И сердце рвется пополам.

11   Poor Lensky! Are we to think that there beyond the grave
news of Olga's fated betrayal
reached the sad poet at the gate of eternal silence,
causing him more distress?
Or, asleep on Lethe's waters,
blissfully insensible,
shut off from sight and sound of the world,
was he already past reach of distress?...
Yes, certain it is that after we die
indifference and oblivion are all that await us.
The voices of enemies, friends and lovers
will quickly fall silent; only our heirs
in angry chorus will start an unseemly wrangle
over our estate.

12   The Larin household didn't hear
the ringing voice of Olga for much longer.
Not being master of his destiny, the lancer
had to ride off with her to join his regiment.
Mrs Larin wept such bitter tears
as she bade her daughter goodbye
that it seemed she might expire with grief.
Tatyána couldn't cry;
but her sorrowful face
took on a deathly pallor.
When they all went out onto the steps,
amid the chaos around the young pair's carriage
as last farewells were said,
it was Tatyána that saw them away.

13   And long she stood there gazing after them,
as through a mist...
Tatyána was now alone, quite alone.
An unkind destiny had carried far off
her little pet,
her soulmate,
her friend of so many years –
had parted them for ever.
Like a ghost, Tatyána wandered aimlessly,
kept looking into the deserted garden...
There was no consolation anywhere,
nothing to give her relief
from the tears she struggled to suppress.
Her heart was breaking in two.

14 И в одиночестве жестоком
Сильнее страсть ее горит,
И об Онегине далеком
Ей сердце громче говорит.
Она его не будет видеть;
Она должна в нем ненавидеть
Убийцу брата своего;
Поэт погиб… но уж его
Никто не помнит, уж другому
Его невеста отдалась.
Поэта память пронеслась
Как дым по небу голубому,
О нем два сердца, может быть,
Еще грустят… На что грустить?..

15 Был вечер. Небо меркло. Воды
Струились тихо. Жук жужжал.
Уж расходились хороводы;
Уж за рекой, дымясь, пылал
Огонь рыбачий. В поле чистом,
Луны при свете серебристом,
В свои мечты погружена,
Татьяна долго шла одна.
Шла, шла. И вдруг перед собою
С холма господский видит дом,
Селенье, рощу под холмом
И сад над светлою рекою.
Она глядит — и сердце в ней
Забилось чаще и сильней.

16 Ее сомнения смущают:
«Пойду ль вперед, пойду ль назад?..
Его здесь нет. Меня не знают…
Взгляну на дом, на этот сад».
И вот с холма Татьяна сходит,
Едва дыша; кругом обводит
Недоуменья полный взор…
И входит на пустынный двор.
К ней, лая, кинулись собаки.
На крик испуганный ея
Ребят дворовая семья
Сбежалась шумно. Не без драки
Мальчишки разогнали псов,
Взяв барышню под свой покров.

14   In that cruel loneliness
Tatyána's passion burnt more fiercely;
and though Onégin was now far off,
the thought of him nagged her with all the more insistence.
She would never see him again:
indeed she was bound to shun him
as the murderer of her brother-to-be.
Lensky had perished... but there was no one now
to remember him: even his bride
had given herself to another.
Memory of the poet had drifted away
like smoke in the bright blue sky.
Two hearts, perhaps, still grieved for him...
But what was the point of grieving?...

15   One evening the sky was darkening; the stream
flowed softly by; a beetle buzzed;
the peasants were dispersing from a dance;
beyond the river smoke was rising
from a fisherman's blazing fire. Tatyána,
immersed in her dreams,
had long been walking alone
through empty fields by the silvery moonlight.
On and on she walked; and all at once from a hilltop
she saw before her a manor house,
a village, a wood at the foot of the hill,
and parkland by the gleaming river.
As she looked, the beating of her heart
came quicker and stronger.

16   She was troubled by doubts:
to go on, or go back?...
True, he was no longer there, and she wasn't known...
She'd take a look at the house, then, and at that park.
So Tatyána walked on downhill,
now scarcely breathing. She glanced around –
a glance full of apprehension...
She entered the empty forecourt.
Dogs rushed at her, barking.
She shrieked with fright,
and a brood of servant children
ran noisily up. The boys
took the young lady beneath their protection
and, not without a tussle, chased the dogs off.

17 «Увидеть барский дом нельзя ли?» —
Спросила Таня. Поскорей
К Анисье дети побежали
У ней ключи взять от сеней;
Анисья тотчас к ней явилась,
И дверь пред ними отворилась,
И Таня входит в дом пустой,
Где жил недавно наш герой.
Она глядит: забытый в зале
Кий на бильярде отдыхал,
На смятом канапе лежал
Манежный хлыстик. Таня дале;
Старушка ей: «А вот камин;
Здесь барин сиживал один.

18 Здесь с ним обедывал зимою
Покойный Ленский, наш сосед.
Сюда пожалуйте, за мною.
Вот это барский кабинет;
Здесь почивал он, кофей кушал,
Приказчика доклады слушал
И книжку поутру читал…
И старый барин здесь живал;
Со мной, бывало, в воскресенье,
Здесь под окном, надев очки,
Играть изволил в дурачки.
Дай Бог душе его спасенье,
А косточкам его покой
В могиле, в мать-земле сырой!»

19 Татьяна взором умиленным
Вокруг себя на всё глядит,
И всё ей кажется бесценным,
Всё душу томную живит
Полумучительной отрадой:
И стол с померкшею лампадой,
И груда книг, и под окном
Кровать, покрытая ковром,
И вид в окно сквозь сумрак лунный,
И этот бледный полусвет,
И лорда Байрона портрет,
И столбик с куклою чугунной
Под шляпой с пасмурным челом,
С руками, сжатыми крестом.

17   "One can't take a look at the manor house, can one?"
Tatyána enquired. The children
rushed quickly off to Anísya
to get the front-door keys.
Anísya herself appeared at once,
and the door swung open before them.
Tatyána entered the empty house
where Onégin had so recently dwelt.
She looked around: in the reception room
on a billiard table there rested a cue
that someone had not put away; on a rumpled couch
lay a riding switch. Tatyána moved on.
The old woman spoke: "This fireplace here
is where the master sat when he was alone…

18   "And here the late Mr Lensky, our neighbour,
used to have dinner with him last winter…
This way please, after me…
Now here you have master's study.
Here's where he used to take a nap, drink coffee,
hear the steward's reports,
and pass the morning reading one of those books of his…
The old master used to spend all of his time here.
Sometimes, of a Sunday, here by the window,
he'd deign to put on his glasses,
and play beat-your-neighbour with me.
May the Lord grant his soul salvation
and give his poor bones rest
there in the grave, in moist Mother Earth!"

19   Tatyána looked round with emotion,
taking everything in –
the desk with its extinguished lamp;
a pile of books; a divan
beneath a bedspread by the window;
the view outside through the moonlit dusk;
the dim half-light itself;
a portrait of Lord Byron;
on a pedestal an iron figurine
with hat, face grimly frowning,
arms tightly folded –
it all seemed to her so infinitely precious;
it all half-painfully
soothed and revived her weary heart.

20 Татьяна долго в келье модной
Как очарована стоит.
Но поздно. Ветер встал холодный.
Темно в долине. Роща спит
Над отуманенной рекою;
Луна сокрылась за горою,
И пилигримке молодой
Пора, давно пора домой.
И Таня, скрыв свое волненье,
Не без того, чтоб не вздохнуть,
Пускается в обратный путь.
Но прежде просит позволенья
Пустынный замок навещать,
Чтоб книжки здесь одной читать.

21 Татьяна с ключницей простилась
За воротами. Через день
Уж утром рано вновь явилась
Она в оставленную сень.
И в молчаливом кабинете,
Забыв на время всё на свете,
Осталась наконец одна,
И долго плакала она.
Потом за книги принялася.
Сперва ей было не до них,
Но показался выбор их
Ей странен. Чтенью предалася
Татьяна жадною душой;
И ей открылся мир иной.

22 Хотя мы знаем, что Евгений
Издавна чтенье разлюбил,
Однако ж несколько творений
Он из опалы исключил:
Певца Гяура и Жуана
Да с ним еще два-три романа,
В которых отразился век
И современный человек
Изображен довольно верно
С его безнравственной душой,
Себялюбивой и сухой,
Мечтанью преданной безмерно,
С его озлобленным умом,
Кипящим в действии пустом.

20   In this contemporary hermitage Tatyána
stood long, as though bewitched.
But it was late. A cold wind had sprung up;
the valley was dark; a mist
enveloped the river below the slumbering woods;
the moon had sunk behind a hill.
It was time, high time,
for the young girl-pilgrim to be home.
Tatyána had concealed her agitation;
but she could not suppress a sigh
as she departed on the journey back.
Before she left she asked permission
to revisit the deserted mansion
and read the books there on her own.

21   She took leave of the housekeeper
outside the gates. Then, one day later,
first thing in the morning, she appeared again
at Onégin's abandoned retreat.
At last she was there alone
in the silent study;
and, oblivious for the moment of the world outside,
she spent a long time crying.
She then turned her attention to the books.
She didn't take to them at first,
but the oddness of the selection
intrigued her. She applied herself
avidly to reading; and, as she read,
a new world opened up before her.

22   As we know, Onégin a long time back
had lost his fondness for books;
there were a few works, nonetheless,
that he'd exempted from disfavour –
the poems of Byron, for example,
and, with them, two or three novels
reflecting the spirit of the age
and portraying contemporary man
with tolerable accuracy –
the amorality, the egotism,
the desiccation of his soul,
his boundless passion for fantasy,
and the fervid and futile turmoil
of his embittered mind.

23 Хранили многие страницы
    Отметку резкую ногтей;
    Глаза внимательной девицы
    Устремлены на них живей.
    Татьяна видит с трепетаньем,
    Какою мыслью, замечаньем
    Бывал Онегин поражен,
    В чем молча соглашался он.
    На их полях она встречает
    Черты его карандаша.
    Везде Онегина душа
    Себя невольно выражает
    То кратким словом, то крестом,
    То вопросительным крючком.

24 И начинает понемногу
    Моя Татьяна понимать
    Теперь яснее — слава Богу —
    Того, по ком она вздыхать
    Осуждена судьбою властной:
    Чудак печальный и опасный,
    Созданье ада иль небес,
    Сей ангел, сей надменный бес,
    Что ж он? Ужели подражанье,
    Ничтожный призрак, иль еще
    Москвич в Гарольдовом плаще,
    Чужих причуд истолкованье,
    Слов модных полный лексикон?..
    Уж не пародия ли он?

25 Ужель загадку разрешила?
    Ужели *слово* найдено?
    Часы бегут; она забыла,
    Что дома ждут ее давно,
    Где собралися два соседа
    И где об ней идет беседа.
    — Как быть? Татьяна не дитя, —
    Старушка молвила кряхтя. —
    Ведь Оленька ее моложе.
    Пристроить девушку, ей-ей,
    Пора; а что мне делать с ней?
    Всем наотрез одно и то же:
    Нейду. И всё грустит она,
    Да бродит по лесам одна.

23   Many pages still retained
the sharp imprint of fingernails.
Tatyána's observant eyes
fastened with livelier interest on these sections.
Her heart beat faster as she noted
the kind of thoughts and comments
that used to shock him,
and those he tacitly accepted.
In margins she encountered marks
he'd made in pencil.
Onégin had inadvertently throughout
given his personality expression
by here a brief word, here a cross,
and there a question mark.

24   And so Tatyána – God be thanked! –
began by stages
to understand more clearly
the man that an inexorable fate
had condemned her to desire.
This gloomy and dangerous maverick,
this creature of heaven or hell,
this angel, this arrogant demon –
what in truth *was* he? Could he be just
an imitation, an empty illusion, or maybe
a man from Moscow masquerading as Childe Harold,
an encyclopedia of other men's oddities,
a dictionary full of the latest clichés...
less copy than caricature?

25   Could it be that she'd solved the riddle?
Had she really discovered the key?
The hours sped by: Tatyána had forgotten
that she was long ago expected home.
A couple of neighbours had called,
and the conversation had turned to her.
"What's to be done? Tatyána's no child,"
old Mrs Larin was saying with a groan.
"Olga was younger than her, you know.
It's really time to get the girl settled.
But what's to be done with her? Tell me!
It's the same blunt answer she gives to all:
'I'm not getting married.' She's always moping
and roaming the woods on her own."

26 «Не влюблена ль она?» — В кого же?
Буянов сватался: отказ.
Ивану Петушкову — тоже.
Гусар Пыхтин гостил у нас;
Уж как он Танею прельщался,
Как мелким бесом рассыпался!
Я думала: пойдет авось;
Куда! и снова дело врозь. —
«Что ж, матушка? за чем же стало?
В Москву, на ярманку невест!
Там, слышно, много праздных мест». —
— Ох, мой отец! доходу мало. —
«Довольно для одной зимы,
Не то уж дам хоть я взаймы».

27 Старушка очень полюбила
Совет разумный и благой;
Сочлась — и тут же положила
В Москву отправиться зимой.
И Таня слышит новость эту.
На суд взыскательному свету
Представить ясные черты
Провинциальной простоты,
И запоздалые наряды,
И запоздалый склад речей;
Московских франтов и цирцей
Привлечь насмешливые взгляды!..
О страх! нет, лучше и верней
В глуши лесов остаться ей.

28 Вставая с первыми лучами,
Теперь она в поля спешит
И, умиленными очами
Их озирая, говорит:
«Простите, мирные долины,
И вы, знакомых гор вершины,
И вы, знакомые леса;
Прости, небесная краса,
Прости, веселая природа;
Меняю милый, тихий свет
На шум блистательных сует…
Прости ж и ты, моя свобода!
Куда, зачем стремлюся я?
Что мне сулит судьба моя?»

26   "She's not in love?" "Who with?
Buyánov proposed, and got turned down;
the same with Iván Petushkóv.
Pykhtín – the hussar – was staying here with us;
my word, how he fell for our Tanya –
couldn't let her alone, the young devil.
'Maybe it'll work,' I thought.
Work how! It all came apart once more!"
"Well, my dear, what's holding you back?
Off to Moscow you go – to the market of brides!
There are plenty of vacancies there, I'm told."
"Ach, my dear sir! On my small income!"
"It'll cover a single winter; if not, well,
I'll give you the money myself, on loan."

27   Such sensible, kindly advice
appealed greatly to Mrs Larin.
She did her sums – and on the spot decided
to leave for Moscow when winter came.
Tatyána heard this news with consternation.
Society set such demanding standards:
must she parade before it
the all-too-obvious marks
of her provincial lack of sophistication,
her dated clothes, her dated mode of speech?
Must she expose herself to the derisive stares
of Moscow's toffs and snobbish beauties?
No: better and safer to stay behind,
deep in her woodlands.

28   From this time on Tatyána
would rise with the sun's first rays
and hurry out into the fields.
There, gazing round her with emotion, she'd say,
"Goodbye, you peaceful dales;
goodbye, you hilltops and woods
I know so well!
Goodbye, you gorgeous sky
and cheerful countryside!
This quiet world I love I'm having to exchange
for the noise and glitter of an empty existence…
Goodbye to you too, my freedom, it's you I'll miss the most.
Where am I going, and what shall I find?
What does my destiny hold in store?"

29   Ее прогулки длятся доле.
Теперь то холмик, то ручей
Остановляют поневоле
Татьяну прелестью своей.
Она, как с давними друзьями,
С своими рощами, лугами
Еще беседовать спешит.
Но лето быстрое летит.
Настала осень золотая.
Природа трепетна, бледна,
Как жертва, пышно убрана...
Вот север, тучи нагоняя,
Дохнул, завыл — и вот сама
Идет волшебница зима.

30   Пришла, рассыпалась; клоками
Повисла на суках дубов;
Легла волнистыми коврами
Среди полей, вокруг холмов;
Брега с недвижною рекою
Сравняла пухлой пеленою;
Блеснул мороз. И рады мы
Проказам матушки зимы.
Не радо ей лишь сердце Тани.
Нейдет она зиму встречать,
Морозной пылью подышать
И первым снегом с кровли бани
Умыть лицо, плеча и грудь:
Татьяне страшен зимний путь.

31   Отъезда день давно просрочен,
Проходит и последний срок.
Осмотрен, вновь обит, упрочен
Забвенью брошенный возок.
Обоз обычный, три кибитки
Везут домашние пожитки,
Кастрюльки, стулья, сундуки,
Варенье в банках, тюфяки,
Перины, клетки с петухами,
Горшки, тазы et cetera,
Ну, много всякого добра.
И вот в избе между слугами
Поднялся шум, прощальный плач:
Ведут на двор осьмнадцать кляч,

29   Tatyána spent longer and longer on these walks.
She couldn't help constantly stopping
to admire the beauty
of hillside or stream.
She was eager to go on conversing
with her woods and her meadows,
as though with friends of long standing.
The brief summer sped by, though,
and golden autumn came.
Nature waited pale and trembling,
like a victim sumptuously arrayed for sacrifice…
Then came the north wind, driving the storm clouds,
gusting and howling – Winter the enchantress
was on her way in person.

30   On arrival she spread herself everywhere –
hung in clumps on the branches of oaks,
lay in undulating carpets
over fields and round hills,
and in a soft, thick shroud
made level the motionless river and banks.
Frosts sparkled. We all enjoy
Mother Winter's antics;
to Tatyána alone they brought no pleasure.
She wouldn't go out to greet the winter season,
breathe clouds of frosty air,
or take the first snow from the bathhouse roof
to wash face, shoulders and chest.
Tatyána was dreading her winter's journey.

31   The day of their departure was long postponed.
Even the "final deadline" passed.
The sledge coach, abandoned and long forgotten,
was inspected, reupholstered and made secure.
The usual convoy of three sledded wagons
was to carry the household paraphernalia:
saucepans, chairs, trunks,
mattresses, jars of jam,
feather beds, caged cockerels,
pots, bowls, et cetera –
plenty of everything, in fact.
Then in the outhouse a hubbub arose
of tearful farewells among the servants.
Eighteen scraggy mares were brought to the yard

32   В возок боярский их впрягают,
Готовят завтрак повара,
Горой кибитки нагружают,
Бранятся бабы, кучера.
На кляче тощей и косматой
Сидит форейтор бородатый.
Сбежалась челядь у ворот
Прощаться с барами. И вот
Уселись, и возок почтенный,
Скользя, ползет за ворота.
«Простите, мирные места!
Прости, приют уединенный!
Увижу ль вас?..» И слез ручей
У Тани льется из очей.

33   Когда благому просвещенью
Отдвинем более границ,
Со временем (по расчисленью
Философических таблиц,
Лет чрез пятьсот) дороги, верно,
У нас изменятся безмерно:
Шоссе Россию здесь и тут,
Соединив, пересекут.
Мосты чугунные чрез воды
Шагнут широкою дугой,
Раздвинем горы, под водой
Пророем дерзостные своды,
И заведет крещеный мир
На каждой станции трактир.

34   Теперь у нас дороги плохи,
Мосты забытые гниют,
На станциях клопы да блохи
Заснуть минуты не дают;
Трактиров нет. В избе холодной
Высокопарный, но голодный
Для виду прейскурант висит
И тщетный дразнит аппетит,
Меж тем как сельские циклопы
Перед медлительным огнем
Российским лечат молотком
Изделье легкое Европы,
Благословляя колеи
И рвы отеческой земли.

32   and harnessed to the manorial coach;
the cooks made breakfast;
the wagons were loaded mountain-high;
serf women and coachmen traded abuse.
Then the bearded team-driver took his seat
on a mare, a lean and shaggy beast;
and the house servants gathered excitedly at the gates
to wave their mistresses off.
The travellers had taken their seats, and the venerable coach
moved slowly and smoothly out of the yard.
"Farewell, secluded haunts!
Farewell, you refuge of tranquillity!
Shall I ever see you?..." and streams of tears
poured down Tatyána's cheeks.

33   As we extend the frontiers
of beneficent civilization,
in due time (to go by the tables
of learned statisticians,
it'll take five hundred years) – in due time, I'm quite sure,
our roads will undergo an enormous transformation.
Russia will be intersected and linked together
by a network of surfaced highways;
broad-spanned iron bridges
will stride across waters;
we'll push aside mountains; we'll boldly
dig tunnels under rivers;
and at every staging post in Christendom
we'll open restaurants.

34   As it is, our roads are bad;
our bridges are rotting from neglect;
and at staging posts the bugs and fleas
deny us a moment's sleep.
Restaurants are non-existent. In a cold shack
there may, for form's sake, hang a price list,
full of pretentious names; but, starved of the food to match,
it stimulates the appetite only to frustrate it.
Meanwhile the village blacksmiths work away
by a sluggish fire,
wielding a Russian hammer
to doctor the fragile workmanship of western Europe –
and heartily grateful they are
to their homeland's ruts and ditches!

35   Зато зимы порой холодной
      Езда приятна и легка.
      Как стих без мысли в песне модной,
      Дорога зимняя гладка.
      Автомедоны наши бойки,
      Неутомимы наши тройки,
      И версты, теша праздный взор,
      В глазах мелькают, как забор.
      К несчастью, Ларина тащилась,
      Боясь прогонов дорогих,
      Не на почтовых, на своих,
      И наша дева насладилась
      Дорожной скукою вполне:
      Семь суток ехали оне.

36   Но вот уж близко. Перед ними
      Уж белокаменной Москвы,
      Как жар, крестами золотыми
      Горят старинные главы.
      Ах, братцы! как я был доволен,
      Когда церквей и колоколен,
      Садов, чертогов полукруг
      Открылся предо мною вдруг!
      Как часто в горестной разлуке,
      В моей блуждающей судьбе,
      Москва, я думал о тебе!
      Москва… как много в этом звуке
      Для сердца русского слилось!
      Как много в нем отозвалось!

37   Вот, окружен своей дубравой,
      Петровский замок. Мрачно он
      Недавнею гордится славой.
      Напрасно ждал Наполеон,
      Последним счастьем упоенный,
      Москвы коленопреклоненной
      С ключами старого Кремля:
      Нет, не пошла Москва моя
      К нему с повинной головою.
      Не праздник, не приемный дар,
      Она готовила пожар
      Нетерпеливому герою.
      Отселе, в думу погружен,
      Глядел на грозный пламень он.

35   Driving in winter's cold, however,
is pleasant and easy.
Winter roads are as smooth
as a meaningless verse in a popular song;
our redoubtable coachmen are alert;
our three-horse teams are indefatigable;
and the mileposts catch the amused attention
of our vacant gaze as they flash past like palings!
Mrs Larin's progress, sadly, was slow:
for fear of costly transport charges
she used, not post horses, but her own.
Tatyána, though, enjoyed
the tedium of the journey to the full.
For seven whole days they travelled.

36   At length they were nearly there. Before them
lay Moscow, city of white stone,
its ancient domes
seemingly aflame with golden crosses.
Ah, friends, how pleased I was
when that semicircle of churches, bell towers,
gardens and palaces
opened up all at once before me!
So often during the sadness of exile,
during the wanderings imposed on me by fate,
I used to think of Moscow…
"Moscow!" – for the Russian soul
that name is a blend of so much,
holds *so* much resonance!

37   Look! There's Petróvsky castle,
in the midst of its oak wood,
sombrely proud of its new-won fame.
Napoleon, elated by his latest success,
had been waiting vainly
for Moscow to do him homage
and surrender the keys of the ancient Kremlin.
But no: my dear old Moscow
refused to abase herself;
and instead of a holiday or presentation
to honour the impatient victor,
she greeted him with a conflagration.
And so from here Napoleon watched and brooded
over the ominous flames.

38   Прощай, свидетель падшей славы,
     Петровский замок. Ну! не стой,
     Пошел! Уже столпы заставы
     Белеют: вот уж по Тверской
     Возок несется чрез ухабы.
     Мелькают мимо будки, бабы,
     Мальчишки, лавки, фонари,
     Дворцы, сады, монастыри,
     Бухарцы, сани, огороды,
     Купцы, лачужки, мужики,
     Бульвары, башни, казаки,
     Аптеки, магазины моды,
     Балконы, львы на воротах
     И стаи галок на крестах.

39   . . . .

40   В сей утомительной прогулке
     Проходит час-другой, и вот
     У Харитонья в переулке
     Возок пред домом у ворот
     Остановился. К старой тетке,
     Четвертый год больной в чахотке,
     Они приехали теперь.
     Им настежь отворяет дверь,
     В очках, в изорванном кафтане,
     С чулком в руке, седой калмык.
     Встречает их в гостиной крик
     Княжны, простертой на диване.
     Старушки с плачем обнялись,
     И восклицанья полились.

41   — Княжна, mon ange! — «Pachette!» — Алина! —
     «Кто б мог подумать? Как давно!
     Надолго ль? Милая! Кузина!
     Садись — как это мудрено!
     Ей-богу, сцена из романа…»
     — А это дочь моя, Татьяна. —
     «Ах, Таня! подойди ко мне —
     Как будто брежу я во сне…
     Кузина, помнишь Грандисона?»
     — Как, Грандисон?.. а, Грандисон!
     Да, помню, помню. Где же он? —
     «В Москве, живет у Симеона;
     Меня в сочельник навестил;
     Недавно сына он женил.

38   Goodbye, then, Petróvsky castle,
you witness to humbled pride! On, on!
We mustn't stop. The columns of the city checkpoint
are already showing white. And now the heavy sleigh's
juddering over Tverskáya Street's ruts.
Glimpses flash past of sentry boxes, serf women,
errand boys, market booths, street lamps,
palaces, gardens, monasteries,
Bukharan merchants, sledges, vegetable plots,
tradespeople, hovels, porters,
boulevards, towers, Cossacks,
chemist shops, fashion houses,
balconies, lion-topped gateways,
and flocks of jackdaws on church crosses.

39   ....

40   This exhausting drive across the city
took them an hour or two.
Then at last the carriage drew up
at the door of a house in St Kharitóny's Lane.
They'd arrived at the home of Tatyána's aunt,
an old lady who for the past three years
had been ill with consumption.
The door was thrown open before them
by a grey-haired Kalmuk servant,
stocking in hand, in glasses and tattered coat.
The princess, who lay in the drawing room
stretched out on a couch, greeted them both with a cry.
The two old ladies burst out in tears and embraced,
amid torrents of exclamations.

41   "Princess, *mon ange*!" "Pachette!" "Aline!"
"Who could have thought it?" "What a long time!"
"How long is it, now?" "My darling cousin!"
"Do sit down. Well, isn't this amazing!
Indeed to goodness, it's a scene from a novel!"
"And this is my daughter Tatyána."
"Ah, Tanya, come to me here.
I feel as though I'm dreaming, delirious…
Cousin, do you remember your hero 'Grandison'?"
"Who? Grandison?… Ah, 'Grandison'!
Yes, remember I do, I do! Where is he, then?"
"In Moscow here, he lives by St Simeon's.
He came to see me on Christmas Eve.
He recently married off his son.

42   А тот… но после всё расскажем,
Не правда ль? Всей ее родне
Мы Таню завтра же покажем.
Жаль, разъезжать нет мочи мне;
Едва, едва таскаю ноги.
Но вы замучены с дороги;
Пойдемте вместе отдохнуть…
Ох, силы нет… устала грудь…
Мне тяжела теперь и радость,
Не только грусть… душа моя,
Уж никуда не годна я…
Под старость жизнь такая гадость…»
И тут, совсем утомлена,
В слезах раскашлялась она.

43   Больной и ласки и веселье
Татьяну трогают; но ей
Нехорошо на новоселье,
Привыкшей к горнице своей.
Под занавескою шелковой
Не спится ей в постеле новой,
И ранний звон колоколов,
Предтеча утренних трудов,
Ее с постели подымает.
Садится Таня у окна.
Редеет сумрак; но она
Своих полей не различает:
Пред нею незнакомый двор,
Конюшня, кухня и забор.

44   И вот: по родственным обедам
Развозят Таню каждый день
Представить бабушкам и дедам
Ее рассеянную лень.
Родне, прибывшей издалеча,
Повсюду ласковая встреча,
И восклицанья, и хлеб-соль.
«Как Таня выросла! Давно ль
Я, кажется, тебя крестила?
А я так на руки брала!
А я так за уши драла!
А я так пряником кормила!»
И хором бабушки твердят:
«Как наши годы-то летят!»

42   Now, *he*... but let's tell all our stories later,
d'you agree? And then tomorrow
we'll show off Tanya to all her relations.
A shame I'm too weak to go out –
I can scarcely drag my legs along.
But you must be shattered after your journey;
let's all of us go and have a rest...
Oh, I've no strength... my chest's worn out...
I even find joy a burden these days,
let alone sorrow... My dear,
I'm fit for nothing now...
when you get old, life is so beastly..."
And at this point, completely exhausted,
she broke into coughing and wept.

43   Tatyána was very touched
by her ailing aunt's attentiveness and ebullience;
but she didn't take well to her new living quarters –
so attached was she to her own familiar bedroom.
Beneath the new bed's silken hangings
she couldn't sleep,
and she was up
as soon as the church bells' early tolling
heralded the morning's chores.
She'd sit down by the window;
but as the night's gloom thinned, she espied
not the countryside she loved,
but an unfamiliar yard,
a stable, kitchen and fence.

44   Each day Tatyána,
listless and abstracted,
was driven from family meal to family meal
to be introduced to grandmammas and grandpapas.
Mother and daughter were greeted everywhere
with effusions, exclamations, invitations
from the relatives they'd come so far to see.
"How Tanya's grown! Was it *so* long ago
that I stood godmother to you at your christening?"
"And to think I used to hold you in my arms like this!"
"And I used to tweak you by the ear like this!"
"And I used to feed you gingerbread like this!"
And a chorus of great-aunts and grandmammas
would chant in unison "My! How our years do fly!"

45   Но в них не видно перемены;
Всё в них на старый образец:
У тетушки княжны Елены
Всё тот же тюлевый чепец;
Всё белится Лукерья Львовна,
Всё то же лжет Любовь Петровна,
Иван Петрович так же глуп,
Семен Петрович так же скуп,
У Пелагеи Николавны
Всё тот же друг мосьё Финмуш,
И тот же шпиц, и тот же муж;
А он, всё клуба член исправный,
Всё так же смирен, так же глух
И так же ест и пьет за двух.

46   Их дочки Таню обнимают.
Младые грации Москвы
Сначала молча озирают
Татьяну с ног до головы;
Ее находят что-то странной,
Провинциальной и жеманной,
И что-то бледной и худой,
А впрочем очень недурной;
Потом, покорствуя природе,
Дружатся с ней, к себе ведут,
Целуют, нежно руки жмут,
Взбивают кудри ей по моде
И поверяют нараспев
Сердечны тайны, тайны дев,

47   Чужие и свои победы,
Надежды, шалости, мечты.
Текут невинные беседы
С прикрасой легкой клеветы.
Потом, в отплату лепетанья,
Ее сердечного признанья
Умильно требуют оне.
Но Таня, точно как во сне,
Их речи слышит без участья,
Не понимает ничего,
И тайну сердца своего,
Заветный клад и слез и счастья,
Хранит безмолвно между тем
И им не делится ни с кем.

45   One saw no change, though, in the authors of these remarks;
everything about them followed the age-old pattern.
Princess Yeléna – "Auntie" –
still wore the same tulle bonnet.
Old Lev's daughter Lukérya whitened her face still.
And from Pyótr's family, Lyubóv still told the same old lies,
Iván was the same old fool,
and Semyón the same old miser.
Pelagéya, Nikolái's daughter,
still had the same old friend Monsieur Finemouche,
the same Pomeranian terrier, and the same husband.
The husband, for his part, still a regular member of his club,
was still as long-suffering, still as deaf,
and still ate and drank enough for two.

46   Their daughters, the young Graces of Moscow,
having greeted Tatyána with a hug,
at first just looked her over
from head to foot in silence.
They found her rather odd,
provincial, straight-laced,
a trifle pale and thin,
but otherwise... not bad at all.
Later they let themselves behave more naturally:
they made friends, brought her to their rooms,
kissed her and squeezed her affectionately by the hand,
fluffed up her curls according to the fashion,
and in ecstatic tones confided to her
the secrets of their girlish hearts:

47   other girls' conquests and their own,
their hopes, their longings and their madcap schemes.
On poured their chatter,
embellished with a little scandal,
but innocent enough for all of that.
Soon they were trading on their intimacy
to press her to lay her own heart bare
in payment for their juvenile effusions.
But although Tatyána heard their talk,
it was like a dream: she didn't pay attention,
it made no sense to her.
She kept to herself the secret of her love.
Her sacred treasure of tears and joy
she shared with no one.

48   Татьяна вслушаться желает
В беседы, в общий разговор;
Но всех в гостиной занимает
Такой бессвязный, пошлый вздор;
Всё в них так бледно, равнодушно;
Они клевещут даже скучно;
В бесплодной сухости речей,
Расспросов, сплетен и вестей
Не вспыхнет мысли в целы сутки,
Хоть невзначай, хоть наобум;
Не улыбнется томный ум,
Не дрогнет сердце, хоть для шутки.
И даже глупости смешной
В тебе не встретишь, свет пустой.

49   Архивны юноши толпою
На Таню чопорно глядят
И про нее между собою
Неблагосклонно говорят.
Один какой-то шут печальный
Ее находит идеальной
И, прислонившись у дверей,
Элегию готовит ей.
У скучной тетки Таню встретя,
К ней как-то Вяземский подсел
И душу ей занять успел.
И, близ него ее заметя,
Об ней, поправя свой парик,
Осведомляется старик.

50   Но там, где Мельпомены бурной
Протяжный раздается вой,
Где машет мантией мишурной
Она пред хладною толпой,
Где Талия тихонько дремлет
И плескам дружеским не внемлет,
Где Терпсихоре лишь одной
Дивится зритель молодой
(Что было также в прежни леты,
Во время ваше и мое),
Не обратились на нее
Ни дам ревнивые лорнеты,
Ни трубки модных знатоков
Из лож и кресельных рядов.

48   Sometimes Tatyána tried to listen in
to the tête-à-têtes and general conversation.
But drawing rooms were wholly taken up
with the most inconsequential and paltry nonsense.
Insipidity and indifference were so pervasive
that even the scandal-mongering was apathetic.
In this arid wilderness of discourse,
questionings, slurs and revelations
you'd wait whole days for a spark of intelligent thought,
even one expressed unconsciously or accidentally;
there'd be no smile from those dull minds,
no tremor of response from those hearts – even to a joke.
So barren indeed is this social life of ours
that even its stupidity can't raise a laugh.

49   One time a group of Archive lads
kept eyeing Tatyána like connoisseurs,
and were ungentlemanly enough
to discuss her among themselves.
One sorry jester
found her "ideal"
and, leaning back against the doors,
began to write her a verse.
One day at the house of a tedious aunt of Tatyána's,
Vyázemsky chanced to sit beside her
and managed to engage her earnest attention.
Noticing them together, an elderly man
straightened his wig
and began to enquire about her.

50   But at the Moscow theatre it was different.
(There actors in tempestuous tragedies
utter protracted wails and wave
their brass-foil cloaks before an unmoved house;
there players act out comedies in a stupor,
oblivious to even well-disposed applause;
the only thing young audiences admire
is the dancing –
it was the same in earlier years,
in our time, yours and mine.)
Tatyána wasn't one, then, to attract
from stalls or boxes
either the opera glasses of modish womanizers
or the lorgnettes of jealous ladies.

51 Ее привозят и в Собранье.
Там теснота, волненье, жар,
Музыки грохот, свеч блистанье,
Мельканье, вихорь быстрых пар,
Красавиц легкие уборы,
Людьми пестреющие хоры,
Невест обширный полукруг,
Всё чувства поражает вдруг.
Здесь кажут франты записные
Свое нахальство, свой жилет
И невнимательный лорнет.
Сюда гусары отпускные
Спешат явиться, прогреметь,
Блеснуть, пленить и улететь.

52 У ночи много звезд прелестных,
Красавиц много на Москве.
Но ярче всех подруг небесных
Луна в воздушной синеве.
Но та, которую не смею
Тревожить лирою моею,
Как величавая луна,
Средь жен и дев блестит одна.
С какою гордостью небесной
Земли касается она!
Как негой грудь ее полна!
Как томен взор ее чудесный!..
Но полно, полно; перестань:
Ты заплатил безумству дань.

53 Шум, хохот, беготня, поклоны,
Галоп, мазурка, вальс… Меж тем,
Между двух теток у колонны,
Не замечаема никем,
Татьяна смотрит и не видит,
Волненье света ненавидит;
Ей душно здесь… она мечтой
Стремится к жизни полевой,
В деревню, к бедным поселянам,
В уединенный уголок,
Где льется светлый ручеек,
К своим цветам, к своим романам
И в сумрак липовых аллей,
Туда, где *он* являлся ей.

51   Tatyána was taken to the Assembly too.
Packed crowds; excitement; heat;
the blare of music, glare of candles;
twirling couples flashing by;
lovely women in delicate dresses;
galleries colourful with people;
a sweeping arc of marriageable girls –
all this is what suddenly assailed her senses.
Men from the smartest set were there,
flaunting their swagger and their waistcoats
and their unheeding eyeglasses.
Hussars on leave, too,
dashed in to be seen,
to dazzle like lightning, set thunder a-rolling,
captivate hearts, and fly off.

52   The night holds many lovely stars,
and Moscow many lovely women.
But brighter than all her celestial companions
in the indigo firmament is the moon.
And like a majestic moon,
she whom I dare not
distress with my verses
shines out uniquely among women and girls.
She condescends to walk on earth,
but retains a heavenly dignity;
her bosom heaves with sensual delight;
and her wonderful eyes are languorous to perfection…
But enough, quite enough! You must stop:
You've paid your folly its due.

53   On went the noise, the laughter, the scampering,
the greetings, the gallop, mazurka and waltz… Meanwhile
Tatyána stood by a pillar between two aunts,
noticed by no one.
She looked on, seeing nothing.
How she loathed this society frenzy!
She felt stifled here… and her imagination
transported her quickly back to her life in the country –
to family estate, poor villagers,
secluded dell
and sparkling brook,
her flowers, her novels,
and shaded avenues of limes –
the very place where *he*'d confronted her.

54   Так мысль ее далече бродит:
Забыт и свет и шумный бал,
А глаз меж тем с нее не сводит
Какой-то важный генерал.
Друг другу тетушки мигнули
И локтем Таню враз толкнули,
И каждая шепнула ей:
— Взгляни налево поскорей. —
«Налево? где? что там такое?»
— Ну, что бы ни было, гляди…
В той кучке, видишь? впереди,
Там, где еще в мундирах двое…
Вот отошел… вот боком стал… —
«Кто? толстый этот генерал?»

55   Но здесь с победою поздравим
Татьяну милую мою
И в сторону свой путь направим,
Чтоб не забыть, о ком пою…
Да кстати, здесь о том два слова:
Пою приятеля младого
И множество его причуд.
Благослови мой долгий труд,
О ты, эпическая муза!
И, верный посох мне вручив,
Не дай блуждать мне вкось и вкрив.
Довольно. С плеч долой обуза!
Я классицизму отдал честь:
Хоть поздно, а вступленье есть.

54   So her thoughts wandered far afield;
smart company and noisy ball were lost to mind.
Meanwhile an impressive-looking general
had been intently staring at Tatyána.
The two aunts traded winks
and nudged her both at once.
Each whispered:
"Quick, quick! Look to the left."
"Left? Where? What's there?"
"Never mind, just look…
in that group, see? In front there,
where there are two more men in uniform…
He's walked away now… Look, now he's turned sideways…"
"Who? That stout general?"…

55   But here we must congratulate
my dear Tatyána on her conquest,
and turn our steps elsewhere,
lest we forget the subject of this epic.
So here's a word or two about him now:
'Tis of a friend I sing, a young friend and his
                    [vagaries legion:
Goddess, thou who of epic verse art patron, a blessing
Grant on this labour of years. With thy faithful staff
                    [now entrust me,
So that I may not wander awry…
Enough! That takes a load from off my shoulders!
I've now invoked the classical tradition –
it may be late, but we've a prologue.

ГЛАВА ОСЬМАЯ

Fare thee well! and if for ever,
Still for ever fare thee well.

—*Byron*

1 В те дни, когда в садах Лицея
   Я безмятежно расцветал,
   Читал охотно Апулея,
   А Цицерона не читал,
   В те дни в таинственных долинах,
   Весной, при кликах лебединых,
   Близ вод, сиявших в тишине,
   Являться муза стала мне.
   Моя студенческая келья
   Вдруг озарилась: муза в ней
   Открыла пир младых затей,
   Воспела детские веселья,
   И славу нашей старины,
   И сердца трепетные сны.

2 И свет ее с улыбкой встретил;
   Успех нас первый окрылил;
   Старик Державин нас заметил
   И, в гроб сходя, благословил.
   ....
   ....
   ....
   ....
   ....
   ....
   ....
   ....
   ....
   ....

CHAPTER EIGHT

Fare thee well! and if for ever,
Still for ever fare thee well.
                                                                    – Byron

1   It was one springtime, in secluded dells
where I could hear the call of swans
and see nearby the gleam of placid waters
that my goddess Inspiration first appeared to me.
Those were the days when I was quietly
opening into flower in the Lyceum park,
eagerly reading Apuleius,
but shirking Cicero.
Then my bare student's room
was suddenly filled with light: my goddess
spread a rich banquet there of youthful inventiveness,
and began to sing of the joys of boyhood,
of the glory of Russia's past,
and of dreams to make the heart throb.

2   The wider world gave her a smiling welcome,
and our early successes lent us wings.
The elderly Derzhávin noticed us
and gave us his blessing as he went down to the grave.

....
....
....
....
....
....
....
....
....
....

3 И я, в закон себе вменяя
   Страстей единый произвол,
   С толпою чувства разделяя,
   Я музу резвую привел
   На шум пиров и буйных споров,
   Грозы полуночных дозоров;
   И к ним в безумные пиры
   Она несла свои дары
   И как вакханочка резвилась,
   За чашей пела для гостей,
   И молодежь минувших дней
   За нею буйно волочилась –
   А я гордился меж друзей
   Подругой ветреной моей.

4 Но я отстал от их союза
   И вдаль бежал… Она за мной.
   Как часто ласковая муза
   Мне услаждала путь немой
   Волшебством тайного рассказа!
   Как часто по скалам Кавказа
   Она Ленорой, при луне,
   Со мной скакала на коне!
   Как часто по брегам Тавриды
   Она меня во мгле ночной
   Водила слушать шум морской,
   Немолчный шепот Нереиды,
   Глубокий, вечный хор валов,
   Хвалебный гимн Отцу миров.

5 И, позабыв столицы дальной
   И блеск и шумные пиры,
   В глуши Молдавии печальной
   Она смиренные шатры
   Племен бродящих посещала,
   И между ними одичала,
   И позабыла речь богов
   Для скудных, странных языков,
   Для песен степи, ей любезной…
   Вдруг изменилось всё кругом,
   И вот она в саду моем
   Явилась барышней уездной,
   С печальной думою в очах,
   С французской книжкою в руках.

3   In those days the capricious prompting of emotion
was the only law I recognized;
my loves and hates I shared with everyone.
I introduced my sprightly goddess
to the noise of banquets and rowdy quarrels –
and to cautions from patrols at midnight.
To those frequenting these wild parties
she brought her gifts:
she'd cast off inhibition like a young bacchante,
and after a glass of wine she'd sing for the company,
while the young bloods of yesteryear
paid her their boisterous attentions.
And I was proud to show off to my friends
this breezy lady love of mine.

4   But I gave up this kind of gathering
and fled to distant parts, my goddess with me,
and many a time, in her engaging way,
she cheered my lonely journey
with the enchantment of a mysterious tale;
many a time
she galloped with me on horseback, like Lenore,
along the moonlit crags of the Caucasus;
and many a time
she led me deep at night by the Crimean shore
to listen to the murmur of the sea,
the never-silent whispering of the Nereids,
the deep and age-long chorus of the breakers,
hymning the Father of the universe.

5   By now she'd driven from mind the distant capital,
its brilliance and its noisy revelry.
In Moldavia's dreary remoteness
she used to visit
the lowly encampments of wandering tribes;
there she became a wild creature,
and forgetting the language of the gods
she picked up in its place strange, rudimentary tongues
and learnt songs of the steppe lands, her new home.
And then a sudden change of scene:
she turned up in my garden
in the guise of a country squire's daughter;
in her eyes was a look of pensive sadness,
and in her hands a novelette in French.

6   И ныне музу я впервые
На светский раут привожу;
На прелести ее степные
С ревнивой робостью гляжу.
Сквозь тесный ряд аристократов,
Военных франтов, дипломатов
И гордых дам она скользит;
Вот села тихо и глядит,
Любуясь шумной теснотою,
Мельканьем платьев и речей,
Явленьем медленным гостей
Перед хозяйкой молодою
И темной рамою мужчин
Вкруг дам, как около картин.

7   Ей нравится порядок стройный
Олигархических бесед,
И холод гордости спокойной,
И эта смесь чинов и лет.
Но это кто в толпе избранной
Стоит безмолвный и туманный?
Для всех он кажется чужим.
Мелькают лица перед ним
Как ряд докучных привидений.
Что, сплин иль страждущая спесь
В его лице? Зачем он здесь?
Кто он таков? Ужель Евгений?
Ужели он?.. Так, точно он.
— Давно ли к нам он занесен?

8   Всё тот же ль он иль усмирился?
Иль корчит также чудака?
Скажите: чем он возвратился?
Что нам представит он пока?
Чем ныне явится? Мельмотом,
Космополитом, патриотом,
Гарольдом, квакером, ханжой,
Иль маской щегольнет иной,
Иль просто будет добрый малый,
Как вы да я, как целый свет?
По крайней мере мой совет:
Отстать от моды обветшалой.
Довольно он морочил свет…
— Знаком он вам? — И да и нет.

6 Today's the first time that I'm bringing
 my goddess to a smart soirée.
 Hers is the austere beauty of the wilds,
 and I'm watching her with jealous apprehension
 as she glides between the crowded ranks
 of aristocrats and foppish officers,
 of diplomats and haughty ladies.
 Quietly seated now, she's looking
 in delighted wonder at the noisy throng,
 at the quick-shifting brilliance of dresses and chatter,
 at the slow-moving line of guests
 waiting to greet the young hostess,
 and at the dark-clad menfolk surrounding the ladies,
 like a frame around a picture.

7 She likes the formalized, harmonious talk
 of this exclusive company,
 its cool, unruffled self-assurance,
 its mingling of rank and age.
 But in this privileged throng one man
 is standing sombre and taciturn. Who is he?
 To everyone he seems a stranger.
 The faces that flash past him –
 they're like a set of troubling phantoms.
 His own expression – is it peevishness,
 or pained presumption? Why is he here?
 Who can he be? "It's not Eugene, is it?
 It can't be, surely?" Yes, it's really him.
 "So the wind's blown him back here! How long since?

8 "Is he the same still? Has he mellowed now?
 Or does he still pose as the maverick? Tell me –
 what role has he assumed for his return?
 What performance will he treat us to this season?
 What part will he play now? Melmoth the Wanderer?
 Childe Harold? Man of the world, or nationalist?
 Dissenter, or bigot?
 Or is there another mask he'll flaunt?
 Or will he now be just a decent chap,
 like you and me and all the rest of us?
 Well, *my* advice is this:
 drop those outmoded affectations.
 He's fooled the world enough."
 You know him, then? "Well, yes and no."

9   — Зачем же так неблагосклонно
Вы отзываетесь о нем?
За то ль, что мы неугомонно
Хлопочем, судим обо всем,
Что пылких душ неосторожность
Самолюбивую ничтожность
Иль оскорбляет, иль смешит,
Что ум, любя простор, теснит,
Что слишком часто разговоры
Принять мы рады за дела,
Что глупость ветрена и зла,
Что важным людям важны вздоры
И что посредственность одна
Нам по плечу и не странна?

10   Блажен, кто смолоду был молод,
Блажен, кто вовремя созрел,
Кто постепенно жизни холод
С летами вытерпеть умел;
Кто странным снам не предавался,
Кто черни светской не чуждался,
Кто в двадцать лет был франт иль хват,
А в тридцать выгодно женат;
Кто в пятьдесят освободился
От частных и других долгов,
Кто славы, денег и чинов
Спокойно в очередь добился,
О ком твердили целый век:
N. N. прекрасный человек.

11   Но грустно думать, что напрасно
Была нам молодость дана,
Что изменяли ей всечасно,
Что обманула нас она;
Что наши лучшие желанья,
Что наши свежие мечтанья
Истлели быстрой чередой,
Как листья осенью гнилой.
Несносно видеть пред собою
Одних обедов длинный ряд,
Глядеть на жизнь, как на обряд,
И вслед за чинною толпою
Идти, не разделяя с ней
Ни общих мнений, ни страстей.

9 Then why do you sound off
 so harshly about him?
 We never tire – do we? – of making trouble
 and criticizing all we can.
 Fiery natures are prone to indiscretions,
 and it's only self-righteous nonentities
 that find these funny or offensive.
 Intelligence relishes freedom, resents restraint.
 We're too often happy to take a rumour for fact:
 fools enjoy flippancy and malice,
 and the more self-important we are
 the more importance we give to such rubbish.
 Content with mediocrity ourselves,
 mediocrity's all we recognize elsewhere.

10 It's a lucky man who's young when he's young,
 who reaches maturity at the proper time,
 and who learns by stages to endure
 with the passing years life's chilling numbness;
 who's not surrendered to outlandish fancies
 nor fallen foul of society's scum.
 At twenty, daredevil or dandy;
 by thirty, profitably married;
 by fifty he's disengaged himself
 from all obligations, private or otherwise.
 He's quietly taken it in his turn
 to win reputation, money and rank;
 and all his life they've kept repeating
 that "so-and-so's a first-rate chap".

11 It's wretched to realize, on the other hand,
 that the gift of youth's been wasted on us,
 that we've repeatedly abused it,
 that *it* has disappointed us,
 and that our noblest aspirations,
 our purest dreams, in quick succession
 have mouldered away,
 like rotting autumn leaves.
 It's insupportable to see nothing ahead
 but a long round of dinners,
 view life as no more than a ritual,
 and trail along behind the respectable throng,
 though we share with them
 no common views or feelings.

12   Предметом став суждений шумных,
        Несносно (согласитесь в том)
        Между людей благоразумных
        Прослыть притворным чудаком,
        Или печальным сумасбродом,
        Иль сатаническим уродом,
        Иль даже демоном моим.
        Онегин (вновь займуся им),
        Убив на поединке друга,
        Дожив без цели, без трудов
        До двадцати шести годов,
        Томясь в бездействии досуга
        Без службы, без жены, без дел,
        Ничем заняться не умел.

13   Им овладело беспокойство,
        Охота к перемене мест
        (Весьма мучительное свойство,
        Немногих добровольный крест).
        Оставил он свое селенье,
        Лесов и нив уединенье,
        Где окровавленная тень
        Ему являлась каждый день,
        И начал странствия без цели,
        Доступный чувству одному;
        И путешествия ему,
        Как всё на свете, надоели;
        Он возвратился и попал,
        Как Чацкий, с корабля на бал.

14   Но вот толпа заколебалась,
        По зале шепот пробежал…
        К хозяйке дама приближалась,
        За нею важный генерал.
        Она была нетороплива,
        Не холодна, не говорлива,
        Без взора наглого для всех,
        Без притязаний на успех,
        Без этих маленьких ужимок,
        Без подражательных затей…
        Всё тихо, просто было в ней,
        Она казалась верный снимок
        Du comme il faut… (Шишков, прости:
        Не знаю, как перевести.)

12 It's insupportable too, you must agree,
  to be the subject of noisy condemnation
  and to be known even to reasonable folk
  as a counterfeit crank,
  pathetic madman,
  satanic monster,
  or even the Demon I once wrote about.
  Onégin – I'm returning to him now! –
  had killed his friend in a duel;
  he'd lived an aimless, idle life
  till the age of twenty-six;
  with no official post, no wife, no business,
  his empty leisure had wearied him,
  but there was nothing he could find to do.

13 A restlessness possessed him,
  a longing for a change of scene
  (a painful condition, this, indeed –
  a cross that few bear of their own free will).
  So he left his estate,
  the seclusion of those woods and fields,
  where daily a bloodstained ghost
  had haunted him;
  and, assailed by one emotion only,
  he embarked on undirected travels.
  But he grew sick of travelling too,
  as of all else on earth.
  So he returned, and found his way,
  like Chatsky, straight from ship to ball.

14 A sudden stir among the assembled guests!
  A whisper ran around the reception room.
  A lady was approaching the hostess,
  escorted by an impressive general.
  Her manner was neither bustling nor frigid;
  she was not one to chatter,
  or stare contemptuously at the company,
  or claim attention to herself,
  or use mysterious grimaces
  or imitative mannerisms.
  She was completely calm and natural.
  She seemed a true example
  of *comme il faut*. (Purists, forgive me:
  I don't know what that is in Russian.)

15   К ней дамы подвигались ближе;
     Старушки улыбались ей;
     Мужчины кланялися ниже,
     Ловили взор ее очей;
     Девицы проходили тише
     Пред ней по зале, и всех выше
     И нос и плечи подымал
     Вошедший с нею генерал.
     Никто б не мог ее прекрасной
     Назвать; но с головы до ног
     Никто бы в ней найти не мог
     Того, что модой самовластной
     В высоком лондонском кругу
     Зовется *vulgar*. (Не могу…

16   Люблю я очень это слово,
     Но не могу перевести;
     Оно у нас покамест ново,
     И вряд ли быть ему в чести.
     Оно б годилось в эпиграмме…)
     Но обращаюсь к нашей даме.
     Беспечной прелестью мила,
     Она сидела у стола
     С блестящей Ниной Воронскою,
     Сей Клеопатрою Невы;
     И верно б согласились вы,
     Что Нина мраморной красою
     Затмить соседку не могла,
     Хоть ослепительна была.

17   «Ужели, — думает Евгений: —
     Ужель она? Но точно… Нет…
     Как! из глуши степных селений…»
     И неотвязчивый лорнет
     Он обращает поминутно
     На ту, чей вид напомнил смутно
     Ему забытые черты.
     «Скажи мне, князь, не знаешь ты,
     Кто там в малиновом берете
     С послом испанским говорит?»
     Князь на Онегина глядит.
     — Ага! давно ж ты не был в свете.
     Постой, тебя представлю я. —
     «Да кто ж она?» — Жена моя. —

15   Women were drawn in her direction;
old ladies gave her smiles;
men made her deeper bows
and strove to catch her eye;
young girls who moved across the room
lowered their voices as they passed.
The general with her held his head
and shoulders higher than the rest.
No one could say she was a beauty;
but nor could anyone find in her
a single thing, from head to toe,
that in the highest London circles
it's fashionable – and so compulsory –
to label *vulgar*. (Apologies again!...

16   It's a word I'm awfully fond of,
but I can't translate it into Russian.
With us it's still a new expression,
not quite acceptable as yet –
good word, though, for an epigram...)
But I must get back to that lady –
her spontaneous charm alone made her attractive.
She was sitting at a table
with splendid Nina Voronskáya,
the Nevá's response to Cleopatra;
yet there's no doubt, you know, that Nina,
bedazzling as she was
with a beauty as of marble,
was quite unable to outshine her.

17   "Surely..." Onégin had been thinking,
"it's surely not her? But it's exactly... No... It can't be!
From that little place buried deep in the wilds!..."
And every few moments he trained
his inquisitive eyeglass onto the woman
whose features brought back troubling recollections
of a face that he'd forgotten.
"Prince, tell me: I don't suppose you know
who that is in the raspberry beret there,
conversing with the Spanish envoy?"
The prince looked at Onégin in surprise:
"Aha! You *have* been out of touch a long time!
Wait here, I'll introduce you."
"Who is she though?" "My wife."

18   «Так ты женат! не знал я ране!
Давно ли?» — Около двух лет. —
«На ком?» — На Лариной. — «Татьяне!»
— Ты ей знаком? — «Я им сосед».
— О, так пойдем же. — Князь подходит
К своей жене и ей подводит
Родню и друга своего.
Княгиня смотрит на него…
И что ей душу ни смутило,
Как сильно ни была она
Удивлена, поражена,
Но ей ничто не изменило:
В ней сохранился тот же тон,
Был так же тих ее поклон.

19   Ей-ей! не то, чтоб содрогнулась
Иль стала вдруг бледна, красна…
У ней и бровь не шевельнулась;
Не сжала даже губ она.
Хоть он глядел нельзя прилежней,
Но и следов Татьяны прежней
Не мог Онегин обрести.
С ней речь хотел он завести
И — и не мог. Она спросила,
Давно ль он здесь, откуда он
И не из их ли уж сторон?
Потом к супругу обратила
Усталый взгляд; скользнула вон…
И недвижим остался он.

20   Ужель та самая Татьяна,
Которой он наедине,
В начале нашего романа,
В глухой, далекой стороне,
В благом пылу нравоученья,
Читал когда-то наставленья,
Та, от которой он хранит
Письмо, где сердце говорит,
Где всё наруже, всё на воле,
Та девочка… иль это сон?..
Та девочка, которой он
Пренебрегал в смиренной доле,
Ужели с ним сейчас была
Так равнодушна, так смела?

18   "You're married, then! I didn't know.
For how long now?" "A couple of years."
"And who is she?" "A Larin." "Not Tatyána?"
"You know each other?" "I'm their neighbour."
"Well, come along then." And the prince approached
his wife and introduced Onégin to her
as a relation and a friend.
The princess looked at him…
but, whatever the turmoil in her heart,
however violent
her surprise and shock,
she showed no outward sign.
Her poise remained unruffled as before,
as did the manner of her greeting.

19   Indeed, there was no fit of trembling,
no turning suddenly white or red,
nor did she flicker an eyelid,
nor even compress her lips.
Onégin watched her with the utmost care,
but he found not the faintest trace
of the old Tatyána. He attempted
to open a conversation with her, but –
but something wouldn't let him. She enquired
if he'd been long in town, and where he'd come from –
was it perhaps from their part of the country?
And then she gave her husband
a look that said "I'm tired", and slipped away –
leaving Onégin rooted to the spot.

20   This wasn't the same Tatyána, surely,
that once, at the beginning of our novel,
he'd had that private meeting with
in those benighted, far-off parts
and in a fit of good intentions
had treated to that moralizing lecture?
This wasn't the Tatyána, surely, whose letter he still kept
– that letter in which the heart had spoken,
that letter free of reserve and inhibition?
The little girl – or was he dreaming? –
that little girl of humble circumstance
that he had disregarded –
surely it wasn't her who'd just conversed
in so offhand, so unabashed a manner?

21   Он оставляет раут тесный,
Домой задумчив едет он;
Мечтой то грустной, то прелестной
Его встревожен поздний сон.
Проснулся он; ему приносят
Письмо: князь N покорно просит
Его на вечер. «Боже! к ней!..
О буду, буду!» и скорей
Марает он ответ учтивый.
Что с ним? в каком он странном сне!
Что шевельнулось в глубине
Души холодной и ленивой?
Досада? суетность? иль вновь
Забота юности — любовь?

22   Онегин вновь часы считает,
Вновь не дождется дню конца.
Но десять бьет; он выезжает,
Он полетел, он у крыльца,
Он с трепетом к княгине входит;
Татьяну он одну находит,
И вместе несколько минут
Они сидят. Слова нейдут
Из уст Онегина. Угрюмый,
Неловкий, он едва-едва
Ей отвечает. Голова
Его полна упрямой думой.
Упрямо смотрит он: она
Сидит покойна и вольна.

23   Приходит муж. Он прерывает
Сей неприятный *tête-à-tête*;
С Онегиным он вспоминает
Проказы, шутки прежних лет.
Они смеются. Входят гости.
Вот крупной солью светской злости
Стал оживляться разговор;
Перед хозяйкой легкий вздор
Сверкал без глупого жеманства,
И прерывал его меж тем
Разумный толк без пошлых тем,
Без вечных истин, без педантства,
И не пугал ничьих ушей
Свободной живостью своей.

21   He left the crowded gathering
and rode home deep in thought. It took him long
to get to sleep that night, and when sleep came
it was disturbed by fantasies now gloomy, now seductive.
On waking he was brought
a letter: the Prince X humbly begged his presence
at a soirée. "Good God! At *her* place!
Oh yes, I'll go, I'll go!" In haste
he scribbled a polite reply.
What dream was this, unsettling and strange?
What was it that had stirred deep down
in that cold, sluggish soul of his?
Vexation? Vanity? Or a return
of the youthful ailment, love?

22   Once more Onégin found himself counting the hours;
once more he couldn't wait for the day to end.
At last ten struck, and off he drove.
He flew at top speed, he reached the porch
and with thumping heart went in to see the princess.
He found Tatyána alone,
and for a few short minutes
they sat together. But from Onégin's lips
words wouldn't come: his manner
was surly and maladroit; he scarcely
made her a single answer. His head
was full of one obstinate thought;
and obstinately though he stared at her,
she sat on, calmly and at ease.

23   Her husband approached, and terminated
this awkward tête-à-tête;
he and Onégin exchanged reminiscences
of amusing escapades of former years,
and soon they were laughing. Other guests arrived,
and now a strong seasoning of social gossip
began to liven up the conversation.
In the hostess's circle the tittle-tattle,
sparkling and light-hearted, was free of silly coyness;
it even gave way from time to time
to thoughtful discussion that avoided hackneyed topics,
unvarying platitudes and intellectual displays,
nor did it cause alarm to those who heard it,
for all its unconstrained vivacity.

24   Тут был, однако, цвет столицы,
     И знать, и моды образцы,
     Везде встречаемые лицы,
     Необходимые глупцы;
     Тут были дамы пожилые
     В чепцах и в розах, с виду злые;
     Тут было несколько девиц,
     Не улыбающихся лиц;
     Тут был посланник, говоривший
     О государственных делах;
     Тут был в душистых сединах
     Старик, по-старому шутивший:
     Отменно тонко и умно,
     Что нынче несколько смешно.

25   Тут был на эпиграммы падкий,
     На всё сердитый господин:
     На чай хозяйский слишком сладкий,
     На плоскость дам, на тон мужчин,
     На толки про роман туманный,
     На вензель, двум сестрицам данный,
     На ложь журналов, на войну,
     На снег и на свою жену.
     . . . .
     . . . .
     . . . .
     . . . .
     . . . .
     . . . .

26   Тут был Проласов, заслуживший
     Известность низостью души,
     Во всех альбомах притупивший,
     St.-Priest, твои карандаши;
     В дверях другой диктатор бальный
     Стоял картинкою журнальной,
     Румян, как вербный херувим,
     Затянут, нем и недвижим,
     И путешественник залётный,
     Перекрахмаленный нахал,
     В гостях улыбку возбуждал
     Своей осанкою заботной,
     И молча обмененный взор
     Ему был общий приговор.

24   Yet this was the flower of Petersburg society –
aristocrats and paragons of fashion,
the faces one meets everywhere,
the fools one can't avoid.
Some ladies past their prime were present,
in bonnets and roses, spiteful-looking;
there were some girls
with lips that never smiled;
an ambassador, too, was there
discoursing about politics,
and an old man with perfumed greying hair,
who told jokes in the old way –
with that exquisite subtlety and wit
that's these days slightly ludicrous.

25   There was there too a gentleman
addicted to aphorisms, angry at everything –
his hosts' excessively sweet tea,
the manners of the men, the ladies' dullness,
the talk about some gloomy novel,
the badge awarded to two little sisters,
the lies in newspapers, the war,
the snow, the foibles of his wife.
. . . .
. . . .
. . . .
. . . .
. . . .
. . . .

26   Prolásov was there, deservedly notorious
for his mean-spiritedness,
whose caricatures in every album
had blunted all the pencils of Saint-Priest.
In a doorway another doyen of the ballrooms
was standing like a fashion plate –
pink as a pussy-willow cherub,
tight-waisted, dumb and motionless.
One man had dropped in from his travels:
over-starched swank he was;
he raised a smile among the guests
by his exaggerated deportment,
and the silent look they all exchanged
was the verdict that they reached on him.

27   Но мой Онегин вечер целый
Татьяной занят был одной,
Не этой девочкой несмелой,
Влюбленной, бедной и простой,
Но равнодушною княгиней,
Но неприступною богиней
Роскошной, царственной Невы.
О люди! все похожи вы
На прародительницу Эву:
Что вам дано, то не влечет,
Вас непрестанно змий зовет
К себе, к таинственному древу;
Запретный плод вам подавай:
А без того вам рай не рай.

28   Как изменилася Татьяна!
Как твердо в роль свою вошла!
Как утеснительного сана
Приемы скоро приняла!
Кто б смел искать девчонки нежной
В сей величавой, в сей небрежной
Законодательнице зал?
И он ей сердце волновал!
Об нем она во мраке ночи,
Пока Морфей не прилетит,
Бывало, девственно грустит,
К луне подъемлет томны очи,
Мечтая с ним когда-нибудь
Свершить смиренный жизни путь!

29   Любви все возрасты покорны;
Но юным, девственным сердцам
Ее порывы благотворны,
Как бури вешние полям:
В дожде страстей они свежеют,
И обновляются, и зреют —
И жизнь могущая дает
И пышный цвет и сладкий плод.
Но в возраст поздний и бесплодный,
На повороте наших лет,
Печален страсти мертвой след:
Так бури осени холодной
В болото обращают луг
И обнажают лес вокруг.

27   Onégin's interest, though, the evening long
was concentrated on Tatyána –
not on the poor, shy, plain
little-girl-in-love,
but on the imperturbable princess
presiding with sublime aloofness
over the imperial city's high society.
You folk are all so very like
your first ancestress Eve:
that which you're given doesn't take your fancy.
The serpent's always calling you
to come to him, to the mysterious tree.
You *must* have the forbidden fruit,
or paradise isn't paradise for you.

28   Tatyána had undergone an amazing change.
She'd entered wholeheartedly into her new role,
and was already quite at ease
with the constricting conventions of her rank.
Who'd have looked for an impressionable young girl
in one who dominated Petersburg salons
with such great dignity and self-possession?
Yet this was the woman Onégin once
had thrown into emotional turmoil!
Because of him she'd lain fretfully in the dark at night,
as girls will, waiting for sleep to come,
turning her weary eyes towards the moon,
and dreaming of one day living out
a humble life with him.

29   There's no age at which we're immune to love.
To hearts that are young and pure,
love's ecstasies are beneficial,
like storms in springtime to the fields.
In the rain of emotion a young heart finds refreshment,
renews itself and grows to ripeness.
Life strengthened thus
produces luxuriant blooms, delicious fruit.
If passion, though, comes late, when years are barren
and life is in decline,
it brings a grim and deathly transformation,
like chilling storms of autumn
that turn the meadows to a quagmire
and strip bare the surrounding woods.

30 Сомненья нет: увы! Евгений
     В Татьяну как дитя влюблен;
     В тоске любовных помышлений
     И день и ночь проводит он.
     Ума не внемля строгим пеням,
     К ее крыльцу, стеклянным сеням
     Он подъезжает каждый день;
     За ней он гонится как тень;
     Он счастлив, если ей накинет
     Боа пушистый на плечо,
     Или коснется горячо
     Ее руки, или раздвинет
     Пред нею пестрый полк ливрей,
     Или платок подымет ей.

31 Она его не замечает,
     Как он ни бейся, хоть умри.
     Свободно дома принимает,
     В гостях с ним молвит слова три,
     Порой одним поклоном встретит,
     Порою вовсе не заметит:
     Кокетства в ней ни капли нет —
     Его не терпит высший свет.
     Бледнеть Онегин начинает:
     Ей иль не видно, иль не жаль;
     Онегин сохнет — и едва ль
     Уж не чахоткою страдает.
     Все шлют Онегина к врачам,
     Те хором шлют его к водам.

32 А он не едет; он заране
     Писать ко прадедам готов
     О скорой встрече; а Татьяне
     И дела нет (их пол таков);
     А он упрям, отстать не хочет,
     Еще надеется, хлопочет;
     Смелей здорового, больной,
     Княгине слабою рукой
     Он пишет страстное посланье.
     Хоть толку мало вообще
     Он в письмах видел не вотще;
     Но, знать, сердечное страданье
     Уже пришло ему невмочь.
     Вот вам письмо его точь-в-точь.

30   The unhappy truth was not in doubt: Onégin
had fallen in love with Tatyána like a youngster.
He spent his days and nights
in anguished dreams of love.
Heedless of reason's stern reproaches,
he drove up every day
to the steps of her house, her glazed-in entrance porch.
He chased her like a shadow,
and was happy if he could merely place
a fluffy boa round her shoulders,
or give her hand an ardent touch, or clear
her way through a motley troop of footmen,
or pick up a handkerchief she'd dropped.

31   Tatyána paid him no attention,
for all his desperate antics.
At home she received whoever came.
When out, she might exchange two words with him;
sometimes she'd greet him with a single nod;
sometimes she utterly ignored him.
No vestige of flirtatiousness was in her –
the highest circles do not stand for that.
Onégin began to look quite pale,
but Tatyána didn't see, or didn't mind.
He also lost a lot of weight; it seemed
he might be suffering from consumption.
Everyone recommended doctors;
and doctors all recommended spas.

32   But he was not for travelling – he'd sooner
be ready to fix an early rendezvous
with his forebears. Tatyána,
as is the way with women, paid no heed.
He was persistent, wouldn't let her be;
still hopeful, went on pestering her.
His ill health lent him new audacity:
with feeble hand he penned the princess
a passionate missive –
and this despite his view (which has some truth)
that generally there's little point in letters.
Clearly the anguish in his heart
was now beyond his power to bear.
So here's his letter for you, word for word:

Письмо Онегина к Татьяне

Предвижу всё: вас оскорбит
Печальной тайны объясненье.
Какое горькое презренье
Ваш гордый взгляд изобразит!
Чего хочу? с какою целью
Открою душу вам свою?
Какому злобному веселью,
Быть может, повод подаю!

Случайно вас когда-то встретя,
В вас искру нежности заметя,
Я ей поверить не посмел:
Привычке милой не дал ходу;
Свою постылую свободу
Я потерять не захотел.
Еще одно нас разлучило…
Несчастной жертвой Ленский пал…
Ото всего, что сердцу мило,
Тогда я сердце оторвал;
Чужой для всех, ничем не связан,
Я думал: вольность и покой
Замена счастью. Боже мой!
Как я ошибся, как наказан.

Нет, поминутно видеть вас,
Повсюду следовать за вами,
Улыбку уст, движенье глаз
Ловить влюбленными глазами,
Внимать вам долго, понимать
Душой всё ваше совершенство,
Пред вами в муках замирать,
Бледнеть и гаснуть… вот блаженство!

И я лишен того: для вас
Тащусь повсюду наудачу;
Мне дорог день, мне дорог час:
А я в напрасной скуке трачу
Судьбой отсчитанные дни.
И так уж тягостны они.

Onégin's Letter to Tatyána

I foresee it all: you'll take offence
at this disclosure of my unhappy secret.
I can already picture the expression
of bitter contempt in those proud eyes of yours.
What am I hoping to achieve? What is my purpose
in opening my heart to you like this?
For probably I'm just affording you
occasion for vindictive merriment.

   When once before I chanced to meet you,
I perceived in you a spark of affection,
but lacked the nerve to place my trust in it:
I didn't allow myself to get know you,
to get to like you…
I wasn't prepared to lose my hateful freedom.
Another thing at that point came between us…
Lensky, unhappily, fell victim…
So then I tore myself away
from all that I held dear –
cut myself off from everyone, renounced all ties.
I thought that freedom and detachment
would do for happiness. Good God,
how wrong I was, how I've been punished!

   I realize now. To see you every minute;
to trail behind you everywhere; to catch a rapturous glimpse
of your smiling lips, your glancing eyes;
to listen to you more and more; to contemplate
inwardly the sum of your perfection;
to be in torment in your presence,
feel faint, turn pale, lose consciousness – there's happiness,
the happiness I've missed!

   I traipse round everywhere
in case I see you.
My days are counted out to me by fate:
each day, each hour, is precious to me;
I waste them, though, in drab futility,
and they're a burden to me now.

Я знаю: век уж мой измерен;
Но чтоб продлилась жизнь моя,
Я утром должен быть уверен,
Что с вами днем увижусь я...

Боюсь: в мольбе моей смиренной
Увидит ваш суровый взор
Затеи хитрости презренной —
И слышу гневный ваш укор.
Когда б вы знали, как ужасно
Томиться жаждою любви,
Пылать — и разумом всечасно
Смирять волнение в крови;
Желать обнять у вас колени
И, зарыдав, у ваших ног
Излить мольбы, признанья, пени,
Всё, всё, что выразить бы мог,
А между тем притворным хладом
Вооружать и речь и взор,
Вести спокойный разговор,
Глядеть на вас веселым взглядом!..

Но так и быть: я сам себе
Противиться не в силах боле;
Всё решено: я в вашей воле
И предаюсь моей судьбе.

33 Ответа нет. Он вновь посланье:
Второму, третьему письму
Ответа нет. В одно собранье
Он едет; лишь вошел... ему
Она навстречу. Как сурова!
Его не видят, с ним ни слова;
У! как теперь окружена
Крещенским холодом она!
Как удержать негодованье
Уста упрямые хотят!
Вперил Онегин зоркий взгляд:
Где, где смятенье, состраданье?
Где пятна слез?.. Их нет, их нет!
На сем лице лишь гнева след...

My time on earth, I know, is predetermined;
but, for my future life to be worth living,
I need each morning to be certain
that I'll be seeing you that day...

I fear that in this abject plea of mine
your stern eye will see nothing
but a sly schemer's shabby machinations –
and I can hear your angry reprimand.
If only you could know how terrible
it is to be racked with thirst for love,
to be aflame – and hour by hour
to try to calm one's fevered pulse by reason;
to be ever longing to embrace your knees,
longing to pour out, sobbing, at your feet
entreaties, declarations and reproaches –
yes, all that I could give expression to –
yet at the same time to be shoring up
my speech and looks with simulated coolness,
to chat with you and not to lose composure,
to look you in the eye with cheerfulness...

But there we are: I've no strength left
to battle with myself.
What's said is said: I'm at your mercy,
and I surrender to my fate.

33   No answer came. He sent another letter.
The second letter, and a third,
brought no reply. One day he drove
to some reception. He'd no sooner entered
than there she was approaching him – how stern
she looked: no gleam of recognition, not a word!
He shuddered at the Epiphanytide coldness
in which she'd now enwrapped herself.
Her lips, it seemed, were stubbornly determined
to contain her indignation.
Onégin stared intently at her face,
hoping to see dismay, or sympathy,
or tear stains... Nothing! Nothing of the sort!
All her expression showed was a hint of anger,

34   Да, может быть, боязни тайной,
        Чтоб муж иль свет не угадал
        Проказы, слабости случайной…
        Всего, что мой Онегин знал…
        Надежды нет! Он уезжает,
        Свое безумство проклинает —
        И, в нем глубоко погружен,
        От света вновь отрекся он.
        И в молчаливом кабинете
        Ему припомнилась пора,
        Когда жестокая хандра
        За ним гналася в шумном свете,
        Поймала, за ворот взяла
        И в темный угол заперла.

35   Стал вновь читать он без разбора.
        Прочел он Гиббона, Руссо,
        Манзони, Гердера, Шамфора,
        Madame de Staël, Биша, Тиссо,
        Прочел скептического Беля,
        Прочел творенья Фонтенеля,
        Прочел из наших кой-кого,
        Не отвергая ничего:
        И альманахи, и журналы,
        Где поученья нам твердят,
        Где нынче так меня бранят,
        А где такие мадригалы
        Себе встречал я иногда:
        È sempre bene, господа.

36   И что ж? Глаза его читали,
        Но мысли были далеко;
        Мечты, желания, печали
        Теснились в душу глубоко.
        Он меж печатными строками
        Читал духовными глазами
        Другие строки. В них-то он
        Был совершенно углублен.
        То были тайные преданья
        Сердечной, темной старины,
        Ни с чем не связанные сны,
        Угрозы, толки, предсказанья,
        Иль длинной сказки вздор живой,
        Иль письма девы молодой.

34   and maybe of a secret fear
lest her husband or the world at large should guess
her act of foolishness, her momentary weakness –
all that my friend Onégin knew.
He saw there was no hope. He drove away,
cursing his crazy obsession.
But, deeply under its influence still,
he once again renounced society.
And in his silent study there came back to him
the time when once before
in the uproar of his social life
a fierce depression had pursued him,
had caught him, seized him by the collar,
and locked him away as in an unlit cell.

35   He again began to read at random.
He got through Gibbon and Rousseau,
Manzoni, Herder, and Chamfort,
Madame de Staël, Bichat, Tissot;
he read all Bayle the Sceptic's books;
he read the works of Fontenelle;
stopping at nothing, he also read
some of our Russian authors. He read too
anthologies, and literary reviews,
in which we're preached the same old sermons –
and in which I'm called to order these days,
though there were times when I'd be fêted
with their most lyrical effusions.
Fine, gentlemen – *è sempre bene*!

36   In fact, it was Onégin's eyes that read;
his thoughts were far away.
Fantasies, yearnings and regrets
kept pressing deep into his soul.
Between the lines of print
his spiritual eyes
read different words,
words that absorbed him totally –
mysterious memories his heart had rescued
from a dim, distant past,
inconsequential dreams,
bad omens, rumours, prophecies,
or long tales full of vivid nonsense –
or letters that a young girl wrote.

37   И постепенно в усыпленье
      И чувств и дум впадает он,
      А перед ним воображенье
      Свой пестрый мечет фараон.
      То видит он: на талом снеге,
      Как будто спящий на ночлеге,
      Недвижим юноша лежит,
      И слышит голос: что ж? убит.
      То видит он врагов забвенных,
      Клеветников, и трусов злых,
      И рой изменниц молодых,
      И круг товарищей презренных,
      То сельский дом — и у окна
      Сидит *она*… и всё она!..

38   Он так привык теряться в этом,
      Что чуть с ума не своротил
      Или не сделался поэтом.
      Признаться: то-то б одолжил!
      А точно: силой магнетизма
      Стихов российских механизма
      Едва в то время не постиг
      Мой бестолковый ученик.
      Как походил он на поэта,
      Когда в углу сидел один,
      И перед ним пылал камин,
      И он мурлыкал: *Benedetta*
      Иль *Idol mio* и ронял
      В огонь то туфлю, то журнал.

39   Дни мчались; в воздухе нагретом
      Уж разрешалася зима;
      И он не сделался поэтом,
      Не умер, не сошел с ума.
      Весна живит его: впервые
      Свои покои запертые,
      Где зимовал он как сурок,
      Двойные окны, камелек
      Он ясным утром оставляет,
      Несется вдоль Невы в санях.
      На синих, иссеченных льдах
      Играет солнце; грязно тает
      На улицах разрытый снег.
      Куда по нем свой быстрый бег

37   So gradually his thoughts and feelings
      would sink into a dreamworld. Imagination
      would deal him one by one, like playing cards,
      a motley pack of visions:
      now he would see a youngster
      lying there motionless on melted snow,
      like someone bedded down for a night-long sleep;
      and hear a voice: "Let's see... Shot dead";
      and then forgotten enemies would appear,
      malicious cowards, scandal-mongers,
      a swarm of fancy-free young women,
      a circle of companions he despised;
      and then a country house, and at the window
      "she" would be sitting... always "she"!

38   So often did he yield to reveries like these
      that he almost lost his mind –
      or turned into a poet
      (that *would* have been a treat!).
      He was, in fact, susceptible to hypnosis
      to such a point that, under my tuition,
      slow as he was to learn, he nearly mastered
      the technicalities of Russian verse.
      For sure, he looked the poet,
      sitting alone in a nook
      by a blazing fire,
      humming 'Benedetta' or 'Idol Mio',
      and letting a slipper or a journal
      drop off into the flames.

39   The days flew past – and frozen winter
      was soon dissolving in the warmer air.
      Onégin hadn't become a poet;
      nor had he died, nor lost his mind.
      The spring revived him. One bright morning
      for the first time that year he quitted
      the double windows and the fireplace
      and the closed rooms where,
      marmot-like, he'd spent the winter,
      and took a sleigh ride by the Nevá.
      On the blue ice, now cracked in slabs,
      the sunlight played; and on the streets
      the churned-up snow was melting into slush.
      Onégin rode on quickly through it. Where

40   Стремит Онегин? Вы заране
        Уж угадали; точно так:
        Примчался к ней, к своей Татьяне
        Мой неисправленный чудак.
        Идет, на мертвеца похожий.
        Нет ни одной души в прихожей.
        Он в залу; дальше: никого.
        Дверь отворил он. Что ж его
        С такою силой поражает?
        Княгиня перед ним, одна,
        Сидит, не убрана, бледна,
        Письмо какое-то читает
        И тихо слезы льет рекой,
        Опершись на руку щекой.

41   О, кто б немых ее страданий
        В сей быстрый миг не прочитал!
        Кто прежней Тани, бедной Тани
        Теперь в княгине б не узнал!
        В тоске безумных сожалений
        К ее ногам упал Евгений;
        Она вздрогнула и молчит;
        И на Онегина глядит
        Без удивления, без гнева…
        Его больной, угасший взор,
        Молящий вид, немой укор,
        Ей внятно всё. Простая дева,
        С мечтами, сердцем прежних дней,
        Теперь опять воскресла в ней.

42   Она его не подымает
        И, не сводя с него очей,
        От жадных уст не отымает
        Бесчувственной руки своей…
        О чем теперь ее мечтанье?
        Проходит долгое молчанье,
        И тихо наконец она:
        «Довольно; встаньте. Я должна
        Вам объясниться откровенно.
        Онегин, помните ль тот час,
        Когда в саду, в аллее нас
        Судьба свела, и так смиренно
        Урок ваш выслушала я?
        Сегодня очередь моя.

40 was he heading? You've already
  guessed it – quite so:
  wayward as ever, he was hurrying
  to "her", to his Tatyána.
  He entered, looking like a ghost.
  No soul was in the vestibule.
  Into the hall he went; and on – still no one.
  He opened a door, and stood dumbfounded
  at what he saw.
  There was the princess sitting alone,
  not fully dressed yet, pallid-faced,
  reading a letter,
  eyes streaming quietly with tears,
  cheek resting on her hand.

41 Who could have failed in that brief moment
  to perceive Tatyána's unvoiced pain?
  Who could have failed to see in the princess
  the poor young Tanya of long ago?
  In agonies of uncontrollable remorse
  Onégin fell down at her feet.
  She shuddered and stayed silent,
  observing him
  without dismay, without resentment.
  His sickly, lifeless gaze,
  his pleading attitude, his mute reproach –
  she took in everything. The simple girl,
  with the feelings and dreams of earlier days,
  now came to life once more within her.

42 She didn't raise him to his feet;
  neither did she withdraw
  her numbed hand from his hungry lips:
  she just stared fixedly at him,
  dreaming – who knows what dreams?...
  There followed a long silence.
  Finally, in a quiet voice, she spoke:
  "Enough. Stand up. I must be frank
  and make myself quite clear to you.
  Onégin, do you recall the time
  when fate brought us together
  in that avenue in the park, and I heard out
  that lecture of yours so meekly?
  Today it's my turn.

43   Онегин, я тогда моложе,
      Я лучше, кажется, была,
      И я любила вас; и что же?
      Что в сердце вашем я нашла?
      Какой ответ? одну суровость.
      Не правда ль? Вам была не новость
      Смиренной девочки любовь?
      И нынче — Боже! — стынет кровь,
      Как только вспомню взгляд холодный
      И эту проповедь… Но вас
      Я не виню: в тот страшный час
      Вы поступили благородно,
      Вы были правы предо мной:
      Я благодарна всей душой…

44   Тогда — не правда ли? — в пустыне,
      Вдали от суетной молвы,
      Я вам не нравилась… Что ж ныне
      Меня преследуете вы?
      Зачем у вас я на примете?
      Не потому ль, что в высшем свете
      Теперь являться я должна;
      Что я богата и знатна,
      Что муж в сраженьях изувечен,
      Что нас за то ласкает двор?
      Не потому ль, что мой позор
      Теперь бы всеми был замечен,
      И мог бы в обществе принесть
      Вам соблазнительную честь?

45   Я плачу… если вашей Тани
      Вы не забыли до сих пор,
      То знайте: колкость вашей брани,
      Холодный, строгий разговор,
      Когда б в моей лишь было власти,
      Я предпочла б обидной страсти
      И этим письмам и слезам.
      К моим младенческим мечтам
      Тогда имели вы хоть жалость,
      Хоть уважение к летам…
      А нынче! — что к моим ногам
      Вас привело? какая малость!
      Как с вашим сердцем и умом
      Быть чувства мелкого рабом?

43   "Onégin, I was younger then,
and better-looking, I suppose;
and I was in love with you. What, then?
What did I find in *your* heart? What response?
Severity, that was all. Isn't that true?
There was no novelty for you, was there,
in the love of a shy young girl?
And even now – good God! – my blood runs cold
when I recall that chilling look,
that sermon!… But that's not
something I hold against you: a dreadful hour
it was for me, but you behaved with honour.
You treated me straightforwardly,
and I thank you from my heart.

44   "At that time, in the lonely countryside,
when we were far away from frivolous gossip,
I didn't take your fancy, did I? Why then
do you pursue me now?
Why have you marked me out?
Isn't it because I'm now obliged
to appear in the highest circles,
because I'm rich and well regarded,
because my husband was wounded in action
and we're treated with special favour by the Palace?
Isn't it because my disgrace would now
be the subject of universal comment
and might bring you in the world at large
some tempting notoriety?

45   "I can't help weeping… If you still remember
the Tanya that you used to know,
be sure of this: were the choice mine,
I'd rather smart from your rebuke,
endure a stern and chilling talk,
than be the object of this offensive passion,
these letters and these tears.
Then at least you showed some pity
towards those childish fantasies of mine,
and some consideration for my age…
But now! What's brought you
grovelling to my feet? So small a thing?
As if you, with your willpower and your brains,
could possibly be slave to a mere emotion!

46 А мне, Онегин, пышность эта,
    Постылой жизни мишура,
    Мои успехи в вихре света,
    Мой модный дом и вечера,
    Что в них? Сейчас отдать я рада
    Всю эту ветошь маскарада,
    Весь этот блеск, и шум, и чад
    За полку книг, за дикий сад,
    За наше бедное жилище,
    За те места, где в первый раз,
    Онегин, видела я вас,
    Да за смиренное кладбище,
    Где нынче крест и тень ветвей
    Над бедной нянею моей…

47 А счастье было так возможно,
    Так близко!.. Но судьба моя
    Уж решена. Неосторожно,
    Быть может, поступила я:
    Меня с слезами заклинаний
    Молила мать; для бедной Тани
    Все были жребии равны…
    Я вышла замуж. Вы должны,
    Я вас прошу, меня оставить;
    Я знаю: в вашем сердце есть
    И гордость и прямая честь.
    Я вас люблю (к чему лукавить?),
    Но я другому отдана;
    Я буду век ему верна».

48 Она ушла. Стоит Евгений,
    Как будто громом поражен.
    В какую бурю ощущений
    Теперь он сердцем погружен!
    Но шпор незапный звон раздался,
    И муж Татьянин показался,
    И здесь героя моего,
    В минуту, злую для него,
    Читатель, мы теперь оставим,
    Надолго… навсегда. За ним
    Довольно мы путем одним
    Бродили по свету. Поздравим
    Друг друга с берегом. Ура!
    Давно б (не правда ли?) пора!

46 "For my part, Onégin, all this glamour,
these gaudy trappings of a life I hate,
my fashionable mansion, my soirées,
my triumphs in the social whirl –
what do they mean to me? I'd gladly
renounce, here and now, this shabby masquerade,
this glitter and noise, this choking vapour,
in return for a shelf of books, for an overgrown park,
for our humble home,
for those same haunts
where first I saw you, Onégin,
and for the lowly graveyard
where under shadowy boughs a cross now marks
the spot where nanny dear, poor thing...

47 "Yet happiness was so possible,
so close!... But now my future's
settled. Maybe
I acted rashly: Mother implored me
with tears and entreaties –
and I was too wretched
to care what happened...
I married... You must
leave me now, I beg you –
I know there's present in your heart
both pride and a true sense of honour.
I do love you – why try to hide it? –
but I'm committed to another man,
and I'll be loyal to him while I live."

48 She left the room. Onégin stood
as though a thunderbolt had struck him;
a savage tempest of emotions
engulfed his heart.
Then all at once there came a clink of spurs:
Tatyána's husband made his entry...
and here, good reader,
at this dire moment for my hero,
we're going to leave him
for long – indeed, for ever. Time enough
we've spent, you and I,
travelling the world together in his wake.
Let's now congratulate ourselves on sighting land.
Hurrah! It's none too soon, eh!

49   Кто б ни был ты, о мой читатель,
      Друг, недруг, я хочу с тобой
      Расстаться нынче как приятель.
      Прости. Чего бы ты за мной
      Здесь ни искал в строфах небрежных,
      Воспоминаний ли мятежных,
      Отдохновенья ль от трудов,
      Живых картин, иль острых слов,
      Иль грамматических ошибок,
      Дай Бог, чтоб в этой книжке ты
      Для развлеченья, для мечты,
      Для сердца, для журнальных сшибок
      Хотя крупицу мог найти.
      За сим расстанемся, прости!

50   Прости ж и ты, мой спутник странный,
      И ты, мой верный идеал,
      И ты, живой и постоянный,
      Хоть малый труд. Я с вами знал
      Всё, что завидно для поэта:
      Забвенье жизни в бурях света,
      Беседу сладкую друзей.
      Промчалось много, много дней
      С тех пор, как юная Татьяна
      И с ней Онегин в смутном сне
      Явилися впервые мне —
      И даль свободного романа
      Я сквозь магический кристалл
      Еще не ясно различал.

51   Но те, которым в дружной встрече
      Я строфы первые читал…
      Иных уж нет, а те далече,
      Как Сади некогда сказал.
      Без них Онегин дорисован.
      А та, с которой образован
      Татьяны милый идеал…
      О много, много рок отъял!
      Блажен, кто праздник жизни рано
      Оставил, не допив до дна
      Бокала полного вина,
      Кто не дочел ее романа
      И вдруг умел расстаться с ним,
      Как я с Онегиным моим.

— К О Н Е Ц —

49   Reader, whoever you are,
       my fan or critic, I should like
       our parting now to be a friendly one. Goodbye, then.
       Whatever you were seeking from me
       here in these slapdash stanzas –
       be it seditious reminiscences,
       a break from work,
       lively descriptions, witty epigrams,
       grammatical mistakes – whatever,
       God grant that in this little book
       you've managed to find at least a scrap
       to amuse you, set you dreaming, stir your emotions –
       or slate in the reviews.
       With that let's part. Goodbye!

50   Goodbye to you as well, rum fellow traveller;
       and you, my true ideal of perfection;
       and you, my book, on whom I've worked so hard:
       small though you are, you've been a constant pal.
       Thanks to you all, I've known all a poet could wish for –
       release from the stormy life of the outside world,
       and the delicious companionship of friends.
       So many, many days have flitted by
       since young Tatyána and Onégin
       first came to me
       in a muddled dream,
       and I had yet to pick out clearly
       in my crystal ball the remoter features
       of this impromptu novel.

51   But there were certain friends I'd meet,
       I used to read them my first stanzas –
       in Sa'di's words of long ago,
       "some now are dead and others far away".
       Onégin's portrait's been achieved without them.
       And she from whom I sketched
       my precious image of Tatyána...
       oh, fate has carried off so much, so much!
       Lucky's the man who leaves life's banquet
       early, before he's drained to the last dregs
       his goblet-full of wine; yes, lucky's the man
       who hasn't read life's novel to the end,
       but has wisely made a sudden break with it –
       as I with my Onégin.

                    — THE END —

Onegin's Journey

Published Excerpts

ОТРЫВКИ ИЗ ПУТЕШЕСТВИЯ ОНЕГИНА

Предисловие Пушкина

Последняя глава «Евгения Онегина» издана была особо, с следующим предисловием:

«Пропущенные строфы подавали неоднократно повод к порицанию и насмешкам (впрочем, весьма справедливым и остроумным). Автор чистосердечно признается, что он выпустил из своего романа целую главу, в коей описано было путешествие Онегина по России. От него зависело означить сию выпущенную главу точками или цифром; но во избежание соблазна решился он лучше выставить, вместо девятого нумера, осьмой над последней главою Евгения Онегина и пожертвовать одною из окончательных строф:

Пора: перо покоя просит;
Я девять песен написал;
На берег радостный выносит
Мою ладью девятый вал —
Хвала вам, девяти каменам, и проч.».

П.А.Катенин (коему прекрасный поэтический талант не мешает быть и тонким критиком) заметил нам, что сие исключение, может быть и выгодное для читателей, вредит, однако ж, плану целого сочинения; ибо чрез то переход от Татьяны, уездной барышни, к Татьяне, знатной даме, становится слишком неожиданным и необъясненным. — Замечание, обличающее опытного художника. Автор сам чувствовал справедливость оного, но решился выпустить эту главу по причинам, важным для него, а не для публики. Некоторые отрывки были напечатаны; мы здесь их помещаем, присовокупив к ним еще несколько строф.

EXCERPTS FROM ONEGIN'S JOURNEY

The Author's Preface

The final chapter of *Eugene Onegin* was published separately, with the following foreword:

> The omitted stanzas have more than once given rise to criticism and ridicule (doubtless well justified and wittily expressed). The author candidly admits that he has dropped from his novel an entire chapter describing Onégin's journey through Russia. It was open to him to mark this omitted chapter with dots or a number; but to avoid further temptation he has decided instead to change the numeral at the head of the last chapter of *Eugene Onegin* from "Nine" to "Eight" and to sacrifice one of the concluding stanzas:
>
> > Time's up: my pen demands a rest;
> > nine cantos I've now written;
> > the ninth wave's carried my boat up
> > onto the welcome shore –
> > well done, nine goddesses of inspiration! Etc.

P.A. Katénin (whose outstanding talent as a poet does not prevent him from being an acute critic too) remarked to us that this excision, advantageous though it might well be for the reader, was detrimental to the work's overall structure; for because of it the transition from Tatyána the provincial squire's daughter to Tatyána the high-ranking noblewoman becomes overly abrupt and unaccountable – a remark that reveals the experienced creative writer. The author himself sensed the truth of this, but decided nonetheless to leave the chapter out for reasons that are important to him, though not to the public. Some excerpts have already been published; we set them out here, supplementing them with several more stanzas.

Евгений Онегин из Москвы едет в Нижний Новгород:

[9] ……………………………
  ……………………… перед ним
  Макарьев суетно хлопочет,
  Кипит обилием своим.
  Сюда жемчуг привез индеец,
  Поддельны вины европеец,
  Табун бракованных коней
  Пригнал заводчик из степей,
  Игрок привез свои колоды
  И горсть услужливых костей,
  Помещик — спелых дочерей,
  А дочки — прошлогодни моды.
  Всяк суетится, лжет за двух,
  И всюду меркантильный дух.

[10] Тоска!..

Онегин едет в Астрахань и оттуда на Кавказ:

[12] Он видит: Терек своенравный
  Крутые роет берега;
  Пред ним парит орел державный,
  Стоит олень, склонив рога;
  Верблюд лежит в тени утеса,
  В лугах несется конь черкеса,
  И вкруг кочующих шатров
  Пасутся овцы калмыков,
  Вдали — кавказские громады:
  К ним путь открыт. Пробилась брань
  За их естественную грань,
  Чрез их опасные преграды;
  Брега Арагвы и Куры
  Узрели русские шатры.

Eugene Onegin travels from Moscow to Nizhny Nóvgorod:

[9]   ....
         .... he saw
the Makáryev market, frenziedly active,
brimming with merchandise galore.
Indians had brought their pearls,
Europeans their poorest wines;
stud owners had driven their duffest horses
in from the steppe in droves;
gamblers had come with their special cards
and their handfuls of weighted dice;
landowners had brought their maturest daughters,
and the daughters their fashions of yesteryear.
All vied for attention and told enough lies for two;
the spirit of commerce was everywhere.

[10]   Such emptiness!...

Onégin travels to Ástrakhan, and from there to the Caucasus:

[12]   Onégin looked on, as the impetuous Terek
bored its way through precipitous ravines.
He saw a majestic eagle soaring,
a stag that stood with antlers lowered,
a camel that lay in the shade of a crag.
A Circassian's horse careered over grasslands;
some wandering Kalmuks
grazed sheep by their tents;
and in the distance he saw the Caucasian massif.
The route to it is open now. Warfare
has forced a way past this natural frontier,
across this perilous bulwark;
and Russian camps have now appeared
beside the rivers Arágva and Kurá.

[13]   Уже пустыни сторож вечный,
Стесненный холмами вокруг,
Стоит Бешту остроконечный
И зеленеющий Машук,
Машук, податель струй целебных;
Вокруг ручьев его волшебных
Больных теснится бледный рой;
Кто жертва чести боевой,
Кто почечуя, кто Киприды;
Страдалец мыслит жизни нить
В волнах чудесных укрепить,
Кокетка злых годов обиды
На дне оставить, а старик
Помолодеть — хотя на миг.

[14]   Питая горьки размышленья,
Среди печальной их семьи,
Онегин взором сожаленья
Глядит на дымные струи
И мыслит, грустью отуманен:
Зачем я пулей в грудь не ранен?
Зачем не хилый я старик,
Как этот бедный откупщик?
Зачем, как тульский заседатель,
Я не лежу в параличе?
Зачем не чувствую в плече
Хоть ревматизма? — ах, Создатель!
Я молод, жизнь во мне крепка;
Чего мне ждать? тоска, тоска!..

Онегин посещает потом Тавриду:

[15]   . . . .
. . . .
. . . .
. . . .
. . . .
. . . .
. . . .
. . . .
Воображенью край священный:
С Атридом спорил там Пилад,
Там закололся Митридат,
Там пел Мицкевич вдохновенный
И посреди прибрежных скал
Свою Литву воспоминал.

[13]   Onégin came to sharp-peaked Mount Beshtáu,
        towering high among its cluster of hills,
        perpetual guardian of the wilderness;
        and to green Mount Mashúk,
        dispenser of healing waters.
        Pallid invalids in crowds
        pressed round its wonder-working streams –
        some, victims of their martial valour;
        some, of their haemorrhoids, or of their love life.
        There were martyrs to pain, who hoped to toughen
        life's fraying thread in the miraculous springs;
        there were compulsive flirts, who hoped to wash away
        the fleeting years' malicious scars, and old men too,
        who hoped, if briefly, to regain their youth.

[14]   Surrounded by this sorry company,
        Onégin nurtured bitter thoughts
        as he gazed regretfully
        at the steaming waters.
        Remorse cast its shadow over him, and he mused,
        "Why hasn't a bullet wounded *me* in the chest?
        Why am *I* not a sickly old man,
        like that pathetic state contractor?
        Why am *I* not lying paralysed,
        like that town councillor from Tula?
        Why don't I even feel in my shoulder
        a twinge of rheumatism? Creator God!
        I'm young, I've the vigour of life within me.
        But what's in store? Just emptiness, emptiness!..."

Onégin then visits the Crimea:

[15]   ....
        ....
        ....
        ....
        ....
        ....
        ....
        ....
        That land is sacred to the imagination.
        There Pylades quarrelled with Orestes.
        There Mithridates stabbed himself.
        And there among the coastal crags
        Mickiewicz wrote inspired verse
        and called to mind his native Poland.

281

[16]   Прекрасны вы, брега Тавриды,
Когда вас видишь с корабля
При свете утренней Киприды,
Как вас впервой увидел я;
Вы мне предстали в блеске брачном:
На небе синем и прозрачном
Сияли груды ваших гор,
Долин, деревьев, сёл узор
Разостлан был передо мною.
А там, меж хижинок татар...
Какой во мне проснулся жар!
Какой волшебною тоскою
Стеснялась пламенная грудь!
Но, муза! прошлое забудь.

[17]   Какие б чувства ни таились
Тогда во мне — теперь их нет:
Они прошли иль изменились...
Мир вам, тревоги прошлых лет!
В ту пору мне казались нужны
Пустыни, волн края жемчужны,
И моря шум, и груды скал,
И гордой девы идеал,
И безыменные страданья...
Другие дни, другие сны;
Смирились вы, моей весны
Высокопарные мечтанья,
И в поэтический бокал
Воды я много подмешал.

[18]   Иные нужны мне картины:
Люблю песчаный косогор,
Перед избушкой две рябины,
Калитку, сломанный забор,
На небе серенькие тучи,
Перед гумном соломы кучи
Да пруд под сенью ив густых,
Раздолье уток молодых;
Теперь мила мне балалайка
Да пьяный топот трепака
Перед порогом кабака.
Мой идеал теперь — хозяйка,
Мои желания — покой,
Да щей горшок, да сам большой.

[16]   The Crimean coastline is magnificent
         when you see it from shipboard,
         as I myself first saw it
         in the light of Venus, the morning star.
         It stood before me in bridal splendour,
         its massive mountains gleaming out
         against a sky of clear, deep blue,
         and its valleys, woods and villages
         spread out before me like a patterned fabric.
         And there among the Tatar cottages...
         there such burning passion woke within me,
         such overpowering desire
         engulfed my flaming heart!...
         But, Inspiration, leave the past behind!

[17]   Whatever emotions lurked within me then
         are there no more.
         They've passed, or changed...
         May they rest in peace, those yearnings of years past.
         In those days my imagination needed
         vast empty spaces, wavecrests of pearl,
         resounding seas and towering crags,
         an unresponsive girl to worship,
         and sufferings I cannot name...
         With new days come new aspirations;
         the soaring imagination of my springtime
         has now come down to earth,
         and into the wineglass of my verse
         I've mixed a goodly dash of water.

[18]   Now there are different pictures
         that take my fancy: a sandy hill slope,
         two rowan trees beside a shack,
         a wicket gate, a broken fence,
         a sky of greyish clouds,
         straw heaped up by a threshing floor,
         and, shaded by thick willow trees,
         a pond, safe home for ducklings.
         Now it's the balalaika that I'm fond of,
         and the *trepák* when danced with a drunken tread
         outside a tavern door.
         My ideal woman's now the housekeeper;
         and my yearnings are for peace – as the saying goes:
         "a mug o' cabbage soup, and master o' meself".

[19]   Порой дождливою намедни
Я, завернув на скотный двор...
Тьфу! прозаические бредни,
Фламандской школы пестрый сор!
Таков ли был я, расцветая?
Скажи, фонтан Бахчисарая!
Такие ль мысли мне на ум
Навел твой бесконечный шум,
Когда безмолвно пред тобою
Зарему я воображал...
Средь пышных, опустелых зал
Спустя три года, вслед за мною
Скитаясь в той же стороне,
Онегин вспомнил обо мне.

[20]   Я жил тогда в Одессе пыльной...
Там долго ясны небеса,
Там хлопотливо торг обильный
Свои подъемлет паруса;
Там всё Европой дышит, веет,
Всё блещет югом и пестреет
Разнообразностью живой.
Язык Италии златой
Звучит по улице веселой,
Где ходит гордый славянин,
Француз, испанец, армянин,
И грек, и молдаван тяжелый,
И сын египетской земли,
Корсар в отставке, Морали.

[21]   Одессу звучными стихами
Наш друг Туманский описал,
Но он пристрастными глазами
В то время на нее взирал.
Приехав, он прямым поэтом
Пошел бродить с своим лорнетом
Один над морем — и потом
Очаровательным пером
Сады одесские прославил.
Всё хорошо, но дело в том,
Что степь нагая там кругом;
Кой-где недавный труд заставил
Младые ветви в знойный день
Давать насильственную тень.

[19]   "When it was raining t'other day,
I dropped into the cowshed, and…"
Ugh! What prosaic drivel,
medley of rubbish, Flemish-style!
That's not how I was in my prime –
witness my *Fountain of Bakhchisaray*!
Those weren't the thoughts
its endless plashing brought to mind
when I stood silently before it
and formed my image of Zaréma…
Well, when Onégin in my footsteps
was, three years later, roaming those same parts,
he stood in the palace's sumptuous apartments,
all empty now, and thought of me.

[20]   I was living then in dusty Odessa…
The skies there are clear for much of the year.
Trade there is brisk and strong
and fills the sails of visiting merchantmen.
The wind there's laden with the smells of Europe;
the whole place glows with the light of the south,
with colour, variety and life.
The language of golden Italy
rings out in the cheerful streets;
proud Slavs walk there,
and Frenchmen, Spaniards,
Armenians, Greeks,
ponderous Moldavians, and Moor Ali,
retired Egyptian buccaneer.

[21]   Our friend Tumánsky wrote some musical verses
about Odessa;
but at the time his view of the city
was over-kind.
He'd no sooner come than, as poets will,
he set off alone for a stroll above the sea,
binoculars in hand – and soon
with magical pen he'd put together
a poem in praise of Odessa's gardens.
All fine – except that in actual fact
it's all bare steppe round about!
Only here and there have labourers lately
compelled young twigs in the heat of the day
to provide some forcible shade.

[22]   А где, бишь, мой рассказ несвязный?
       В Одессе пыльной, я сказал.
       Я б мог сказать: в Одессе грязной —
       И тут бы, право, не солгал.
       В году недель пять-шесть Одесса,
       По воле бурного Зевеса,
       Потоплена, запружена,
       В густой грязи погружена.
       Все домы на аршин загрязнут,
       Лишь на ходулях пешеход
       По улице дерзает вброд;
       Кареты, люди тонут, вязнут,
       И в дрожках вол, рога склоня,
       Сменяет хилого коня.

[23]   Но уж дробит каменья молот,
       И скоро звонкой мостовой
       Покроется спасенный город,
       Как будто кованой броней.
       Однако в сей Одессе влажной
       Еще есть недостаток важный;
       Чего б вы думали? — воды.
       Потребны тяжкие труды...
       Что ж? это небольшое горе,
       Особенно, когда вино
       Без пошлины привезено.
       Но солнце южное, но море...
       Чего ж вам более, друзья?
       Благословенные края!

[24]   Бывало, пушка зоревая
       Лишь только грянет с корабля,
       С крутого берега сбегая,
       Уж к морю отправляюсь я.
       Потом за трубкой раскаленной,
       Волной соленой оживленный,
       Как мусульман в своем раю,
       С восточной гущей кофе пью.
       Иду гулять. Уж благосклонный
       Открыт Casino; чашек звон
       Там раздается; на балкон
       Маркёр выходит полусонный
       С метлой в руках, и у крыльца
       Уже сошлися два купца.

[22]   Dear me, though, where's my disjointed story?
"In *dusty* Odessa" I had said.
I might rather have said "in *muddy* Odessa" –
and, really, I wouldn't have lied.
For five or six weeks of the year,
the storm god Zeus wills that Odessa
be swamped and flooded,
and drowned in thick mud.
Each house is two foot deep in mire.
Pedestrians are in need of stilts
before they dare to ford the street.
Coaches and townsfolk flounder, founder;
and oxen struggle forward with lowered horns,
harnessed to carriages in place of puny horses.

[23]   But rescue's at hand! Sledgehammers even now
are smashing slabs of stone; and soon the town
will be arrayed in resonating pavements,
as though with armour plating from the forge.
In this wet city of Odessa, though,
there's one important shortage.
Shortage of what, do you suppose? Of water!
"Major construction works are needed…"
But why? There's no great problem,
especially when the wine's
imported duty-free!
Yes, southern sun, the sea…
what more could you want, my friends?
Charmed regions, those!

[24]   When I was there, no sooner had the cannon
roared its dawn salvo from the guardship,
than I'd run down the cliffs
and head straight for the sea.
Then after that, invigorated by the brine,
I'd sit behind a freshly lighted pipe,
just like a Muslim in his paradise,
and drink a coffee thick with oriental grounds.
I'd take a walk. The casino club by now, obligingly,
would be open. You'd hear from that direction
a jingle of cups; the billiard-room attendant,
still half-asleep, would come out on the terrace
with broom in hand; and by the entrance steps
a couple of merchants would have met already.

[25]   Глядишь — и площадь запестрела.
Всё оживилось; здесь и там
Бегут за делом и без дела,
Однако больше по делам.
Дитя расчета и отваги,
Идет купец взглянуть на флаги,
Проведать, шлют ли небеса
Ему знакомы паруса.
Какие новые товары
Вступили нынче в карантин?
Пришли ли бочки жданных вин?
И что чума? и где пожары?
И нет ли голода, войны
Или подобной новизны?

[26]   Но мы, ребята без печали,
Среди заботливых купцов,
Мы только устриц ожидали
От цареградских берегов.
Что устрицы? пришли! О радость!
Летит обжорливая младость
Глотать из раковин морских
Затворниц жирных и живых,
Слегка обрызгнутых лимоном.
Шум, споры — легкое вино
Из погребов принесено
На стол услужливым Отоном;
Часы летят, а грозный счет
Меж тем невидимо растет.

[27]   Но уж темнеет вечер синий,
Пора нам в оперу скорей:
Там упоительный Россини,
Европы баловень — Орфей.
Не внемля критике суровой,
Он вечно тот же, вечно новый,
Он звуки льет — они кипят,
Они текут, они горят,
Как поцелуи молодые,
Все в неге, в пламени любви,
Как зашипевшего Аи
Струя и брызги золотые...
Но, господа, позволено ль
С вином равнять do-re-mi-sol?

[25]   You'd see the square, too, full of colour;
         the town had sprung to life. People were rushing
         to and fro on business, or on no business –
         but mostly busy anyhow!
         Merchants, living off risk and calculation,
         were on their way to inspect ships' flags,
         to learn if Heaven had sent them
         the vessels they'd been banking on.
         What cargoes freshly arrived
         were undergoing clearance by port-health?
         Had the expected casks of wine come in?
         What news of plagues?
         Where'd there been conflagrations? And no
         new famines, wars or suchlike?

[26]   We carefree youngsters, on the other hand,
         in contrast to those anxious merchants,
         were just awaiting oysters
         from the beds round Istanbul.
         "What about oysters? They've arrived! O joy!"
         And off we'd fly, young gluttons,
         to swallow down those plump recluses
         live from their seashells,
         with a light sprinkling of lemon.
         Then uproar, argument – the attentive
         Automne had brought us a light-bodied wine
         up from the cellars to table.
         The hours flew by; and all the while
         the awesome bill, unheeded, mounted up.

[27]   But soon the evening dimmed to indigo,
         and it was time we hurried to the opera.
         Rossini was on there – intoxicating maestro,
         darling of Europe, modern Orpheus.
         He pays no heed to hostile critics –
         always the same, yet always fresh!
         He pours forth melodies
         that fizz, that froth, that sizzle –
         like youthful lovers' kisses, always
         lingering, yet incandescent;
         or like the hissing streams and golden spray
         of champagne from Ay...
         But, gentlemen, are we allowed
         to liken notes of music to a wine?

289

[28]   А только ль там очарований?
А разыскательный лорнет?
А закулисные свиданья?
A prima donna? а балет?
А ложа, где, красой блистая,
Негоцианка молодая,
Самолюбива и томна,
Толпой рабов окружена?
Она и внемлет и не внемлет
И каватине, и мольбам,
И шутке с лестью пополам...
А муж — в углу за нею дремлет,
Впросонках фора закричит,
Зевнет и — снова захрапит.

[29]   Финал гремит; пустеет зала;
Шумя, торопится разъезд;
Толпа на площадь побежала
При блеске фонарей и звезд;
Сыны Авзонии счастливой
Слегка поют мотив игривый,
Его невольно затвердив,
А мы ревем речитатив.
Но поздно. Тихо спит Одесса;
И бездыханна и тепла
Немая ночь. Луна взошла,
Прозрачно-легкая завеса
Объемлет небо. Всё молчит;
Лишь море Черное шумит...

[30]   Итак, я жил тогда в Одессе...

[28]   Music wasn't the only fascination there.
        What of those prying opera glasses?
        those backstage assignations?
        the prima donna, the corps de ballet?
        And what of that box where
        a businessman's young wife was radiating beauty,
        so vain, so yielding,
        encircled by a crowd of devotees?
        She heard the aria, and didn't hear it;
        she heard, and didn't hear, their pleas,
        their banter mingled half-and-half with flattery...
        The husband? He dozed on at the back behind her,
        half woke to shout "encore" –
        then yawned, and snored again.

[29]   Thunderous finale over, the theatre emptied;
        carriages departed quickly with a clatter.
        By light of lanterns and the stars
        crowds flocked into the square.
        Some merry Italians crooned
        a catchy tune
        they'd couldn't get from their minds.
        We roared a recitative.
        But it grew late. Odessa was sleeping softly.
        The noiseless night
        was warm and muggy. The moon had risen;
        a thin transparent veil
        enshrouded the sky. No sound was heard,
        except the Black Sea plashing on the shore...

[30]   So I was living in Odessa then...

291

Note on the Text

Eugene Onegin and Onegin's Journey

Pushkin published *Eugene Onegin* in separate chapters (except Chapters Four and Five, which came out together) over seven years between 1825 and 1832. He published the complete work for the first time in 1833, and he brought out a second edition (with few changes) in 1837, just before he died. I have followed normal practice in basing both the Russian text and the translation on the 1837 edition, though (again in common with other editors and translators) I have incorporated a few changes (e.g. correction of obvious printing errors; reversal of the changes made in Chapter Two at the censor's behest; the filling-in of names of Pushkin's contemporaries, which he sometimes indicated only by asterisks). The same applies to the text of *Onegin's Journey*, which is appended here as it was to the 1833 and 1837 editions.

Pushkin's endnotes

The other component of the 1833 and 1837 editions was a set of endnotes (forty-four in the 1837 edition), printed between the end of the novel and *Onegin's Journey*, containing Pushkin's own explanations and comments. A number of these, including some of the longest, relate to literary issues (e.g. acknowledgements to contemporary writers, answers to critics) of interest to Pushkin's contemporaries, but not to modern readers. I have not therefore included Pushkin's notes in this edition, though where a note gives information of continuing relevance I have incorporated the substance of it in my commentary.

Missing lines and stanzas

In the editions of *Onegin* published during his lifetime, Pushkin omitted certain lines and stanzas for reasons which are not always clear. He may have been told, or feared, that the lines would fall foul of the censorship; he may have grown dissatisfied with a particular passage; or he may have wanted for artistic reasons to introduce a pause or break the continuity of the narration. In most cases we know the text of the missing passages, either because Pushkin had the material published separately, or because scholars have found the drafts in his notebooks. Pushkin marked the omissions by lines of dots and by counting omitted stanzas in the numerical sequence. Where (in Chapter Two) we are fairly certain that these omissions were due to the censorship, I have, in common with most modern editors, reinstated Pushkin's text. But where the omissions are apparently due to other motives, I have left the text as Pushkin published it, commenting on the lacuna in the notes. I have set out omitted passages in full in the Appendix where the text was published by Pushkin during his lifetime; but where we only know of what was omitted through Pushkin's unpublished drafts or from the reminiscences of others, I have simply recorded the gist of the absent lines in the commentary.

References

For abbreviated references to the text I have used Roman numerals to refer to chapters of the work and Arabic numerals to refer to stanzas (thus "V, 23" refers to Stanza 23 of Chapter Five). Because Pushkin did not assign stanza numbers to *Onegin's Journey*, I have put square brackets round my own numbers ("Stanza [20]") – see further on *Onegin's Journey*, page 363 below.

Notes and Commentary

As mentioned above, the chapters of *Eugene Onegin* were published separately over eight years. To some degree Pushkin wrote them, and expected them to be read, as separate compositions. I have accordingly prefaced the notes to each chapter with introductory material about that chapter.

Epigraph to the novel

"He was vanity through and through; yet he possessed in even greater measure the sort of pride which acknowledges deeds both good and bad with the same indifference – pride that springs from a consciousness of superiority that is perhaps imagined. – From a private letter" (French). On the surface this epigraph is a straightforward summing-up of the character of the hero, Eugene Onégin. Yet it also prefigures the nature of the novel in more subtle ways. The reference to the hero's consciousness of superiority as

"perhaps imagined" ("*peut-être imaginaire*") introduces the element
of deliberate ambiguity that permeates Pushkin's characterization
of Onégin and to an extent of all the main characters. Whenever
we think we have understood their true nature and their real
motivations, Pushkin shows us another facet of their personalities,
or offers us another interpretation of their actions, that forces us
to regard our previous assessment of them as "perhaps imagined".
We end up as unsure as in real life who people really are behind
the masks they present to society – and perhaps to themselves.

This equivocal realism, or realistic equivocality, so characteristic
of the novel, is underlined by the nature of the epigraph itself.
No one has yet identified the "private letter", whether Pushkin's
or someone else's, from which the epigraph is allegedly taken.
Commentators generally assume that Pushkin made the quotation
up for the purpose of the book. So even the epigraph itself is
"*peut-être imaginaire*".

Dedication
Addressed to P.A. Pletnyóv (1792–1865), a scholar, teacher, enthusiast
for literature and friend of Pushkin's, who later became Rector of
St Petersburg University. He was a man of gentle and sympathetic
character. It was Pletnyóv who took on the task of publishing
successive chapters of *Eugene Onegin* as Pushkin finished them. He
also published the first complete edition in 1833.

The lines first appeared, dated 29th December 1827 and with
Pletnyóv named as the dedicatee, in the first edition of Chapters
Four and Five in early 1828; but Pushkin clearly intended them to
cover the whole set of chapters. In the 1837 edition – the last to be
published before he died – he had the dedication, without Pletnyóv's
name, printed at the head of the whole novel.

Notes to Chapter One

Pushkin began work on Chapter One on 9th May 1823, during his
posting in Kishinyóv (now Chişinău, capital of modern Moldova).
He completed it that October in Odessa (apart from Stanzas 18,
19 and 33, which were added within the next twelve months). It
was published in St Petersburg in February 1825, while the poet

was still living in detention at Mikháylovskoye. The chapter was introduced by two pieces. The first was a short preface, as follows:

This is the beginning of a large poetical work, which will probably not be completed.

Several cantos, or chapters, of *Eugene Onegin* are now ready. Written as they were under the influence of favourable circumstances, they bear the stamp of that lightheartedness that marked the earliest works of the author of *Ruslan and Lyudmila* [see note on Stanza 2 below].

The first chapter offers something self-contained. It incorporates a description of the social life of a young person in St Petersburg at the close of 1819 and recalls *Beppo*, a jovial work by the gloomy Byron.

Far-sighted critics will, of course, remark on the lack of a plan: everyone is free to pontificate about the plan of a complete novel once they have read its first chapter. There will be criticism of the antipoetical nature of the chief character, who is reminiscent of the Prisoner in the Caucasus [the misanthropic hero of Pushkin's earlier narrative poem of that name]; also of certain stanzas that are written in the languid manner of recent elegiac poetry in which "a feeling of melancholy has engulfed all else" [quoted from a piece of contemporary literary criticism by Pushkin's poet-friend Vilgelm Kyukhelbéker – see note to IV, 32]. But let us be permitted to draw the attention of readers to merits that are rare in a satirical writer: the absence of anything to give personal offence, and the maintenance of strict propriety in the humorous description of social behaviour.

Between this preface and the beginning of Chapter One, Pushkin inserted another piece – an ironic dialogue in 192 lines of verse entitled 'Conversation between a Bookseller and a Poet', in which the reluctant poet is at length persuaded by a bookseller to negotiate a payment for the publication of his new work. The dialogue has (as Nabókov remarks) very little to do with *Eugene Onegin* and evokes less interest today than it would have done in early nineteenth-century Russia, where the concept of poets earning a living from their work was still a novelty.

According to the novel, Eugene Onégin was born in about 1795 (VIII, 12), four years before Pushkin. Having entered St Petersburg society at the age of about seventeen, in around 1812, he spent the next eight years there in a life of dissipation (IV, 9). Onégin's departure for his uncle's country estate is set in the early summer of 1820; Onégin is now about twenty-five.

At first sight Chapter One might seem a rather formless and fragmented composition, with its abrupt start and lengthy flashbacks to Onégin's early life in St Petersburg, interspersed with Pushkin's own expansive reflections. In fact, though, the chapter follows a disciplined concentric plan, in which one reaches the centre of the design through layers which then repeat themselves in reverse. At the centre of Chapter One is the description of a typical day in Onégin's life in St Petersburg (15–36); on either side of that are sections on Onégin's upbringing and early love affairs (3–12) and his disenchantment with love, learning and youth (36–48); enclosing that are passages touching on Pushkin's friendship with Onégin and Onégin's father's indebtedness (2–3 and 45–51), with the outermost layer dealing with Onégin's journey to his uncle's estate (1–2 and 52–54). The last six stanzas (55–60) are a coda of entirely autobiographical material.

Epigraph: A line from Prince Pyótr Vyázemsky's poem 'The First Snow' (dated November 1819), which is also referred to in V, 3. Vyázemsky (1792–1878) was a poet, critic and wit, and a close friend of Pushkin's.

In celebrating the first snow of winter the poet imagines a young couple enjoying the exhilaration of a country sleigh ride. He goes on:

Their swift ride as on wings, like a brief winter gust,
slices the snow with even furrows
and, throwing it up from the ground in a sparkling cloud,
envelopes them in silvery dust.
Time is for them foreshortened to one wingèd moment.
Just so do impetuous youngsters glide over life,
in a hurry to live, in haste for experience!
Vainly they follow every new impulse;
led far astray by their limitless desires,
they find refuge nowhere.

O happy years, those times of heartfelt longing!
But what am I saying? One fleeting day,
gone in a flash, like a false dream, a phantom's shadow,
carries off with it what is but a cruel mirage!
Even love itself betrays us likewise,
and teaches us wisdom the hard way;
it wears out our feelings and leaves on our lonely hearts
the scar of hope disappointed.
But what the heart has lost lives on in the heart's recollections.
Memory, like a resourceful magician,
summons up the past from cold ashes,
gives voice to what has gone silent
and life to what is dead and decayed...

In using one line of this poem for his epigraph to Chapter One, Pushkin no doubt had in mind how Vyázemsky's poem sets a trajectory for the whole of the chapter: it foreshadows the description of the young Onégin's thirst for experience, and subsequent satiety and disillusion; it anticipates ("One fleeting day, gone in a flash, like a false dream...") the description of Onégin's day in the middle of the chapter; and it also points forward to Pushkin's comments on the role of memory in his own love poetry in Stanzas 57–59.

Pushkin placed this epigraph at the head of Chapter One only after he had completed the whole novel: it first appeared in the edition of the complete work published in 1833. Previously separate printings of Chapter One had been headed only by the epigraph ("*Pétri de vanité...*") that subsequently became the epigraph for the whole work.

1   *Man of the highest principles*: The very first line of the novel gives an example of how Pushkin uses literary echoes that would have resonated with his readers to deepen the surface meaning of his words. The phrase "of the highest principles" is taken from a fable published in 1819 by the contemporary writer Iván Krylóv (1769–1844). In the fable, 'The Donkey and the Yokel', it is the donkey that is described as "of the highest principles". So when Onégin uses these words of his uncle, Pushkin is hinting that Onégin subconsciously thinks of his uncle as an ass,

thus introducing us from the start to the flippancy and contempt with which he habitually regards others.

In the fable the yokel has placed the donkey in his vegetable garden to scare the birds away, a role for which the animal is innately unsuited; and the donkey's asinine behaviour makes havoc of the garden. Is Pushkin suggesting that Onégin too, like the ass, is about to be placed in a situation in the country for which he is temperamentally unsuited and where his own thoughtlessness will create havoc?

Furthermore, the situation adumbrated in this stanza is a typically Pushkinian crystallization of a situation described much more diffusely in the epistolary novel *Clarissa* by the then still popular English author Samuel Richardson (1689–1761), whom Pushkin and his Russian contemporaries would have read mostly in French translation. Richardson's novels are alluded to several times in *Eugene Onegin* (e.g. II, 29, 30; III, 9, 10; IV, 7). *Clarissa* is about a rakish and unprincipled anti-hero, Lovelace, who seduces and cruelly mistreats the saintly heroine. In Volume III of the novel Lovelace learns of his wealthy uncle's illness and expected demise. Warned, as the presumptive heir, that his presence at his uncle's bedside would not be amiss and that his uncle wants to see him before he dies, and anxious to secure his uncle's loose cash, he travels out from London in a carriage-and-six to the old man's country seat in Berkshire, already worried about how to keep a straight face: "…how to act (I, who am no hypocrite) in the days of condolement! What farces I have to go through; and to be a principal actor in them!…" Lovelace (unlike Onégin) arrives in time to find, to his chagrin, that the uncle is still alive and subsequently complains to his correspondents that the old man "endures not to have me out of his sight for one half-hour" and "makes him sit hours together entertaining him…" (*Clarissa* Vol. III letters 37, 47, 49, 50, 56, 93). In opening his work in this way, Pushkin seems to be signalling that Eugene Onégin, reflecting in his personality sombre English models rather than French or German ones, will turn out ot be a similar anti-hero to Lovelace.

2   *as he rode post-haste*: Onégin's use of relays of post horses to pull his carriage (allowing continuous travel, without

the lengthy breaks required for resting proprietary horses) bears witness to the urgency, and financial importance, of his journey.

Lyudmíla and Ruslán: The heroine and hero of Pushkin's first major work, his mock-epic poem *Ruslan and Lyudmila*, completed and published in 1820. Though its fairy-tale subject matter could hardly be more different from that of *Eugene Onegin*, the two works share a lightness of touch and a detached, ironic and digressive style of narration.

but the north disagrees with me now: A reference, both tactful and ironic, to the disfavour with which the authorities in St Petersburg viewed the young Pushkin and which led them in 1820 to exclude him from the capital and post him compulsorily to the far south of Russia. Pushkin, still banned from visiting St Petersburg, wrote this in mid-1823 at Kishinyóv in modern Moldova. See Extra Material, pages 376 and 378.

3   *monsieur... madame*: The French Revolution, which began in 1789, had caused many members of the French aristocracy, bourgeoisie and clergy to flee abroad, where, often destitute, they were obliged to take up what employment they could find. By the first decade of the nineteenth century – the period of Onégin's boyhood – many were living in Russia as tutors or governesses to noble households, where a knowledge of French had long been regarded as an essential social prerequisite.

The French monsieur (a godforsaken cleric): In Samuel Richardson's *Clarissa* (Vol. II, letter 92) Lovelace's childhood tutor was "an honest parson".

Summer Park: The Letny Sad was (and is) a small and fashionable park by the Nevá, adjoining Peter the Great's modest Summer Palace.

4   *dressed like a London dandy*: The young Onégin "came out" into St Petersburg society in about 1812, at the time when, as a result of the French invasion of Russia under Napoleon, the long-standing dominance of French fashions among the upper classes had yielded to an enthusiasm for things English.

6   *make out an inscription*: The famous equestrian monument to Peter the Great (the "Bronze Horseman" of Pushkin's poem of the same name), erected in St Petersburg about forty years earlier by the Empress Catherine II, is inscribed on one side in Latin: "*PETRO PRIMO CATHARINA SECUNDA MDCCLXXXII*" ("Catherine II to Peter I, 1782"). It would not require a great proficiency in Latin to decipher such an inscription – and in any case a Russian translation is helpfully provided on the opposite side.

      Juvenal: Latin writer of around 100 AD who composed scathing satires on contemporary Roman society.

      vale: Latin for "farewell", often used at the end of letters.

      Aeneid: The famous epic poem by the Latin poet Virgil (70–19 BC).

      Romulus: Legendary founder of Rome in (according to tradition) 753 BC.

7   *tell an iambus from a trochee*: Two units of poetic metre: an iambus is a short (or unstressed) syllable followed by a long (or stressed) one; a trochee has the syllables in the reverse order.

      Theocritus or Homer: Classical Greek poets: Homer from early in the first millennium BC; and Theocritus from the third century BC.

      Adam Smith: Scottish economist (1723–90), who taught that agriculture and industry were more important to a country's prosperity than money.

8   *Ovid*: The Roman poet Publius Ovidius Naso (43 BC – 17 or 18 AD) wrote brilliant, witty and often erotic poetry. One of his most famous works, his *Ars amatoria* or "Art of Love", offended the Emperor Augustus, who was trying to raise standards of sexual morality in Rome. For this, and for an unspecified political misdemeanour, Ovid was exiled from Rome in 8 AD; he was sent to the distant frontier of the Roman Empire at Tomis on the shore of the Black Sea (modern Constanţa in Romania), just across the Danube delta from Moldavia. There he spent the last eight years of his life complaining of the harsh conditions and begging to be allowed back to Rome. His request was never granted.

There is a striking coincidence (which Pushkin had in mind when he wrote this passage) between Ovid's career and Pushkin's, whose libertine verses had offended the Emperor Alexander I and provoked him to banish Pushkin from the imperial capital to Kishinyóv in Moldavia-Bessarabia on the southern frontier of the Russian Empire. Although Pushkin's St Petersburg and Ovid's Rome are 2,500 km (and eighteen hundred years) apart, there is only about 350 km between the two disgraced poets' places of exile.

9 Pushkin composed a Stanza 9, but deleted it before printing. In it he observed that many of us, impatient for experience of life, learn about love from reading fiction instead of waiting to feel it for ourselves; Onégin, nonetheless, had managed to learn a lot about women. We do not know why Pushkin dropped the stanza: he may have decided that the sentiment about learning of love from reading was of out of character for Onégin, whose education had left much to be desired (I, 3–7) and who, we are later informed, got little from books (I, 44).

12 *ex-pupils of the same school*: The Russian text reads literally "ex-pupils of Faublas". Faublas was the main character in a multi-part novel by the French author Louvet de Couvray (1760–97), about a young seducer of other men's wives and girlfriends.

 those conceit had blinded to their state: Pushkin refers here to "the haughty horn-bearer". The wearing of horns was traditionally symbolic of cuckoldry.

13, 14 These stanzas did not get beyond the rough-draft stage. Stanza 13 gave additional examples of Onégin's cunning in the pursuit of women, and Stanza 14 compared his stratagems to those of a cat stalking a mouse or a hungry wolf hunting down a lamb. As it is, the gap (as Michael Basker points out in his notes to the Penguin Classics edition of 2003) performs a compositional function, separating the characterization of Onégin from the description of his day beginning in Stanza 15.

15 *a youngsters' dance*: This would have been a kind of junior ball, arranged for girls of between thirteen and sixteen years old, accompanied by their mothers, the menfolk

being from a wider age range. Because these functions were held early, they allowed male guests time to go on to theatres and proper balls afterwards.

wide-brimmed hat Bolívar-style: A style of hat associated with the South American liberator and republican Simón Bolívar (1783–1830), who by 1819 had embarked on the most successful phase of his campaign to oust the Spanish royalists from north-western South America; such hats were fashionable in St Petersburg at the time, especially among those of more liberal views.

Boulevard: Part of the Nevsky Prospékt, at that time planted with trees.

watch from Paris: Literally "Breguet", named after A.L. Breguet (1747–1823), who established a famous watch-making business in Paris in 1775. Pocket watches made by him were furnished with a mechanism whereby, if the wearer pressed a catch, he could hear the hour chimed without the need to open the watch case.

16   *Talon's*: Talon was a well-known French restaurateur in St Petersburg, whose establishment stood at the beginning of the Nevsky Prospékt (actually quite close to the "Boulevard" where Onégin had been strolling).

Kavérin: Teasingly hidden by asterisks in the 1837 edition. Pyótr Kavérin (1794–1855) was a hussar, man about town and friend of Pushkin's in St Petersburg.

vintage champagne: Literally "wine of the comet". The year 1811, in which a comet appeared, was a vintage year for champagne, and a comet was depicted on the corks of that year's wine.

Strasbourg pâté: I.e. *pâté de foie gras*, also known at the time as "Strasbourg pie", a pâté of goose livers larded with truffles that was (as Stanley Mitchell points out) imported to Russia in tins (hence "ever-fresh").

Limburg cheese: A strong, soft Belgian cheese that runs when it is cut.

Note the foreignness of all the fashionable luxuries, sartorial and culinary, in which Onégin indulges in Stanzas 15 and 16.

17   *the new ballet had now begun*: Theatrical performances normally began at 6 p.m.

    entrechat: A balletic term for a vertical leap in which the dancer repeatedly crosses the feet and beats them together.

    Phèdre... Cleopatra... Moëna: The references are to heroines of various plays, operas or ballets apparently performed in St Petersburg in 1818 or 1819. *Phèdre* was the heroine either of Racine's tragedy or of an opera based on it; the exact *Cleopatra* that Pushkin had in mind is uncertain; *Moëna* was the heroine of Ózerov's Celtic tragedy *Fingal*.

18   The stanza commemorates the Russian theatre of the late eighteenth and early nineteenth centuries. The playwrights referred to are the satirist Denís Fonvízin (1745–92), a versatile writer and progressive thinker of his day; Yakov Knyazhnín (1742–91); Vladisláv Ózerov (1769–1816); Pavel Katénin (1792–1853), a friend of Pushkin's, who wrote tragedies much influenced by French models; and Alexánder Shakhovskóy (1777–1846), writer of comedies similarly imitated from the French. Yekaterína Semyónova (1786–1849) was a renowned tragic actress of the time. Charles-Louis Didelot (1767–1837) was a French ballet master and choreographer associated with the St Petersburg ballet between 1801 and 1830.

19   *How sad it is I have to ask*: When Pushkin wrote this he had been in enforced absence from St Petersburg for three years and was out of touch with developments in the theatrical world there that he loved.

    a Russian Terpsichore: in classical mythology, Terpsichore was one of the nine Muses, the goddesses of the arts; Terpsichore was the Muse of dancing.

20   *boxes... stalls, pit*: At that time ladies (accompanied or not) sat only in the boxes and circles; stalls and pit (standing room behind the stall seats) were reserved for men.

    Istómina: Avdótya "Dunyásha" Istómina (1799–1848) was an attractive and gifted ballerina of Pushkin's time, taught by Didelot (see note on Stanza 18 above). Pushkin had courted her once. In 1823 she appeared in St Petersburg in a ballet based on Pushkin's verse tale *A Prisoner in the Caucasus*.

like fluff on a puff of the wind: Literally "like fluff from Aeolus's lips". In Greek mythology Aeolus was god of the winds.

24 *Rousseau*: Jean-Jacques Rousseau (1712–78), the French writer and philosopher. He also wrote a popular epistolary romance called *Julie, ou la nouvelle Héloïse,* first published in 1761, to which Pushkin refers in II, 29 and III, 9–10.

Grimm: Frédéric Melchior Grimm (1723–1807), the French encyclopedist. In a note on these lines, Pushkin quotes from Rousseau's *Confessions* on the encounter between the two men, when Grimm persisted in Rousseau's presence in polishing his fingernails with a purpose-made brush. Pushkin comments: "Grimm was ahead of his age: nowadays, all over enlightened Europe, people clean their nails with a special brush."

25 *Chaadáyev*: The name is concealed by asterisks in the 1837 edition. Pyótr Chaadáyev (1793–1856) was a friend of Pushkin's and a notable personality of the period. Famous for his meticulous attention to dress, he was also a philosopher and, later, a religious mystic.

26 *pantalons, frac and gilet*: French for "trousers", "dress coat" and "waistcoat".

Russian Academy's Lexicon: A dictionary, published in six volumes between 1789 and 1794, the policy of whose compilers was to exclude all "unnecessarily imported" foreign words.

30–34 Though many attempts have been made, it is impossible now to identify with any certainty the several pairs of delicate feet that have left their tantalizing imprint on these stanzas, in which Pushkin recalls various romantic encounters during his years in the south and earlier.

32 *Diana... Flora... Terpsichore*: Pushkin is here referring to the traditional artistic representation of certain mythological subjects. Diana, the Roman goddess of hunting and virginity, was usually portrayed dressed in a short tunic fastened over one shoulder and leaving the

other breast bare. Flora, the Roman goddess of flowering plants, was shown as a young girl with rosy cheeks. For Terpsichore, the goddess of dancing, see note on Stanza 19; she was normally portrayed barefoot.

Elvína: One of the conventional names for girls mentioned in love poetry of this period, and probably a literary fiction here. Zhukóvsky (see note on epigraph to Chapter Five) wrote a ballad about a fictional Elvína in 1814. When still at school in 1815, Pushkin addressed one of his early love lyrics to an Elvína, which may be a pseudonym for a real person or again represent a figment of Pushkin's imagination. It is hard to see why Pushkin has introduced Elvína in this stanza except to provide a convenient rhyme with "hearth" (*kamína*) three lines later.

33   *a young Armida's lips*: Armida was a beautiful sorceress in the poem *Gerusalemme liberata* (*Jerusalem Liberated*) (1581) by Torquato Tasso (1544–95).

35   *dawn drum roll*: The reveille for the guards' regiments quartered in various parts of the city.

      an Okhta dairy girl: Okhta was an outlying suburb of St Petersburg, where at the request of Alexander I in 1817 English Quakers had set up a modern farm that supplied dairy and other produce to the capital.

      Halbtür: German for "half-door", "hatch". The unusual (and un-Russian) word Pushkin uses here is *vasistas*, a French name, as Nabókov explains, for "a small spy window... with a mobile screen or grate", out of which a shopkeeper might pass his goods; Pushkin aptly uses it in the context of a German baker's shop because it is derived from the German *Was ist das?* (literally "What is it?"). Presumably this is what a German shopkeeper would say on opening his hatch to a customer outside, or perhaps the coiners of the word, ignorant of the right name for the fitment, referred to it as a "whatsit".

38   *Childe Harold*: The restless and gloomy hero of Lord Byron's long poem *Childe Harold's Pilgrimage*, published between 1812 and 1818, a work that had a strong influence on Pushkin and many of his contemporaries across Europe.

39–41   There is no evidence that these three stanzas ever existed. Nabokov comments, perhaps overfancifully, that "the gap… produces the impression of a tremendous yawn of ennui".

42   Pushkin appends the following note to this superficially misogynistic stanza:

> The whole of this ironical stanza is none other than a subtle panegyric to our lovely fellow-countrywomen. It is in this way that Boileau, under the guise of criticism, praises Louis XIV. Our ladies combine enlightenment with amiability, and a strict purity of morals with that oriental allure that so captivated Madame de Staël (see her *Dix ans d'exil*).

Irony? Or double irony?

Say and Bentham: Jean-Baptiste Say (1767–1832), French political economist, and Jeremy Bentham (1748–1832), English jurist and philosopher. Both were popular subjects of discussion in progressive circles at the time.

47   In this and the following stanza Pushkin imagines himself of a summer night (the "white nights", when in St Petersburg the daylight never really fades) standing with Onégin above the Nevá on the Palace Embankment near the Winter Palace.

image of the moon: Pushkin refers to "Diana's visage"; Diana was the goddess of the moon (and other things) in Roman mythology.

48   *our "bard"*: Pushkin is referring to verses by the minor poet Mikhaíl Nikítich Muravyóv (1757–1807) entitled 'To the goddess Nevá', four lines of which read:

> The enraptured bard beholds the goddess
> before him, the benign Nevá;
> a sleepless night he spends, arms resting
> upon the granite parapet.

the night-watch sentries: Probably the guards in the Peter and Paul Fortress, across the river from the Palace

Embankment and fashionable St Petersburg; it housed political prisoners in imperial Russia.

Milyónnaya Street: The street parallel to the Palace Embankment, one block back from the river.

the faraway sound of a horn and a jaunty song: It was the custom of some St Petersburg grandees to cruise on the Nevá with a band of musicians and singers. This may be what Pushkin has in mind here.

But sweeter still: A literal translation of the last sentence of this stanza would be: "But sweeter amid nocturnal pastimes [would be] the singing of Torquato's octaves". Torquato Tasso's *Gerusalemme liberata* was written in eight-line stanzas (octaves). Verses from it were often sung by Venetian gondoliers.

49   *River Brenta*: A river that flows into the Adriatic near Venice.

us poets: Literally "grandsons of Apollo". In Greek mythology Apollo was patron god of the arts, including poetry.

from Byron's noble verses: Literally "through the proud lyre of Albion". Byron had lived in Venice between 1816 and 1819 and described it several times in his poetry.

in golden Italy I'll spend: In the event Pushkin never realized his wish to visit Italy or anywhere in Western Europe.

Petrarch: the famous fourteenth-century Italian poet, author of many love poems.

50   This stanza was written in autumn 1823 in Odessa, the port city which stands on low cliffs above the Black Sea: see Extra Material, page 379.

Africa, my home: A reference to Pushkin's African great-grandfather – see Extra Material, page 375.

52   *he did receive... take his leave*: Compare Richardson's *Clarissa*, Vol. III, where Lovelace writes: "I have this moment intelligence from Simon Parsons, one of [my uncle] Lord M.'s stewards, that his lordship is very ill. Simon, who is my obsequious servant, in virtue of my presumptive heirship, gives me a hint in this letter that my

presence at M. Hall will not be amiss..." (letter 37) and "[I] found Simon Parsons, my lord's Berkshire bailiff... waiting for me with a message... to press me to go down, and that at my lord's particular desire; who wants to see me before he dies" (letter 50).

55   *far niente*: "To do nothing" (Italian).

57   *This was how... Bakhchisaráy*: A more literal translation of this sentence would be: "This was how, with so little trouble, I sang of the maid of the mountains, my ideal, and of the (female) captives of the banks of the Salgír." Pushkin is referring to the heroines of two of his earlier narrative poems, *A Prisoner in the Caucasus* and *The Fountain of Bakhchisaráy*. The Salgír is the longest of the Crimean rivers, flowing northwards from the Crimean mountains through Simferópol into the Sea of Ázov; it passes within about twenty miles of Bakhchisaráy, the former residence of the Crimean khans.

59   *clutters the margin*: Pushkin's notebooks, many of which survive, are noted for the abundance of marginal doodles, especially sketches of friends' profiles, hands, feet, etc.

    a twenty-five-canto-long epic: Pushkin, noted as an author for his brevity, never came near to writing such a work.

60   *the censor*: A reference to the imperial censorship in St Petersburg, which had to approve books for publication. The censors gave Pushkin a lot of trouble over the years.

    So off you go... off to St Petersburg: Again, written by Pushkin during his banishment in Odessa – see the opening of Ovid's *Tristia*, the first set of poems he sent back to Rome from his exile on the shores of the same Black Sea: "*Parve, (nec invideo) sine me, liber, ibis in urbem: / ei mihi, quod domino non licet ire tuo!*" ("Off you go without me to the city, little book. I don't begrudge it you; but how I regret that your author can't go too!").

Notes to Chapter Two

Pushkin composed Chapter Two between October and December 1823 in Odessa (though Stanzas 35, 39 and 40 were written later). It was published in Moscow in October 1826, shortly after Nicholas I had recalled the author from exile.

The events of this chapter take place in the summer of 1820. By the time of his arrival in the country, Lensky is probably just eighteen; Tatyána is seventeen, and her sister Olga about a year younger. Praskóvya Lárina, their mother, who could well have been in her late teens when she was married in 1802 or a little earlier, will still be only around forty. Her recently deceased husband, Dmitry Larin, to judge by his military rank and service (Stanzas 36 and 37), must have been at least in his mid-thirties when he married and his mid-fifties when he died.

In Chapter Two, as in Chapter One, it is possible to trace a pattern of concentric layers, revolving this time around the brief and prosaic portrait of Olga in Stanza 23. On either side of Olga are fuller descriptions of Lensky and Tatyána, in similarly dreamy and idealistic terms, that tempt us to anticipate Onégin's tactless remark to Lensky in the next chapter: "If I'd been a poet like you, it's the other one I would have chosen" (III, 5). Outside Lensky and Tatyána are descriptions of Onégin and the Larin parents, contrasting their attitudes to country life: the bored bachelor reforming country institutions and avoiding neighbours' visits (2, 4), and the contented couple observing country customs and receiving neighbours' visits (34, 35). There is also a contrast between the lives and deaths of two of the older generation: Onégin's miserly, reclusive and largely unmourned uncle (3), and the kindly, sociable and lamented Dmitry Larin (34–37).

Epigraph: There is a play on words in the original. It reads (in Latin) "*O rus!*" – a quotation from the Roman poet Horace, meaning "O countryside!" – and then (in Russian) "*O Rus!*" – an invocation of the ancient and poetic name for Russia. Horace (65–8 BC) was a poet who (like Pushkin) enjoyed country life. The quotation in this epigraph is from his *Satires* (II, 6), where he talks of his longing to see the countryside again and to forget the vexations of city life in reading, sleeping and general inactivity. Taken as a whole, then, the epigraph evokes specifically a love for the traditional Russian countryside, which is a recurring theme not only of Chapter Two but of the whole central section of the novel from Chapters Two to Seven.

1   *secluded manor house*: The picture given here could almost be a description of the Pushkin family's country residence at Mikháylovskoye, which he had visited several times since the summer of 1817 and where he was later to spend over two years of exile. The house at Mikháylovskoye, too, stands on a steep hill, surrounded on three sides by a wooded park and on the fourth enjoying extensive views across the River Sorot to the countryside beyond.

2   *tsars' portraits*: This is what Pushkin originally wrote; but for reasons of censorship ("tsars were not to be mentioned in such an offhand way," comments Nabókov), he changed it to read "portraits of ancestors" in the published text.

4   *The serfs*: Apparently the censor objected to the use of the word *раб* ("serf"), as the issue of the emancipation of the serfs was already a highly sensitive one. Consequently all the editions of Chapter Two published during Pushkin's lifetime replace *И раб* at the beginning of line 8 with the less politically loaded *Мужик* ("peasant").

5   *freethinking masons*: In the original *farmazón*, an ignorant and prejudiced mispronunciation of "freemason". Masonic organizations at the time were centres of liberal thought, and their members tended to be regarded by conservatives as revolutionaries. The Emperor Alexander I banned Masonic lodges in Russia in 1821, the year after Onégin's arrival in the country.

    Red wine in tumblerfuls: An accusation not so much of alcoholism as of extravagance in preferring an expensive, often imported drink to the home-made kvass and fruit cordials normally drunk in traditional households.

6   *Göttingen alumnus*: Göttingen University (founded in 1737 by King George II of England as Elector of Hannover) had become one of the leading universities of Western Europe with a reputation for intellectual freedom and liberalism. In the eighteenth century it had been a centre for German

poets of the "sentimental" school, who rebelled against the constrictions of Enlightenment rationalism and were forerunners of German romanticism.

Kant: Immanuel Kant (1724–1804), German idealist philosopher.

8–10   In these stanzas, as elsewhere in the novel (e.g. IV, 27, 31; VI, 20–23, 36–37), Pushkin is drawing an implicit contrast between Lensky's woolly, high-minded and self-consciously earnest style and his own much more incisive, down-to-earth and irreverently ironic approach. He is also, through Lensky's thought and poetry, gently parodying the attitudes and verses of friends, such as Zhukóvsky and Kyukhelbéker, who admired the same German models as Lensky.

8   *to be humanity's... endow the world with bliss*: These lines were omitted from the published text of this chapter during Pushkin's lifetime, apparently because of objections from the censor. Perhaps the censor thought that Pushkin's words, submitted for publication in 1826, could be read as an ironic comment on the recently deceased Emperor Alexander I's mystical belief in the destiny of the Románov dynasty.

9   *Schiller and Goethe*: Friedrich von Schiller (1759–1805), German poet, playwright and historian; Johann Wolfgang von Goethe (1749–1832), renowned German poet, dramatist, novelist, statesman and thinker. Nabókov comments: "Pushkin had even less German than he had English, and only very vaguely knew German literature. He was immune to its influence and hostile to its trends. The little he had read of it was either in French versions... or in Russian adaptations" – by, for instance, Pushkin's friend Zhukóvsky.

12   *Come to me in my golden chamber*: This is the first line of an aria from a Russian comic opera (adapted from a German original with music by Ferdinand Kauer) entitled *The Rusalka of the Dniepr* – first staged in St Petersburg in 1803, but still popular in Pushkin's day. The words of this aria were calculated to leave young eligibles like Lensky in no doubt about the singer's aspirations:

Come to me in my golden chamber,
come to me, my dearest prince,
there you'll gather all you wish for,
there you'll find a loving bride.
Come, and learn how much I love you,
how I'm burning with desire.

…

I'll burn with love only for you.
Yours, yours alone I want to be,
'tis only you I want to love.

16   *The social contract... and the arts*: A reference to the ideas put forward in two of Jean-Jacques Rousseau's socio-philosophical works, his *Du contrat social* (1762) and his *Discours sur les sciences et les arts* (1750), which continued to generate discussion in Russian intellectual circles.

     northern verse: Nabókov takes this to refer to the legendary Celtic bard Ossian, whose supposed epic fragments were much in vogue in Europe at that time. But it seems to me much more likely that Pushkin was making a typically ironic reference to his own and his contemporaries' Russian poetry.

29, 30   *Richardson... Grandison... Lovelace*: For Richardson and Lovelace, see note on I, 1. Another popular novel of Richardson's, besides *Clarissa*, was *The History of Sir Charles Grandison* (1753), about a model hero of this name who shows every good quality.

29   *Rousseau*: See note on I, 24.

     His wife: Pushkin is said to have modelled Praskóvya Lárina on Praskóvya Ósipova, widowed mother of several daughters of Pushkin's age and younger, who lived at Trigórskoye, a neighbouring estate to the Pushkins' Mikháylovskoye. Pushkin had met the Ósipov family during his summer stay at Mikháylovskoye in 1817 and remained on friendly terms with the mother and members of her family all his life.

30   *Aline*: A fashionably Western-European-sounding version of the Russian name Alexándra, adopted in the same spirit as "Pauline" and "Céline" – see Stanza 33 below.

31 *Routine... happiness*: This is Pushkin's vernacular version
    (as he acknowledges in his notes) of a sentence in the novel
    René (1802) by Chateaubriand (for whom see note on IV,
    26): "*Si j'avais la folie de croire encore au bonheur, je le
    chercherais dans l'habitude.*"

32 *like an autocrat*: In Russian самодержавно, the word used
    in Pushkin's manuscript draft of this line. It comes from
    the word самодержец ("autocrat"), a title often applied
    to the reigning emperor. The editions printed in Pushkin's
    lifetime substitute the word единовластно ("like a
    monarch"), because (it is presumed) the censor once again
    objected to what he took to be a flippant reference to the
    imperial regime (see note on Stanza 2).

    chose serfs for soldiers: Literally "shaved foreheads".
    From time to time landowners were expected to provide
    serfs to serve in the army. At recruiting times those serfs
    considered suitable for service had their forelocks shaved;
    those unsuitable were shaved on the back of the neck.
    Service was typically for twenty-five years, tantamount
    to a life sentence, and selection was often imposed as a
    punishment.

33 *to call Céline "Akúlka" once again*: In other words, she
    went back to using Russian names instead of chic French
    ones like Céline. "Akúlka" is a familiar form of the
    Russian girl's name Akulína (i.e. Aquilina, the name, like
    Tatiana, of a third-century Christian martyr and saint).

35 *They kept the Church fasts*: Pushkin omitted lines 5–11
    of this stanza from editions published during his lifetime,
    apparently in response to objections from the censor.
    Nabokov explains that "such homely and perhaps 'satirical'
    descriptions of churchgoing were taboo". Most modern
    editors have reinstated them from Pushkin's fair copy.

    songs for telling fortunes: Telling fortunes was an
    especially popular pastime at *svyátki*, the festive period
    between Christmas and Epiphany (6th January) – see V,
    7–8. One custom was for girls to drop their rings into
    a covered bowl of water before singing carols or other
    songs; as the carols were sung, the rings were taken out
    at random one by one, and each girl's fortune was said to

be revealed by the words and tune of the song being sung when her ring came out of the bowl.

they'd shed... bunch of buttercups: On Trinity Day, which usually falls in June, people often brought a birch-tree branch or a bunch of wild flowers to church. The tradition in some regions was for worshippers to count their sins by the number of dewdrops on the foliage they carried and to shed a tear for each sin. The implication here is that the Larins were good folk with few sins to repent of.

kvass: A traditional Russian drink made from rye dough and malt.

had dishes served in order of their rank: An old Russian custom, obsolete in the capitals by Pushkin's day.

36   *brigadier*: The army rank of brigadier had been abolished by the Emperor Paul in 1799. Evidently Dmitry Larin had retired from the army in that year (if not earlier) and had then, within the next couple of years, arranged his marriage and withdrawn to the country.

37   *Poor Yorick*: Pushkin adds a note here: "Hamlet's exclamation over the jester's skull – see Shakespeare and Sterne." Although later Pushkin learnt enough of the language to read English literature in the original and became an enthusiastic admirer of Shakespeare, at this stage in his career (1823) his English was rudimentary and he knew English writers mainly through French translations. As his note suggests, his knowledge of *Hamlet* would have come initially through French versions of Laurence Sterne (1713–68). In Sterne's *Tristram Shandy* and *A Sentimental Journey*, "the Reverend Mr Yorick" is respectively a minor character and the narrator of the story. In one episode of the latter work the Reverend Yorick is comically mistaken for Shakespeare's Yorick.

Lensky is clearly thinking of more than Hamlet's two-word exclamation in Shakespeare's play. More fully the passage reads: "Alas, poor Yorick! I knew him, Horatio: a fellow of infinite jest, of most excellent fancy; he hath borne me on his back a thousand times..." (Act V, Scene 1). The quotation typifies Pushkin's distinctive blend of pathos and humour, even when dealing with death.

> *Ochákov*: A fortress on the Black Sea, east of Odessa, which Russian forces under Potyómkin captured from the Turks in 1788.

40 *Lethe's waters*: Lethe, in ancient mythology, was the river of the underworld whose waters were said to bring forgetfulness. There is an allusion here to a poem by Pushkin's contemporary Konstantín Bátyushkov (1787–1855), *Vision on Lethe's Banks*, which referred to the works of incompetent poets "drowning in the waters of oblivion".

> *peaceful arts*: The original reads "peaceful Aonids". The Muses, Greco-Roman goddesses of the arts, had their principal shrine on Mount Helicon, in the district of Greece known as Aonia. Hence the Roman poet Ovid used the term Aonids (women from Aonia) to denote the Muses.

Notes to Chapter Three

Pushkin composed Chapter Three in Odessa and Mikháylovskoye between February and October 1824. The chapter was only published in its entirety in St Petersburg in October 1827. In a brief preface Pushkin wrote:

> The first chapter of *Eugene Onegin*, written in 1823, appeared in '25. Two years later the second was published. These delays were due to extraneous circumstances. From now on publication will proceed in uninterrupted sequence, one chapter immediately after another.

The action takes place in the summer of 1820.

It is again possible to trace a concentric plan in the structure of the chapter, centred on the bedroom scene where Tatyána converses with her old nurse (17–21), preceded and followed by stanzas describing and contrasting Tatyána's and other women's attitudes to love (15–16, and 22–25). This central section is framed by two often ironic digressions, one on women's reading (12–14) and one on their ability to express themselves in speech and writing (26–29). Beyond that, in both directions, there are specific examples of Tatyána's reading (9–10) and of her writing (between 31 and 32), the first including a fictional love letter and the second consisting of an actual letter. Further out still we have stanzas about the effect on Tatyána of her feelings for Onégin and of her embarrassment at the inquisitiveness of neighbours (6–8 and 32–35). The outer frame for the whole chapter is formed by accounts of the first (1–5) and second (36–41) visits of Onégin to the Larin household, both passages featuring a mention of country fruits and country customs (3 and 39 plus the peasant girls' song); both accounts, however, curiously stop short of describing the couple's actual encounter.

Epigraph: Jacques Clinchamps de Malfilâtre (1732–67) was a minor French poet; the quotation comes from his poem *Narcisse, ou l'île de Vénus*, published in 1768. Pushkin seems to have drawn the quotation from the compilation of teaching material on literature entitled *Lycée, ou Cours de littérature* (1799) by Jean-François de La Harpe (1739–1803), a publication that Pushkin knew from school. The passage continues as follows:

> *Elle était fille; elle était amoureuse.*
> *Elle tremblait pour l'objet de ses soins.*
> *...*
> *Et, pour Écho, sa faute est excusable.*
> *Si cette nymphe est coupable en ceci,*
> *Je lui pardonne; Amour la fit coupable*:
> *Puisse le sort lui pardonner aussi!*

– which may be roughly translated:

> She was a girl, a girl in love.
> She was trembling for the object of her desires.
> ...
> And, as for Echo, her fault is forgivable.
> If this nymph is guilty here,
> I pardon her; Love made her guilty:
> May destiny pardon her too!

The passage, whose subject matter is taken from Ovid's *Metamorphoses*, refers to the nymph Echo, who (in ancient mythology) fell in love with the youth Narcissus; but Narcissus did not return her love because he was in love with his own reflection. Thus the apparently inconsequential epigraph carries within it a summary of the chapter as a whole.

2   *this shepherdess of yours*: "Phyllis", in Pushkin's original: a conventional girl's name in classical pastoral poetry.

3   *cowberry juice*: Cowberries are small red berries from a low shrub (*Vaccinium vitis-idaea* – of the same genus as bilberries) that grows wild in the Russian countryside. Pushkin is contrasting the Larins' homely lifestyle with Onégin's extravagant taste for imported "red wine in tumblerfuls" (II, 5).

     Pushkin drafted lines 9–14, which gave a few more details of the young friends' visit to the Larins'; but he deleted them from the published version for reasons that are unclear.

5   *'silent / and dejected', like Svetlána*: Svetlána was the heroine of a ballad (1812) of the same name by Pushkin's poet friend Zhukóvsky, who describes her in these terms – see note on the epigraph to Chapter Five.

9, 10 The literary references here are as follows. Julie Wolmar ("Julie" in Stanza 10) is the Swiss heroine of Rousseau's epistolary novel *Julie, ou la nouvelle Héloïse* (see note on I, 24); Julie falls in love with her tutor Saint-Preux. He goes abroad and returns years later to find her married to someone else. Malek-Adhel is the hero of *Mathilde*, a novel (1805) by Sophie Cottin (1770–1807); he is a Muslim general at the time of the Crusades who has a love affair with Mathilde, an English princess; but her religious, political and family obligations prevent them from marrying before he is killed in combat. De Linar was a young Swede in love with Valérie in the epistolary novel of that name (1803) by Madame de Krüdener (1764–1824). Werther was the hero of Goethe's sentimental romance, largely in epistolary form, *Die Leiden des jungen Werthers* (1774), about a young painter in love with a married girl, who eventually kills himself. For Grandison and Clarissa see notes on II, 29, 30. Delphine d'Albémar is the heroine of Madame de Staël's epistolary novel *Delphine* (1804), about a young widow in love with a married man.

Significantly, in each of these novels, except *Sir Charles Grandison*, moral obligations, usually over the sanctity of marriage, prevent the heroine from being united with the man that loved her. Even in *Sir Charles Grandison* a secondary heroine renounces marriage with him for religious reasons. Pushkin has chosen the novels on Tatyána's reading list to prepare her for her future.

9   *Grandison / (who sends us all to sleep)*: See Sir Walter Scott, writing in his *Prefatory Memoir to the Novels of Samuel Richardson* of 1824 – the same year in which Pushkin composed Chapter Three. Scott refers to:

> the numerous and long conversations upon religious and moral topics, which compose so great a part of [*Sir Charles Grandison*] that a venerable old lady, whom we well knew, when in advanced age she became subject to drowsy fits, chose to hear *Sir Charles Grandison* read to her as she sat in her elbow chair, in preference to any other work, "because," said she, "should I drop asleep in course of the reading, I am sure, when I awake, I shall have lost none of the story, but shall find the party, where I left them, conversing in the cedar parlour."

11   In the concentric scheme for this chapter described above, this stanza matches Stanza 30. It is possible therefore to see Stanza 11 as a covert message of sympathy, support and encouragement to his disgraced friend the poet Baratýnsky – see note on Stanza 30.

12   *fables of British writers*: The literary references are as follows. The vampire superstition is mentioned in Byron's poem *The Giaour* (1813) and was used by him later; but, as Pushkin makes clear in a note, the reference here is to the horror tale *The Vampyre* (1819) by Byron's physician John Polidori (1795–1821), which was initially attributed to Byron and probably based on an oral improvisation

by him. Melmoth is the chief character in *Melmoth the Wanderer* (1820), by the Irish author Charles Maturin (1782–1824), another grisly story of the supernatural. The legend of the Jew who, having refused to help Jesus Christ on his way to Calvary, was condemned to roam the world for eternity, was widely used by Byronic writers of the Romantic era. *The Corsair* (published 1814) was a poem of Byron's about a "lone, wild and strange" adventurer, thought to have been based in part on the character of Napoleon. The "mysterious Sbogar" is Jean Sbogar, hero of a novel of that name (1818) about a young and wild Dalmatian brigand by the French writer Charles Nodier (1780–1844), a non-British interloper in this stanza.

These books are all works of Pushkin's (and Onégin's) time, while Tatyána's reading (Stanzas 9 and 10) comes from an earlier generation of writers. She does not encounter Byron and his confrères until she browses through Onégin's library in VII, 20–24.

13   *defying Phoebus's threats*: Phoebus (Apollo) was the ancient god of poetry and the other arts.

18   *"Then how did you get married, nanny?"*: Tatyána is aghast that her nurse could have been forced by her family to enter a loveless marriage. But the irony of the passage is that in the end Tatyána will be pressed by her own family into just such a marriage.

      as they undid my plait: In old Russia, when a girl was married, her single plait was retressed in two braids, amid customary lamentations..

22   *Abandon hope for ever*: According to Dante's *Inferno*, the inscription over the gate of Hell ended: *Lasciate ogni speranza, voi ch'entrate!* ("Abandon all hope, you who enter here!"). Pushkin comments in his note on this line: "Our bashful author has translated only the first half of this famous verse."

23   *more gentle*: Russian *нежней*, the reading of Pushkin's earlier editions. The 1837 edition reads *важней* ("more grave"), which modern editors have taken to be a misprint.

26   *She didn't know her Russian well*: Girls like Tatyána would of course have been fluent in the spoken Russian of

319

everyday life; and they would have had some familiarity with the Old Slavonic of Orthodox church services and religious texts. Pushkin is here commenting on their weaknesses in Russian grammar and on their lack of practice with the written Russian of books and letters.

27 *that rag The Well-Intentioned*: *The Well-Intentioned* (*Blagonamérenny* in Russian) was a literary journal published during the 1820s, of which Pushkin had a low opinion. In a note written later he describes it as "a journal once edited, rather carelessly, by the late A. Izmáylov", who had died in 1831. The journal was known for the lack of discrimination and good taste in the material it published, which was sometimes deemed unsuitable for young ladies. In the early 1820s Izmáylov had clashed with poets of Pushkin's circle (including Baratýnsky – see Stanza 30 below) over literary issues.

29 *the verses of Bogdanóvich*: Ippolít Fyódorovich Bogdanóvich (1743–1803) was a Russian poet and translator admired by Pushkin.

Parny's frank expressions... no longer in fashion: Evarist-Désiré de Parny (1753–1814) was a French poet famed for both the elegance and the frankness of his love poetry; he influenced Pushkin as well as Russian writers of the preceding generation. In referring to Parny being "no longer in fashion" Pushkin seems to be referring ironically to the views of his friend the poet and literary critic Kyukhelbéker, who had published an article in 1824 – see note to IV, 32 – in which he criticized Parny harshly, describing him as "a pygmy of French literature".

30 *my dear Baratýnsky*: Pushkin does not name Baratýnsky in the text, though he identifies him in a note. Yevgény Abrámovich Baratýnsky (1800–44) was a friend of Pushkin's, whose poetry Pushkin regarded highly. Baratýnsky was born in Tambóv province. At the age of sixteen he was expelled from the Corps of Pages by order of the Emperor for a misdemeanour, and he withdrew into the country in disgrace. Back in St Petersburg in 1819 he met Pushkin. The next year, in order to rehabilitate himself, he joined the army as a private and was posted to Finland, where

he stayed till 1824. His elegy *Feasts* was written in Finland in 1820. The nostalgic poem evokes a happier time with poet friends in the St Petersburg of 1819. He later wrote a narrative poem *Eda: A Finnish Tale* (published 1826), about a Finnish girl seduced by a Russian soldier; the poem contained a description that Pushkin admired of a Finnish winter (see V, 3).

31   *Freischütz*: A popular opera by Weber (1786–1826), first produced in Berlin in 1821. Its brilliant overture is often performed separately. The wife of Pushkin's close friend Prince Pyótr Vyázemsky was staying in Odessa while Pushkin was there in the early summer of 1824 and had been sent a copy of the piano score earlier in the year; so Pushkin might well have heard it being practised in her apartment.

Tatyána's letter: Commentators find here numerous echoes of French novels of the kind Tatyána had been reading (Stanzas 9 and 10).

Tatyána's letter exemplifies the way Pushkin manipulates the boundaries between fiction and reality. Pushkin claims to have the French original of the letter in his possession; and after six stanzas of rambling and apologetic hesitation he purports to produce a "lame and inadequate" Russian translation of it. In reality, however, there is no French original, and the Russian text is not a translation. Paradoxically, the purpose – and effect – of this procedure is to have us believe in the reality of a text that is doubly non-existent (no French original, no letter at all).

By the conventions of her time it was, of course, wildly indiscreet – and dangerous – for Tatyána to write a secret love letter to a man she hardly knew. One feature of the letter that does not come over easily in English translation is Tatyána's use of second-person pronouns. Russian, like French (in which, we are told, Tatyána composed her letter), has two forms for addressing a single person: the familiar form (French *tu*), used only for family and close friends, and the polite form (French *vous*), used in all other cases. Tatyána begins her letter using – appropriately – the polite form; but in the middle of the letter she abandons convention and daringly starts to address Onégin with the familiar pronoun. Then in the final sentence, as if ashamed of the familiarity, she reverts to the polite form. In the absence of alternative second-person pronouns in modern English, I have inserted the appellation "Eugene" in the text in a couple of places to signal Tatyána's use of the familiar form; and at the end I have signalled her return to formality by having her address Onégin as "sir".

Heaven has willed it: The reading *То воля неба…* is from the 1833 edition. The 1837 edition reads *Но воля неба…* ("But Heaven has willed…"). Modern editors take the 1837 version to be a misprint.

38   *leapt to the other porch… straight into the garden*: Tatyána is here unwittingly giving Onégin a taste of his own medicine. Tatyána escaping Onégin via her back door ironically parallels Onégin escaping his neighbours via *his* back door – see II, 5. But Onégin was evading his visitors because he liked and respected them too little, while Tatyána was avoiding her visitor because she liked and respected him too much.

39   *Song of the Peasant Girls*: This is not an actual folk song, but a pastiche composed by Pushkin to further his literary purposes on several levels. He inserts it at this point to heighten the narrative suspense. He uses it to colour in the rustic background of traditional Russian peasant life, as a foil to the Europeanized sensibility of gentry like the Larins. He draws a piquant contrast between the playful archness of the peasant girls' attitude to the opposite sex and the passionate sincerity and sponaneity of Tatyána's reaction to Onégin: the girls in the song are, for fun, luring on an amorous young man they do not love, with the intention of chasing him away again, while Tatyána, in deadly earnest, is running away from the unresponsive man that she does love, although she wishes to attract him. In this way Pushkin uses the song to throw Tatyána's emotions into stronger relief.

Pushkin's song is composed of eighteen seven-syllable lines in a trochaic rhythm. He uses an intricate pattern of internal rhymes and assonances, which it would be impossible to reproduce in English without an unacceptably clumsy or inaccurate outcome. My own translation alternates Pushkin's seven-syllable trochaic trimeters with ten-syllable iambic pentameters and in compensation reduces the number of lines to fourteen, with an end-of-line rhyme for each couplet. This gives the translation more freedom to reflect the sense of the original faithfully, while preserving the folk-song flavour.

Notes to Chapter Four

Pushkin composed Chapter Four between October 1824 and the first week of January 1826: it was therefore written entirely during the period of his house arrest at Mikháylovskoye. Chapter Four was first published together with Chapter Five in St Petersburg at the end of January 1828.

This chapter spans the summer and early winter of 1820. We are told that the closing scene (Stanzas 47–50) takes place in the week before Tatyána's name day, Saturday 12th January 1821 (last line of 48, and first two lines of 49). On the assumption that there is no overlap between the end of Chapter Four and the beginning of Chapter Five, which opens in the small hours of (Wednesday) 3rd January, then the conversation between Onégin and Lensky must take place between 31st December 1820 and 2nd January 1821. Accordingly the wedding between Lensky and Olga must have been planned for the week beginning Sunday 13th January (first two lines of 50).

A concentric structure for this chapter is less marked, but still discernible. The "bookends" of the chapter are two passages contrasting men's attitudes towards women – predatory and coldly apathetic on the part of the likes of Onégin (7–10) and sentimentally idealistic on the part of Lensky (48–50), the final stanza (51) commenting briefly on the two standpoints. Within that are two passages that give a somewhat mellower picture of Onégin than hitherto (11–17 and 44–49). The middle of this chapter contains, amid a series of digressions, stanzas on Tatyána's continuing unhappiness (23–24) and Onégin's relative contentment

(37–38), with as a centrepiece a much interrupted account of the relationship between Lensky and Olga (25–35).

Epigraph: Again, a brief and apparently bland motto that hides several layers of underlying significance. Jacques Necker (1732–1804) was a Genevan banker who entered politics in France and became director general of finance under Louis XVI. The remark of his that Pushkin quotes was recorded by his daughter Madame de Staël (1766–1817) in Chapter 20 of Part 2 of her *Considérations sur les principaux événements de la révolution française* (*Reflections on the Principal Events of the French Revolution*), published posthumously in 1818. The chapter deals with the death in 1791 of the Comte de Mirabeau, the opportunist renegade aristocrat and revolutionary leader who had in public been an outspoken opponent of her father. In the chapter she is making the point that, for all his ruthless self-seeking and populism, Mirabeau latterly showed himself also to be a conciliator and man of principle. She writes:

> I have held in my hands a letter of Mirabeau's written to be shown to the King; in it he offered his every assistance in providing France with a monarchy that would be strong and prestigious, but limited; he used, among others, the following striking expression: "I would not wish the only outcome of my work to be one vast destruction." The whole letter did honour to the reasonableness of his viewpoint. His death was a great tragedy, at the time when it happened: an overwhelming superiority of intellect always presents great opportunities. "You are too clever," Monsieur Necker said one day to Mirabeau, "not to recognize sooner or later that morality is in the nature of things."

Later in the chapter, after recounting the widespread mourning in Paris at Mirabeau's death, she sums up:

> There is in the destiny of nearly everyone, when we take the trouble to look, the clear proof of a moral and religious purpose, of which they are not always themselves aware and towards which they step out unconsciously.

Pushkin seems to have had more than one motive in choosing this remark of Necker's as the epigraph to Chapter Four. Madame de Staël is quoting her father in support of her own contention that there is an innate morality that shows itself, sooner or later, in the behaviour of nearly everyone, however ruthless and self-seeking they may have been. On one level Pushkin is suggesting that Onégin's uncharacteristically gentle treatment of Tatyána in Chapter Four is a manifestation of this "innate morality". But Pushkin is also punning here: in French (and Russian) the word *morale* ("morality") can also mean "moralizing"; so this is also a sardonic reference (*"moralizing* is in the nature of things") to Onégin's "sermon" in Stanzas 12–16 and Lensky's choice of reading in Stanza 26. On a third level it is possible to read a political subtext: Pushkin completed Chapter Four on 6th January 1826, just over three weeks after the abortive Decembrist uprising in St Petersburg. The aim of some at least of the Decembrists was to establish in Russia a constitutional monarchy of the same kind that Mirabeau had been manoeuvring to establish in France at the time of his death. Whether fully consciously or not, Pushkin seems to have had this passage of Madame de Staël's in mind at that time because her regret at the failure of Mirabeau's attempts at political compromise in France mirrored his own reactions to the failure of the Decembrists in Russia.

1–6   Pushkin composed the first four stanzas of this chapter, but then decided against including them in the published text. He did, however, in October 1827 have them published separately in the *Moscow Herald* under the title 'Women'. They give a frank and personal account of his relations with women and the conclusions he draws from his experience. The four published stanzas are given in the Appendix. It is unclear why Pushkin left these stanzas out of the published versions of his novel. He may well have felt that the preamble to the resumption of the narrative in Stanza 11 was long enough without them.

    Pushkin never seems to have produced a completed version of Stanzas 5 and 6.

7   *such Lovelaces*: For Lovelace, the anti-hero of Richardson's *Clarissa*, see notes on I, 1 and II, 29–30 above.

14   *marriage*: Literally "Hymenaeus" (Hymen), the Greco-Roman god of marriage, often used, even in classical literature, as a synonym for marriage or married life.

19   *there is no slander... rumour-monger*: "The Garret" was the name given to the upper floor of a St Petersburg mansion where the playwright-impresario Prince Alexánder Shakhovskóy used to give parties for the young bloods of the city during Pushkin's St Petersburg days (1818–20). At the time of Pushkin's disgrace and banishment from St Petersburg in 1820, one of the members of this set, the disreputable Count Fyódor Ivánovich Tolstóy (1782–1846), spread a malicious rumour that Pushkin had been subjected to a flogging in the secret chancellery of the Ministry of the Interior. This rumour enraged Pushkin when he heard of it after his departure from the capital. Six years later, after his exile, he challenged Tolstóy to a duel, though they were later reconciled.

26   *Chateaubriand*: French writer, diplomat and politician, (1768–1848) whose writings, including the novel *René* (1802), were renowned at the time for the romantic "naturalism" of their descriptions of landscapes and human feelings, a naturalism that was at variance with the idealistic Lensky's penchant for moralizing and sentimentality. See also note for II, 31.

27   *shrine of Venus*: Literally "temple of Kiprída". *Kiprída* is a Russian form of the Greek *Cypris*. Cypris ("the woman from Cyprus") was a Greek title, used in Homer onwards, for Aphrodite (a.k.a. Venus), goddess of love, because two of her main sanctuaries were in Cyprus.

28   *"Qu'écrirez-vous sur ces tablettes?"... "toute à vous, Annette"*: Entries written, fashionably, in French verse: "What will you in this note book write?"; "all yours, Annette".

30   *Tolstóy*: This refers to Count Fyódor Petróvich Tolstóy (1783–1873), who was a well-known and fashionable artist.

       Baratýnsky's: See note on III, 30.

31   *Yazýkov*: Nikolái M. Yazýkov (1803–46) was a minor poet and acquaintance of Pushkin's.

32   *one of our sterner critics*: Pushkin's old school friend, the poet and critic Vilgelm Kárlovich Kyukhelbéker (1799–1846) had written an article in 1824 'On the Direction of Our Poetry, Especially Lyric Poetry, in the Last Decade'. The article attacked the preponderance of elegiac romanticism in contemporary verse writing. Kyukhelbéker favoured the formal ode (see next note but one) as a vehicle for poetry. Pushkin is here (as in the preface, composed at about the same time, to Chapter One – see page 295) taking issue, in a good-humoured way, with Kyukhelbéker's main ideas.

      the classical trumpet, mask and dagger: In the ancient world the dagger was an attribute of Melpomene, one of the nine Muses (or goddesses of the arts); Melpomene was patroness of tragic drama; masks were an attribute both of Melpomene and of Thalia, the Muse of comedy. The trumpet may also symbolize tragic drama, or, through its association with war, epic poetry. So Pushkin may have in mind here classical tragedy alone, or he may be thinking of all three of the "heavier" categories of classical poetry: epic, tragedy and comedy. Pushkin was at this time (1825) working on his full-length drama *Boris Godunov*, which he modelled on Shakespeare in reaction against the dramatic conventions of the ancient world and their French imitators.

      odes: For Pushkin the term "ode" suggested bombastic and heavy pieces in the eighteenth-century Russian manner; his own preference was clearly for the romantic "elegy", by which term he would have described love lyrics and any other short contemplative verses. The mock debate conducted in this and the following stanza reflects an actual dispute between "archaists" (like Kyukhelbéker) and "modernists" (like Pushkin and many of his other friends) of that time.

33   *Remember Dmítriev's lampoon*: The passage reads literally, "Remember what the satirist said! Surely you don't find the crafty ode-writer of *Another's View* more bearable..." Iván Ivánovich Dmítriev (1760–1837) was a Russian writer of satires, including one of 1795 called

Another's View, in which contemporary ode-writers are mocked for their venality and hypocrisy.

35   *my old nurse*: Arína Rodiónovna Yákovleva (1758–1828), an old serf woman belonging to Pushkin's mother's family, who served as nanny to the Pushkin children. Pushkin remained very attached to her. She looked after him during his exile at Mikháylovskoye between 1824 and 1826, and was often his only companion. She was the source of some of the folk tales that Pushkin later incorporated into his poetry.

    smother him with a tragedy: Apparently a reference to Pushkin's historical drama *Boris Godunov*, which he was engaged in writing at this time.

36   This stanza was included in the first printing of Stanzas 4 and 5, but omitted from later editions. The text is given in the Appendix. Nabókov characterizes it as "an extremely poor stanza". Maybe Pushkin agreed and dropped it accordingly.

37   *in the tradition of Byron*: Literally, "imitating the singer of Gulnare". Gulnare was the heroine of Byron's poem *The Corsair*.

    swimming the Hellespont: The Hellespont is part of the narrow straits between the Black Sea and the Aegean Sea, now known as the Dardanelles. A story from classical times tells of a young Greek called Leander who used to swim across the strait nightly to visit his lover Hero, who lived on the other side – a distance of two kilometres each way, before allowing for the strong currents. When Byron, an exceptionally good swimmer, visited the Dardanelles in 1810 he made a point of swimming across the strait at the same place.

    Pushkin too, when living in the country, would start his day with a bathe in the Sorot (the smallish river that flows at the foot of the hill on which Mikháylovskoye stands) – a somewhat lesser feat than Byron's.

37, 38   The last one and a half lines of Stanza 37 and the whole of Stanza 38 are preserved in Pushkin's manuscript. They take forward the subject of Onégin's dress by particularizing the unconventional garments that he wore in the country –

strongly reminiscent of the garments Pushkin himself used to wear – and the outrage they caused in the neighbourhood. He may well have decided to omit them from the published text because the eccentricity of the clothing was too obviously Pushkin's and too improbably Onégin's.

39 We have already noted the physical similarity between Onégin's country seat and Pushkin's Mikháylovskoye (note on II, 1 above). There are similarities too, even without Stanza 38 (see note above), between Onégin's solitary way of life in the country and the author's: Pushkin too indulged in the pastimes mentioned in this stanza (including the companionship, from time to time, of a pretty young serf girl, Olga Kaláshnikova), as well as early-morning swims in the river (Stanza 37), ice baths, solo billiards (Stanza 44) and reading Walter Scott's historical novels (Stanza 43).

now and again a young, fresh kiss / from a fair-skinned, dark-eyed girl: See preceding note. These lines are a virtually word-for-word translation of a verse from the French poet André Chénier's 'Au Chevalier de Pange': "*...et quelquefois, les soirs, / le baiser jeune et frais d'une blanche aux yeux noirs*".

42 *Outside frosts crackled too*: In the first two sentences of this stanza, which make up its first four lines in verse, Pushkin is making a joke about rhymes that is untranslatable in English. The meaning is literally: "And look! Already crackling are hoarfrosts (*morózy*) / and showing silver among the fields... / (Reader, you are now expecting the rhyme 'roses' (*rózy*): / there you are then – take it quickly!)" Beyond the obvious parody of a banal rhyme, Pushkin is making a subtler literary point in contrasting the crisp realism of winter frost on the fields with the inane romantic cliché of roses (in a Russian midwinter!).

43 *Pradt*: Dominique de Pradt (1759–1837), a prolific French political writer.

Walter Scott: Pushkin greatly admired Scott's historical novels and poetry and referred to him as "the Scottish wizard".

44 *Childe Harold*: See note on I, 38.

45   *as though from a sacred spring*: Literally "like Hippocrene". Hippocrene was a spring on Mount Helicon in Greece, regarded in ancient times as sacred to the Muses, and therefore as a source of inspiration for poets.

    its resemblance to... this or that: This seems to be a jibe at the censors, who had objected to a passage in Baratýnsky's *Feasts* (see note on III, 30) about the qualities of champagne from Ay (see note on next stanza). Baratýnsky had written:

> [champagne] seethes with liberty;
> like an ardent mind, it cannot bear captivity,
> it bursts the cork with its impetuous liquor,
> and the joyous froth spurts forth –
> resembling youthful life...

    my last poor farthing: Another covert political jibe. The poet Zhukóvsky had addressed a poem to Alexander I containing a reference to the needy spending their "last poor farthing" on a portrait of the Emperor; Pushkin, however, who was no fan of Alexander's, preferred to spend *his* last poor farthing on a glass of champagne. (Pushkin received news of Alexander's death at the beginning of December 1825, shortly before completing this chapter.)

46   *Ay*: A French town in the Marne valley near Épernay, famous for its champagne.

47   *twixt dog and wolf*: Pushkin is referring to the French expression *entre chien et loup*, meaning dusk, the time when the domestic dog comes home, to be replaced outside by the nocturnal wolf, and when it is becoming too dark to distinguish the one from the other.

49   *the Saturday's Tatyána's name day*: The name day is the day in the church calendar dedicated to the saint after whom one is named. In Russia in Pushkin's time a person's name day was regarded as more significant than their birthday and was celebrated as their principal personal anniversary. The church commemorated St Tatiana on 12th January, which was therefore Tatyána's name day.

50   *married life… marriage*: Literally "Hymen" – see note on
        Stanza 14.
        Lafontaine: August Lafontaine (1758–1831), a German
        writer of numerous novels of family life.

Notes to Chapter Five

Pushkin commenced Chapter Five on 4th January 1826 (five years
and one day after commencement of the chapter's action) while still
in detention at Mikháylovskoye, and he reached Stanza 24 within
a few weeks, after which there was a prolonged break. Nicholas I
recalled Pushkin from banishment that September. He resumed work
on the chapter in the autumn, and completed it during a voluntary
return visit to Mikháylovskoye in November 1826. Chapter Five was
published together with Chapter Four at the end of January 1828.

The chapter takes place between 3rd January 1821 and Tatyána's
name day on 12th January – see note on IV, 49. Tatyána's pre-
Epiphany fortune-telling beginning in Stanza 8 must take place on
the night of the 3rd, 4th or 5th January, since the snow on the
ground (Stanza 9) had only fallen early on the 3rd (Stanza 1).

There is no discernible concentric pattern to this chapter; instead,
it is structured in two parallel sections. The first section (Stanzas
1–21) describes successively a winter morning, a fortune-telling,
a nightmare party, a nightmare encounter with Onégin and a
nightmare quarrel; the second section (Stanzas 21–45) similarly
describes in succession a winter morning, a fortune-telling, a real
dinner party, a real encounter with Onégin and a real quarrel.

Epigraph: Pushkin's friend and mentor the poet Vasíly Andréyevich
Zhukóvsky (1783–1852) wrote the ballad *Svetlana* (which became
very popular in Russia) between 1808 and 1812. It is an adaptation
of the German ballad *Lenore* (1773) by Gottfried August Bürger
(1747–94). (Pushkin refers to *Lenore* directly in VIII, 4.) In
Zhukóvsky's story, Svetlána, "silent and dejected" in the absence
of her lover, tried to conjure him up by magic; he did appear,
and carried her off to his grave – but it all turned out to be a
nightmare: Svetlána's lover soon after returned in real life, safe
and sound, and they got married.

There are several echoes of Zhukóvsky's *Svetlana* in *Eugene Onegin*. In III, 5, Lensky quotes from Stanza 2 of the ballad in describing Tatyána as "silent and dejected". The Epiphany-tide fortune-telling in Tatyána's household in V, 8 is strongly reminiscent of the activities of Svetlána's friends in Stanzas 1 and 2 of the ballad. Svetlána's conjuring experiment in Stanzas 4–6 of the ballad is mentioned explicitly in V, 10 in connection with Tatyána's abortive attempt to conjure up her lover. And Tatyána's nightmare in V, 11–21 has some points of contact with Svetlána's nightmare in Zhukóvsky's poem.

Zhukóvsky dedicated the poem to his niece, who was shortly to be married herself and whom he nicknamed Svetlána after his heroine. He ends the ballad in Stanza 20 with good wishes and prayers for his niece's happiness: "My Svetlána, be you spared / all such dreadful nightmares…" There is therefore a sad irony in Pushkin's choice of these words for his epigraph for Chapter Five: despite the wish, his Tatyána was spared neither a nightmare nor its horrific fulfilment.

2   *jubilant peasant*: Apparently there was a saying that "a snowfall on the night of the second" meant there would be a good harvest.

3   *Another poet*: Pushkin, as he acknowledges in a note, is referring to his friend Prince Vyázemsky's poem 'The First snow' – see note to the epigraph to Chapter One. Here and in III, 41 and 42 above Pushkin is drawing a tersely "realistic" picture of a country winter in friendly contrast with Vyázemsky's more conventionally aristocratic and elegant (and longer-winded) portrayal in 'The First Snow'.

     Baratýnsky: The reference is to Baratýnsky's poem *Eda: A Finnish Tale* – see the note above on III, 30.

4   *evenings around Epiphany*: The celebration of Epiphany – 6th January – and of the twelve days leading up to it from Christmas (*svyátki* in Russian) is given more emphasis in the Eastern Orthodox Church than in the West. Russian folklore divided *svyátki* between "holy evenings" (25th–31st December) and "fearsome evenings" (1st–5th January). It was a favoured time for fortune-telling – a

throwback to pagan customs. Tatyána's fortune-telling in the stanzas to come must have taken place on one of the "fearsome evenings".

6   Pushkin too was superstitious. Towards the end of 1825 – a few weeks before writing these stanzas – he set off from the Mikháylovskoye estate, where he was under house arrest, for St Petersburg in defiance of his detention. The consequences for him could have been severe; but he soon turned back after seeing both a hare and a monk.

8, 9, 10 There are references here to several traditional methods of telling fortunes, used particularly by women and girls at the Christmas-Epiphany season.

One custom was to pour molten wax into cold water: the shapes the wax took were interpreted prophetically. There was also the singing of so-called "dish divining" songs – see note on II, 35. On this occasion the words of Tatyána's song seem to foretell wealth and position; but the tune portends a death. The song of the "she-puss" was a popular one because it was believed to presage a marriage. Training a mirror on the moon was another method of divination: the reflected face in the mirror was supposed to resemble that of the future husband. Or a girl would go into the street and ask the name of the first stranger she encountered: that would be the name of her future husband. Another device for discovering the identity of a future husband was for a girl (like Svetlána – see note on the epigraph to this chapter) to conjure up his spirit in an all-night vigil. Another *svyátki* ritual, not referred to directly by Pushkin, was for young people to put on fancy-dress and visit neighbouring households as mummers (see Leo Tolstoy's *War and Peace*, Vol. 2, Part IV, chapters 10 and 11). In his *Pushkin*, Yury Mikháylovich Lotman reports that one of the favourite traditional disguises was as a bear. This custom may have influenced Tatyána's dream that night (see Stanza 11).

9   *He stared, / and replied, "Agafón"*: See preceding note. Not only was "Agafón" not "Eugene"; it was (as Pushkin himself points out in a note elsewhere) an uncommon, archaic-sounding Russian name, likely to be found predominantly

among the peasantry. Nonetheless, could "Agafón" have been the name of the man Tatyána eventually married? Pushkin teasingly never tells us Tatyána's husband's name. Although "Agafón" had old-fashioned and low-class connotations, so too did "Tatyána", as Pushkin acknowledges (II, 24).

10 *in the bathhouse*: Chosen probably because in the bathhouse there were no Christian icons to counteract the magic.

took off her silken girdle: In Russian folkore a girdle was a protection against witchcraft and evil powers. So the mention of Tatyána taking off her girdle, as of her use of the love charm and the mirror, implies that she is deliberately exposing herself to the influence of the occult as she sleeps, in the hope of learning the identity of her future husband.

a love charm: Literally, "Lel" – according to nineteenth century Russian folklorists, the pagan Slavic god of love.

11–20 Tatyána's dream: Although, on the surface at least, Tatyána's disturbing dream speaks for itself, commentators have variously interpreted its images by reference to psychology, folklore and pagan myth. In fairy tale, folk-song and folk mythology, for instance, crossing a river can symbolize marriage (or death); and in the lore of dreams a bridge of sticks is the means by which a girl may be led into the married state by her future husband. Bears too are connected in folklore with marriage. Thus the large bear who helps Tatyána across the river and brings her to his "pal" Onégin's hut could prefigure the "stout general" that Tatyána eventually marries and who in Chapter Eight reintroduces her to his "relation and friend" Onégin.

Events in Onégin's hut can also be seen as combining elements of a funeral wake with an upside-down wedding feast: at a wedding it was the bridegroom (with his best man) who would normally enter the feast room to be given a friendly greeting by the waiting guests; in the dream it is Tatyána who arrives at the feast to be given a hostile reception by the waiting monsters (it was indeed Tatyána who turned convention upside down by taking the initiative to declare her love to Onégin). More obviously, the party in the hut, with its rowdy and terrifying guests, its mortifications for Tatyána and its murderous consequences, is also to be taken as presaging Tatyána's imminent name-day party with its (for her) noisy and intimidating company, private embarrassments and equally dire sequel. Again, Pushkin is writing on several different levels, and commentators have been busy identifying these – and others that never entered Pushkin's mind.

22   *Virgil or Racine / or Scott or Byron or Seneca*: Virgil (70– 19 BC), Latin pastoral and epic poet; Jean Racine (1639– 99), French tragedian; Walter Scott (1771–1832), British novelist and poet; Lord Byron (1788–1824), British poet and controversialist; Seneca (4 BC–65 AD), Latin tragedian and philosopher – an ironic and random collection of authors that were *not* likely to be engrossing Tatyána. Although Scott and Byron were among Pushkin's favourite writers, we know from III, 9–12 that they were not yet by Tatyána's bedside; her taste was still for the more sentimental writers of the previous generation.

Journal of Ladies' Fashions: Pushkin seems to be referring to a French magazine, the *Journal des dames et des modes*, which had a wide European circulation at this period.

Martin Zadeck: The name, or rather pseudonym, of a compiler of several collections of prophecies and dream interpretations, published both in Russia and in Germany.

leading astrologer: Literally "head of Chaldean sages". The Chaldeans of ancient Mesopotamia were renowned for their expertise in astrology.

23   *an incomplete Malvina*: A lengthy six-part French novel by Sophie Cottin (see note on III, 9 and 10), published in 1800.

Marmontel: Jean-François Marmontel (1723–99), French encyclopedist and short-story writer. The third volume of Marmontel's collected works (the eighteen-volume set of which Pushkin had in his library) contained his *Moral Tales*.

25   *with crimson hand... with the sun*: To inaugurate his account of Tatyána's name day Pushkin is parodying (as he admits himself in a note) an extravagant formula for the dawning of an anniversary used by the early Russian polymath, scientist and poet Mikhaíl Vasílyevich Lomonósov (1711–65) at the opening of his *Ode on the Anniversary of the Ascent to the Throne of Her Majesty Empress Elizavéta Petróvna* of 1748. The 240-line ode begins as follows:

> With crimson hand Dawn
> ushers from the placid waters of morning
> the sun, and with the sun
> a new year of your reign...

Pushkin has made only one change in quoting the first three lines: conscious that in European Russia the sun rises over land and not over sea, he has corrected Lomonósov's "placid waters" to "plains".

    pug dogs barking... squalling kids: The intonation of these four lines is deliberately reminiscent of lines 7 and 8 of Stanza 17. Tatyána's nightmare is already coming true.

26   *Pustyakóv... Buyánov*: The names Pushkin gives to the guests are deliberately comic ones: Pustyakóv ("Trifle"), Gvozdín ("Clout"); Skotínin ("Brute"), Petushkóv ("Cockerel"). Buyánov ("Rowdy") was the hero of a popular and racy poem by Pushkin's uncle, Vasíly Pushkin (1766–1830); as his uncle's literary offspring he was thus, playfully, Pushkin's cousin. Buyánov is described by Vasíly Pushkin as "with moustache unclipped, with hair dishevelled, his clothes all fluff, and wearing a peaked cap".

27   *Tambóv*: About 500 km south-east of Moscow. It was one of the towns to which French prisoners of war were sent after the fighting of 1812.

29   *God above! The poet!*: In Russian a single word, "*Tvoréts*", (literally "Creator"), which can be used either of God or of a poet. Mrs Larin's ambiguous exclamation, interpreted by Onégin as a welcome to Lensky alone, may have contributed to Onégin's annoyance.

30   *right opposite Tatyána*: As the party was to celebrate Tatyána's name day, the seat opposite her would be for the guest of honour; and, although Onégin and Lensky were in fact placed there on the spur of the moment because they had come late, the arrangement would have suggested both to Onégin and to Tatyána that the company expected them soon to become engaged. Hence the acute embarrassment they both felt.

32   *blancmanger*: Not quite the modern blancmange, but a sweet and inexpensive milk jelly, often flavoured with almond.

       sparkling Russian wine: Literally "Tsimlyánskoye wine", a sparkling red wine from the lower Don region, north-east of the Sea of Azov. In contrast to Onégin's sumptuous meal of imported delicacies in I, 16, and even to the informal hospitality he offers in the country (IV, 45), here at the Larins' everything – pie, *blancmanger*, even the wine – is home-produced. Mrs Larin is not well off.

       Zizí: A family nickname for Yevpráxia Vulf (1810–83), daughter by a first marriage of Praskóvya Ósipova, owner of Trigórskoye, neighbouring estate to Pushkin's Mikháylovskoye. Zizí could brew an excellent punch, which Pushkin enjoyed on more than one occasion when visiting the family during his enforced stay at Mikháylovskoye in 1824–26. Pushkin flirted with her then and later, and she remained a lifelong friend. Pushkin may have been joking about her waist: Zizí, later in life at least, was really rather plump.

       In the Orthodox Church St Eupraxia the Elder (Yevpráxia in Russian), a saint from the fourth century, is commemorated on 12th January, the same day as St Tatiana; so it was appropriate that Pushkin should have included Zizí in Tatyána's name-day celebration.

35   *Boston... ombre... whist*: Card games widely played in Europe. Ombre, a trick-taking game for three, originally from Spain, used a pack of forty cards (no eights, nines or tens); one player (*el hombre*) sought to win the pool; it was especially popular in the seventeenth and eighteenth centuries. Whist also dated (by this name at least) from the

seventeenth century, but proved more enduringly popular. Boston was a form of whist, popular in late-eighteenth-century France, the name of which is said to originate from the siege of Boston (1775–76) in the American War of Independence. Play would normally have been for money; but at households like the Larins' stakes would have been nominal.

36   *eight rubbers*: A rubber in whist was a series of three hands, at the end of which scores were settled and players changed places. Eight rubbers would have taken well over two hours to play.

chiming watches: In Russian *брегет* ("Breguet"), for which see note on I, 15.

in describing feasts… Homer: Homer (early first millennium BC), the Greek poet credited with the composition of the *Iliad* and *Odyssey*, was famous for his descriptions of feasting.

37, 38   The text of these stanzas, included in the first printing of Chapters Four and Five but omitted from Pushkin's full editions, is given in the Appendix. In them Pushkin continues "in brackets" to address his ancient predecessor Homer with a jocular comparison between the *Iliad* and his own *Eugene Onegin*.

We do not know why Pushkin dropped these two stanzas. Perhaps even he felt on reflection that this was a digression too far, particularly in view of his vow in Stanza 40 to keep Chapter Five "clear of digressions".

39   *heart-throb*: In the original "Paris", the handsome shepherd-prince of Troy, whose seduction of Helen ignited the Trojan War. This ironic allusion to Homer would have had more resonance before the dropping of Stanzas 37 and 38.

40   *Albani*: Francesco Albani (1578–1660) was an Italian painter much admired in the eighteenth and early nineteenth centuries.

41   *All were astonished*: The astonishment would be not only at Onégin's choice of Lensky's betrothed for the dance, but also at his neglect of Tatyána (see also stanza 44), in view of the local expectation that Onégin was her favoured suitor.

43   This stanza is preserved in manuscript, and all but the first four lines were printed in the first edition of 1828. Thereafter Pushkin dropped it. See the Appendix for the text.

44   *conducted Tatyána and her sister / over to Onégin*: A feature of the mazurka was that at the opening one man would offer another a choice of partner from two ladies he had already invited to dance.

cotillion: Traditionally the final dance of the ball.

Notes to Chapter Six

Pushkin apparently composed most of Chapter Six in the spring or summer of 1826, while still under house arrest at Mikháylovskoye, before the completion of Chapter Five. The last three or four stanzas were added in August 1827, after his release and return to metropolitan life. Chapter Six was published in St Petersburg at the end of March 1828. At the end of the chapter was added a list of corrections to the chapters – One to Five – already published; the list ended with the words: "End of first part", suggesting that at that time it was Pushkin's intention to write several more chapters at least, the agenda for which he summarizes in Stanza 42.

The main events of this chapter – Stanzas 8–35 – take place on 13th and 14th January 1821, the start of the week of Lensky's and Olga's proposed wedding.

Chapter Six starts with three stanzas describing the end of Tatyána's name-day party (1–3) and ends with four autobiographical stanzas (43–46). The rest (4–42), a narrative of the duel and its outcome, is once more structured with a hidden concentric symmetry of matching and contrasting elements. This narrative section is flanked by two contrasting equestrian portraits – the drunk and disreputable Zarétsky, falling off his stallion into the hands of the French during the Napoleonic Wars (5); and the reflective and sensitive young horsewoman pausing by Lensky's memorial to read its inscription (41). In the vicinity of the first portrait we learn the sleazy realities of Zarétsky's long life (4–7); and in the vicinity of the second we contemplate the more honourable potentialities of Lensky's curtailed life (36–39). One step further towards the middle of the chapter, Zarétsky calls on Onégin to deliver Lensky's challenge (8–9); and at the other end, Zarétsky parts from Onégin to remove Lensky's body (35). Further in again, we learn of Onégin's state of mind, first after receiving Lensky's challenge (10–11), and later after shooting Lensky dead (33–35).

The chapter's core extends from Lensky's misconceived joy at receiving Onégin's acceptance of the challenge (12) to the unmistakable tragedy of his death (30–32). Its first half describes the sentiment of Lensky's final encounter with Olga and subsequent poetic effusion (13–22); it contains a stanza (18) on the failure of communication on the part of various characters that prevented a reconciliation; and it ends with Lensky's abrupt awakening from a brief sleep (23). The core's second half begins with Onégin's belated awakening from a lengthy sleep (24); and describes in entirely unsentimental language the uncomfortable realities of the duel itself (25–30); it contains a stanza on Lensky's and Onégin's failure to communicate with each other over a reconciliation (28).

Epigraph: The Italian quotation is taken from one of the poems in *Rime in vita di Laura* (*Poems during Laura's Life*) by Petrarch (1304–74).

Petrarch, exchanging his usual topic of love for that of war, wrote this poem in support of the proposed crusade of 1334. In the lines leading up to Pushkin's epigraph Petrarch refers to "a part of the world that lies under perpetual ice and snow, far from the path of the sun". He then goes on to describe the inhabitants of this region, a nation "innately averse to peace", in the terms of the two lines of the epigraph. (Although the words evoke Russia well, Petrarch actually had Germany in mind.) The thrust of the whole passage is that this nation is facing up to the new struggle against a heathen enemy with even more than its usual zeal and determination.

As previously, the epigraph can be read on several different levels. It can simply be taken as a comment on the readiness of many young Russian aristocrats of Pushkin's day (including Pushkin himself) to hazard their lives in duels on a point of honour. But in choosing to take his epigraph from this poem Pushkin seems also to be drawing an ironic parallel between the unexpected and supposedly high-principled reorientation of both Petrarch and Lensky, normally pacific love poets, towards violent conflict and revenge.

But Pushkin would also have been thinking of his friends among the Decembrist conspirators such as Ryléyev and Kyukhelbéker, who in December 1825 risked their careers as poets and their lives by taking up arms unsuccessfully against what they saw as a cynical and corrupt autocracy. Ryléyev and four other leading conspirators were in fact executed a few months later. News of the executions reached Pushkin on 24th July 1826, while he was working on Chapter Six.

2   *the moon*: Literally "Diana", in Roman mythology goddess of the moon.

3   *as though a black... yawning at her feet*: The image is reminiscent of the beginning of Tatyána's dream – V, 11 – where Tatyána is confronted by a "thundering chasm" that she will only be able to cross by "an unsteady and perilous footbridge" with the help of a terrifying bear – for the symbolism see note on V, 11–20.

4   *(though bachelor) a family man*: Implying a serf mistress and illegitimate offspring.

5   *at a dozen yards*: A typical distance for the space between the "barriers" at a duel, which mark the inner limits for firing at an opponent – see Stanzas 29 and 30.

     Kalmuk: The Kalmuk (or Kalmyk) region is in southern Russia, near the mouth of the River Volga at the north end of the Caspian Sea. The Kalmuk people are of Mongolian extraction and are famous for their horses.

     latterday Regulus: An ironic reference to the heroic Roman general, Marcus Atilius Regulus (d. *c*.250 BC), who, after his capture by the Carthaginian enemy, was released on parole to return to Rome to negotiate for peace. Once back in Rome he insisted instead that the war be continued. Although he knew that he would pay for this with his life, he then returned to captivity, as he had promised, and was executed.

     at Véry's: Nabokov tells us that the Café Véry was a Parisian café-restaurant situated up to 1817 in the Jardin des Tuileries and celebrated for its exceptionally fine cuisine.

7   *in the shelter of his bird cherries and laburnums*: an ironic quotation from a poem 'The Muses' Arbour' (1817) by Pushkin's older contemporary Konstantín Bátyushkov (see note on II, 40), in which a world-weary poet is imagined in mellow old age resting "in the shelter of his bird cherries and his laburnums".

         like Horace: See note to the epigraph to Chapter Two.

15, 16   A copy of these stanzas has survived. Stanza 15 is a heartfelt description of the torments of jealousy. In Stanza 16 Pushkin addresses a woman who in his younger days had aroused in him both intense love and intense jealousy, but who is now dead. The woman was probably Amalia Riznić, the attractive young Viennese wife of an elderly Dalmatian grain merchant, with whom Pushkin had had an affair in Odessa in 1823–24, but who (Pushkin heard later) had at the same time been encouraging the attentions of at least one other suitor. Amalia had left Odessa for Italy in the spring of 1824 for health reasons, and Pushkin had lost touch with her. In July 1826, when already working on Chapter Six, he was shocked to receive news that she had died in Trieste over a year earlier. The memory of her had apparently induced him to dash off these two stanzas. He excluded them from published versions of the chapter.

17–19   In his notes to the Penguin Classics edition of 2003, Basker draws attention to the "differing forms of mutual incomprehension" and failures to communicate explored by Pushkin in this chapter and refers in particular to the "poignant silences" in these stanzas, "where the dramatic effect of words left unsaid anticipates Chekhov".

20   *Schiller*: See note on II, 9. Pushkin parodies the high-flown and idealistic style of Schiller's poetry, and of his imitators like Lensky, in the following stanzas.

         Delvig: Baron Antón Delvig (1798–1831), minor poet and one of Pushkin's closest friends since schooldays, who used to do poetic improvisations at parties.

23–30   The duel: Duels – fought originally with swords, more recently with pistols – had long been a way of settling disputes of "honour" between members of the upper classes in European countries. To ensure that both parties played fair and "honourably", detailed rules and procedures were devised governing the choice of weapon, where the opponents should stand at the outset, how close they could come, when and how many times they could fire, and so on, though much would be left for agreement between the parties. Because the two antagonists would not normally be on speaking terms, it was customary for each to appoint a "second". The second would normally be a friend or acquaintance of the same social standing as his principal and preferably with some experience of duelling. The seconds would act as channels of communication between the main contestants; in the first place, their duty was to try to effect a reconciliation; failing that, they were to negotiate, on behalf of their principals, the arrangements for the duel, prepare the weapons, and agree on the precise procedures that would apply.

In this case it would have been for Zarétsky and Guillot to agree the thirty-two paces' initial separation between the duellists, and the distance from those outer limits to the "barrier" (commonly marked on the ground by the contestants' cloaks) that delimited the central no man's land, within which they were not allowed to fire at each other. Onégin and Lensky had advanced nine paces each before Onégin fired and were thus fourteen paces apart at that point. The no man's land was commonly twelve paces wide (see Stanza 5), but could be more or less, as the seconds decided.

Duels did not necessarily end in death. Often forcing an opponent to undergo the experience of a duel was reckoned punishment enough, and a reluctant or generous dueller would shoot to miss, or aim at a non-vital organ such as a leg or arm. This made Onégin's killing of Lensky, unless it was a careless accident, the more inexplicable and shocking.

By the 1820s many countries, including Russia and Britain, had outlawed duelling. But because the concepts of pride and honour were so deeply ingrained in the upper classes, duels continued to be fought out of the public eye. The need for secrecy was one reason why duels were often fought in lonely spots at dawn.

Pushkin himself had already been involved in several non-fatal duels: hence the precision of his description, both of the procedure and of the combatants' states of mind. The duel between Lensky and Onégin proved to be a strange case of fiction foreshadowing fact. In 1837, some ten years after describing how the poet Lensky had been killed in a January duel defending his fiancée's honour, the poet Pushkin was himself killed in a January duel defending his wife's honour.

25   *Lepage's*: Jean Lepage (1779–1822) was a famous Parisian gunsmith. By convention each party presented a pair of (new) pistols; the pair to be used would then be chosen by lot.

26   *Onégin came over with apologies*: The combatants were due to ride to the meeting place "ere daybreak" (Stanza 12), so that the preparations could be made for the duel to take place at first light, before other people would be around. According to Lotman, on 14th January 1821 the sun would have risen in those parts at 8.20 a.m. Onégin was still in bed long after that, so could hardly have arrived at the meeting place till about 10.30 or 11.00 a.m., more than two hours late. By that time Lensky and Zarétsky could have left the field with honour; but evidently Lensky, as the injured party, was still angry and did not wish to seem to be funking the encounter; and Zarétsky, as an aficionado of duels, would have made little effort to talk him out of it. The careless improprieties of Onégin's conduct, on the other hand – his lateness, his last-minute appointment of a social inferior as his second – suggest that he, for his part, regarded the duel as unimportant and had no strong urge to kill his opponent.

27   *Zarétsky bit his lip*: The seconds, Zarétsky and Guillot, should make a last attempt before the duel to bring about a reconciliation; but Zarétsky evidently has no wish to do so. This may explain why Onégin, puzzled at the silence, addresses his question "Well, shall we start?" direct to

Lensky, again in breach of the etiquette of duelling, which disallowed direct communication between the principals on the field.

38   An incomplete copy of this rejected stanza is known from the source that preserved Stanzas 15 and 16. It was one of a piece with Stanzas 37 and 39, in which Pushkin reviews the might-have-beens of Lensky's career. In Stanza 38 he considered the possibility that Lensky might have made a name for himself, for good or ill, in public life as a Napoleon, a Nelson, or an executed Decembrist revolutionary. We do not know why Pushkin dropped the stanza: perhaps on reflection he considered its scenarios too improbable for Lensky; perhaps he felt it made the chapter too long; or he anticipated the censor's veto.

44   *My dreams... become of my youth*: There is an untranslatable play on words in these two lines. The following two sentences read literally: "What has become of their sweetness (*sládost*)? What has become of its ever-present rhyme, youth (*mládost*)?"

    soon be thirty: A slight poetic exaggeration: Pushkin had not long been twenty-eight when he wrote this.

46   *One last look back*: This seems to be a wistful farewell by Pushkin to his two and a half years in detention in the country at Mikháylovskoye, from which he returned to metropolitan life late in 1826.

    In one of his notes to the complete edition of the novel Pushkin records that Stanza 46 is a conflation of two stanzas from Chapter Six as first published in 1828. The original text of the two stanzas is given in the Appendix.

Notes to Chapter Seven

Pushkin is thought to have begun Chapter Seven at the end of July 1827 during a stay at Mikháylovskoye, and he composed the Moscow stanzas there during the summer and autumn; he returned to work on the chapter in St Petersburg the following February; and he completed it on 4th November 1828 during a stay at Malínniki, one of the estates belonging to Praskóvya Ósipova, Pushkin's neighbour at Mikháylovskoye. Chapter Seven was first published in its entirety in St Petersburg in March 1830. It was much less well received by the reviewers than the previous six chapters had been, on the grounds that it lacked substance and that the picture it presented of Russia was already outdated, criticisms that Pushkin rejected in an unpublished preface of autumn 1830 to the final instalment of the novel.

The chapter opens in the spring of 1821 and closes in the early months of 1822.

Chapter Seven (like Chapter Five) is structured in two parallel (and slightly overlapping) sections, which chronicle two stages in the development of Tatyána's understanding of the world and her adjustment to it: Stanzas 1–30 describe Tatyána's continuing life in the country and centre on her exposure to Onégin's library; and Stanzas 29–54 describe Tatyána's new life in the city and centre on her exposure to Moscow society. The synchronization of these two phases in Tatyána's development with the changing seasons from spring to winter suggests both the inevitable and irreversible process of growing up and the accompanying transformation of the character from something fluid, spontaneous, warm and beautiful into something still indeed attractive in its way, but cooler, harder and more fixed. There are many other artfully concealed parallels of detail between these two sections, too numerous to itemize here.

Epigraphs: *Dmítriev*: See note above on IV, 33. The quotation is from Dmítriev's poem *The Liberation of Moscow* (1795), which contains an encomium of Moscow as the city where the tsars were crowned, with its ancient walls and golden domes, its treasures, and its courageous menfolk and attractive girls. (This picture gained an extra resonance from the heroic – as it was seen – sacrifice of Moscow that the Russians made in 1812 in order to trap and turn back the invading French under Napoleon.)

Baratýnsky: See note on III, 30. The quotation is from Baratýnsky's *Feasts*. In a much more informal passage he acknowledges Moscow's traditions, its architecture, its chiming bells and its gossip, but admits that what he really likes about the city is its cheerful social life and sumptuous banquets.

Griboyédov: Alexánder Sergéyevich Griboyédov (1794–1829) – contemporary of Pushkin, author of a famous comedy (1824) *Woe from Wit* (or *The Misfortune of Being Clever*), from which this quotation is taken. In Act I, Scene 7 of the play the caustic (anti-)hero Chatsky arrives back suddenly in Moscow from abroad after an absence of three years. He turns up in the house of Sófya, the girl he loves, where there is to be a party that evening, and after a few minutes' repartee the following exchange takes place:

> *Chatsky*: What new has Moscow got to show me? One ball last night, two more tomorrow. Someone's been courting – with success; someone else has tried and failed. Still just the same talk, just the same verses in autograph albums.
> *Sófya*: Disparage Moscow! What it is to know the world! Just tell me somewhere better.
> *Chatsky*: Where there's none of us.

These three epigraphs express three different qualities that Pushkin and his contemporaries found in Moscow, Russia's old capital before the creation of St Petersburg: the richness of Moscow's monuments and history; the hospitality and clubbiness of its noble families; and the provincial vapidity of its social intercourse – all of which feature in the picture of the city presented in this chapter by Pushkin, who was himself born in Moscow and spent the first twelve years of his life there.

4   *enlightened Epicureans*: Epicurus (*c*.342–*c*.270 BC) was a Greek philosopher who taught that the aim of life is pleasure, which he equated with a self-sufficient tranquillity.

        armchair agriculturalists: Literally "fledglings of Lyóvshin's school". Vasíly Lyóvshin (1746–1826) was the author of numerous tracts on gardening and agriculture.

        prolific squires: Literally "country Priams". Priam was in Greek mythology a king of Troy, famous among other things for his very large family – fifty sons and twelve daughters.

8, 9   Pushkin prepared a rough draft of these two stanzas (which described a fraught visit to the grave by Olga), but dropped them in the fair copy, save for six lines, which he transferred to the end of Stanza 11.

11   *Lethe's waters*: see note on II, 40.

19   *Lord Byron… figurine*: Pushkin does not name the figurine, but the image of Napoleon would have been unmistakable to contemporaries. The message from both portrait and figurine is of a westward-leaning disaffected radicalism at odds with the rigid formality and traditionalism of Russian politics and society.

21   Pushkin originally drafted a different ending to this stanza followed by a different Stanza 22, in which Tatyána discovers among Onégin's books an "album" (or diary) of his. Pushkin then proposed to follow these stanzas with a selection of entries from this album, and his notebooks contain unfinished drafts of these. Pushkin composed the album entries in the form of rhymed lines in his normal metre, but grouped into a dozen passages of unequal length, not in the usual fourteen-line stanzas. The entries consist of Onégin's disjointed jottings, for the most part recording or commenting tersely on his social encounters in St Petersburg. After discarding the album idea, Pushkin incorporated seven-odd lines from the first entry into Stanza 9 of Chapter Eight.

22   *the poems of Byron*: Literally "singer of the Giaour and of Juan". *The Giaour* (Turkish for "infidel") is the title of a celebrated narrative poem by Byron, first published in 1813. The first two cantos of *Don Juan*, perhaps Byron's most famous work, were published in 1819; Byron eventually composed sixteen cantos and even then left it unfinished. When he had written no more than the first chapter of *Eugene Onegin* Pushkin described his novel as "in the manner of *Don Juan*"; but he later changed his mind: "You compare the first chapter [of *Onegin*] with *Don Juan*," he wrote to a friend in 1825. "No one esteems *Don Juan* more than I do… but it has nothing in common with *Onegin*… Where is the *satire* in my work?…" (letters of 4th November 1823 to Prince Vyázemsky; and of 24th March 1825 to A. A. Bestúzhev).

24   *Childe Harold*: See note on I, 38.

        At an early stage Pushkin proposed at the end of this stanza to revert to Onégin and describe his departure from the country and the beginning of his journey to distant parts.

27   *snobbish beauties*: Literally "Circes". Circe was a beautiful sorceress encountered by Odysseus on his wanderings (Homer, *Odyssey*, x). She lived on a remote island and used her magic to turn all human visitors into animals.

33   *the tables / of learned statisticians*: Pushkin has in mind here the works of the French statistician and engineer Baron Charles Dupin (1784–1873) published in the 1820s, notably his *Forces productives et commerciales de la France* (1827), which contained tabulated data comparing the economic resources and development of various European countries including Russia.

      bridges... tunnels: Lotman quotes the following from *Pushkin: Comparative Historical Studies* by M.P. Alexéyev (Leningrad 1972): "The first issue of the *Moscow Telegraph* for 1825 contains the information: 'Suspension bridges are entering into general use. In St Petersburg such a bridge has been built across the Móyka. In England (*sic*) the Isle of Anglesey has been joined to the mainland by a bridge of this type...' In England too, the same *Moscow Telegraph* states enviously, 'work has commenced on an underground crossing that will be dug beneath the Thames.'" Pushkin had evidently read this article.

34   *blacksmiths*: Literally "Cyclopes". The Cyclopes were a mythical race of one-eyed giants, renowned for their skill in metalworking (Virgil, *Georgics* IV, 170*ff*., *Æneid* VIII, 416*ff*.).

35   *redoubtable coachmen*: Literally "Automedons". In Homer's *Iliad* Automedon was the skilled charioteer of the Greek warrior Achilles.

36   *Moscow... its ancient domes*: To one approaching Moscow in Pushkin's day the first sight would have been of innumerable, mostly gilded church domes and bell towers. Lotman notes that at the beginning of the 1820s there were five cathedral churches, about 270 Orthodox parish churches, cemetery churches, etc. (in 1784 there had been 325, but the conflagration at the time of Napoleon's occupation had reduced the number), and six churches of other denominations; in addition, within the city limits there were twenty-two religious houses, each with

several churches and some with as many as six to eight. Certainly, a sight to gladden weary travellers, even those not returning, like Pushkin and Mrs Larin, from years of absence.

Ah, friends: Pushkin is here remembering his arrival in Moscow in September 1826, when he was abruptly summoned from Mikháylovskoye by the new Emperor Nicholas I to receive his pardon and release from detention.

37   *Petróvsky castle*: A chateau built in 1776 in an oak wood in the grounds of the old St Peter's monastery (hence its name). It was situated near the St Petersburg road about two miles from Moscow's Tver gate. As Pushkin explains, Napoleon had first used the castle on his approach to Moscow at the climax of his 1812 Russian campaign: he had waited there vainly for the city's surrender. Having occupied the city, he had later taken refuge there again when driven back by the fires that engulfed it. The castle, as rebuilt in 1840, has survived to the present.

38   *city checkpoint*: On entering the city travellers had to stop at a checkpoint consisting of a barrier and sentry box, where they had to register their names and the reason for their journey. The Tver checkpoint, on the St Petersburg road, was situated in the vicinity of today's Belorússky Station, on the north-western side of the city. Lotman notes that at that date a triumphal arch was under construction at the spot, in memory of the Russian forces who took part in the allied victories over the French at the end of the Napoleonic Wars. It is presumably the white stone columns of the new arch that Pushkin refers to in this sentence. (The triumphal arch was removed under Stalin to the Kutúzovsky Prospékt, where it still stands.)

Bokharan merchants: Bokhara was a Central Asian trading city in what is now Uzbekistan.

Cossacks: Cossacks were sometimes employed to run errands on horseback.

flocks of jackdaws on church crosses: Lotman passes on an amusing story about this line. Reportedly Filarét, Metropolitan of Moscow, complained to Count Benkendorf

(Nicholas I's head of police and security, and overseer of the censorship) about the words, considering them sacrilegious. The censor responsible for approving the passage, when called upon to explain, said that, for all he knew, jackdaws really did perch on Moscow church crosses, but that, in his opinion, the main fault lay with the Moscow police superintendent for allowing it, not with the poet or censor. Benkendorf, for once taking Pushkin's side, replied diplomatically to Filarét that it was not a matter that merited the attention of such a respected spiritual leader.

39   There is no trace of Pushkin's ever having drafted a Stanza 39. Commentators surmise that he deliberately left the number vacant to stress the duration of the "exhausting drive through the city" or (in Nabókov's words) "to suggest the blurry repetition of trivial impressions".

40   *in St Kharitóny's lane*: St Kharitóny's was a parish in east Moscow (hence the Larins' need to travel right through the city from the Tver Gate on the north-west). Between 1801 and 1808 the Pushkin family had lived in Great Kharitóny's Lane.

      Kalmuk servant: See note above on VI, 5.

41   *mon ange*: "My angel" (French).

      Pachette: The normal affectionate diminutive in Russian for Mrs Larin's Christian name Praskóvya (II, 33) would be Pasha. Here her gushing cousin offers her a double endearment by adding the French diminutive suffix *-ette*.

      Grandison: See II, 30 and note.

      It should be noted that the trajectory of Mrs Larin's final intervention in the novel in this chapter – life in the country socializing with neighbours and managing the estate (25–27); travelling from the country to Moscow for the purpose of an arranged marriage (31–40); and gossiping with Princess Aline about Richardson's hero Grandison (41) – is precisely the reverse of her first appearance in the novel in Chapter Two – gossiping with Princess Aline about Richardson and Grandison (II, 29, 30); travelling to the country from Moscow as a result of an arranged marriage (II, 31); and managing the estate and socializing with neighbours in the country (II, 34, 35).

45   *his club*: Probably the English Club, founded in Moscow in 1770 and modelled on the gentlemen's clubs of London.

49   *Archive lads*: Young men from well-connected families who held cushy jobs at the Moscow archives of the Ministry of Foreign Affairs. A number of them belonged to a literary-philosophical society called the *Lyubomúdry* ("Lovers of wisdom"), some members of which were friends of Pushkin – hence Pushkin's jocular tone. While Pushkin was in Moscow in the last months of 1826, he may well have been present at a gathering of these young literati at which the first two chapters of *Eugene Onegin* and their characters were discussed; Chapter Two was published in Moscow that October.

     Vyázemsky: Named as "V…" in the published text; see note to the epigraph to Chapter One.

     an elderly man: According to Vyázemsky, this may be a reference to the poet Dmítriev – see note on IV, 33. Dmítriev would now have been in his sixties.

50   A literal rendering of this stanza would read roughly as follows:

> But there, where the protracted wail of tempestuous Melpomene is given voice, where she waves a brass-foil cloak in front of a cold house, where Thalia quietly dozes and does not notice friendly applause, where the young spectator marvels only at Terpsichore alone (which was likewise in former years, in your time and mine), there were not turned on her [i.e. Tatyána] either the lorgnettes of jealous ladies or the opera glasses of fashionable experts from boxes or rows of stalls.

The names refer to three of the Muses, Greek goddesses of the arts: Melpomene was patroness of tragedy, Thalia of comedy, and Terpsichore of dancing.

     Pushkin's gloomy account of Tatyána's visit to the theatre in Moscow matches, in reverse, his enthusiastic description of the St Petersburg theatre in I, 17–21. Over the intervening years Pushkin had fallen out of love with the prevailing French style of serious drama and had developed an admiration for Shakespeare.

from stalls or boxes: see note on I, 20. There is a contrast between Tatyána's self-effacement in the Moscow theatre here and Onégin's brashness in the St Petersburg theatre in I, 21.

51   *the Assembly*: I.e. the Assembly of Nobility, also known as the Nobles' Club (*Club de la Noblesse*). The Assembly was housed in the Dolgorúky Palace near the Kremlin, a white three-storeyed mansion, with interior colonnades. As well as balls, theatrical performances and other social events for the nobility were held there.

52   *she whom I dare not / distress*: It is not known for certain who was in Pushkin's mind here. Pushkin's friend Prince Vyázemsky later identified her as probably Alexándra Rímskaya-Kórsakova (1803–60); Pushkin had visited her at her mother's home in Moscow after his return from exile in 1826.

55   *'Tis of a friend I sing*: Pushkin is here playfully imitating the prologue of a classical epic poem, such as Homer's *Odyssey* (which begins: "Tell me, Muse, of a resourceful man and his many wanderings…") or Virgil's *Aeneid*, (which begins: "'Tis of arms and a man I sing…"). Although Pushkin contains the parody within the regular metre of his fourteen-line stanza, I have taken advantage of my normally unmetrical translation to render the passage into three and a half lines of dactylic hexameters, the metre used by Homer and Virgil.

Notes to Chapter Eight

Pushkin began Chapter Eight in St Petersburg on Christmas Eve 1829. He largely completed the chapter at the family estate of Bóldino in September 1830, finishing it off at Tsárskoye Seló in the summer and autumn of 1831; the last part of the chapter to be written was Onégin's letter, which he composed in October 1831. Chapter Eight was first published in St Petersburg in January 1832. For the short preface published with it see the introduction to *Onégin's Journey* below (page 363).

The action of this chapter stretches from autumn 1824 to early spring 1825. Onégin will now be nearly thirty, and Tatyána twenty-one or twenty-two. Tatyána will have been married since the autumn of 1822 or thereabouts. Nabókov noted that 7th November 1824 was the date of the catastrophic St Petersburg flood that is commemorated in Pushkin's later poem *The Bronze Horseman*, following which the authorities for a time prohibited balls and "routs". He deduced from this that the action in the chapter up to Stanza 34 must have taken place by the beginning of November 1824, after which Onégin went into hibernation till the spring.

The axis of this chapter is Stanza 29, containing a reflection on the effect of love on people of different ages. Around it is arranged an account of four successive encounters (or series of encounters) between Onégin and Princess X in St Petersburg – Stanzas 14–20; Stanzas 21–28; Stanzas 30–34; and Stanzas 39–48. Each of these four sections is marked by an intensification of Onégin's passion for the princess and by a stiffening of her resistance to him. They are prefaced, and conclude, with a discussion of Onégin's character and conduct (7–13 and 42–47). The content of the outermost sections of the chapter (1–7 and 48–51) is autobiographical and literary.

Epigraph: In English in the original. The quotation is the opening couplet of Byron's 'Fare Thee Well', one of his 'Poems of Separation'. The poem was addressed by Byron to his high-minded wife when in 1816 he had reluctantly agreed to her demand for a formal separation after a year of often torturous marriage and was about to leave England, never to return. The words – a blend of bitter reproof, self-pity and seemingly sincere devotion – express both pain at her rejection of him and an assurance of his continuing love (a love that he had not always shown during their life together). The brief epigraph thus provides us intertextually with Onégin's final apologia and valediction to Tatyána and offers us an insight into Onégin's character and state of mind at the close of the novel. The poem ends:

> Fare thee well! – thus disunited,
>   Torn from every nearer tie,
> Sear'd in heart, and lone, and blighted,
>   More than this I scarce can die.

1–7   In these stanzas Pushkin refers to episodes in his life from his schooldays to the time of writing. He imagines himself accompanied through these times by his muse in the role of a girlfriend who personifies his poetic inspiration and who takes on various guises reflecting the vicissitudes of Pushkin's career and his successive literary preoccupations, including finally his work on *Eugene Onegin* itself. See below for more detail.

1   *My goddess Inspiration*: literally "the Muse": see note above.

Lyceum: Or, in its French form, *Lycée*, Pushkin's school – see Extra Material, page 376. The Lyceum took its name from a park near Athens where Aristotle (384–322 BC) established his school of philosophy.

Apuleius... Cicero: Two contrasting Latin authors. Lucius Apuleius (*fl. c.*150 AD) is most famous as the author of a lengthy romance called *The Golden Ass*, which contains within it numerous lively, entertaining and sometimes erotic tales. (It is curious that the first stanzas of both the first and last chapters of *Onegin* – see also note for I, 1 – contain veiled references to a fabulous ass.) Marcus Tullius Cicero (106–43 BC) was a Roman orator and statesman and writer of political, literary and philosophical works that were heavier and less appealing to schoolboys.

my goddess... make the heart throb: Pushkin is recalling that his poetic activity began while he was still at school, with pieces that consisted largely of light-hearted verses addressed to his fellow students, items with a historical and patriotic flavour (like the 'Recollections of Tsárskoye Seló' mentioned in the following note), and numerous early love lyrics.

2   *Derzhávin*: Gavríla Derzhávin (1743–1816) was the greatest Russian poet of the eighteenth century. On 8th January 1815, the aged Derzhávin attended a school examination at the Lyceum at which the sixteen-year-old Pushkin recited one of his poems, 'Recollections of Tsárskoye Seló'. This work, which delighted the elderly poet, described the park adjoining the imperial palace and its monuments to Russian victories. Pushkin's title recalls a poem of Derzhávin's called

'An Excursion in Sárskoye Seló' (1791), which similarly began with a description of the park at Tsárskoye Seló in the evening, and mentioned placid waters and the cries of swans – images that Pushkin invokes again in Stanza 1 above.

The missing lines of this stanza exist only in Pushkin's manuscript. They recorded the early encouragement given to the young Pushkin by other eminent writers of the time, namely Dmítriev (see note on IV, 33), the poet and historian Nikolái Mikháylovich Karamzín (1766–1826), and Zhukóvsky (see note on the epigraph to Chapter Five). Why Pushkin dropped these lines is unclear.

3–5   Here Pushkin alludes to the course of his life after leaving school and to some of the works he composed during this period – see Extra Material, pp. 376–378. Stanza 3 describes his riotous life as a young man in St Petersburg up to 1820. Stanza 4 refers to his banishment from St Petersburg and his travels in the Caucasus and the Crimea in 1820, which inspired his *A Prisoner in the Caucasus*, *The Fountain of Bakhchisaray* and numerous lyrics. Stanza 5 recalls his continuing exile in Moldavia-Bessarabia (1820–23), where he spent some of his leisure roaming with the local gypsies (an experience reflected in his poem *Gypsies*); and goes on to refer to his subsequent exile to his country estate at Mikháylovskoye (1824–26), where he wrote most of Chapters Three to Six of *Eugene Onegin*.

4   *Lenore*: Heroine of the German romantic ballad *Lenore* (1773) by Gottfried Bürger (1747–94), in which Lenore's absent lover, of whose death she is ignorant, appears and carries her off on horseback over moor and mountain to his tomb. Perhaps Pushkin, in casting himself here as the horseman, is likening his exile in the south of Russia to a kind of death.

Crimean: Literally "of Tavrída"– see note on *Onegin's Journey* [15–19].

Nereids: In ancient mythology the Nereids were sea nymphs, so called because they were daughters of Nereus, a sea god.

5   *the language of the gods*: I.e. poetry in the classical manner.

6   *soirée*: Pushkin uses a transliteration of the English term "rout", which denoted at that time a large gathering or reception without dancing.

8   *Melmoth the Wanderer*: See note on III, 12.

        Childe Harold: See note on I, 38.

12   *Demon*: Pushkin refers to his poem 'The Demon' (1823), in which he speaks of having been haunted in his youth by an "evil genius", a spirit of negation and doubt who mocked the ideals of beauty, love and freedom.

13   *undirected travels*: For more information on these see *Onégin's Journey* and the relevant notes.

        Chatsky: The hero of Griboyédov's comedy *Woe from Wit* (1824) – see the note on the third epigraph to Chapter Seven. The acerbic Chatsky, after three years abroad, turns up on the day of a party at the Moscow house of his girlfriend (who later rejects him).

14   *Purists*: In the published editions of this chapter the addressee of this aside is indicated only by a row of asterisks. But from manuscript notes of Pushkin and his friends, as well as from the context, it is clear that the hidden name was "Shishkóv". Admiral Alexánder Semyónovich Shishkóv (1754–1841), statesman and publicist, was leader of a backward-looking group of Russian writers formed in 1811 to protect the "purity" of their language. He campaigned against both foreign expressions and liberal thought in Russian letters.

16   *good word... for an epigram*: Pushkin is no doubt thinking of the similarity in sound between the word "vulgar" and the name of his enemy, the writer, critic and police agent Faddéy B. Bulgárin (1789–1859), who had already been the target of at least one of Pushkin's epigrams.

        Nina Voronskáya: There is no agreement among commentators as to whom Pushkin might be referring to under this name. It is often assumed that he is sketching a composite portrait of more than one society belle. Michael Basker sees in her a reference to "Princess Nina", fictional heroine of the narrative poem *The Ball* of 1825–28 by Pushkin's friend Baratýnsky (see note on III, 30). In the poem Baratýnsky portrays Princess Nina as an extravagantly dressed and arrestingly beautiful wife of an aristocrat, who was nonetheless selfish, sexually promiscuous and contemptuous of other women. When eventually Princess Nina becomes infatuated with a man, she wants to run off abroad with him, deserting her husband and her role in society. As it is, her unfulfilled passion destroys her. Nina, with her cold, hard, marble-like beauty, thus presents a clear contrast, in character as well as appearance, to the Tatyána whom, in Pushkin's eyes, she is "quite unable to outshine" – a Tatyána of tenderness, restraint, loyalty and good taste.

Nabókov points out that, just as Tatyána had supplanted the "*belle Nina*" in Monsieur Triquet's song in V, 27, she now eclipses an incarnate Nina in St Petersburg.

Cleopatra: 69–30 BC, Queen of Egypt, notorious for prostituting her exceptional beauty. Her capital Alexandria stood on the shore of the Nile delta, just as St Petersburg stands on the shore of the Nevá delta.

17 *raspberry-coloured beret*: Why "raspberry-coloured"? The only previous mention of raspberries was in the peasant girls' song at the end of Chapter Three, which pointed up a contrast between their attitude to the opposite sex and Tatyána's (see note there). Is Pushkin now signalling subliminally to us – and to Onégin – that Tatyána has changed? She too, like the raspberry-picking peasant girls, is now about to attract a man, only to drive him away.

21, 22 *On waking he was brought / a letter*: Receiving invitations in bed, counting the hours by his chiming watch, driving off to a social gathering in a grand mansion: all this is a replay – in a different key – of the themes in I, 15, 27, 28.

23 *reminiscences / of amusing escapades of former years*: This, and the easy tone of their conversation in VIII, 17–18 (where they both use the familiar form of the pronoun "you"), suggests that Tatyána's husband (contrary to Tchaikovsky's operatic portrayal of "Prince Gremin") is not many years older than Onégin. At that time it was quite common for a well-regarded officer to rise to general by his mid-thirties.

24–26 The vignettes in these stanzas read like pen portraits – or caricatures – of real people encountered by Pushkin in the salons of St Petersburg; in some cases further details are given in the drafts of these stanzas in Pushkin's notebooks. Nevertheless, commentators have not succeeded in establishing the identity of the originals.

Pushkin seems to have had a lot of difficulty over this passage, which went through many revisions. His drafts, nonetheless, contain no complete and coherent text of the three stanzas. Although a complete draft of Stanza 25 does appear, the lines cut from the final text were largely reused in the final version of Stanza 26. Perhaps Pushkin found it difficult to make the allusions precise enough to be credible and funny, without becoming so obvious as to cause embarrassment or offence. In the end he seems to have found it necessary to blur his draft sketches slightly.

Nabókov points out the similarity between these three stanzas and Byron's *Don Juan* XIII, 84–88, where he satirically (but more wordily than Pushkin) enumerates the guests at an English country house party.

25 *the badge awarded to two little sisters*: In a draft Pushkin refers to the "two little sisters" as "two little orphans". The "badge" was a jewelled monogram of the Empress's initials awarded to those appointed as her maids-of-honour.

26 *Prolásov*: Roughly "Social climber", a comic name. The name, which is taken from one of Pushkin's drafts, was left blank in the editions of the chapter published during Pushkin's lifetime, suggesting that he had a real person in mind.

Saint-Priest: Count Emmanuel Saint-Priest (1806–28) was the son of a French émigré and a noted caricaturist. The young man had already committed suicide by the time Pushkin wrote this stanza.

pink as a pussy-willow cherub: Pussy willow is the English name for the twigs of sallow (a shrub of the willow family) that bear furry catkins in early spring. Pussy-Willow Week was the name given in Russia to the week before Easter (Holy Week), beginning with Palm

Sunday, during which fairs were held at which peasants sold figures of cherubs made of coloured paper or wax.

One man... over-starched swank: Nabókov explains that "over-starched" refers to the neck-cloth or cravat, which according to fashion should have been only slightly starched.

In a draft of these lines the "over-starched swank" is described as a "resplendent London swank". This may refer to the much-travelled English dandy Tom Raikes (1777–1848), whom Pushkin met in St Petersburg in the winter of 1829–30. Or (as Nabókov suggests) Pushkin may have been thinking of Count Mikhaíl Vorontsóv, Governor General of southern Russia, whom Pushkin despised, having worked under him in Odessa in 1823–24; Vorontsóv, son of a Russian ambassador to London, had been educated in England, was zealously pro-English and continued to affect English manners.

28   *sleep*: Literally "Morpheus", the god of sleep and dreams in classical mythology.

31, 32   *doctors all recommended spas. / But he was not for travelling*: Maybe Onégin's reluctance to travel to a spa was partly due to his dismal memories of the mineral waters of the Caucasus recorded in Stanzas [13] and [14] of *Onégin's Journey*.

Onégin's letter: It is noteworthy that Onégin (unlike the immature Tatyána years before – see note on Tatyána's letter in Chapter III) does not forget himself to the extent of using the familiar second-person pronoun at any point in his letter. (Nor does Tatyána, in her spoken reply in Stanzas 42–47, repeat her earlier indiscretion.)

33   *Epiphanytide coldness*: This reference to Epiphany and cold near the end of the novel echoes the Epiphanytide scenes at the novel's centre – V, 1-9. Then Tatyána, an excited teenager, recklessly disregarded the cold of Epiphanytide to invite a romantic liaison she longed for. Now, older and wiser, she uses Epiphanytide cold to protect herself from a romantic liaison she dreads.

35   The new literary references are as follows: Edward Gibbon (1737–94), the English historian; Alessandro Manzoni (1785–1873), Italian novelist and poet of the Romantic school; Johann

Gottfried von Herder (1744–1803), German philosopher; Sébastien-Nicolas Chamfort (1741–94), French writer famous for his maxims and epigrams; Madame de Staël (see notes on III, 10 and IV, Epigraph); Marie François-Xavier Bichat (1771–1802) French physician and anatomist. "Tissot" is either Simon-André Tissot (1728–97), famous Swiss doctor and writer on medicine, or Pierre François Tissot (1768–1854), a participant in the French Revolution and later supporter of Napoleon, who wrote on Latin poetry and French history. The remaining figures are Pierre Bayle (1647–1706), French sceptical philosopher and Bernard Fontenelle (1657–1757), French rationalist philosopher and man of letters.

he also read / some of our Russian authors: His reading could have included Chapter One of *Eugene Onegin*, which was first published this very winter, in February 1825.

è sempre bene: "It's fine always" (Italian).

37   *Imagination... pack of visions*: Literally "in front of him imagination deals him its motley faro". Faro (or pharaoh) was a card game, popular at the time among gamblers, in which the dealer (or "banker") dealt cards from a pack, placing them alternately to his right and his left, and the "player" placed bets on the appearance of a chosen card in the pile on the dealer's left. A fuller description of the game is given by Nabókov in his note on Pushkin's discarded stanzas following II, 17.

38   *Benedetta... Idol mio*: 'Benedetta sia la madre' ('Blessed be the Mother') was a popular Venetian barcarole. "*Idol mio, più pace non ho*" ('My idol, I have no more peace') was the refrain from a duet by Vincenzo Gabussi (1800–46).

46   *the spot where nanny*: Tatyána is unable to finish the sentence. Pushkin's throat tightens here too: his own nurse Arína Rodiónovna Yákovleva, to whom he was very attached and who had kept him company during his banishment at Mikháylovskoye (see for example IV, 35), had died in 1828.

48   *we're going to leave him... for ever*: However, Pushkin allows Onégin a final rejoinder, in the words of Byron's poem that furnished the epigraph to this chapter – see note on epigraph above.

48, 49   The abrupt ending of the narrative in Stanza 48 followed by Pushkin's self-deprecating remarks in Stanza 49 about the contents of the work mirror in reverse the abrupt opening of the narrative in the first stanza of Chapter One preceded by his self-deprecating description of the work in the Dedication. Note, for example, how the mention of "these slapdash stanzas" in 49 echoes the Dedication's reference to "the slapdash product of my leisure hours".

51   *Sa'di's words*: The quotation originates from the *Bustan* (*Garden*), a collection of poems by the Persian poet Sa'di (*c*.1193–*c*.1291). Pushkin had used a longer version of this quotation as the epigraph to his narrative poem *The Fountain of Bakhchisaray* (1821–23). There it reads: "Many like me have visited this fountain; but some are no more, and others are travelling afar." Pushkin did not quote Sa'di directly, but from an earlier quotation by the Irish romantic poet Thomas Moore (1779–1852) in his "oriental romance" *Lalla Rookh* (1817), which was known to Pushkin in a French translation by Amédée Pichot.

Four years after the composition of *The Fountain of Bakhchisaray* Pushkin's adaptation of Sa'di's lines acquired a more sombre significance. Early in 1827 the writer Polevóy published an article in the form of a letter to a Russian friend in New York, in which he bewailed the stagnation of Russian literature over the previous two years. "I look at the circle of our friends," he wrote, "that was once so full of life and merriment, and often, with you in mind, I sadly repeat the words of Sa'adi (or of Pushkin, who passed Sa'adi's words on to us): 'Some are no more, others are travelling afar.'" (*Moscow Telegraph*, 1827, first issue, p. 9).

Polevóy's words, and the quotation of Sa'di, were read at the time as a reference to the Decembrists, liberal members of the Russian intelligentsia and officer corps, who had risen abortively against the tsarist autocracy in December 1825 and who had subsequently either been executed or sentenced to long periods of hard labour and imprisonment in Siberia. A number of the Decembrists had been Pushkin's close friends and fellow writers, and more still had been admirers of his poetry. Thus, when in 1830 Pushkin used a further adaptation of Sa'di's supposed words in this stanza of *Eugene Onegin,* he was himself now referring, in a code which many of his readers would understand, to the Decembrists, who had still been at liberty at the time when the first four chapters of *Onégin* were written and the first was published.

Onégin's portrait... image of Tatyána: Commentators have been unable to identify any single prototype for Pushkin's portrayal of either Onégin or Tatyána. Probably Pushkin drew on a number of different models in each case.

Notes to Onégin's Journey

Pushkin did not assign numbers to the published stanzas of *Onégin's Journey.* For ease of reference I have numbered them according to the system used by Nabókov and some Russian editions, enclosing my numbers in square brackets. This system allows for the surviving stanzas that Pushkin drafted but decided not to publish.

Pushkin composed the stanzas of *Onégin's Journey* at different times. The stanzas about Odessa, [20–30], he wrote at the beginning of 1825, only six months or so after leaving the city. These stanzas were first published in a Moscow journal in 1827. At that time Pushkin's intention was to include them in Chapter Seven of the novel, the second part of which was to describe Onégin's departure from the country after the death of Lensky and his travels through Russia.

Pushkin wrote the other stanzas in 1829–30. He had the Crimean stanzas, from [16] to line 10 of [19], published in a literary journal at the beginning of 1830. By then Chapter Seven had already taken its present form, and Pushkin's plan was to devote a whole chapter between Chapter Seven and what is now Chapter Eight to an account of Onégin's wanderings up to his return to St Petersburg more than three years later, thus making *Eugene Onegin* a nine-chapter work. But, having drafted all or most of the chapter, he then decided to drop it entirely, as he explained in a preface to Chapter Eight when it first came out in 1832. In preparing the first complete text of the novel for publication a year later he included some of the discarded stanzas – those already published in journals, plus a few others – in an appendix, with a short explanatory introduction. This is how *Onégin's Journey* appeared in the two full editions (1833 and 1837) of the novel published during Pushkin's lifetime, and it is this presentation that I have reproduced here. A few more stanzas and part stanzas that Pushkin never published survive in manuscript drafts.

According to the chronology of the novel, Onégin leaves his country estate after Lensky's death early in 1821; his return to St Petersburg in Chapter Eight takes place in the autumn of 1824. The journey described in the aborted chapter bridges these dates.

The incompleteness of the material that Pushkin has left us prevents us from reconstructing Onégin's exact itinerary. From a combination of the published and unpublished stanzas, however, it appears that, having left his country estate shortly after Lensky's death, he moves first to St Petersburg. Departing from there on 3rd July 1821 he travels to Nóvgorod the Great and then via Valdáy, Torzhók and Tver on the upper Volga to Moscow. Leaving Moscow by late 1821 (before Tatyána's arrival in the early weeks of 1822), he travels on eastwards to Nizhny Nóvgorod at the confluence of the Oká and Volga rivers, where he visits the summer fair that ran between June and August. From Nizhny Nóvgorod Onégin sails down the Volga to Ástrakhan on the Volga delta, arriving in the late summer of 1822. Driven from there by the heat and mosquitoes, he makes his way round the north-western side of the Caspian Sea to the foothills of the Caucasus and the mineral springs around Pyatigórsk. Next, having travelled through the plains of the Kubán and across the straits of Kerch, he reaches the Crimea by 1823. From there he goes on to the Black Sea port of Odessa, where (according to Pushkin's drafts) he renews his acquaintance with the poet. This would be in early or middle 1824, not long before Pushkin was sent to exile in Mikháylovskoye – he left on 1st August. Onégin at this point decides to return to St Petersburg, by which route the surviving material does not specify. If the reference to "from ship to ball" in VIII, 13 is taken to imply that Onégin arrives in the capital by sea, then presumably his journey from Odessa takes him via a Russian port on the eastern coast of the Baltic such as Riga.

Introduction: *nine goddesses of inspiration*: "nine Camenae" in the original. "Camenae" was the Roman name for the Greek Muses, the goddesses of the arts, of whom, according to Greek mythology, there were nine.

Katénin: Pavel Alexándrovich Katénin was a friend of Pushkin's and a literary critic; see also I, 18 and note.

reasons that are important to him, though not to the public: Why was it that Pushkin decided to omit the chapter on Onégin's journey? There are various theories. Pavel Katénin (see preceding note) claimed to have been told by Pushkin himself that the full chapter contained an account of a visit by Onégin to the notorious military-agricultural settlements set up after the Napoleonic wars by Arakchéyev, one of Alexander I's ministers, where men were forced to combine the rigours of military discipline with the hardships of peasant life. According to Katénin, Pushkin later realized that his portrayal of these settlements was too harsh to pass the censorship and therefore discarded the whole chapter. However, there is no trace among the surviving drafts of any reference to the settlements; and it would be odd for Pushkin to reject the whole chapter on account of a single episode. It is possible that, more generally, Pushkin, for all his ingenuity, could find no way of composing a more than commonplace account of Onégin's tour of Russia without including critical comments that would have been unacceptable to the regime. Certainly the surviving stanzas steer clear of any comment on contemporary politics, nor do they advance our understanding of Onégin's character; and the stanzas included in the published appendix are much fuller of Pushkin's travels and impressions than of Onégin's. So, for all the chapter's poetic brilliance and topographical interest, it may well be that Pushkin decided that the chapter was insufficiently relevant and therefore superfluous to the main work.

[1–4] Pushkin ended up by using Stanzas [1], [3] and [4] as Stanzas 10–12 of Chapter Eight. Stanza [2] was simply an extension of Stanza [1].

[5–9] These draft stanzas trace Onégin's journey from St Petersburg via Moscow to Nizhny Nóvgorod.

[9]   *Nizhny Nóvgorod*: An old mercantile city some 400 km east of Moscow, known as Gorky in the Soviet era. Its long-standing importance as a trading centre was enhanced, in the absence of good roads, by its situation at the confluence of two major navigable rivers, the Oká and the Volga.

Makáryev market: Makáryev was a monastery and settlement about 80 km down the Volga from Nizhny Nóvgorod. An ancient annual market fair used to be held each midsummer outside the monastery wall; over time it came to attract traders from abroad as well as from within Russia and became one of the foremost Russia's markets, remaining open from June to August. Between 1804 and 1809 modern commercial facilities were constructed there; but the site was unsatisfactory, being close to marshy ground and liable to flooding, and in 1816 the whole complex was devastated by fire. The imperial government then transferred the fair to temporary accommodation in a better position at the mouth of the Oká opposite Nizhny Nóvgorod. Such was the economic importance of the fair, however, that Alexander I immediately charged the Spanish-born engineer and planner Agustín de Betancourt (1758–1824) with the planning and construction of extensive new facilities, including canals, locks, bridges and fine permanent buildings. The new facilities were first opened for use in July 1822 in the presence of over 200,000 merchants, visitors and sightseers, presumably including Onégin. At the time it was said to be the finest market complex in all Europe. A popular international fair is still held on the site annually.

[10, 11] The drafts of these two stanzas tell of Onégin's voyage down the Volga by ship, his arrival in Ástrakhan, and his journey onwards to the Caucasus.

[12]   *Terek*: A river that rises high on the northern slopes of the Caucasus range and, after plunging northwards through the mountains, flows east into the Caspian. The Georgian Military Highway, the one safe and practicable route linking the Russian territories to the north with Georgia, in Transcaucasia, ascended the Caucasus along the valley of the Terek.

the rivers Arágva and Kurá: The Arágva rises on the southern slope of the Caucasus, just over the watershed from the source of the Terek. Its valley, down to its confluence with the Kurá just upstream of the Georgian capital Tbilisi, provided the southern section of the route of the Georgian Military Highway. The Kurá is the major river of Transcaucasia, flowing eastwards through Georgia and Azerbaijan into the Caspian. Russia annexed Georgia in 1801, commenced work on the Georgian Military Highway in 1811, and spent much of the ensuing half-century trying to pacify the rest of the region including the freedom-loving tribes of the Caucasus itself.

[13]   Pushkin is talking of the area around Pyatigórsk, in the northern foothills of the Caucasus, famous for its mineral springs; he visited the area in 1820 and again in 1829.

victims of their love life: Pushkin wrote "victims of Kiprída" – for Kiprída see note on IV, 27.

[15–19] *Crimea*: Pushkin generally uses the name Tavrída (the Russian form of the old Greek name *Tauris*) for the Crimea. In ancient times the Crimean seaboard was an outpost of Greek civilization and later of the Roman and Byzantine empires. After the Golden Horde had overrun much of eastern Europe in the thirteenth century the Crimea fell into the hands of the Tatars, who in due course set up an independent Muslim khanate there, which later became a vassal state of the Turkish Empire. The Tatars made their capital at Bakhchisaráy, where the khans' palace can still be seen. The Crimean Tatars lived largely by pillage and slave-trading, and made frequent raids into the Christian Polish and Russian territories to the north for this purpose. Controlling as they did much of the northern coastline of the Black Sea, they remained an obstacle to Russian imperial expansion until they were finally subdued and their lands annexed under Catherine the Great in 1783, only forty years before Onégin's visit. At the time of Onégin's visit (and Pushkin's three years previously) the Crimea still struck visitors not only with the beauty of its mountains and the Mediterranean mildness of its coastal climate, but also with the lingering oriental exoticism of its human history and geography.

[15]   In Pushkin's draft the missing lines contained a continuation of Onégin's musings from Stanza [14], and a brief mention of his journey from the Caucasus to the Crimea.

Pylades quarrelled with Orestes: Agamemnon, King of Mycenae, returning home after his victory in the Trojan War, was murdered by his wife Clytemnestra. Their son Orestes (here called "Atríd" after his grandfather) then killed his mother in revenge. For this crime Orestes was forced to flee from home, accompanied only by his loyal friend Pylades. In the course of his wanderings he came to the Crimea, then inhabited by a wild people whose law it was to sacrifice all strangers to the goddess Artemis. The priestess of Artemis (actually Orestes's long-lost sister Iphigenia, but unrecognized by him) offered to spare one of the two friends so that she could have him take back a message to Greece. This led to the quarrel between Orestes and Pylades over who should die and who should be spared, each of the two friends wanting to die for the other. In the end Orestes, Pylades and Iphigenia all escape. The story would have been most familiar to Pushkin from its retelling by the Roman poet Ovid (see note on I, 8 above) in his *Epistulæ ex Ponto* III, 2.

Mithridates: King of Pontus (in the north-east of modern Turkey), who opposed the expansion of the Roman Empire in the first century BC, at first with some success. Eventually, however, he was defeated by the Romans, and fled to the Crimea. There in 63 BC, faced with the disaffection of his army and the treachery of his son, he decided to take his own life. Having failed to kill himself with poison, because of the antidotes he had taken earlier in life, he had one of his attendants stab him to death.

Mickiewicz... Poland: Adam Mickiewicz (1798–1855), the famous Polish poet, who spent from 1824 to 1829 in Russia and became a friend of Pushkin's at that time. He visited the Crimea in 1825 and recorded his impressions in his *Crimean Sonnets*.

Pushkin wrote "Lithuania" (*Litvá*) for Poland. Poland and Lithuania joined in a united commonwealth in 1569, which lasted until the country was partitioned between its neighbours in 1795. Pushkin treated the two names as synonyms.

[16]   *Venus: Kiprída* in the Russian – see note on IV, 27.

such burning passion: Almost certainly a reference to the beautiful Yekaterína Rayévskaya (1797–1885), eldest daughter of General Nikolái N. Rayévsky (1771–1829). Pushkin stayed with the Rayévsky family in the Crimea in the late summer of 1820 – see Extra Material, page 377 – and was strongly attracted to Yekaterína, whom he had previously met in St Petersburg. Yekaterína was known to be fascinated by the planet Venus and linked with it in the minds of her family, so the reference to Venus and to "bridal splendour" earlier in the stanza could be a subliminal glimpse of Pushkin's dream that a renewal of their acquaintance might lead to marriage.

[19]   *Flemish-style*: I.e. in the manner of the painters of the fifteenth- and sixteenth-century Flemish school with their ultra-realism and passion for detail.

Fountain of Bakhchisaráy… Zaréma: In 1820, on the way back from his holiday on the Crimean coast to take up his official duties in Bessarabia, Pushkin visited the old palace of the Crimean khans at Bakhchisaráy and saw the fountain that afterwards inspired his romantic narrative poem *The Fountain of Bakhchisaray* (published in 1824). Zaréma was one of the heroines of this poem.

[20]   *Odessa*: For Pushkin's stay in Odessa in 1823–24 see Extra Material, page 379. The cheerful tone of this celebrated description of Pushkin's life there is in interesting contrast with the mood of I, 50 of the novel, written while Pushkin was still in the city.

The Russians had founded Odessa as recently as 1794, following their annexation of the northern seaboard of the Black Sea from the Turks a few years earlier. They had encouraged foreigners, as well as Russians, to trade, work and settle there. In the early nineteenth century a large proportion of the population were foreigners, nearly a half of them Italians. Odessa, as an already thriving port still under development, was a city of excitement and opportunity. In 1819 the city was declared a tax-free zone, so many goods, including wine, were available to the inhabitants more cheaply than elsewhere.

Moor Ali: A merchant skipper and (allegedly) ex-pirate, originally from North Africa, who had settled in Odessa. He became an acquaintance of Pushkin's there.

[21]   *Tumánsky*: Vasíly Ivánovich Tumánsky (1800–60) was a minor poet, a friend of Pushkin's, and a colleague of his in the Governor General's office. A poem of his of 1823 about Odessa contained the couplet: "Beneath the light canopy of evening clouds / the fragrance of the gardens overwhelms us."

[23]   *Shortage... Of water*: One of the projects of Count Vorontsóv, Governor General of New Russia, on whose staff Pushkin reluctantly served in Odessa, was to provide the city with a good supply of drinking water.

[24]   *casino club*: This institution, which incorporated a large oval columned hall, combined the functions of gentlemen's club, venue for balls, gaming house and mercantile exchange.

[26]   *Automne*: César Automne was a popular Odessan restaurateur.

[27]   *Orpheus*: In Greek mythology a minstrel who charmed everyone and everything – even animals and inanimate objects – with the beauty of his music.

     Ay: See note on IV, 46.

     But, gentlemen: These last words are addressed to the censors – see note on IV, 45.

[28]   *businessman's young wife*: This seems to be a reference to Amalia Riznić – see note on VI, 15–16.

[29]   *merry Italians*: literally "sons of merry Ausonia". Ausonia was an ancient name for Italy.

[30-...] Pushkin left drafts of five more stanzas in his notebooks. They describe his reunion with Onégin in Odessa and their departures, Pushkin's for exile in Mikháylovskoye, and Onégin's for St Petersburg.

Note on "Chapter Ten"

We know from remarks by Pushkin's friends and from notes in his private papers that Pushkin had it in mind to continue the story of Onégin in a so-called "Chapter Ten", and indeed drafted at least seventeen stanzas. The subject matter of "Chapter Ten" was to be much more political than the earlier parts of the novel: it would deal with the events of Alexander I's reign and would chronicle the revolutionary movement that led to the Decembrist uprising of 1825, perhaps having Onégin join the rebels.

Pushkin disliked Alexander I both because of his reactionary policies and because he had been responsible for Pushkin's six-year banishment from St Petersburg between 1820 and 1826, and the "Chapter Ten" fragments that we have contain scathing references to the late Emperor. Pushkin realized the acute political sensitivity of this material and committed the stanzas he had composed to code.

By the second half of 1830, however, Pushkin was at last engaged to be married, with the blessing of the current Emperor, and planned to settle down to a less adventurous and controversial life than hitherto. He seems to have calculated that writing mockingly of Alexander, even in coded unpublished manuscript, would too much imperil his future plans. In his short story 'The Blizzard', therefore, which he was composing during October 1830, he included a passage in almost effusively laudatory terms about Alexander's role in the Napoleonic Wars, and in the margin at the end of this manuscript he recorded that he had incinerated "Chapter Ten" on 19 October. However, by oversight he left short fragments of fourteen encoded stanzas among his papers, plus three more stanzas, two complete and one unfinished. The enciphered stanza fragments were not decoded until 1910, and it is from these that we derive most of our knowledge of the gist of the chapter.

Because of the disjointed and incomplete nature of these fragments, and because Pushkin never approved them for publication, they are not included in this volume.

Extra Material

on

Alexander Pushkin's

Eugene Onegin

Alexander Pushkin's Life

Aléxander Sergéyevich Pushkin was born in Moscow in *Family, Birth and*
1799. He came of an ancient, but largely undistinguished, *Childhood*
aristocratic line. Some members of his father's family took a
part in the events of the reign of Borís Godunóv (r. 1598–1605)
and appear in Pushkin's historical drama about that Tsar.
Perhaps his most famous ancestor – and the one of whom
Pushkin was most proud – was his mother's grandfather,
Abrám Petróvich Gannibál (or Annibál) (*c.*1693–1781), who
was an African, most probably from Ethíopia or Cameroon.
According to family tradition he was abducted from home at
the age of seven by slave traders and taken to Istanbul. There
in 1704 he was purchased by order of the Russian foreign
minister and sent to Moscow, where the minister made a
gift of him to Tsar Peter the Great. Peter took a liking to the
boy and in 1707 stood godfather to him at his christening
(hence his patronymic Petróvich, "son of Peter"). Later he
adopted the surname "Gannibál", a Russian transliteration of
Hannibal, the famous African general of Roman times. Peter
sent him abroad as a young man to study fortification and
military mining. After seven years in France he was recalled
to Russia, where he followed a career as a military engineer.
Peter's daughter, the Empress Elizabeth, made him a general,
and he eventually died in retirement well into his eighties on
one of the estates granted him by the crown.

Pushkin had an older sister, Olga, and a younger brother,
Lev. His parents did not show him much affection as a child,
and he was left to the care of his grandmother and servants,
including a nurse of whom he became very fond. As was usual
in those days, his early schooling was received at home, mostly
from French tutors and in the French language.

School In 1811 at the age of twelve Pushkin was sent by his parents to St Petersburg to be educated at the new Lyceum (Lycée, or high school) that the Emperor Alexander I had just established in a wing of his summer palace at Tsárskoye Seló to prepare the sons of noblemen for careers in the government service. Pushkin spent six happy years there, studying (his curriculum included Russian, French, Latin, German, state economy and finance, scripture, logic, moral philosophy, law, history, geography, statistics and mathematics), socializing with teachers and fellow students, and relaxing in the palace park. To the end of his life he remained deeply attached to his memories and friends from those years. In 1817 he graduated with the rank of collegial secretary, the tenth rank in the civil service, and was attached to the Ministry of Foreign Affairs, with duties that he was allowed to interpret as minimal. While still at the Lyceum Pushkin had already started writing poetry, some of which had attracted the admiration of leading Russian literary figures of the time.

St Petersburg 1817–20 Pushkin spent the next three years in St Petersburg living a life of pleasure and dissipation. He loved the company of friends, drinking parties, cards, the theatre and particularly women. He took an interest in radical politics. And he continued to write poetry – mostly lyric verses and epigrams on personal, amatory or political subjects – often light and ribald, but always crisply, lucidly and euphoniously expressed. Some of these verses, even unpublished, gained wide currency in St Petersburg and attracted the unfavourable notice of the Emperor Alexander I.

Pushkin's major work of this period was *Ruslan and Lyudmila*, a mock epic in six cantos, completed in 1820 and enthusiastically received by the public. Before it could be published, however, the Emperor finally lost patience with the subversiveness of some of Pushkin's shorter verses and determined to remove him from the capital. He first considered exiling Pushkin to Siberia or the White Sea, but at the intercession of high-placed friends of Pushkin's the proposed sentence was commuted to a posting to the south of Russia. Even so, some supposed friends hurt and infuriated Pushkin by spreading exaggerated rumours about his disgrace.

Travels in the South Pushkin was detailed to report to Lieutenant General Iván Inzóv (1768–1845), who was at the time Commissioner for the Protection for Foreign Colonists in Southern Russia based at

Yekaterinosláv (now Dnepropetróvsk) on the lower Dnieper. Inzóv gave him a friendly welcome, but little work to do, and before long Pushkin caught a fever from bathing in the river and was confined to bed in his poor lodgings. He was rescued by General Nikolái Rayévsky, a soldier who had distinguished himself in the war of 1812 against Napoleon. Rayévsky, who from 1817 to 1824 commanded the Fourth Infantry Corps in Kiev, was travelling through Yekaterinosláv with his younger son (also called Nikolái), his two youngest daughters María and Sófya, a personal physician and other attendants; they were on their way to join the elder son Alexander, who was taking a cure at the mineral springs in the Caucasus. General Rayévsky generously invited Pushkin to join them, and Inzóv gave his leave.

The party arrived in Pyatigórsk, in the northern foothills of the Caucasus, in June. Pushkin, along with his hosts, benefited from the waters and was soon well again. He accompanied the Rayévskys on long trips into the surrounding country, where he enjoyed the mountain scenery and observed the way of life of the local Circassian and Chechen tribes. In early August they set off westwards to join the rest of the Rayévsky family (the General's wife and two older daughters) in the Crimea. On the way they passed through the Cossack-patrolled lands on the northern bank of the Kubán river and learnt more about the warlike Circassians of the mountains to the south.

General Rayévsky and his party including Pushkin met up with the rest of the family at Gurzúf on the Crimean coast, where they had the use of a villa near the shore. Pushkin enjoyed his time in the Crimea, particularly the majestic coastal scenery, the southern climate, and the new experience of living in the midst of a harmonious, hospitable and intelligent family. He also fell in love with Yekaterína, the General's oldest daughter, a love that was not reciprocated. Before leaving the Crimea Pushkin travelled with the Rayévskys through the coastal mountains and inland to Bakhchisaráy, an oriental town which had till forty years before been the capital of the Tatar khans of the Crimea and where the khans' palace still stood (and stands).

After a month in the Crimea it was time for the party to return to the mainland. During the summer General Inzóv had been transferred from Yekaterinosláv to be governor of Bessarabia (the northern slice of Moldavia, which Russia had annexed from Turkey only eight years previously). His new headquarters was in Kishinyóv (modern Chişinău, capital of Moldova), the chief town of Bessarabia. So it was to Kishinyóv that Pushkin went back to duty in September 1820. Pushkin remained there (with spells of local leave) till 1823.

Bessarabia 1820–23   Kishinyóv was still, apart from recently arrived Russian officials and soldiers, a raw Near-Eastern town, with few buildings of stone or brick, populated by Moldavians and other Balkan nationalities. Despite the contrast with St Petersburg, Pushkin still passed a lot of his time in a similar lifestyle of camaraderie, drinking, gambling, womanizing and quarrelling, with little official work. But he wrote too. And he also, as in the Caucasus and Crimea, took a close interest in the indigenous cultures, visiting local fairs and living for a few days with a band of Moldavian gypsies, an experience on which he later drew in his narrative poem *Gypsies*.

In the winter of 1820–21 Pushkin finished the first of his "southern" narrative poems, *A Prisoner in the Caucasus*, which he had already begun in the Crimea. (The epilogue he added in May 1821.) This poem reflects the experiences of his Caucasus visit. The work was published in August 1822. It had considerable public success, not so much for the plot and characterization, which were criticized even by Pushkin himself, but rather, as he himself acknowledged, for its "truthful, though only lightly sketched, descriptions of the Caucasus and the customs of its mountain peoples".

Having completed *A Prisoner in the Caucasus*, Pushkin went on to write a narrative poem reflecting his impressions of the Crimea, *The Fountain of Bakhchisaray*. This was started in 1821, finished in 1823 and published in March 1824. It was also a great popular success, though again Pushkin dismissed it as "rubbish". Both poems, as Pushkin admitted, show the influence of Lord Byron, a poet whom, particularly at this period, Pushkin admired.

Just before his departure from Kishinyóv in 1823, Pushkin composed the first few stanzas of Chapter One of his greatest work, the novel in verse *Eugene Onegin*. It took him eight years to complete. Each chapter was published separately (except Chapters Four and Five, which came out together) between the years 1825 and 1832; the work was first published as a whole in 1833.

Odessa 1823–24   In the summer of 1823, through the influence of his friends in St Petersburg, Pushkin was posted to work for Count

Mikhaíl Vorontsóv, who had just been appointed Governor General of the newly-Russianized region south of the Ukraine. Vorontsóv's headquarters were to be in Odessa, the port city on the Black Sea founded by Catherine the Great thirty years previously. Despite its newness Odessa was a far more lively, cosmopolitan and cultured place than Kishinyóv, and Pushkin was pleased with the change. But he only remained there a year.

Pushkin did not get on well with his new chief, partly because of temperamental differences, partly because he objected to the work Count Vorontsóv expected him to do, and partly because he had an affair with the Countess. Vorontsóv tried hard to get Pushkin transferred elsewhere, and Pushkin for his part became so unhappy with his position on the Count's staff that he tried to resign and even contemplated escaping overseas. But before matters came to a head the police intercepted a letter from Pushkin to a friend in which he spoke approvingly of the atheistic views of an Englishman he had met in the city. The authorities in St Petersburg now finally lost patience with Pushkin: he was dismissed from the service and sent into indefinite banishment on his mother's country estate of Mikháylovskoye in the west of Russia. He left Odessa for Mikháylovskoye on 1st August 1824; he had by now written two and a half chapters of *Eugene Onegin*, and had begun *Gypsies*.

Pushkin spent more than two years under police surveillance *Exile at Mikháylovskoye* at Mikháylovskoye. The enforced leisure gave him a lot of time for writing. Within a couple of months he had completed *Gypsies*, which was first published in full in 1827. *Gypsies* is a terser, starker, more thoughtful and more dramatic work than *A Prisoner in the Caucasus* or *The Fountain of Bakhchisaray*; along with *Eugene Onegin* it marks a transition from the discursive romanticism of Pushkin's earliest years to the compressed realism of his mature style. At Mikháylovskoye Pushkin progressively completed Chapters Three to Six of *Eugene Onegin*, many passages of which reflect Pushkin's observation of country life and love of the countryside. He also wrote his historical drama *Boris Godunov* at this period and his entertaining verse tale *Count Nulin*.

In November 1825 Alexander I died. He left no legitimate *The Decembrist Revolt* children, and there was initially confusion over the succession. *1825* In December some liberal-minded members of the army and the intelligentsia (subsequently known as the "Decembrists") seized the opportunity to attempt a *coup d'état*. This was put down by the new Emperor, Nicholas I, a younger brother of Alexander's. Among the conspirators were several old friends of Pushkin, and he might well have joined them had he been at liberty. As it was, the leading conspirators were executed, and many of the rest were sent to Siberia for long spells of hard labour and exile. Pushkin feared that he too might be punished.

Rehabilitation 1826–31 The following autumn Pushkin was summoned unexpectedly to Moscow to see the new Emperor. Nicholas surprised Pushkin by offering him his freedom, and Pushkin assured Nicholas of his future good conduct. Pushkin complained that he had difficulty in making money from his writing because of the censorship, and Nicholas undertook to oversee Pushkin's work personally. In practice, however, the Emperor delegated the task to the Chief of the Secret Police, and, despite occasional interventions from Nicholas, Pushkin continued to have difficulty with the censors.

After a few months in Moscow Pushkin returned to St Petersburg, where he spent most of his time in the coming years, though he continued periodically to visit Moscow, call at the family's estates and stay with friends in the country. In 1829 he made his only visit abroad, following the Russian army on a campaign into north-eastern Turkey. During the late 1820s he made several attempts to find a wife, with a view to settling down. In 1829 he met Natálya Goncharóva, whom he married early in 1831.

It was during the four years between his return from exile and his marriage that he wrote Chapter Seven (1827–28) and most of Chapter Eight (1829–31) of *Eugene Onegin*. In 1828 he also wrote *Poltava* (published in 1829), a kind of historical "novella in verse". This seems to have been the first attempt in Russian at a work of this kind based on the study of historical material. In its application of the imagination to real events, it prefigured Pushkin's later novel in prose *The Captain's Daughter* and helped to set a pattern for subsequent historical novels in Russia. It is also notable for the terse realism of its descriptions and for the pace and drama of its narratives and dialogues.

In the autumn of 1830 a cholera epidemic caused Pushkin to be marooned for a couple of months on another family estate, Bóldino, some 600 kilometres east of Moscow. He took advantage of the enforced leisure to write. This was when he virtually completed Chapter Eight of *Eugene Onegin*. He also composed at this time his collection of short stories in prose *The Tales of Belkin*, another verse tale, *The Little House in Kolomna*, and his set of four one-act dramas known together as *The Little Tragedies*.

The 1830s were not on the whole happy years for Pushkin. *The Final Years 1831–37* His marriage, it is true, was more successful than might have been expected. Natálya was thirteen years his junior; her remarkable beauty and susceptibility to admiration constantly exposed her to the attentions of other men; she showed more liking for society and its entertainments than for intellectual or artistic pursuits or for household management; her fashionable tastes and social aspirations incurred outlays that the pair could ill afford; and she took little interest in her husband's writing. Nonetheless, despite all this they seem to have remained a loyal and loving couple; Natálya bore him four children in their less than six years of marriage, and she showed real anguish at his untimely death.

But there were other difficulties. Pushkin, though short of money himself and with a costly family of his own to maintain, was often called upon to help out his parents, his brother and sister and his in-laws, and so fell ever deeper into debt. Both his wife and the Emperor demanded his presence in the capital so that he would be available to attend social and court functions, while he would much have preferred to be in the country, writing. Though Nicholas gave him intermittent support socially and financially, many at court and in the government, wounded by his jibes or shocked by his supposed political and sexual liberalism, disliked or despised him. And a new generation of writers and readers were beginning to look on him as a man of the past.

In 1831 Pushkin at length completed *Eugene Onegin*. The final chapter was published at the beginning of 1832, the first complete edition of the work coming out in 1833. But overall in these years Pushkin wrote less, and when he did write he turned increasingly to prose. In 1833 he spent another productive autumn at the Bóldino estate, producing his most famous prose novella, *The Queen of Spades*, and one of his finest narrative poems, *The Bronze Horseman*. He also developed in these years his interest in history, already evident in *Boris Godunov* and *Poltava*: Nicholas I commissioned him to write a history of Peter the Great, but alas he left only copious notes for this at his death. He did, however, complete in 1833 a history of the eighteenth-century peasant uprising known as the Pugachóv rebellion, and he built on his research into this episode to write his longest work of prose fiction, *The Captain's Daughter* (1836). Over these years too he produced his five metrical fairy stories; these are mostly based on Russian folk tales, but one, *The Golden Cockerel* (1834), is an adaptation of one of Washington Irving's *Tales of the Alhambra*.

Writings   From his schooldays till his death Pushkin also composed well over 600 shorter verses, comprising many lyrics of love and friendship, brief narratives, protests, invectives, epigrams, epitaphs, dedications and others. He left numerous letters from his adult years that give us an invaluable insight into his thoughts and activities and those of his contemporaries. And, as a man of keen intelligence and interest in literature, he produced throughout his career many articles and shorter notes – some published in his lifetime, others not – containing a wide variety of literary criticism and comment.

It is indeed hard to name a literary genre that Pushkin did not use in his lifetime, or it would be truer to say that he wrote across the genres, ignoring traditional categories with his characteristic independence and originality. All his writing is marked by an extraordinary polish, succinctness and clarity, an extraordinary sense for the beauty of sounds and rhythms, an extraordinary human sympathy and insight, an extraordinary feel for what is appropriate to the occasion and an extraordinary directness and naturalness of diction that is never pompous, insincere or carelessly obscure.

Death   Early in 1837 Pushkin's career was cut tragically short. Following a series of improper advances to his wife and insults to himself, he felt obliged to fight a duel with a young Frenchman who was serving as an officer in the Imperial Horse Guards in St Petersburg. Pushkin was fatally wounded in the stomach and died at his home in St Petersburg two days later. The authorities denied him a public funeral in the capital for fear of demonstrations, and he was buried privately at the Svyatýe Góry monastery near Mikháylovskoye, where his memorial has remained a place of popular pilgrimage.

Eugene Onegin

What is *Eugene Onegin*? This question is less simple to answer than one might expect. The work has a uniqueness that defies categorization. Pushkin himself describes the work as a "novel in verse". *What is Eugene Onegin?*

This translation does not attempt to replicate Pushkin's metre or rhyme scheme. But in order to give the reader some impression of Pushkin's original, I begin with a short description of the verse form. The work consists of 366 regular stanzas, grouped into eight chapters (this excludes the twenty-odd stanzas of *Onegin's Journey*). Each stanza has fourteen rhyming lines (like a sonnet); the lines are iambic tetrameters (i.e. they have eight or nine syllables with the stress falling on the even-numbered syllables); and the rhymes follow the pattern: *Onegin as Verse*

a b a b e e c c i d d i f f

where the vowels represent two-syllable "feminine" rhymes and the consonants one-syllable "masculine" rhymes.

The structure of this complex stanza (which Pushkin created specifically for *Onegin*) is easier to grasp from an example. Here is Stanza 20 of Chapter One from Stanley Mitchell's verse translation (published by Penguin Classics in 2008), where Pushkin describes a visit to the ballet in St Petersburg:

> The house is full; the boxes brilliant;
> Parterre and stalls – all seethe and roar;
> Up in the gods they clap, ebullient,
> And, with a swish, the curtains soar.
> Semi-ethereal and radiant,
> To the enchanting bow obedient,
> Ringed round by nymphs, Istomina
> Stands still; one foot supporting her,
> She circles slowly with the other,
> And lo! a leap, and lo! she flies,
> Flies off like fluff across the skies,
> By Aeolus wafted hither thither;
> Her waist she twists, untwists; her feet
> Against each other swiftly beat.

In addition to the regular stanzas, *Onegin* contains a seventeen-line opening Dedication and two letters in Chapters Three and Eight, all in the same metre, but with an irregular sequence of rhymes not arranged in stanzas. Chapter Three also contains an eighteen-line peasant girls' song with a quite different metre and rhyme pattern.

There is no dispute among Russians and students of Russian that the quality of Pushkin's verse-writing in *Onegin* (as in his other verse works) is superb. The spontaneity and aptness of rhythms and rhymes, the matching of words to metre and of sentences to stanzas, the combination of sounds to enhance meaning or entrance the ear through such devices as onomatopoeia, alliteration or assonance – all these bring the verse writing in *Onegin* to a level that is invariably excellent and often near perfect. But this word music is only accessible in Pushkin's Russian original. To reproduce it in a foreign language is simply impossible; and the attempt to translate Pushkin's words into an English replica of his verse form must not only fail to recapture his word music, it inevitably also obscures and distorts transmission of the work as a whole, including its many other qualities, which are much more susceptible to clear, accurate and readable translation. I discuss my own approach to translating *Onegin* in the Translator's Note on page 396. Here let us concentrate on identifying those other qualities of the work that it is both possible and worthwhile to convey in translation.

Onegin as a Novel   *Eugene Onegin* tells a story, like any other good novel, of imagined but believable characters leading believable lives, experiencing believable emotions, reacting to believable situations. A striking feature of *Onegin* is its balanced realism – its detached and ironic depiction of people and events, in which the author does not obtrude his own judgements, but offers us alternative interpretations.

Story and Character   The story of *Onegin* is set in the St Petersburg, the Moscow and the Russian countryside of Pushkin's own day, between 1819 and 1825, years that overlap the period of its composition (1823–31). The setting is one that we can observe independently through other accounts by Pushkin himself and his contemporaries. The human behaviour it depicts in Russia's new and ancient capitals and on the country estates of Russian landowners – the way the characters, major and minor, pass their time in learning, reading, talking, writing, working, idling, eating and drinking, dancing and playing, loving, quarrelling, travelling, marrying, worrying, decaying, dying and being laid finally to rest – is all recognizable, not only as behaviour credible for the early 1820s, but also, with allowance for changing circumstances, as behaviour credible today. As with any other good novel, it validates itself not only against what we know historically of human behaviour at the time it portrays, but also against what we know intuitively from our own experience to be credible human behaviour in our own time. The novel, like any good novel, informs us, and reminds us, of ourselves.

Pushkin understood people well. The characters in *Onegin* are drawn with originality, subtlety, humour and truth. Though "extras", like the guests at the Larins' name-day party, are often little more than entertaining satirizations, those even minor characters that have a personal role in the plot come over as real human beings – like Tatyána's loyal, if slow-witted, old nurse in Chapter Three, or the pedantic busybody Zarétsky in Chapter Six, or Mrs Larin's ailing but effusive cousin, Princess Aline, in Chapter Seven.

Pushkin treats most of the characters in the book with a detached irony, sometimes gently mocking, rarely unsympathetic, always perceptive. His picture of the attractive but shallow Olga Lárina in II, 23 is an excellent example of this. So is his portrayal of Lensky: the sheltered and idyllic upbringing in the country; the saturation in German idealistic philosophy; the vapidly romantic verses, which Pushkin parodied so well; the uncritical infatuation with Olga; and the fatal oversensitivity that causes the final breach with Onégin. Nonetheless, inadequate though Lensky has been as a thinker, writer, lover and friend, Pushkin causes us to feel to the full the tragic waste of his early death. The pathos is even increased by our consciousness of Lensky's weaknesses: through them we feel Lensky's life to be more human, and his death more unnecessary, than if he had been drawn as a more heroic figure.

Pushkin treats the two main characters with more overt seriousness. Tatyána he frankly idealizes, calling her explicitly "my ideal of perfection". This is in fact Pushkin's most committed characterization in the whole novel: there is no trace of irony in Pushkin's picture of Tatyána, save possibly in her choice of books. Clearly Pushkin believes in her, fervently, and succeeds in getting us to do so too. But nonetheless one senses that his (and therefore our) belief in Tatyána (unlike the other characters) is a belief founded less on the observations of a realist than on the hopes and longings of a romantic. The Tatyána of Chapter Eight, for example, reads like a template for the wife he was in the course of marrying.

Onégin's is the most interesting characterization of all. This is partly because here above all Pushkin presents us with two alternative personas, and leaves the choice tantalizingly to us. On the one hand Pushkin allows us to see him as a flip, superficial, idle young man who has driven himself to insensitivity and exhaustion through a frantic search for pleasure in St Petersburg's playhouses and casinos, restaurants and salons, ballrooms and boudoirs. Bored with the capital, and unexpectedly enriched by his inheritance, he goes to the country, where he alienates his neighbours by his boorish behaviour and ill-considered reforms. He patronizingly rebuffs the advances of a shy young girl who has imprudently fallen for him. His only friend – young Lensky – he deliberately and gratuitously provokes by flirting with his fiancée, and in the ensuing duel cold-bloodedly kills him. Exposed as

> ...just
> an imitation, an empty illusion...
> an encyclopedia of other men's oddities,
> a dictionary full of the latest clichés... (VII, 24)

– in short, as an empty poser – he travels abroad for several years. On his return, having met the girl he had disdained years before and who is now well married in St Petersburg society, he allows himself to fall for her and tries selfishly – and ineffectually – to entice her from her husband.

Against this unattractive but plausible portrait, Pushkin presents us with a different interpretation of Onégin (see especially VIII, 9–12). Onégin is more to be pitied than criticized. He is not alone in having misspent his youth – and in having lived to regret it. His disillusion with society is due, at least in part, to the malice he has suffered from others and to the stifling conventions of the day. He could have seduced the local girl who fell for him in the country, but instead he lets her down gently and gives her sensible advice. His friendship with Lensky is good for both of them until the overenthusiastic youngster badgers Onégin against his better judgement into attending the sort of local gathering he hates. Onégin bitterly regrets the resultant quarrel and duel, the outcome of which will haunt him for the rest of his life. On his return to St Petersburg he realizes the mistake he has made in rejecting the country girl who had fallen for him years before; since she still loves him, he tries vainly to persuade her that it would be best for them both even now to seek happiness together.

Throughout the novel Pushkin builds up these alternative (or complementary?) interpretations of Onégin's personality. Pushkin carefully never delivers his own verdict on his hero and leaves us free to decide on ours. This deliberate ambivalence of characterization (which applies too in a less developed way to other characters) is one of the most fascinating features of the work.

We have omitted mention of one minor character in the novel – the author himself. Pushkin, as well as narrating the story, gives himself a role in the plot as a St Petersburg friend of Onégin's. This enables Pushkin to develop Onégin's character by comparison and contrast. In Chapter One, for example, having likened Onégin's premature disillusion with St Petersburg society to his own, Pushkin then takes an opportunity to contrast Onégin's boredom in the countryside with his own love of it. This gives him the cue to point out that he is not following Byron in drawing the hero of his novel in his own image.

But Pushkin's presence with us as we read *Onegin* is much more pervasive even than as the author-narrator and as a character in the story. He constantly chats to us like a friend, reminiscing about his own life and activities, and commenting on this or that subject of interest. He talks to us autobiographically about his upbringing, his early life in St Petersburg, his exile and travels in the Russian south, his life under detention in his family estate in the country, and his eventual release; he mentions his daily routine, his writings, his love affairs, his friendships, his taste in wines, his aspirations. As commentator he gossips away to us about education, language, the theatre, literature, history, philosophy, the transport system, the natural world, people, life and death. (He would no doubt have been glad to comment more openly on the political background too if that had not been barred by the oppressive imperial censorship.) If we approach *Onegin* as

Autobiography and Comment

an ordinary novel, we may be irritated by the author's constant interruption of his narrative with other material. But that is to miss an important part of the charm and artistry of the work. Pushkin is indeed an affecting and amusing storyteller, but he also has a gift for talking interestingly and entertainingly to us on a whole variety of topics. In the digressions, as in the narrative, we can enjoy the company of a fascinating and inexhaustible conversationalist and friend.

Reality and Fiction   All this has one more effect. Because we come to know Pushkin as our own friend as well as a personal friend of Onégin's, and because Pushkin keeps dividing his attention between us, his real-life friends and the characters in the story, the boundary between reality and fiction becomes blurred; we begin to think of Pushkin's narrative not as a creation of his imagination, but as remembered fact. Pushkin shows us documents his characters have produced: their handwritten letters, poems and entries in autograph albums. Again, at the beginning of the last chapter he leads us via a stylized account of his own personal and literary development into the very St Petersburg salon where Onégin, after years of travelling, is about to renew his acquaintance with Tatyána. By these devices Pushkin brings his story to life in the same way as a baroque sculptor brings his subjects to life by having them step out to us beyond their architectural frame.

There are other ways in which Pushkin tries to destroy our consciousness of the boundary between reality and fiction. The action of the novel is set in the real world of Pushkin and his friends, amid the streets, palaces, theatres and restaurants of St Petersburg and Moscow with which his first readers would have been familiar, and in the sort of country estates in rural Russia that they would have immediately recognized. The work contains numerous references to books – to the poetry, novels and other works of Russian and Western European literature that Pushkin's contemporaries would have read, or at least would have seen collecting the dust on their bookshelves. Pushkin portrays several of his principal characters as avid readers of these books. Indeed, the characters of Tatyána and her mother, of Lensky, and even of Onégin himself, are obviously much influenced by the books they have chosen to read, and this paradoxically helps to give them an existence that is independent of the author's imagination. In short, this coexistence in a common physical environment, this awareness of the same authors and exposure to the influence of the same books, gave Pushkin's first readers, and can still give us to a lesser degree, the impression of sharing a common reality with the characters of the novel.

If it were just a *novel* in verse, *Onegin* would already have the makings of an original, interesting and attractive composition. *Other Features of Eugene Onegin* But what gives the work even more originality, interest and attraction is the rich concoction of other ingredients that are blended in with the novel. There is the *structure* that Pushkin builds into *Onegin* – the elegant balance of the story, the shape of each chapter, the links between chapters, the parallels and symmetries of the work as a whole. And there is the *poetry*, in the broad sense of vivid and evocative word pictures – either as descriptions that enrich the background of the narrative, or as imagery that gives the narrative itself added colour and impact. And there is Pushkin's inimitable *style* of writing. I deal more fully with each of these ingredients below.

It may seem surprising even to consider the structure of a *Structure* work which occupied the author off and on for over seven years. Pushkin admits himself that –

> young Tatyána and Onégin
> first came to me
> in a muddled dream,
> and I had yet to pick out clearly
> in my crystal ball the remoter features
> of this impromptu novel. (VIII, 50)

We know too that for a time Pushkin contemplated a longer novel perhaps of a dozen chapters, later of ten, and penultimately of nine grouped in threes, instead of the eight that finally emerged. And yet the finished work has an undeniable symmetry and proportion that are underpinned by a complex if artfully concealed substructure.

At the highest level, the story has a striking simplicity and balance. A girl meets a man, falls in love, writes him a love letter, and is rejected. A quarrel and a killing drive them apart. Several years later, the same man meets the same woman; he falls in love, writes her a love letter, and is rejected.

But the work also contains many more complex symmetries, links and cross-references. The elaborate structures of individual chapters I analyse briefly in the notes that preface the commentary on each chapter. Other more detailed points I cover in notes on specific stanzas. I concentrate here on the broader structural features.

There is a circular motion through the novel. For nearly the whole of Chapter One the action is in the polished, superficial world of St Petersburg's high society. For Chapter Two it moves to the country, with a side glance at Moscow and Mrs Larin's family there; and it remains in the country till halfway through Chapter Seven, when it shifts in earnest to Moscow and Mrs Larin's family, before coming back to the high society of St Petersburg for nearly the whole of the last chapter.

This circular motion is emphasized by other parallels between Chapters One and Eight. We meet Onégin abruptly at the very beginning of Chapter One, and we part from him abruptly at the end of Chapter Eight. The early stanzas of Chapter One contain an account of Onégin's schooling and early youth; Chapter Eight begins with six (very different) stanzas that relate to Pushkin's schooling and early youth. Chapter One near the end tells of Onégin's departure from St Petersburg; and Chapter Eight near the beginning tells of his return there. The autobiographical material in both Chapters One and Eight contains references to two of Pushkin's earlier narrative poems. Early in Chapter One we learn of Onégin's successes in seducing married women he does not love; near the end of Chapter Eight we read of his failure to seduce one married woman he does love. Onégin is joined in both chapters by his friend Pushkin. In both chapters Onégin tries to take up reading and writing as pastimes, in both cases unsuccessfully.

There are similar parallels between the next two chapters moving inwards, Chapters Two and Seven. Chapter Two ends near a country grave; Chapter Seven begins near one; in both cases we read the inscription on the tombstone. In Chapter Two, Mrs Larin is brought from her family (Princess Aline) and friends ("Grandison") in Moscow into the country by reason of an arranged marriage (her own); in Chapter Seven she is transported back from the country to her family (Princess Aline) and friends ("Grandison") in Moscow for the purpose of an arranged marriage (her daughter's). Chapter Two contains the novel's first mention of Lensky, Olga, Mrs Larin and Princess Aline; Chapter Seven the last. In Chapter Two we have a first description of Onégin's country house, we meet his housekeeper, and hear about his uncle's way of life; in Chapter Seven we have a second account of the house, the housekeeper and the uncle. Chapters Two and Seven both open with descriptions of idyllic pastoral scenery. Napoleon is recalled in both chapters. And so on.

Let us now look at the opposite side of the circle that begins with Chapter One and ends with Chapter Eight. Geometrically, this is the beginning of Chapter Five (Nabókov tells us that V, 5 contains the exact centre of the novel, equidistant from the beginning and the end). Here, instead of being among the sophisticates of the Russian capital's aristocratic society, we find ourselves momentarily surrounded by rural peasantry. And instead of the cold or cynical rationality of St Petersburg conversation we hear the excited gasps of housemaids telling fortunes and discussing omens. We have arrived in a world of folk magic, superstition and nightmare, as far distant as can be imagined from where we began or from where we shall end. Pushkin, though superstitious himself, tackles the subject with his usual lightness, and we are ready to giggle with the girls about the silly prophecies of "a soldier husband and a war" for both Olga and Tatyána; it is only later when we get to Chapters Seven and Eight that we realize with a frisson that for both of them the "silly prophecies" are well on their way to fulfilment. The forecasts of "wealth and fame", and of a loss, in Tatyána's divination song also come true. No doubt the reason why Pushkin never tells us the name of Tatyána's husband is to keep us guessing whether it was "Agafón" (see V, 9). In relating to us all these strange goings-on, Pushkin, I am sure, remains tongue-in-cheek; but by including them where he does at the start of Chapter Five he allows them to cast a deeper shadow over the drama that plays itself out in the second half of the novel.

There is another, more obvious way of analysing the structure of *Onegin*. If we split the novel in the middle – between Chapters Four and Five – we observe a different parallelism between the two halves. Both Chapters One and Five contain scenes of socializing, feasting and dancing, albeit in a very different class of company and decor. This parallel is underlined by Pushkin's recollection in V, 40 of his digression in Chapter One about women's feet. Chapter Two marks the entry of Lensky into the story: it describes his friendship with Onégin and leaves him standing in a country graveyard meditating on death. Chapter Six marks the exit of

Lensky from the story: it describes his enmity towards Onégin and leaves him lying in a country grave, dead. In Chapter Three Tatyána is reading her own novels, which mislead her into falling in love with Onégin; in Chapter Seven she reads Onégin's books, which lead her into a truer estimation of him. The close of Chapter Three finds Tatyána standing forlorn and silent among the trees of the park, nervously face-to-face with Onégin; the close of Chapter Seven finds her standing forlorn and silent among the pillars of the Assembly of Nobility in Moscow exchanging nervous looks with her future husband. In Chapters Three and Four Tatyána, infatuated with Onégin, writes him a letter which Pushkin allows us to read; there is no written reply; later she tries to avoid meeting Onégin by rushing out into the park, where he eventually finds her and delivers her, by word of mouth, a cool rejection. In Chapter Eight, Onégin, now infatuated with Tatyána, writes her a letter which Pushkin allows us to read; there is no written reply; later he tries to see her by rushing across St Petersburg to her mansion, where she delivers him, by word of mouth, a cool rejection. Chapter Four ends with a kind of affirmation of marriage in the form of Lensky's anticipation of his imminent wedding to Olga; Chapter Eight ends with a kind of affirmation of marriage in the form of Tatyána's decision to remain faithful to her husband despite Onégin's advances.

One can only wonder at Pushkin's skill in building such a complex structure of links, parallels, counterparallels and circularities beneath the artless surface of his novel. It is scarcely credible that he did so consciously when we know that its gestation was spread over such a long period and when he had already published the early chapters before he could have had any clear idea of what the later ones would contain – indeed, before he even knew how many later chapters there would be. And yet these structural features are too numerous and significant to be fortuitous. It is these devices, well concealed as they mostly are, that help to give the work the indefinable balance, proportion and symmetry that the reader senses in spite of Pushkin's apparent spontaneity.

Poetry: Description and Imagery   Another element of *Onegin* that we identified earlier was its poetry – poetry in description and poetry in imagery.

Each chapter has many memorable descriptions. In the middle of the first chapter alone we have Onégin's visit to the theatre; his dressing room; his arrival at a ball; his drive home through St Petersburg early on a bright winter's morning; and (in I, 47–48) an evocative account of a calm summer night in the same city, when the sun hardly sets. In later chapters the descriptions of the countryside at various seasons of the year are equally evocative and memorable, as is the slideshow of old Moscow (VII, 38), witnessed by Tatyána through the window of the old family coach as it jolts its way along the uneven streets.

Pushkin's imagery, too, is memorable for its succinct clarity, its aptness and, often, its originality. Usually sparing in his similes, he gives us several in quick succession to fill out his description of the death of Lensky (VI, 31–32). After a striking picture of a mountain avalanche he includes, as a parting tribute, three conventional romantic metaphors in Lensky's own style – a spent storm, a wilted flower, an extinguished altar flame – then finishes with the most memorable image of all, the abandoned house with its windows whitewashed over.

Then there is the element of Pushkin's style of writing. One *Pushkin's Style* feature of Pushkin's style is his *brevity*: the whole novel, with its unhurried narration and frequent digressions, amounts to less than 35,000 words in this translation, far less than the typical works of other nineteenth-century novelists. Another quality of Pushkin's writing is its *simplicity*: his preference for simple constructions, short sentences, everyday language, expressing apparently uncomplicated thoughts – though Pushkin's simplicity is often the smooth surface not of a shallow lagoon, but of ocean depths. There is also a *directness* of attitude and thought, an absence of posturing and falsity, a disarming sincerity and generosity of spirit, exemplified in the unpretentious but warmly felt dedication at the start of the work. Throughout there is a refreshing absence of sentimentality and sermonizing. Pushkin never talks down to his readers: he treats us as equals, presents us with the story "as it happened", and leaves us to draw our own conclusions. Then there is Pushkin's *clarity*, of two sorts: first, his clarity of vision, through which he can see, and point out to us, a wealth of fascinating and memorable detail in Russian life in city and countryside; and secondly his clarity of expression: his thought is always clearly conceived and clearly expressed.

A pre-eminent quality of Pushkin's style in *Onegin* is his pervasive *irony and humour*. Nearly every chapter glints mischievously with parody – parody of other writers, of other

393

styles of writing. He satirizes his real-life contemporaries and their manners, but with restraint: in an early introduction to part of the work he drew the attention of his readers to "merits that are rare in a satirical writer: the absence of anything to give personal offence, and the maintenance of strict propriety in the humorous description of social behaviour". This gives his style what Walter Arndt has called a "caustic elegance". Pushkin also pokes fun at each of his fictional characters (except Tatyána). But his habitually wry treatment of them gives him scope on occasion for an earnestness that avoids the sentimentality and melodrama that another writer might fall into: because Pushkin usually treats his characters with detachment and irony, we take him seriously and trustingly when he describes real emotion and tragedy. Nor does Pushkin spare himself from his jokes: he can laugh about a flock of wild ducks flying off from the lake to escape the sound of him declaiming his own verses (IV, 35).

It is these qualities together that give Pushkin's writing in *Onegin* its extraordinary *lightness*. Although the main characters experience much anguish in the novel, and although it ends without their having found fulfilment, the general feel of the work is very far from being tedious or dispiriting; indeed, it is a remarkably entertaining and heartening work to read. It is not that Pushkin is unmoved, or leaves us unmoved, by Tatyána's or Onégin's suffering; but he has an infectious resilience, an unquenchable brightness of outlook, a persistent *joie de vivre* that quickly replaces sadness with something of beauty or fun.

The Russian poet Alexándr Blok spoke about his appreciation of Pushkin as follows:

> Our memory retains from childhood one cheerful name: Pushkin... There are sombre names of emperors, warlords, inventors of murderous weaponry, life's tormentors and life's tormented. And beside them this buoyant name: Pushkin.
> (Speech given at the gathering to celebrate the 84th anniversary of Pushkin's death in 1921.)

Censorship The relaxed geniality of Pushkin's writing might suggest that he worked under a regime that allowed wide freedom of expression. Not so. Publishing in imperial Russia during Pushkin's productive lifetime was subject to a government censorship that was designed to uphold the political, religious and moral authority of the state, but which often manifested itself in trivial and unpredictable ways. Pushkin had hoped that his special relationship with Nicholas I from the autumn of 1826 (see page 380) would protect him from the most arbitrary interventions of the censorship apparatus, but in this he was frequently disappointed. The only part of *Onegin* clearly to show the marks of the censor's blue pencil is Chapter Two (see notes on Stanzas 2, 4, 8, 32 and 35). But Pushkin always subjected himself to rigorous self-censorship, as is clear from the ostensible absence of political and religious comment throughout the published novel (when he comments freely on almost everything else) and from the fate of the overtly political "Chapter Ten" (see page 371). Those political comments that he does make he buries deep in the subtext of his epigraphs and other literary quotations (see, for example, the notes on the epigraphs to Chapters Four and Six, and on IV, 45 and VIII, 51).

So does this mean that that *Onegin* as a whole is a lightweight *Entertainment or a* work of entertainment lacking in serious purpose? Critics since *Serious Message?* Pushkin's time have drawn out messages from *Onegin* about art and human existence, though Pushkin's artistry is such that an agreed version of these messages has proved hard to decipher. As with Onégin's ambivalent characterization (see above) Pushkin presents to us ideas that are often tongue-in-cheek or equivocal or even contradictory, and he leaves us to interpret the uncertainties for ourselves, just as we have to interpret the ambiguities and contradictions that we meet in real life.

Some critics have been so dazzled by the quality and variety of Pushkin's writing that they have seen the work primarily as a virtuoso exercise in style and the creative process; but that is surely to undervalue the work's many merits of substance. For some the main message of the novel has been the debilitating and corrupting effects of political oppression, or the destructive power of social convention, or the inexorability of fate; for some it has been a confrontation between sophistication and innocence, or contrivance and sincerity, or modernity and tradition; for some it has been the futile search for love and human happiness; or the triumph of altruism and fidelity; or the havoc wrought by selfishness and depravity; for some the work is preoccupied with death, for others it is a celebration of life. Much has been written in support of these and other readings, and there is no space here to explain, let alone discuss, the many theories. I prefer, therefore, like Pushkin, to let readers, having first enjoyed the story and its telling, reach their own judgement on the masterpiece's deeper significance.

Translator's Note

Principles A translator's two prime duties must surely be: first, faithfully to communicate the *meaning* of the text to English readers; and secondly – almost as important – faithfully to convey the *spirit* of the original, to match its character, style and "tone of voice". To fulfil these two apparently uncontentious duties is the aim of my new translation of *Eugene Onegin*.

A Literal Translation? Although I have striven above all to produce a version that is true to Pushkin's meaning, my translation is not a strictly literal one. It does not set out to reproduce in English the grammatical structure and individual words of Pushkin's sentences: to attempt this would result in a difficult and unnatural English that, as well as being unreadable, would be untrue to Pushkin's easy and natural Russian and to the spontaneity of his "impromptu novel", as he himself termed it (VIII, 50). A translator must take account of the specific features of the English language that differ from Russian, such as word order, word rhythms, grammar and sentence structure. A translator must also consider how modes of expression differ between verse and prose, and between the nineteenth and twenty-first centuries.

Conveying the Spirit of the Work The spirit of the writing in *Onegin* resides in the diction – Pushkin's choice of language and the way he uses it. Pushkin wrote in a Russian that is particularly fluent and natural, using a vocabulary, grammar and sentence structure that were normally up-to-date and always apt to context. His default style is informal, playfully conversational; but, as Pushkin himself acknowledges in his dedication, he modulates his "tone of voice" across a wide range of registers according to the effect he wants to produce – from the solemn to the flippant, from the serious to the ironic, from the heartfelt to the cynical, from the affectionate to the acid, from the lyrical to the down-to-earth. In this translation, against a backcloth of Pushkinian informality, I have striven to replicate the constantly shifting textures of his writing.

Ideally, another duty of the translator should be to reproduce *Treatment of* the *form* of the original work. *Onegin* is a "novel in verse", and the *Verse Form* verse form into which Pushkin has cast his novel is an innovative and tightly disciplined one (see page 383 above for the detail). How far should the translator aim to reproduce the *verse form* of *Onegin*? Nearly all previous translators of the work into English have set themselves this aim; but I believe them to be mistaken in this, for two main reasons. The first is word music: Pushkin is unrivalled in the brilliance and beauty of his verse-writing; but Pushkin's rhymes are Russian rhymes, made up from the sounds of the Russian language. To try to recreate Pushkin's rhymes in English is futile. The rhymes of an English translator, however skilful (and none will be as skilful as Pushkin), can only ever be *different* from Pushkin's; they can never produce *the same* word music. So to attempt to convey the effect of Pushkin's rhymes through a rhymed English version can only be to chase a mirage. The second, still more important reason for freeing a translation from the verse form of the original relates to meaning, style and intonation. It is in most cases impossible to replicate in English the strict metre and rhyme scheme of a foreign original of any length without unacceptably distorting meaning, style and tone and obscuring other qualities of writing (plot, characterization, imagery, etc.). This is especially so with Russian, where rhymes are much more plentiful than in English, and where the highly inflected nature of the language gives the author much more flexibility of word order than an English writer has. Nabókov in his commentary frequently pokes fun at previous translators – in most cases legitimately – for their clumsy and fanciful attempts to fit meaning to metre.

As Pushkin's work is a "*novel* in verse", an alternative *A Novel in Prose* approach is to give up on the verse and to make the work available to the English reader in straight prose as a novel. My previous translation of *Eugene Onegin* (published by Wordsworth Classics in 2005) did precisely this. As *Onegin* is a novel, I still believe it was right to make it available to the English reader as a straight novel and to extend knowledge and admiration of Pushkin's work to those (and I suspect they are many) who shun a lengthy work in verse form.

However, a straight prose translation inevitably loses certain important features of the original that, unlike rhyme, *can* be reflected in an English version without distorting the source text's meaning, style and tone. One of these features is the regular flow of the fourteen-line stanzas with their closing couplets that are so apt for pointing up a jibe or a joke or an aphorism or a touch of irony, or simply for closing off an episode in the neatest way; the distinct stanzas are like successive waves breaking on the beach, similar in form but different in content, only occasionally merging for special effect (as in III, 38–39). Another feature is the pattern of line breaks, its normal evenness again sometimes interrupted for dramatic purposes (e.g. in the opening lines of V, 21).

Nabókov's Solution   Vladímir Nabókov, in his monumental edition of the work first published in 1964, included a controversial translation that reflected some of the thinking I have outlined above. Nabókov rejected rhyme and regular tetrameters in his translation because he felt, like me, that it should be his primary aim to remain true to Pushkin's words and meaning; he nevertheless set his translation out in fourteen-line stanzas, like Pushkin, with a rhythm that, while free, was still reminiscent of Pushkin's. Within that framework, however, Nabókov aimed at a strictly literal translation; and his obsessive literalness, combined with an idiosyncratic use of archaisms, neologisms and inversions, results in a bizarre rendering that, in my view and that of many others, is quite untrue to the spirit of the original with its lightness, fluency and informality.

My Approach   It seemed to me, in undertaking the present translation, that there should be a middle way between prose novel and rhymed verse that, while being (in a truer way than Nabókov) faithful to Pushkin's meaning and spirit, also preserves the regular sea swell of his stanza form and something of his word rhythms.

I have therefore set this translation out in fourteen-line stanzas that correspond to Pushkin's; I have also, for the most part, followed Pushkin's line breaks. Within each stanza I have not attempted to reproduce Pushkin's rhymes or strict tetrameters because I wished to avoid importing an alien and discordant word music and forcing myself to distort Pushkin's sense and style. Instead I have used unrhymed lines of varying length, as the English text required, introducing suitable word rhythms in a free and spontaneous way, where this did not interfere with an accurate rendering and where the rhythms might indeed help to catch Pushkin's intonation, particularly at the climax of sentences and stanzas. I have also tried to make up for the absence of rhyme by producing a translation that *sounds* attractive in other ways – notably through appropriate repetitions, alliterations and assonances. In ways like this I hope I have produced a version that will give the English reader, through its sounds, a little of the same pleasure that the Russian reader receives from Pushkin's writing.

In this way the present translation, in avoiding the distraction of an English imitation of Pushkin's rhymes, will help readers focus their attention on the many other qualities of *Onegin*, including the story itself, the characterization, the interplay of imagination and reality, the poetry of imagery and description, and the wealth of comment, irony and humour. My hope is that this translation, by conveying these features more clearly, accurately and readably, will enable Pushkin's masterpiece at last to be esteemed and enjoyed in the English-reading world as greatly as it deserves.

I believe that this translation of *Eugene Onegin* rescues meaning from metre, conveying more faithfully than any of its predecessors the sense and spirit of Pushkin's original. Printed face to face with the Russian text, it should therefore be invaluable both to students of Russian and to readers of Russian literature in English.

In transliterating Russian names I have used the British *Russian Names* Standard method in its simplified version. This still leaves the reader without guidance on stress, which is both important and unpredictable in Russian. I have, therefore, normally marked the stressed syllable of Russian names with an acute accent on the appropriate vowel, except where these are monosyllables or words of two syllables with the stress on the first (e.g. "Pushkin", "Lensky", "Larin").

For the given names of Russians I have normally transliterated the Russian, rather than substituting an English equivalent, except where this would seem excessively awkward or unfamiliar (e.g. *Eugene* Onegin, not Yevgény; *Alexander* Pushkin, not Alexándr).

Most Russian surnames have a feminine form for women. In accordance with usual practice I have used the feminine form when referring to women by their own names, but not when referring to them by their husband's names prefixed by a title – e.g. "Praskóvya Lárina", but "Mrs Larin".

– Roger Clarke
March 2011

Select Bibliography

Books about Pushkin and His Work:

Arinshtein, Leonid Matveyevich, *Pushkin: Neprichosannaya Biografiya* (Moscow: Rossiysky Fond Kultury, 2007)

Bayley, John, *Pushkin: a Comparative Commentary* (Cambridge University Press, 1971)

Binyon, T.J., *Pushkin: a Biography* (London: HarperCollins, 2002)

Briggs, A.D.P., *Alexander Pushkin: a Critical Study* (London: Croom Helm, 1983)

Lotman, Yury Mikhaylovich, *Pushkin* (St Petersburg: Iskusstvo-SPB, 1995)

Tertz, Abram (Sinyavsky, Andrey), *Strolls with Pushkin* (New Haven and London: Yale University Press, 1993)

Tomashevsky Boris Viktorovich, *Pushkin* (Moscow-Leningrad: Izdatelstvo Akademii Nauk USSR, 1956)

Wolff, Tatiana, ed. and tr., *Pushkin on Literature* (London: The Athlone Press, 1986)

Russian Text of Eugene Onegin:

Texts are available in numerous collections of Pushkin's works, published in the Soviet Union and in Russia during the last half-century and more, notably: *Sobranie Sochineniy Pushkina*, Vol. IV (Moscow: Gosudarstvennoye Izdatelstvo Khudozhestvennoy Literatury, 1959–62). This ten-volume collection is also available online through the *Russkaya Virtualnaya Biblioteka* at www.rvb.ru/pushkin/toc.htm.

Books about Eugene Onegin:

Briggs, Professor A.D.P., *Pushkin: Eugene Onegin* (Cambridge: Landmarks of World Literature, Cambridge University Press, 1992), a very readable and perceptive appreciation of Pushkin's artistry in *Eugene Onegin* and discussion of some of the issues the work raises

Dalton-Brown, S., *Pushkin's Eugene Onegin* (Bristol: Bristol Classical Press, 1997): A useful survey of the extensive critical literature published about *Eugene Onegin* in Russian and other languages

Eugene Onegin: English Translations and Commentaries:

Eugene Onegin, translated into English, with commentary, by Vladimir Nabokov, in four volumes (New York: Bollingen Foundation, 1964)

Eugene Onegin, a Novel in Verse, by Alexander Pushkin, translated by Charles Johnston, with introduction and notes by Michael Basker (London: Penguin, 2003)

Eugene Onegin, translated into English verse, with introduction and notes, by Stanley Mitchell (London: Penguin, 2008)

Other Suggestions:

A beautiful modern example of a novel in verse in the Pushkinian manner, using the *Onegin* stanza, is Vikram Seth's *The Golden Gate* (New York: Random House, 1986).

Acknowledgements

My thanks go to two people especially – to Alessandro Gallenzi of Alma Classics for entrusting me with the happy task of retranslating and re-editing Pushkin's masterpiece; and to Elizabeth, my wife, for her unfailing support and help throughout my work.

I am grateful to others too – to Simon Blundell, librarian of the Reform Club in London, who provided me with generous and willing assistance in my early research; to Elena Bassil-Morozow and the late Stanley Mitchell, who were generous with their time and knowledge in giving me comments on my previous translation that have enabled me to make this one better; and to the editorial team at Alma Classics, for their efficiency and patience in processing the text and in accommodating my sometimes idiosyncratic requests. Remaining faults are my own.

Appendix

Стихи и строфы *Евгения Онегина*, пропущенные Пушкиным из издания 1837 года, но ранее им публикованные

ГЛАВА ЧЕТВЕРТАЯ

1   В начале жизни мною правил
     Прелестный, хитрый, слабый пол;
     Тогда в закон себе я ставил
     Его единый произвол.
     Душа лишь только разгоралась,
     И сердцу женщина являлась
     Каким-то чистым божеством.
     Владея чувствами, умом,
     Она сияла совершенством.
     Пред ней я таял в тишине:
     Ее любовь казалась мне
     Недосягаемым блаженством.
     Жить, умереть у милых ног —
     Иного я желать не мог.

2   То вдруг ее я ненавидел,
     И трепетал, и слезы лил,
     С тоской и ужасом в ней видел
     Созданье злобных, тайных сил;
     Ее пронзительные взоры,
     Улыбка, голос, разговоры —
     Всё было в ней отравлено,
     Изменой злой напоено,
     Всё в ней алкало слез и стона,
     Питалось кровию моей...
     То вдруг я мрамор видел в ней,
     Перед мольбой Пигмалиона
     Еще холодный и немой,
     Но вскоре жаркий и живой.

Passages of *Eugene Onegin* excluded by Pushkin from
the 1837 edition, but published by him earlier

CHAPTER FOUR

1   In early life the weaker sex
governed me with its charm and guile.
At that time the rule I set myself
was to do its pleasure, nothing else.
As soon as I first felt the fire of love,
each woman to my eyes became
a sort of pure divinity.
She held my mind, my feelings in her power,
radiating perfection.
I melted silently when in her presence:
to me her love seemed
bliss beyond attainment.
To love, to die at my beloved's feet
was everything I could desire.

2   Then suddenly I came to hate her:
I trembled, I shed tears;
I saw in her, with horror and distress,
a creature of dark, evil forces;
her piercing eyes,
her smile, her voice, her talk –
all of her was infused with poison,
was steeped in malice and deceit,
all in her craved my tears and groans,
gorged itself on my blood...
Then all at once she took on a new form –
a marble figure, cold and dumb at first, who
in answer to Pygmalion's prayers
soon took on warmth and life.

3   Словами вещего поэта
     Сказать и мне позволено:
     Темира, Дафна и Лилета —
     Как сон забыты мной давно.
     Но есть одна меж их толпою...
     Я долго был пленен одною —
     Но был ли я любим, и кем,
     И где, и долго ли?.. зачем
     Вам это знать? не в этом дело!
     Что было, то прошло, то вздор;
     А дело в том, что с этих пор
     Во мне уж сердце охладело,
     Закрылось для любви оно,
     И всё в нем пусто и темно.

4   Дознался я, что дамы сами,
     Душевной тайне изменя,
     Не могут надивиться нами,
     Себя по совести ценя.
     Восторги наши своенравны
     Им очень кажутся забавны;
     И, право, с нашей стороны
     Мы непростительно смешны.
     Закабалясь неосторожно,
     Мы их любви в награду ждем,
     Любовь в безумии зовем,
     Как будто требовать возможно
     От мотыльков иль от лилей
     И чувств глубоких и страстей!

---

36   Уж их далече взор мой ищет...
     А лесом кравшийся стрелок
     Поэзию клянет и свищет,
     Спуская бережно курок.
     У всякого своя охота,
     Своя любимая забота:
     Кто целит в уток из ружья,
     Кто бредит рифмами, как я,
     Кто бьет хлопушкой мух нахальных,
     Кто правит в замыслах толпой,
     Кто забавляется войной,
     Кто в чувствах нежится печальных,
     Кто занимается вином:
     И благо смешано со злом.

3   I too may quote
    an eloquent poet's words:
    "Thémire and Daphne and Lileta
    I've long forgotten, like a dream."
    There's one among the many, though...
    there's one that I was long held captive by.
    But was I loved in my turn? And who was it?
    And where? And for how long?... But why
    do you need know this? It's no matter!
    What's past is past, it's meaningless;
    the matter now is this: from that time on,
    my heart has grown quite cold,
    it's shut love out,
    inside all's dark and void.

4   I've learnt now that our lady friends themselves
    can't help but be amazed at us,
    if they (false to their inner natures)
    make an honest appraisal of themselves.
    They find our uncontrollable emotions
    highly diverting;
    It's true too, I admit –
    we're inexcusably absurd:
    we're fool enough to make ourselves their slaves,
    and then expect their love as a reward;
    we insanely try to summon love
    as though you could realistically demand
    deep feelings and intense emotions
    from lilies or from butterflies!

---

36   ...until they've vanished from my sight.
    The marksman creeping through the trees, though,
    damns poetry, and hisses
    as he uncocks his gun with care.
    Each has his sport,
    his favourite pastime:
    one shoots at ducks,
    another's crazy about rhymes (that's me),
    one swats at cheeky flies,
    one aims to rule a nation,
    one plays at war,
    one savours melancholy feelings,
    another spends his time on wine:
    good things and bad – a mix.

ГЛАВА ПЯТАЯ

37 В пирах готов я непослушно
С твоим бороться божеством;
Но, признаюсь великодушно,
Ты победил меня в другом:
Твои свирепые герои,
Твои неправильные бои,
Твоя Киприда, твой Зевес
Большой имеют перевес
Перед Онегиным холодным,
Пред сонной скукою полей,
Перед Истоминой моей,
Пред нашим воспитаньем модным;
Но Таня (присягну) милей
Елены пакостной твоей.

38 Никто и спорить тут не станет,
Хоть за Елену Менелай
Сто лет еще не перестанет
Казнить Фригийский бедный край,
Хоть вкруг почтенного Приама
Собранье стариков Пергама,
Ее завидя, вновь решит:
Прав Менелай и прав Парид.
Что ж до сражений, то немного
Я попрошу вас подождать:
Извольте далее читать;
Начала не судите строго;
Сраженье будет. Не солгу,
Честное слово дать могу.

———————————

43 . . . .
. . . .
. . . .
. . . .
Подковы, шпоры Петушкова
(Канцеляриста отставного)
Стучат; Буянова каблук
Так и ломает пол вокруг;
Треск, топот, грохот — по порядку:
Чем дальше в лес, тем больше дров;
Теперь пошло на молодцов:
Пустились, только не в присядку.
Ах! легче, легче: каблуки
Отдавят дамские носки!

CHAPTER FIVE

37   When it comes to feasts, for all your inspiration
I'm not ashamed to pit myself against you.
But I'm magnanimous enough to own
that there are areas where you've bettered me:
your savage heroes,
your uneven battles,
your Aphrodite and your Zeus
outdo by far in gravitas
my chill Onégin,
the dreamy tedium of my landscapes,
my ballet dancers
and all our fashionable sophistication.
I'll vouch for this, though: my Tatyána's
much nicer than your sleazy Helen...

38   ...no one will quarrel with me here,
though Menelaus spend a hundred years more
in ravaging the lands around poor Troy
for Helen's sake,
and though the conference of Trojan elders
round good King Priam, catching sight of her,
reach the conclusion that
Menelaus and Paris, both, were justified.
But as for fighting, I must ask you, readers,
to wait in patience for a little longer:
kindly read on;
don't criticize to soon;
there *will* be fighting: I'll not let you down;
my word of honour I can give you.

-----

43   ....
....
....

....
That office clerk (retired) Petushkóv's
metal studs and spurs
ring out; Buyánov's boots
are also threatening to smash the floor;
stamp, tramp and rumble, in succession –
the deeper the forest, the more's the wood.
And now the young men take their turn:
they're dancing lower, almost squatting.
Aah! Easy, easy there! Those boots
will crush the ladies' toes!

ГЛАВА ШЕСТАЯ

В место строфы 46

46   Дай оглянусь. Простите ж, сени,
Где дни мои текли в глуши,
Исполнены страстей и лени
И снов задумчивой души.
А ты, младое вдохновенье,
Волнуй мое воображенье,
Дремоту сердца оживляй,
В мой угол чаще прилетай,
Не дай остыть душе поэта,
Ожесточиться, очерстветь,
И наконец окаменеть
В мертвящем упоеньи света,
Среди бездушных гордецов,
Среди блистательных глупцов,

47   Среди лукавых, малодушных,
Шальных, балованных детей,
Злодеев и смешных и скучных,
Тупых, привязчивых судей,
Среди кокеток богомольных,
Среди холопьев добровольных,
Среди вседневных, модных сцен,
Учтивых, ласковых измен,
Среди холодных приговоров
Жестокосердой суеты,
Среди досадной пустоты
Расчетов, душ и разговоров,
В сем омуте, где с вами я
Купаюсь, милые друзья.

CHAPTER SIX

(In place of Stanza 46)

46   One last look back – to say goodbye
to the sheltered spots where in seclusion day by day
I used to indulge my emotions, indolence
and wistful dreams... But my youthful inspiration
– please not "goodbye" to that!
May it wing its way more often to my corner,
to stir my imagination
and enliven the musings of my soul,
so that my poet's heart may not grow cold
and hard and stale,
and not be turned at last to stone
in society's lethal frenzy,
amid soulless grandees,
amid illustrious fools...

47   ...amid the devious, the fainthearted,
the children spoilt and uncontrolled,
the scoundrels laughable and tedious,
the critics quarrelsome and dim,
amid the sanctimonious flirts,
amid the eager sycophants,
amid the daily fashion shows,
amid the snubs polite and suave,
amid the icy verdicts voiced
by those who are vain and cruel-hearted,
amid the sickening emptiness
of calculation, thought and chatter –
in this morass, friends, where we're all
wallowing together, you and I!

Notes on the Appendix

Chapter Four

2   *Pygmalion*: In Greco-Roman mythology Pygmalion was a sculptor who, having carved the figure of a girl, fell in love with it. In answer to Pygmalion's prayers Aphrodite, goddess of love, brought the statue to life and they were married.

3   *Thémire and Daphne and Lileta*: Commonplace girls' names in French and Russian pastoral verse. The two lines are a quotation from a poem by Pushkin's friend Antón Delvig, 'To Fanny'. Pushkin refers to Delvig again in VI, 20.

Chapter Five

37, 38   These stanzas contain an extended and facetious reference to Homer's account of the Trojan War in his *Iliad*. Paris, a son of the Trojan King Priam, had abducted Helen, the beautiful wife of Menelaus, King of Sparta, and brought her back home to Troy. Menelaus and his brother then led a Greek force against Troy to recover Helen, besieging the city for ten years before taking it. The Olympian gods, Zeus, Aphrodite and others, assisted one side or the other as they chose. At one point in his account Homer describes a meeting between King Priam and his elder statesmen on one of Troy's gate towers; he relates how: "When [the elders] saw Helen approaching the tower, they said to each other, 'You can't condemn the Trojans and Greeks for enduring hardships for so long over such a woman: she's stunningly like the immortal goddesses in her looks...' " (*Iliad* III,154–58). Pushkin is hinting here at an ironic parallel between Paris's abduction of Helen from her husband Menelaus, which brought about the disastrous Trojan war, and Onégin's imminent seduction of Lensky's fiancée Olga, which will bring about their fatal duel.

37   *Aphrodite*: Pushkin refers to *Kiprída* – for whom see note on IV, 27.

37   *my ballet dancers*: Pushkin wrote: "my Istómina" – for whom see note on I, 20.

38   *the lands around poor Troy*: Literally "the poor Phrygian land". Phrygia was the name of a region of western Asia Minor (now Turkey), sometimes used by ancient authors to refer to the area around Troy.

     conference of Trojan elders: Literally "conference of the elders of Pergám". Pergamos was a name used by Homer for the citadel of Troy.

Chapter Six

47   The first twelve lines of this stanza were used by Tchaikovsky for the middle section of Prince Gremin's famous aria in the last act of the opera *Eugene Onegin*.